And Jakob Flew The Fiend Away

by

Ursula Hartlein

This book is a work of historical fiction. Apart from the well-known actual people, locales, and events which feature in the narrative, all references to historical events, real people, or real places are used fictiously. All other characters, events, incidents, and dialogues are products of the author's imagination. Any resemblance to actual events, locales, or persons, living or dead, is entirely coincidental.

http://www.facebook.com/AndJakobFlewTheFiendAway

Dedicated to the brave, righteous people of The Netherlands who served in the Resistance instead of being silent or active collaborators
and
To all my fellow limpers, past, present, and future, particularly Curly
and
In loving memory of all my loved ones who left the material world before my lifelong dream of publication finally came to fruition

All glories to Hashem, without whom I wouldn't have been given a gift for writing from such a young age, and without whom my brain wouldn't have been wired according to Divine Will.

Ursula Hartlein

Weapons are instruments of fear; a curse seems to follow them....
Weapons are unblessèd things; they are not things a wise man resorts to.
He uses them only when he has no choice.
Peace and quiet are dear to a good soldier's heart,
And victory no cause for rejoicing.
Rejoicing over victory is the same as delighting in killing.
If you delight in killing, you cannot fulfill yourself.
....[W]ar is conducted like a funeral.
When many people are being killed,
They should be mourned in heartfelt sorrow.
Thus, a victory must be observed like a funeral.
(*The Tao Te Ching*, Chapter 31)

Cast of Characters:

Jakob Eliezer DeJonghe (called Jaap, Jaapje, and Jaapetje), born 9 May 1926.

Luisa Mirjam Hartog, his mother, born 10 March 1886.

Rudolf Jozua DeJonghe (Ruud), his father, born 1 August 1885 and coerced into suicide the day the story begins, 10 October 1940.

Emilia Zahava DeJonghe, his little sister, born 1937, who mysteriously disappears without a trace in the wake of Ruud's murder. She is never seen, but often mentioned.

Ruud's three assassins

Augusta Ruth Kikkert (Gusta), an old family friend and Luisa's midwife, whom Jakob and Luisa move in with after Ruud's murder, born 1896.

Cornelius Sebastiaan ter Avest (Kees), her husband, born 1896.

Bram ter Avest (called Brammetje), their adult son.

Floor ter Avest (called Floortje), their adult daughter.

Vrouw Ryskamp, the mother of Emilia's friend Saskia.

Other residents of the neighborhood where Emilia was last seen

Anselma Specht (Elma), one of Jakob's friends, born 1926.

Alexander Zeeger (Sander), his other close friend from school, born 1926.

Luuk Klein, Jakob's enemy, who'd rather emulate the suicidal Zealots than fight back like the Maccabees, born 1926.

Debora Tholberg, one of Jakob's school friends, born 1926.

Gertruida Vervloet (Trudie), one of Jakob's classmates, born 1926.

Juffrouw Arendonk, Jakob's teacher at religious school.

Heer Eikenboom, the principal of religious school.

Dutch police and soldiers, German soldiers, and Nazis participating in the February 1941 raids in Amsterdam.

Vrouw Rebekka Antema, a family friend and neighbor who hosts the first-night Seder in 1941.

Adriaan Antema, her only son left after losing her husband and two older sons in one of the February 1941 raids.

Elisabeth Antema (Elsje), her daughter, born 1924.

Heer Marquering, one of Jakob's teachers at his segregated school.

Bank teller

Fat Nazi with a disgusting deep, hacking cough

Vrouw Daube, the co-owner of an art supplies store Jakob frequents.

Vrouw Zaal, a family friend who hides some of Jakob and Luisa's possessions for safekeeping, along with Jakob's bicycle and Kees's car.

Tall, thin NSBer

Liver-spotted Nazi

Ugly bald Nazi at Amsterdam police station

Westerbork registrar

Westerbork inmates

Westerbork guards

Man who engineers escape from death train

Andries Quackenboss (Dries), a member of the Dutch Resistance, part of a group specializing in sabotage and assassinations, and eventually in the Princess Irene Brigade with Jakob, born 1924.

Leendert van den Hoff, one of their comrades, born 1925.

Govert Vrooman, one of their comrades, born 1923.

Jeronymus Schermerhorn, one of their comrades and a major playboy, born 1921.

Vrouw Heleen Visser, a woman in the underground who hides Jakob in her basement for seven months and periodically hosts him while he's in the partisans.

Dr. Gustaaf Xylander, the underground doctor smuggled in to treat Jakob's broken foot and ankle.

Commander Jurriaan van der Beek, in charge of Jakob's partisan unit.

Other partisans

NSB chauffeur

Bernhard (Ben, called Bentje), the Kooikerhondje dog Jakob and Dries find on one of their missions and adopt into their group, born 1943.

Rachel Susanna Roggenfelder (called Gepje), a very progressive, spirited girl whom Jakob falls in love with after their first chance meeting in October 1943, born 27 March 1926.

Julia van Acker (Juli), her extremely shy, passive best friend, born 2 April 1924.

Sgts. Pieter van Donk, Stefan van Rossem, and Lodewijk van Willigen, members of the Princess Irene Brigade who convey their commander's decision about which partisans to induct into the official Army.

Other members of the Princess Irene Brigade.

Queen Wilhelmina, Queen of The Netherlands, in exile for most of the war, then returns in early 1945 to meet the Princess Irene Brigade, born 31 August 1880.
Wehrmacht combatants
Members of the Canadian military
Nazis, NSBers, and collaborators being punished in The Hague
Jeweler in Hooghalen
Marriage registrar in Winschoten
Taxi driver
Old family friends who secretly have Ruud buried in a placeholder spot in their church cemetery, then have him reinterred at the DeJonghes' ancestral Jewish cemetery and given a proper headstone.
Seven volunteers who make a minyan at the cemetery
Willem Brinkerhoff, Elma's fiancé, later husband, born 1926.
Colonel Onderdonk, one of Jakob's commanding officers.
Jakob's commanding officer in the Dutch East Indies campaign
Indonesian guerrillas
Members of the British and British Indian armed forces
Indonesian woman who runs an arts and crafts stall in the Surabaya market
Officials at the American Embassy in Amsterdam
Heer Prinsen, the director of an Amsterdam orphanage for war orphans, Jakob's boss during his last two months in Amsterdam.
Ursula (Urseltje), a little girl at the orphanage who grows very attached to Jakob and Ben, born 1941.
Other orphanage children
Orphanage cooks
Sanitarium warden

Part I:
Angry in His Nightmare

(October 1940–April 1941)

Chapter 1: Jakob's Nightmare Begins

Jakob DeJonghe looked away from a German soldier as he and his mother Luisa headed home from the Waterlooplein market. Tomorrow, at Yom Kippur services, he planned to pray for these fiends to leave his country. Five months of occupation were about all he could take. In the meantime, he was looking forward to making chocolate cake when they got home.

"You're the world's best cook, *Moeder*." Jakob shifted a heavy bag of groceries to his other arm. "I wish I were still as little as Emilia so I could lick the spoon."

He and Luisa halted at unfamiliar voices coming from the open back door of their home. His father Rudolf sat on the floor sobbing as three Nazis stood above him. One had an oddly-shaped nose; another was chubby and had a face full of measles or chickenpox scars; and the third was a bit short for a man and had a scar on his forehead. *So much for so-called Aryans being the master race,* Jakob thought as he drew back.

Jakob grabbed Luisa's arm and pulled her back. "Don't go in there, Mama," he whispered. Since his bar mitzvah last year, he'd stopped calling his parents Mama and Papa, but he sometimes still called Luisa Mama in emotional situations. "They can't see us. It might make more trouble if we go in there. I don't want anyone to hurt you."

Luisa looked towards the man who'd been her husband for thirty-four years, then back at the firstborn child she'd waited forty years for. Her face a mask of pain, she stepped back to Jakob, shaking.

"No matter what happens to *Vader*, I'll protect you." Jakob was sick to his stomach as he observed the scene inside the house, unable to believe he'd just been thinking of something as trivial as chocolate cake.

"Here you go." One of them pushed a gun into Ruud's hand. "Tell us again how much you hate us for conquering your pathetic little country. And then you're going to kill yourself."

"I'm only fifty-five years old! I'm not going to take my own life!"

"Would you rather we do it for you?"

"I want you to get out of my house!"

"We're not going anywhere. This country is ours now. We can do whatever we want with whomever we want. Your days of controlling the world are over. You're lucky we let some of your kind continue to exist."

"Quit stalling for time and pull the damn trigger," the second one snarled. "We don't have all day."

"I have a wife, a son, and a daughter! And I'm a successful businessman!"

"Like we care," the third one sneered. "Just pull the trigger, vermin."

Ruud began weeping again. "If you spare me, I'll take my family and we'll go far away! Just leave me in peace to live out my life!"

"That's not an option, louse." The ringleader lit a cigarette. "Either you pull the trigger and shoot yourself in the head, or we'll do it for you. Please keep in mind we'll shoot you all over and make your death even more painful and agonizing. If you're lucky, maybe some neighbors will stop by before tomorrow and bury your inferior body before we come back to dispose of it."

"This is a gross injustice! I'm going to complain to my local representatives and take my case to The Hague if I have to! You can't break into a law-abiding citizen's house and try to make him kill himself! I've never done anything wrong! I've been moral all my life, by both the laws of God and man!"

The second one glared down at him. "We are the authorities now. Complaining to the pathetic people we overthrew won't do anything. Now are you going to kill yourself, or do you want us to do it for you?"

"You should be embarrassed," the third one said, in a very high-pitched voice. "A grown man weeping like a baby."

"You're trying to make me end my own life for no reason! I'd only kill myself if I were very sick and wanted out of my misery!"

"Your misery is only beginning." The ringleader took a puff on his cigarette.

The second one raised his boot and positioned it inches from Ruud's head. "Are you going to put the gun to your head or not?"

"I have a wife and two children! My son is only fourteen, and my daughter is only three! My wife and I waited so long to have those children! I deserve to see them grow up after waiting longer than most men to become a father! Do you realize what a miracle it was that my wife had our daughter when she was fifty-one?"

"No, and we don't care either." The ringleader bent down and blew smoke into Ruud's face. "Why would we care about the reproduction habits of vermin? By the time we get done with your pathetic little country, you might not have anyone left in your family. Now pull the damn trigger and stop wasting our valuable time."

The third one grabbed Ruud's hand and led the gun to the side of his head, then pushed his fingers towards the trigger. "Are you going to do the right thing, or will we have to send you to Hell ourselves?"

"I haven't even reached sixty yet! My daughter is only three! My wife shouldn't have to be such an old mother all by herself!"

The three butchers began laughing, and their laughter sent waves of hatred through Jakob's body. He desperately wished he could run in there and tackle them, but that would make the situation even worse. The butchers laughed even more when Ruud began hyperventilating and struggling for breath.

"Perhaps you should've thought of these things before you decided to reproduce when you were old enough to be a grandfather. Did you think you were following after Abraham and Sarah?" The ringleader blew smoke into his face again.

"With any luck, your wife and kids will soon join you," the second one said, in a bullfrog-like voice. "Your so-called miracles were for nothing. Now pull the trigger and stop wasting our time."

"Pull the damn trigger or we'll burn this house down and hunt down your wife and kids! You have one more minute left to do the right thing, or we'll end your life on our terms."

"This isn't right! I'm only fifty-five! You have no sense of justice or humanity! I want to live! I don't want to end my own life for no reason!" Ruud began hyperventilating even harder.

"Now, scum!" the third one shouted. "Remember what we said would happen if you didn't obey us. You're dreaming if you think we're going to leave."

Ruud looked around at the cold, steely faces of the goons who'd broken into his home and decided to use him as their entertainment. They weren't relenting. As the ringleader advanced towards him, he placed the gun above his right ear, said the Sh'ma in his frantic, gulping breaths, and pulled the trigger.

Jakob felt even sicker when he saw his father's blood and brain fluid splattered against the doorway. Luisa stood frozen in her tracks, unable to process what they'd just witnessed. Their grocery bags fell to the ground with a thud. Then the three barbarians looked up and finally realized there had been witnesses.

"Who the hell are you?" the ringleader asked.

"This is our house," Luisa stammered. "Have we done something to offend you?"

"You exist. That's reason enough." He looked Luisa and Jakob up and down. "You look even less Aryan than that thing who just deceased himself. At least his hair and eyes weren't jet black. Now get the hell out of here and there won't be any trouble. As I told your husband before he ended his pathetic, useless life, maybe some neighbors will come by and bury the corpse before we return to dispose of it our way."

"Didn't you hear us?" The third one spat on the floor. "Get the hell out of here before we make you kill yourselves too. I suppose your daughter isn't with you. It's not our racket if she can't find you when she comes home."

"Is the girl Mongoloid?" the second one asked. "What right did people of an inferior race have to reproduce when they were in their fifties?"

"She's normal," Luisa said, her voice shaking. "May we gather important possessions before we go?"

"Of course not. You have your groceries, the clothes on your backs, and your worthless lives. I assume you have people who'll agree to take you in, or enough money for a hotel or new home."

Jakob burnt with hatred as they picked the bags up and turned around, retracing their steps down Zwanenburgwal. He struggled to repress his urge to vomit, while Luisa was still too shocked to do or say anything. Suddenly the cool October air felt a whole lot colder.

"Do you think they'll forget about it and let us go home soon?" Luisa finally asked as they turned onto Jodenbreestraat.

"They didn't relent when they were torturing *Vader*! He wouldn't have taken his own life unless he were being tortured!"

Three buildings down, the front door of a red apartment opened and a well-dressed woman came out. She smiled when she recognized them, until she saw the looks on their faces. Luisa was in a daze, and Jakob's eyes burnt with fury. Both of them were visibly shaking.

"Did something happen to you? You're welcome to come sit down and tell me about it. Kees won't mind if he comes home from work and sees unexpected visitors."

"My mother is now a widow," Jakob ranted. "My father is a dead body with half his face blown away. Three Nazi goons broke into our home while we were out, and when we came back, they were torturing him and coercing him into suicide."

"We have to get Emilia," Luisa said. "She can't come home to the sight of her dead, disfigured father and her mother missing. We might never see her again. Gusta, can you ask Kees to go to our house and leave a note? Alida Peerenboom in Oude Pijp is hosting Emilia's playgroup this afternoon. Thank God Alida's Christian."

Jakob went up the stairs to the third-story apartment and dumped his grocery bag on the nearest table. He practiced punching the air with both fists as his mother and Augusta Kikkert climbed the stairs and entered the apartment what felt like an excruciatingly long time later.

"I'm going back to our house tonight," he announced. "You can come with me too, *Moeder*. We need to get our belongings before they're stolen. I don't want Nazi or NSB bastards to burn our family pictures or heirlooms."

"Jaapje, you heard what they said!" Luisa sank into the nearest chair. "We could be shot if we're found there!"

"There are no laws keeping us inside after dark, and by law, that's our house. Everything inside it is ours. I memorized their dirty faces, so they're living on borrowed time. As soon as I'm old enough, I'm joining the military."

"No you're not. They were soundly defeated in May. The last I heard, their remnants fled to England and became a splinter group with the British military. You're not going to go to England to try to find them, and you're certainly not joining the military when you're only fourteen. I wouldn't even let you join the military at sixteen. You're all I have now."

Jakob decided not to pursue the matter of revenge further at the moment and turned back to the matter of getting their most important possessions out of the house. "Those bastards have probably already forgotten about it. If we go back tonight, I think we'll be safe. It's a good thing Kees has a car. We'll have more room to stash our things."

Gusta took down her teapot and began rummaging through her wooden crate of imported teas. "I'm still in shock that my dear friend Ruud is dead, and by forced suicide no less. Only last week we celebrated Rosh Hashanah together."

"I'm more angry than shocked." Jakob began punching the air again.

"We can't let all our belongings sit there and be open to theft," Luisa said, her face shaking. "It probably is a good idea to go back there and get the most important ones. Jaapje, you can go after dark with Kees, but you can't linger long. After what we saw and heard, I don't think they were bluffing. Just get what we need and get out. Make sure to get Emilia's things too. Hopefully Alida will make inquiries and find out where we are. You don't mind, do you, Gusta, keeping us overnight? I don't like the idea of staying in a hotel without Ruud for protection."

"Both of your children were born into my hands. Of course you can stay overnight. Please, take Bram and Floor's old rooms. They never stay overnight when they visit."

Jakob leaned out the window and looked up and down the street, now starting to fill with people coming home from work and heading out for shopping. "Do you think it's safe for us to stay here? We're still in Jodenbuurt. The Nazis and NSB hate us. Maybe we should move to another neighborhood just to be safe. If you and *Vader* weren't so emotionally attached to this place despite no longer being working-class, we could've moved years ago."

"Nonsense. They just want to scare us. Good always wins over evil. Before long, we'll get a full apology and compensation for your father's murder. The murderers will be punished, and no sane jury would consider him a real suicide." Luisa took off her hat. "All we have to do is patiently wait for this crime to be avenged. I see that look in your eyes. Don't even think about revenge or sneaking off to join the military."

"One of my teachers at religious school said God wants us to be active participants in our fate. We shouldn't sit around passively waiting for miracles and believe everyone has our best interests at heart. Sometimes you have to take matters into your own hands or nothing will ever happen. We were slaves in Egypt for four hundred years, but Moshe Rabeynu wasn't called till our ancestors began crying out to God and stopped accepting slavery."

2

That night, after Kees ter Avest had come home from work and the new household of four had had supper, Jakob put his jacket and shoes on and headed out to the street. He stalked around the blue Peugeot, keeping his eyes peeled for any potential friends or foes who might ask what he was doing there at that hour. Those filthy Nazis had probably deliberately chosen this day to torture and coerce Ruud into suicide, knowing Yom Kippur started the next evening. It was a mockery of everything sacred and beautiful, and Jakob wasn't about to let this wrong go unpunished.

"What took so long?" he demanded when Kees came outside after minutes lasting an eternity.

"Hold your horses. Your house is only a street away. How'd you like me to take you to Rembrandt's house tomorrow before Kol Nidre? You're excused from school and I'm excused from work, and it's the perfect opportunity to do something fun to take your mind off this tragedy."

"Right now I only care about avenging my father. I don't care this is the street Rembrandt lived on. I can visit a museum anytime, but I won't be able to get revenge so easily."

"Take it easy. This tragedy was an isolated incident. Already the world sees what the Nazis are capable of. They won't be allowed to trample all over Europe much longer. By the time this war ends, you probably won't be old enough to join the military yet."

Jakob climbed into the car and slammed the door. "I'll be a little happier once I have my belongings back in my hands, but I'll be happiest when I aim a gun at those murderers and blow their brains away."

Kees got into the driver's seat and pulled out of his parking spot. "You're thinking with anger now. You don't want to be so angry and hateful on the eve of Yom Kippur, even after what's happened. Once you calm down and start grieving your father normally, you'll see things differently."

Jakob was on pins and needles the entire short drive back to Zwanenburgwal. As soon as Kees parked as close to the four-story brick rowhouse as possible, Jakob flung his door open and jumped out. He dug the key out of his pocket and unlocked the front door, then stormed inside and flipped the lights on.

"Is he still here?" Kees asked. "Burying your father takes precedence over collecting clothes, books, and heirlooms."

Jakob went over to the back door, which was now closed. Ruud's body was gone, though there were dried blood and brain fluid on the doorway. At this point, he didn't know what to believe. He only hoped the butchers had been right about coming back for the body in the morning. Maybe one of their friends or neighbors had come by and seen the crime scene. Not all of their neighbors were Jewish. Perhaps he was in safe hands now, with people who wouldn't be suspected of anything. Part of Jakob was relieved he wouldn't have to see his father's dead body with half his face blown away again.

"We have no time to waste," Kees said. "Get your suitcases and start filling them up. Anything else that's important can be carried to the car in another trip. Your legal documents are the most important things to collect."

Jakob went up to his third-story room and pulled his three suitcases out of the closet. He tossed them on his bed and began aimlessly dumping in clothes, books, photographs, school supplies, and religious articles. He didn't stop to look at the family photos or open the books to see the inscriptions from his parents and other relatives.

After finishing up in his room, he headed into his mother's room. He found her suitcases and then began loading them up as carelessly as he'd packed his things. When he put in her clothing, he tried not to look at or really touch her undergarments.

"Jaapje, did you hear the intruders upstairs when you were last here?" Kees called from down the hall. "A lot of Emilia's things are missing."

Jakob dropped his mother's wedding dress on her bed and came running into his little sister's room. His heart began racing when he saw what Kees was talking about. Emilia's little bed was stripped bare, even of the pillows, and all her toys, dolls, and stuffed animals were gone. Her little bookshelf was also stripped bare. Only her shiny red tricycle, which she'd just received a few months ago, some art supplies, and a few items of clothing remained in the room.

"Whoever did this did a really thorough job," Kees said. "I thought the Nazis or NSB did it at first, but now I'm not so sure. Do you think it's possible Alida came here while Ruud's body was still in the doorway, and decided to keep Emilia for safety? Perhaps she assumed you and Luisa were also murdered, or arrested. It's too bad she lives in Oude Pijp, so we can't go by to inquire at this hour."

"We can visit after Yom Kippur. I hope you're right. It would be too mean even for the Nazis and NSB to steal toys from a three-year-old girl." Jakob picked up his sister's tricycle. "But in the meantime, we can take what's left. She'll come home soon, God willing, and she'll be very sad if she doesn't have her tricycle."

Kees went into the file cabinet of important legal and religious documents. Without looking through each folder, he grabbed them and started stacking them on top of the file cabinet. He paused when he realized Emilia's folder was absent.

"This is really getting strange. Whoever took Emilia's things also felt the need to make off with her personal papers. Why would anyone want a three-year-old's birth certificate or the document of her religious naming?"

Jakob tensed up when he heard a car driving in front of the house. He crept up to a window and peered out from behind the curtain.

"It's just a normal car. At least things aren't as bad here as I've heard about in Germany and Austria."

"We need to start moving these suitcases into my car. You can carry out your things, and I'll tie your bicycles to the top. Then we'll carry out the rest of the things together. You might want to gather up some of your father's things too, to remember him by."

Jakob did as he was told, all while fantasizing about catching the three Nazi murderers, pulling out the most heavy-duty gun in existence, making them beg and plead for their worthless little lives, just as they'd made Ruud beg, and then taking them out one by one with the same unfeeling attitude. The entire way back to his new residence, he smiled as he thought about how his father's three murderers were now living on borrowed time.

Chapter 2: U'Netaneh Tokef

Jakob always stood for Kol Nidre, but this year he remained seated so he could keep his arm around his sobbing mother. He was glad his family had joined the new Progressive synagogue that opened eight years ago. If they were still members of the old-fashioned synagogue, he'd have to sit apart from his mother and feel tortured the entire service, knowing she was crying alone in another part of the building.

"I think God will understand if I spend the day plotting revenge instead of fasting," he whispered before the cantor began.

Kees fixed him with a sharp look. "You'll do no such thing, and you know your father wouldn't have wanted you to do that either. Since when is a death in the family, even if it's a murder, an acceptable reason to not fast? Unless you're very sick and haven't told us, you're going to make this the second year you've fasted all the way through."

"You're the man of your house now," Gusta agreed. "Your mother needs you to be strong for her. That's the last any of us wants to hear about revenge or joining the military underage."

Jakob rolled his eyes after Gusta and Kees stood up and the cantor started chanting Kol Nidre. During each of the three renditions, Jakob only half listened. The other half of his mind was far away, thinking about how the words of the prayer would be turned on their head. Kol Nidre only spoke about nullifying all religious vows and oaths one had made in the past year. It didn't deal with matters of vows and oaths between people, nor did it say anything preventing one from making new vows in the new year. And right now, he was making a vow to rid the world of the evil people who'd destroyed his life yesterday.

"Do you think I'm being disrespectful by not praying?" Luisa asked after she finally composed herself. "Even if we're not Orthodox, it's the most important day of the year. When Yom Kippur falls on the Sabbath, it's even holier."

"God probably understands." Jakob hadn't picked up a Machzor either. "I'm sure even the Orthodox would understand why a new widow isn't following the service."

Jakob had always enjoyed the special, beautiful prayers and melodies used only during the High Holy Days and Days of Awe, but tonight they almost made him sick to his stomach. Right now praising God and thinking about atonement were the furthest things from his mind. Already his family's Rosh Hashanah celebration of last week seemed like a million years ago. He'd still had a father then, and a little sister.

As the other congregants prayed the Amidah and thought about being written and sealed in the Book of Life, Jakob daydreamt about creating his own Book of Life. He didn't know the names of the evil ones who'd murdered his father, but he wrote their descriptions on the page for people whose time was up in the coming year:

Murderer with cigarette, average height, light brown hair, pale blue eyes, eyebrows too thick and close together, moustache, thick mouth, nose oddly shaped on the right side.

Second murderer, a little short for a man, blonde hair, dark green eyes, big Adam's apple, scar on the forehead, thin mouth, bullfrog voice.

Third murderer, average height, brown hair, hazel eyes, short beard, very feminine eyelashes, reddish skin, high-pitched voice, slightly chubby, face full of ugly measles or chickenpox scars.

Then he signed his name at the bottom of the page and sealed it with a wax seal worthy of the exiled Queen Wilhelmina and Princess Juliana. As he looked into the eyes of the murderers, he slammed the book shut and gave them the same cold, unfeeling look they'd given Ruud. He laughed as they pled for their worthless little lives, then pulled out a gun and shot each one. To make sure his fantasy came true to the letter, he'd have to read up on how to shoot to kill.

"Why are you smiling?" Gusta asked. "The service is over, and everyone is leaving. You're the only one still sitting here doing nothing. Something tells me this isn't a good smile."

"Oh, it's a very good smile. I'll tell you my reason later."

"Something tells me you're smiling because you're thinking about running away to join the military, or going on a stupid, suicidal scouting mission to catch the *kankerhonden* who murdered your father," Kees said. "Put those ridiculous thoughts out of your head right now if you know what's good for you."

"Cornelius ter Avest!" Gusta gasped. "You dare to use such language on the holiest day of the year?"

"I'm not the one who thinks he's going to play an avenging hero and go against everything he was ever taught was moral." Kees straightened his white tie and looked down at Jakob. "Are you coming home with us?"

"I'd prefer to go home to my real house and sleep in my real bed," Jakob grumbled as he stood up and followed after the others.

"That's not an option either. I hope you're over this ridiculous revenge fantasy by the end of the holiday season."

Luisa began sobbing again as soon as they were out of the building and going down the street. Jakob rushed to hug her, wishing it were acceptable for a boy his age to cry too. Even if it were, or if he saw nothing unmanly about it regardless, he had to be strong for his mother. He cursed the Nazis for forcing him into the role of man of the house at only fourteen years old.

"I can't lose you too, Jaapje. I've already lost your father and probably Emilia too. You need to promise me you'll be a good boy and take care of our family. That doesn't include trying to be a hero. I didn't wait forty years to become a mother just to see my only child left get himself killed acting out a crazy revenge fantasy. I've seen the looks on your face since yesterday, and I know it means your mind is working overtime. Just worry about getting good marks in school and helping around our new home, not being a boy soldier."

He nodded, not convinced at all, but wanting to make his mother feel better. Perhaps it wasn't such a bad idea to wait a little while and formulate a better revenge plan, instead of immediately going on the warpath. Revenge was a dish best served cold, and his father had always told him never to act or speak in the heat of anger to avoid doing or saying anything he might later regret.

2

Every year since he'd graduated from the children's service to the adult service, the highlight of the Rosh Hashanah and Yom Kippur service for Jakob was U'Netaneh Tokef. His religious school teacher told his class last year that the story behind the prayer was probably apocryphal and not grounded in known historical facts, but that didn't take away from the power and beauty of the prayer. Its impact didn't rest on whether the story of its creation were truth or fiction.

Jakob didn't follow along with the prayer, but read it at his own pace on the Dutch side of the Machzor. He let the words sink in, numb with horror when he thought about how Ruud had been by his side only last week when they listened to U'Netaneh Tokef during Rosh Hashanah. Little had anyone known Ruud's name hadn't been written in the Book of Life and that his destiny had already been decided.

Jakob wished the prayer had a modern section. Most people in the modern era, in the developed world, no longer died by being gorged by beasts, for example.

We shall ascribe holiness to this day, for it is awesome and terrible. Your kingship is exalted upon it. Your throne is established in mercy. You are enthroned upon it in truth.

In truth, you are the judge, the exhorter, the all-knowing, the witness, he who inscribes and seals, remembering all that is forgotten. You open the book of remembrance which proclaims itself, and the seal of each person is there.

A still small voice is heard. The angels are dismayed, they are seized by fear and trembling as they proclaim: Behold the Day of Judgment! For all the hosts of heaven are brought for judgment. They shall not be guiltless in your eyes, and all creatures shall parade before you as a troop. As a shepherd herds his flock, causing his sheep to pass beneath his staff, so do you cause to pass, count, and record, visiting the souls of all living, decreeing the length of their days, inscribing their judgment.

On Rosh Hashanah it is written; on Yom Kippur it is sealed.

How many shall pass away and how many shall be born, who shall live and who shall die, who in the fullness of years and who before, who shall perish by water and who by fire, who by sword and who by beast, who by famine and who by thirst, who by earthquake and who by plague, who by strangulation and who by stoning, who shall have rest and who shall wander, who shall be at peace and who shall be pursued, who shall be at rest and who shall be tormented, who shall be exalted and who shall be brought low, who shall become rich and who shall be impoverished.

But teshuvah, and tefilah, and tzedakah avert the severe decree.

For your praise is in accordance with your name. You are difficult to anger and easy to appease, for you do not desire the death of the condemned, but that we turn from our path and live. Until the day of our death, you wait for us. Should we turn, you will receive us at once. In truth, you are our Creator, and you understand our inclination, for we are but flesh and blood.

Our origin is dust, our end is dust. We earn our bread by exertion and are like a broken shard, like dry grass, a withered flower, like a passing shadow and a vanishing cloud, like the breeze that blows away and dust that scatters, like the dream that flies away. But you are King, God who lives for all eternity! There is no limit to your years, no end to the length of your days, no measure to the hosts of your glory, no understanding the meaning of your name. Your name is fitting unto you and you are fitting unto it, and our name has been called by your name. Act for the sake of your name and sanctify your name through those who sanctify your name.

All people were numbered and accounted for, not just the righteous. While sometimes bad people did repent, Jakob was sure his father's murderers would never repent. Those high and mighty Nazis thought their empire would last for a thousand years, but he'd help to hasten its early downfall. He'd also make sure to include those murderers among the people destined to die before the fullness of years and headed for a year of being brought low, tormented, pursued, and impoverished. Most importantly of all, they weren't among the people meant to live very much longer. He began smiling as the prayer ended.

Chapter 3: Mysterious Disappearance

When Jakob came home from school on Monday, he found Kees assembling a sukkah on the back balcony of the apartment. Luisa sifted through a crate of the old Sukkot decorations made by Gusta and Kees's children Bram and Floor, deciding which ones to hang up around the sukkah. A big pile of schach was in a corner.

"My boss let me off earlier than usual," Kees said. "I think he wants to join the NSB. That's the talk all around the office. I hope we drive these fools out of our country before they do any further damage and I'm out of a job."

Jakob set his schoolbag down. "You said we'd go to see the Peerenbooms today. Won't it be nice if we can bring Emilia home and celebrate the next holiday with her? She must be really sad and lonely."

"You're assuming she's still with them," Luisa said. "We don't know anything. My gymnasium Latin teacher taught me to never assume anything. There are lots of other children in the playgroup. Perhaps she ended up with one of those other families in the meantime. Those people are all our friends. Why wouldn't they try to find us or make inquiries?"

"People don't always act right when they're afraid." Kees began hammering a piece of plywood to the bottom of the balcony above them. "We should be glad we still have more freedom than the people in Germany and Austria, and that most of the people in this neighborhood are our own kind."

"The more time we let go by, the harder it'll be to learn any information," Jakob said. "My father told me to always strike while the iron is hot. Good detectives never let years or months go by before they start to investigate a crime or mystery. If you won't let me play soldier, you can let me play detective."

"Both Alida and Willem work," Luisa said. "If they still had Emilia, where would they put her during the day? They have no servants, and no relatives live with them. If you want to play detective, you might as well start questioning all the parents of the children in Emilia's playgroup."

"That sounds like a good idea." Jakob pulled a notebook and pen out of his schoolbag. "Do you remember all their names and addresses? I'm surprised you're not the one who's most eager to try to find her.

Emilia's your little miracle baby. I don't know anyone else who had a baby in her fifties."

"Of course I'm worried about her! But running all over the city trying to play detective won't turn back time. God willing, she'll come back to us soon, but not because you played detective. Did you ever stop to think you might get the authorities suspicious if you do that, after what already happened? Perhaps she truly is safer wherever she is now."

"I don't care if she is in a safe place with nice people. She belongs with us."

"Do you really think it's a good use of my time and energy to spend all day mourning her? Don't you hear me crying every night for your father and sister? What'll it accomplish if I do that during the daytime as well? I have to be a good mother to my one child left and focus my energies on things I can do. Just let me live my way."

Kees climbed off of his stepladder and put the hammer on the balcony floor. "I suppose it won't hurt to visit them, and I'm all for it if it'll get you to stop having such a one-track mind. You can wait by the car, and I'll be out after I wash up."

Jakob patted Luisa on the arm. "You can get ready to go too, *Moeder*. I bet you can't wait to see our Emilia again."

"I'm staying here and holding down the fort. Someone has to stay in the house in case something happens. We can't take any chances these days."

"Gusta will probably be home presently," Kees said. "She went out about an hour ago to deliver Vrouw Westenberg. Since it's her fifth child, the delivery will probably go very quickly. Gusta says the more children a woman has, the quicker each birth passes."

"Someday, God willing, it'll be your wife in labor, Jaapje." Luisa smiled at him. "But I can't become an *oma* if you're killed as a boy soldier."

Jakob rolled his eyes and headed out to the car. He wasn't as antsy to go as he'd been the night he and Kees went back to the house for his belongings, but it still felt like hours had passed by the time he finally saw Kees heading out to the Peugeot. On their drive across the city, he looked out the window and began making up a story to tell Emilia on the drive home. As for what had happened to Ruud, he'd tell her their father had gone off to England to serve their country's Free Forces. When she was old enough, she'd learn the truth, but for now, she needed a beautiful lie to sugarcoat the awful truth.

"Can we stop at that toy store so I can buy a present for Emilia?" Jakob asked when they were one block away from the Peerenbooms' house.

"Once again you're putting the cart before the horse, my boy. You'll feel terrible if we don't find her. You're already keeping her tricycle for her, and it's depressing enough every time we look at that. Adding a doll or toy would make it even worse."

"She deserves a really special treat to make up for spending the last five days away from her family."

"Clearly you don't remember your early childhood very well. The normal three-year-old is satisfied with so little, unless you're raising a spoilt brat. Small children go from being very sad to very happy in minutes. I'm sure she'll be more than happy just to see you and your mother again. That is, if there is an Emilia waiting for us."

Jakob scrambled out of the car as soon as Kees parked in front of the four-story brick rowhouse. Smiling more than he had since Thursday afternoon, he rang the bell.

A woman who wasn't Vrouw Peerenboom answered the door. Jakob stepped back a little, his heart starting to beat a little quicker. This was one thing he hadn't bargained on.

"Are you visiting Heer Krusen and Vrouw Peerenboom? I don't recall meeting you before."

"I never met these people. My family just moved into this house the other day. We were told it just went on the market, right as we were moving from an apartment to a real house. I'm sorry I can't be of any assistance."

Jakob tried to take all this information in. "Did you hear any talk about why they moved?"

"All I know is my husband and I just moved in here with our three children the other day. Perhaps some of the neighbors can tell you more. Some friends these people are, not telling anyone they were moving."

He nodded politely, his heart beating even faster. "I see. Thank you for your time."

Kees shook his head after the door closed. "That is very strange, people suddenly moving and not alerting their friends. I hope this doesn't have anything to do with the Nazis or NSB."

Jakob tried the house on the left and was relieved when he recognized Vrouw Ryskamp, the mother of Emilia's friend Saskia. Vrouw Ryskamp turned white when she saw who her visitor was.

"Am I seeing a ghost? Alida and Willem told everyone you were all murdered on Thursday!"

"What? My father was the only one who was murdered!"

Vrouw Ryskamp stepped back from him. "I like you, Jakob, but I don't think it's a good idea to invite you in. The people who murdered your father probably want you dead as well, and we all know how awful those Nazis are. At least, some of us know. Some of the people in this neighborhood have joined the NSB. I hope they're all executed as traitors when the invaders are chased out and our Queen returns home."

"Do you know anything about where Alida and Willem went?" Kees asked.

"When did they move?" Jakob asked. "The same day those new people moved in?"

"I didn't know they were moving. All they said was you and your parents were murdered. They saw your poor father's dead body and blood against the doorway, and assumed you and your mother had been taken away and murdered too."

Jakob feared his heart might leap out of his chest, the way it was beating so rapidly by now. He bid goodbye to Vrouw Ryskamp in a shaking voice and then headed for the house on the right.

This door was answered by someone he didn't recognize. At this point, all he cared about was finding someone who knew what had happened, even if he didn't hear it from a friend.

"Hello. I'm a family friend of Willem Krusen and Alida Peerenboom. I just found out they moved recently, and wanted to know if they happened to tell you where they were going."

"I'm sorry, but I don't know much more than you do. My husband and I couldn't sleep on Thursday night because of a lot of noise from next door, and when my husband went to inquire, he was told they were packing up to move. When he asked what in the world they were doing packing in the middle of the night, and why they were moving out of the blue, they only told him they had to get out of Amsterdam."

"So you know for sure they're not in the city anymore?" Jakob hoped his eyes weren't too wide from shock.

"That's the story they gave my husband. They claimed their lives might be in danger, and they couldn't take any chances staying in the city longer than they needed to. On Friday night, they loaded all their things into a big truck and drove God knows where."

"Did you happen to notice if there were a little girl in the house besides their daughter Juliana?"

"Why would they have had another child with them? If they did, it sure was well-concealed from us. If you know anything about why they left town and felt their lives were in danger, I'd advise you to stay quiet about it. You never know who's a traitor these days. There are NSBers in this neighborhood, and it makes me sick."

"We understand perfectly," Kees said. "We won't bother you further. Thank you for providing what little information you could."

Jakob fumed as they walked back to the car. He slammed the door and sat in stony silence during the entire drive back to Jodenbreestraat. The people who'd been most likely to have information on Emilia's whereabouts were gone without a trace. He hadn't struck while the iron was hot enough. Now he was even more determined to do something, anything, to get revenge on these evil people before his family was split in half again.

"I'm sure they'll come home after we get rid of the Germans," Kees said as they arrived home. "If they did have Emilia with them, you should be thankful they took her out of harm's way. This situation can't last forever. You'll have a sister again in no time."

"The previous war lasted four years! That was supposed to be the war to end all wars! We don't even have help from the Americans! Didn't they learn their lesson from the last war, when they joined the fight so late?"

"It's not my country to know why they feel it's in their best interests to stay out of this war. Maybe they'll join soon and help us. But in the meantime, we have a lot of other countries doing their part. Like we've told you, all you need to worry about at your age is doing well in school and helping with housework."

Jakob stalked up to the third floor and flung himself onto the davenport. He shook his head in resignation when Luisa came into the room.

"If there still is an Emilia, she's not in Amsterdam. Heer Krusen and Vrouw Peerenboom are gone, and no one knew why or where they went. I wish I could behead those murderers!"

"Now you're up to wanting to behead them?" Luisa asked. "I wish we had money for a psychotherapist, because you really need one."

"I don't need a fancy mind doctor to analyze my dreams and make me lie on a couch. I'll be happy again when I get revenge. That's all the therapy I need."

Luisa sat beside him and put her arm around him. "Sukkot begins on Wednesday night, and Simchat Torah comes at the end of Sukkot. Do you know the significance of that holiday? It was always one of your favorites."

"What are you quizzing me about holidays for? I'm at home now, not in religious school!"

"Why do we start at the beginning after we get to the end of the Torah and have so much celebration over reaching the end?"

He looked down at his hands, realizing what she was trying to get at. "To show it's a constant cycle of renewal, and because it's not really the end, just a new beginning that came from an ending. We're not supposed to stop celebrating or reading, because the ending and beginning are the same."

"Exactly. Very few things are ever really an ending, just the start of something new and different. We're not looking forward to the ending of the Torah because we want it to be over, but because it means we can celebrate and start all over again, every single year. It ends with the death of Moshe Rabeynu and starts with the creation of life."

He nodded. "But it'd still make me feel a lot better if I could be the author of our new beginning."

"If you're truly meant to have a role in driving these invaders out and getting justice for your father, a way to do it will open up to you. You shouldn't force it just because you're angry and upset. That would be like trying to make someone love you if she didn't want to be your wife. It's not always all about you and what you want. Understand?"

"Yes, *Moeder*."

"Good. Now you can go wash up, and in about twenty minutes you can help me start dinner. We can make that chocolate cake we were going to make the day your father was murdered."

"I'm sorry I said I wished I could lick the bowl and spoon. Emilia should be here to do that."

"She'll come back to us soon enough. I'm sure she will. But in the meantime, you're my only baby left, and you get to lick the extra frosting and batter. By next year at this time, we'll all be together again in our real house."

Chapter 4: Heroes and Cowards of History

This year, Chanukah came "late," compared to the Gregorian calendar. The first night was on Christmas Eve. While most of the people of Amsterdam had fancy Christmas trees in their windows and bright lights and decorations, Jakob's new home had chanukiyot in the window. When he was a boy, Jakob had asked his father why the Christians had their big Christmas celebration on December fifth when the actual holiday was twenty days away, and Ruud had told him perhaps they were trying to make up for how their religion didn't have so many holidays. Now Jakob wondered if Emilia had gotten presents from Sinterklaas earlier in the month, and if Heer Krusen and Vrouw Peerenboom, if they still had her, were raising her as a Christian.

"I never thought I'd live to see a day when we'd be in the same position as our ancestors during the first Chanukah," Kees commented as he put a heaping spoonful of applesauce on his plate. "Then again, I also believed the last war was truly the war to end all wars."

"We'll emerge victorious soon enough," Gusta said as she cut up a latke. "Only this time we have large, professional armies to save us, and don't need to depend on a group like the Maccabees."

Jakob stabbed at his latkes and shoved them into his mouth, chewing very loudly. "I don't believe the armies of the world care about us. All they want to do is defeat Germany. I really doubt they're in this war to defend our religious liberties. How can you still deliver babies when they're coming into an occupied country? The babies of our own people are even worse. You're letting their mothers give birth in a time of danger. If I were a little older and had a wife, I sure wouldn't get her pregnant or let her keep a pregnancy in a time like this."

Luisa fixed him with the sharp look she always used when she was annoyed with him. "Gusta's money is helping us get by. I don't make enough money from my part-time work in the bookstore. You should be thankful Gusta and Kees let us live with them and took on two additional people without advance notice. If Gusta is in business long enough, your children might be born into her hands someday."

"All my current clients were expecting before the invasion," Gusta said. "It's simple math. What are they teaching in biology these days that you wouldn't know how long human gestation takes on average?"

Jakob opened the box of sufganiyot Kees had bought from one of the local Sephardic bakeries. He carefully inspected each doughnut to see what type of jelly they contained before finally making his selection, a doughnut with strawberry jelly. He gnawed off a large hunk of it and chewed forcefully, his eyes burning with anger.

"You've got religious school on Sunday," Luisa continued. "I'm sure your teacher will also make a comparison between the Maccabees and our situation today. And I'm sure she'll tell you exactly what we're telling you, that we don't need a partisan army in modern times to defend civilians."

"Of course we need people to defend our own. You've seen how things have been going since the invasion in May. We've started finding out who our real friends are, and who never really liked us. We can't count on outsiders to stand up for our best interests. Sometimes you have to take action yourself."

"And sometimes you have to listen to your mother and your elders. Just because you're in gymnasium now doesn't mean you know better than we do. If these are the kinds of things you're hearing at school, maybe I should consider changing your academic track. They probably don't have such radical thoughts at the ordinary secondary school."

Jakob selected another doughnut, then put five latkes on his plate and topped them with an overly generous spoonful of sour cream. "I get my ideas from myself and my friends. My teachers don't talk politics, but I know some of them are in the NSB. Other of my teachers are pacifists. Only an idiot would be a pacifist in a war like this. You can't defeat an evil occupying force with sweet speeches and presents."

"No, but you can't defeat them with an army of fourteen-year-old boys either," Kees said.

"I won't be fourteen forever. I'm less than six months away from fifteen."

"I wouldn't even let you join any branch of the military if you were seventeen," Luisa said. "If you truly want a military career, you can wait till you're out of school. By the time you've graduated, the war will be over. You'll laugh at how silly you were."

Jakob stabbed his fork into another latke. "Whether you agree with me or not, I'm taking the right side. One day I'll be able to tell my grandchildren what I did in this war, and that won't include sitting around waiting to turn eighteen or get justice and an apology from a government that hates us."

2

Every Sunday morning, Jakob attended classes at the religious school built by the Progressive synagogue his family attended. It was a pain to attend classes six days a week, but he put up with it because there were no real tests or textbooks. Now that he was in his ninth year of school, religious school mostly consisted of sitting in a circle and talking about things like famous rabbis, lessons from the Bible they could apply to their modern lives, and interesting episodes in Jewish history. He enjoyed learning some of these things, since his parents never had this kind of education. That made him smarter than they were. Only three months ago, he'd taught Ruud interesting stories from the Talmud.

"Does anyone else think it's kind of exciting to be living through this historic time?" the teacher, Juffrouw Arendonk, asked. "Perhaps we'll all have a chance to be like the Maccabees and play a part in vanquishing these evil foreigners from our country."

"My parents think we should leave the country or go into hiding until things get better," Debora Tholberg said. "We've been talking about this every night. My entire family agrees it's stupid to act like we're still in the ancient world by taking the law into our own hands."

Sander Zeeger nodded. "My parents feel the same way. The Nazis and NSB are overgrown bullies heading for a fall. My father says they have more bark than bite. They just want to scare us and make us behave. No one in my family thinks they're going to do anything like the Greeks did in the Maccabees' day. Our religion isn't outlawed, and our synagogues haven't been made into churches or had pigs brought into them."

Jakob stared around the room at his classmates, many of whom looked to be in agreement with Debora and Sander. He stopped drawing a picture of the three murderers begging him for their lives and raised his hand.

"Yes, Jakob?"

"I no longer have a father because of those *kankerhonden*. Are you all blind and deaf to think they mean us no harm? Don't any of you follow the news or remember what happened in Germany and Austria two years ago? All the synagogues and businesses were set on fire and looted. I'm sure that'll happen here too if we don't stand up and fight. The people in Germany let this happen because they didn't protest.

They let it happen there, but I'm not going to let it happen here. I'm going to do exactly as the Maccabees did and fight to liberate our country and get religious freedom back."

"That's stupid," Trudie Vervloet said. "This is the twentieth century. People our age earned the right to enjoy being young and not do adult things. We need to let the adults handle this. Maybe the people in Germany didn't protest because they were too scared of punishment. Normal people don't want to risk their lives by playing heroes."

"So you'd let someone get robbed or beaten up because you were too afraid to save him? What if an attack happened in broad daylight in front of lots of people, but everyone thought the other people would save the day? Sometimes you have to be that person who steps up and takes charge."

Juffrouw Arendonk shifted in her seat and twisted her coral necklace around her fingers. "Now that we've discussed that topic, can anyone tell us about some other heroic groups like the Maccabees? Who else do you admire in Jewish history, people you imagine might protest and revolt if they were here today?"

Luuk Klein put his hand up and spoke without waiting to be called on. "The Zealots at Masada were great heroes too. They're my favorite heroes in Jewish history because of how brave they were."

Jakob snorted. "The Zealots were first-class cowards! They did absolutely nothing heroic! They committed mass suicide rather than stand and fight the Romans! They even dragged women and children into their cowardly mass suicide!"

"They held out as long as they could, and when they realized they were outnumbered and would be defeated, they took their own lives rather than staying to be taken prisoner or killed by enemies. How is that cowardly?"

"Cowards kill themselves instead of fighting back! That sends a horrible message to the world and makes us look bad! Don't you realize a lot of people don't take us seriously as a people because we don't have enough Maccabees in our history? When I have children, I'll sure as hell never teach them not to fight back when people bully them. When people threaten you, you stay and defend yourself, not run away!"

"Oh, come on," Debora said. "We're the People of the Book, not the People of the Sword. You're in the wrong religion if you expect us to have lots of famous warriors in our history. The Zealots were heroes who did the best they could under the circumstances. I'm sure even you would do exactly as they did. My mother says everything is always perfect in a fantasy, but when you experience something in real life, you change your mind a lot."

Jakob stabbed at his notebook with his pen, leaving big ink splotches and little holes in the paper. "Being threatened by a dangerous enemy is a lot different than changing your mind about something like how many kids you want or what you want to do for a living. It's a matter of life and death. I'm going to stand and fight in whatever way I can."

"How would the Zealots have defended themselves against the Romans?" Sander asked. "They didn't have a bigger group or stronger weapons."

"Maybe, instead of hiding themselves on top of a mountain in the desert, they should've trained for warfare and scouted the area to come up with a good attack plan. Praying all day and living in caves gets you nowhere when people are trying to kill you."

"You're hardly one to talk about suicide being cowardly, since your own father killed himself rather than fight back," Luuk said in a very smug tone of voice.

Jakob threw his notebook and pen across the room and lunged at Luuk. Juffrouw Arendonk stood up and clapped her hands, but Jakob ignored her pathetic attempt at breaking it up. He pushed Luuk against the wall and began wildly kicking and punching him, dodging all of Luuk's weak attempts at defending himself. When he decided he'd had enough of pummeling him against the wall, he threw Luuk onto the floor, jumped onto his legs, and started punching him in the face. The other students stood by in shocked silence as Juffrouw Arendonk left the room.

"Now who's going to call my father a coward? You weren't even there! I saw and heard probably almost everything! Don't you compare my father to the Zealot cowards! My father is a holy martyr, not a coward who killed himself to avoid fighting back!" He punched Luuk in the eye and smiled when Luuk's eye started bleeding. "There, that should probably hold you for awhile and teach you a lesson. I never liked you, and now I like you even less."

Juffrouw Arendonk came back with the principal, Heer Eikenboom. Heer Eikenboom stopped and stared down at Jakob's notebook.

"This is yours, Heer DeJonghe?" he asked, holding it up in the air.

Jakob got off of Luuk and faced the principal. "Yes, that's my notebook. Sometimes I like to draw during class, but I'm still listening and paying attention."

"What is the meaning of this picture? Are these supposed to be Luuk and other boys in your class? Why would you draw a picture like this?"

"No, they're the three murderers who killed my father the day before Yom Kippur. No matter what, I'm going to find them and get justice. I'll make them beg for life and justice just like they made my father beg. Then I'll shoot them one by one. I'll laugh as they beg for life. What goes around comes around."

"Your father was not murdered!" Luuk shouted, holding his hand over his swollen, bleeding right eye. "He killed himself!"

"Under extreme duress, not because he wanted to!"

Heer Eikenboom handed him the notebook. "Collect the rest of your things and come with me. You're going home early, and will be suspended from religious school until Juf Arendonk and I decide you've learnt your lesson and it's safe to invite you back."

"Fine by me. Most of the people in this class are cowards. At least I know what's really going on and don't think it's no big deal to live under enemy occupation." He set his schoolbag on a chair and shoved his notebook and pen into it, then went to the wall to get his coat off of its peg.

Elma Specht went up to him as he was putting his coat on. "You punch pretty good, Jaap," she whispered. "I never knew anyone who could punch so good with both hands before. You'll probably be a really good soldier if you're allowed to join the military or Resistance."

"Thanks."

"You did the right thing. I hate Luuk. He's such an annoying, smug *Bokkelul.* Maybe now he'll think twice before he opens his big fat mouth."

Heer Eikenboom glared over at him. "Are you coming? I'm sure your mother will be very displeased to hear you started a fight at religious school and possibly blinded a fellow classmate because he had a difference of opinion. And during a happy holiday, too."

Jakob buttoned up his coat and slung his schoolbag over his shoulders. He kicked at Luuk lying on the floor one final time before he headed out of the building. Only because his teacher and principal were watching did he refrain from kicking Luuk in the head or kidney.

"Perhaps this suspension will give you some time to think about how hotheaded and on-edge you've been lately," Heer Eikenboom said as they started down the street. "Your father's death was a tragedy, but you're hardly the first boy in history who's lost his father during a time of war or enemy occupation. I don't think any of those other young men reacted like you. Sooner or later, you and your mother will get a full apology."

"My mother isn't getting a widow's pension, and we can't go back to our real house! My little sister is gone! We're not dealing with a normal enemy. These people aren't like any other enemies we've seen before. Our enemies in the ancient days were more civilized. Nobody is doing anything real to stop these people. If no one in power wants to do anything, it's up to us to fight back. It's pathetic how we let ourselves be conquered in just five days. A country like the United States or England would never let their people be occupied so easily."

"We're a much smaller country, and we don't have a large military like they do. And we wanted to stay neutral for this war anyway."

"Neutrality is for people without spines. It's evil to be neutral when there's a big emergency and people need help. It's just as bad how the United States isn't getting involved in this war. Maybe we would've been saved by now if they'd helped us."

During the twenty-minute walk home, Jakob periodically leaned down to scoop up snow and threw the snowballs against walls. He held back his urge to throw them at the NSBers and Nazis walking in the streets. At least he was allowed to remain on the same street. He'd heard stories about how people in Poland were made to get off the street if a Nazi passed them.

Luisa looked up from her crocheting when the door opened and Jakob came in with Heer Eikenboom. She threw her head back, already expecting to hear the worst. "Now what happened?"

"Your son decided it would be a great idea to start a fight with another boy, Luuk Klein. Luuk now has a bloody, swollen right eye and probably bruises all over his body from being punched and kicked so violently over and over again. I found a very violent drawing in his notebook. Your son the aspiring artist spent his class time drawing himself gunning down the people who coerced your husband into suicide."

Luisa sighed. "We've all tried to restrain him and get him to act and talk normally. Apparently he still needs more time to readjust after our tragedy."

"Jakob has also been suspended from religious school until further notice. Before he left, he made sure to announce that he thinks most of his classmates are cowards who like living under German occupation."

"Luuk said *Vader* was a coward for committing suicide." Jakob threw his schoolbag across the room. "He had such a smug look on his face. I've always hated that *Bokkelul*. So I had to teach him a lesson."

Heer Eikenboom stuffed his hands into his coat pockets. "This is why you're suspended till further notice. At least you haven't been suspended from gymnasium yet for this type of behavior."

"I only act like that when someone pushes my buttons. Unlike Luuk's heroes the Zealots, I don't think it's heroic to run away or back down when someone's attacking me."

Heer Eikenboom looked around quickly, then headed for the door. "Enjoy your modern-day Maccabee, Vrouw Hartog. Maybe you'll get him under control in time for him to come back before his birthday."

"From your mouth to God's ear." Luisa went back to her crocheting as Jakob sat down with his notebook and started drawing again.

Chapter 5: Nowhere to Run

Though he was forbidden to have anything to do with it, Jakob was very excited to discover the existence of several Jewish self-defense groups in the city, including one in his own neighborhood. At least one of these groups had ties to the Communist Party, which even his parents had always found too radical, but he didn't care. Political affiliation didn't matter so long as these people had weapons and plans of attack.

"Can I go out and join them?" Jakob begged during dinner. "I can hear them fighting from up here, and the gunfire is calling my name."

"Of course not!" Luisa reached for the platter of fish. "It's a blessing in disguise our Emilia is gone. I have to believe that wherever she went, she's a lot safer than she'd be here."

He speared a big piece of fish and plopped it onto his plate, then began talking with his mouth full. "As much as I'm itching to fire a gun, a bomb would be even better. Even a thousand people with guns can't do as much perfect damage as a big bomb in an important place like the town hall or NSB headquarters."

"Fourteen-year-old boys aren't supposed to be streetfighters," Kees said. "Even if it's morally justified, it's never respectable. Respectable freedom fighters join the military and fight in a professional battle, instead of in a residential neighborhood with amateur, disorganized ranks."

"Can I at least go outside after supper to see what's going on? I can lurk in the background to see what the score is."

"I can't take that risk," Luisa said. "What if you were killed by a stray bullet? Then I'd have no children left. No woman in her right mind waits forty years to become a mother only to give her miracle firstborn permission to get involved in a street fight."

"Don't try to sneak out after we're in bed either," Kees said. "We have that stupid midnight curfew, so you'd get in trouble even if you weren't fighting or helping resistance groups."

"But I'm not doing anything now. All those guys are being useful while I'm sitting at home like a pampered mama's boy who's afraid of fighting."

"At least a mama's boy is safe, unlike the streetfighter who cares only for himself," Luisa said.

"I'd be fighting because I care so much about our country and our family. As soon as we toss these *kankerhonden* out, the sooner you can be safe again, and the sooner we can get Emilia back. I'm not one of those stupid intellectuals who cares only about ideas and books, instead of living in the real world. Those brave fighters out there are the only ones in this country living in the real world."

"Soon they won't be living in the world at all, if they continue fighting street battles. They'll be overpowered."

"We should be thankful no one broke into our home during the raids a few days ago," Gusta said. "They're obviously here again now, so we should be even more thankful our home wasn't one of the ones disturbed."

"We might be next," Jakob said. "We should all be prepared to defend ourselves, even if it's only with an axe, a brick, a wooden pole, anything."

"You're not going out there after supper," Luisa repeated. "You can read about it in the newspaper later, or hear about it from your friends at school."

He roughly sawed away at his fish. "You told me I was the man of the house now, and I'm being the man of the house. One day you'll thank me for how I tried to do my part to defend our family."

2

The next day, while Jakob, Luisa, and Gusta were shopping in the Waterlooplein market, a rumbling was heard. Jakob ran off to the nearest side street and craned his neck to try to find the source of the noise. He ran back to his mother and Gusta when he saw Dutch police and German soldiers.

"Is it okay if I throw some of our eggs and fruit at them?" he begged. "I knew this would happen someday. Now we're unarmed, and have no choice but to defend ourselves."

"You're staying right here," Luisa warned.

Jakob heard the words the evil occupiers and their collaborators broadcasted as they stormed into the marketplace, but he couldn't quite understand what it meant. Luisa held him back when he tried to rush forward after several young men nearby began attacking a German soldier.

"Excuse me, but what exactly are you doing?" Gusta asked a Dutch policeman. "What's the reason for this?"

"Are you deaf? We just told you terrorists we're blocking off this dangerous neighborhood to avoid further skirmishes and attacks on our officers. Hendrik Koot is in the hospital after the severe injuries some of these terrorists gave him yesterday!"

"I think we should go home now," Luisa said. "We can get the rest of our groceries another day."

"But that's letting the Nazis and NSB win!" Jakob protested. "I have to see what they're doing so I can figure out an escape plan!"

"The only escape we're making is going home to avoid getting in anyone's way."

Jakob dragged his feet the entire way home, frequently lagging behind to see the progress of the operation. He fantasized about rolling these people up in their own barbed wire and strangling them with it, and throwing them off the bridges they were opening to create new boundaries. When they were going up the steps of the apartment, he picked up a rock and threw it at a German soldier whose back was turned. He smiled when the rock hit the soldier's back and the soldier screamed in pain and surprise. Before the soldier could turn around to discover the culprit, Jakob ducked into the building.

"Why are you smiling?" Luisa asked. "This is a horrible day!"

"I just threw a rock at one of those overgrown bullies. I hope I hit his kidney, or, better yet, his spine."

Luisa's eyes widened. "You threw a rock at an officer?"

"I wish it'd been a much bigger rock, so I might've knocked him to the ground or killed him."

"Do you think the other two Jewish neighborhoods are being closed off too?" Gusta asked.

"They probably will be." Jakob began punching the air. "We were chosen first because we're the oldest and most famous."

Luisa sank into a chair and fanned herself. "This might mean you won't be able to go to school anymore, though Jewish gymnasium students haven't been expelled yet like the university students. Kees and I both work outside of the neighborhood. We might not be able to go to work anymore either."

"About half my current clients live outside the neighborhood," Gusta said. "That's another big loss of income."

Jakob counted on his fingers. "May to February is nine months. So you should probably be delivering the last of your clients who were pregnant before the invasion. I hope you do the right thing and tell them to stop having babies, or help the newer clients end their pregnancies."

"Why would I tell a valued customer to stop adding to her family unless she were on her fifteenth child or had a serious medical condition? I'm not going to help women end their pregnancies just because we're under occupation. That's not given as an acceptable reason anywhere in the Bible or Talmud."

Jakob went to the window and saw five of the invaders coming up the steps. "Do you think they'd go to so much trouble to go after someone who only threw a rock? That idiot didn't see who did it."

They heard the intruders going into the apartments on the first floor and storming around. They assumed the intruders only wanted the people there until they heard footsteps coming up the stairs. Jakob put his ear to the floor and heard screaming, cursing, and demands for weapons.

"We need to run out the fire escape and grab what we can before they come up here too," he said, his heart pounding.

"Where would we go?" Luisa demanded. "Kees is still at work. He wouldn't know where to find us. We have nowhere left to run now."

"We can't leave our apartment open to looting," Gusta said.

"Thank God Emilia is no longer with us. She was scared enough by the invasion and the early days of occupation. I can only imagine how terrified she'd be by the events of the past week."

Jakob froze when he heard banging on the door. The three of them looked back and forth at one another for several very long moments.

"Would you terrorists like us to shoot or break your door down? All of you will be beaten and taken away if you don't open up right now!"

"We're not terrorists," Gusta said. "We had nothing to do with the street fights. We have no ties whatsoever to any of those renegade groups."

"We'll believe that when we're done searching your dirty home. All you terrorists are the same, insisting you're innocent. Innocent people don't attack the authorities and almost kill an important officer. Now open the door or we'll take you all to prison."

Gusta went to get the door and was shoved back by one of the

Dutch policemen. Jakob slipped his hand into Luisa's, standing up as straight as possible to try to look taller.

"Where do you keep your weapons?" one of the German soldiers asked. "If you don't tell us, we'll have to search the place and find them ourselves."

"We have no weapons," Gusta repeated. "Only kitchen knives."

"Then I suppose we'll have to search your home. We can't risk you people having weapons after what you've done to us."

The second Dutch policeman looked at them. "Is there no man of the house?"

"My husband is still at work," Gusta said. "My friend and her son live with us. They moved in after some of your friends coerced her husband into suicide."

"What a brilliant idea. Perhaps if we'd done that more often, we wouldn't have so many people taking up arms and thinking they're better than us." The policeman stormed into the kitchen.

The five intruders looked through every room, closet, drawer, and box for the next thirty minutes. Jakob saw several of Luisa's hairs turning gray, and cursed these people even more for causing his mother to start going gray right in front of him.

"You were right," one of the German soldiers said in disgust. "At least some of you people are law-abiding citizens and obey our decrees."

Kees came into the apartment and saw the mess all over the floor and the five strange men. They turned to look at him.

"You're the husband of the other woman?" the second Dutch policeman asked. "Now that you're home, you won't mind letting us frisk you before we leave."

"What have my wife and our friends done to warrant this visit?"

"You exist. That's reason enough." The German soldier who appeared to be the ringleader lit a cigarette.

Jakob's eyes burnt in furious remembrance. Those were the exact words used by the ringleader who murdered Ruud. That murderer had also been smoking a cigarette. He was somewhat disappointed none of these people were the ones he was waiting to murder in revenge. No amount of warnings or physical restraint by Luisa or Gusta could've made him hold back from killing them with his bare hands.

Kees held his arms up and let one of the other German soldiers frisk him. After finding no weapons on him either, the five invaders slammed the door and left. Jakob imagined himself reaching into his pocket for a small gun that transformed into a huge machine gun and shooting all five of them in the back, then kicking their bloodied, mangled corpses down the stairs.

"What happened?" Kees asked. "I came home and had to be cleared by a police checkpoint, and saw all this barbed wire around our neighborhood. What is this, the Middle Ages?"

"They wish," Jakob sneered. "In the Middle Ages, we let ourselves be put into ghettos because we were so busy studying holy books and teaching children not to fight back. Today we know about self-defense. I'm sure all those idiots in my religious school feel really stupid now. When I'm allowed to go back, I'm going to laugh in all their faces. I was right and they were wrong. Only a fool would still believe the Nazis and NSB mean us no real harm after today."

"Do you suppose the barbed wire will be taken down eventually?" Luisa asked. "After a decent period passes without another fight, they'll realize things are back to normal and ease up."

"I'd like to tear it down myself. They left us with our knives, so I can use those. Would any of you like to join me?"

"After what just happened, you know full well none of us are going to do anything so stupid. Now you might as well help us start supper. That's something useful you can do, not getting us in even more trouble. When you've got nowhere to run, you don't want to make your little space even more cramped."

Chapter 6: A Short-Lived Glimmer of Hope

Instead of working on his algebra homework, Jakob was bent over a detailed map of the city, a pen tightly gripped in his hand. Every so often, he looked up from the map to practice with the toy pistol he'd found in his new room. It was one of the toys that was left behind when Kees and Gusta's son Bram moved out some years back. A toy was better than nothing, and it wouldn't make him as nervous as handling a real firearm when he'd never used one before.

Jakob looked up from his map when Kees came in from work. "Have you been to the van Woustraat recently? These women are keeping me from going there and joining in the fun, so I have to content myself with planning my own attack from home."

Kees's eyes narrowed. "What are you talking about? What's happened at the van Woustraat? Somehow I think whatever happened is hardly what I'd consider fun, knowing your one-track mind."

Gusta wrung her hands. "This could be the beginning of the end for us, even worse than what's already happened. Thank God he listened to us and stayed put instead of heading over there to take part in that riot, or protest, or whatever he thinks would be fun to participate in."

"I can't wait to go back to the Koco ice-cream parlor," Jakob went on. "Before I just liked going there for the delicious ice-cream, but now I'll like going there even more because its owners are heroes. Finally, someone really stood up and did something to fight back against these barbarians."

"Do you listen to him talking?" Luisa asked. "You really think there won't be any punishment for this? I'm sure Ernst Cahn and Alfred Kohn will both be arrested and severely punished. If there still is a Koco ice-cream parlor after this week, I can almost guarantee you it'll be under entirely new management."

"Some Nazis decided to pay a visit and were sprayed with ammonia released through pipes," Gusta explained. "At least we know Jaapje didn't have anything to do with this."

"How could I have anything to do with it when you only let me leave the house to go to school, synagogue, or the market?" Jakob pretend-fired the toy pistol at a wall.

"And that's exactly what you'll continue doing," Luisa said. "We need you to behave now more than ever. If there are reprisals, your name can't be linked to any of the groups involved. You should be thankful you're still allowed to go to gymnasium and leave the neighborhood five days a week."

Kees went into the kitchen for a snack. "Why would ordinary people be punished? Even the Nazis and NSB aren't that awful they'd target normal people who had nothing to do with this."

"Now might be an excellent time to move to the center of action," Jakob said. "This isn't where the major underground groups are headquartered. Most people here aren't smart enough to get involved with real resistance groups. Those people who were defending us weren't in official resistance groups. They were like a child's version of the Army. We're easy targets in Jodenbuurt. Just look at that damned barbed wire, those stupid signs, and those police checkpoints. They're closing in on us like a hunter chasing a bear."

"We'll be easy targets anywhere we go," Luisa said. "Are you already forgetting we were forced to register last month? Now our religion is a matter of public record."

"The resistance is starting to rise, *Moeder*. The days of our people being helpless cowards are over. When enough people stand up and take back control, even a powerful invading force has to back down."

"And sometimes a small country conquers a great country by submitting to it. You have my permission to borrow my copy of *The Tao Te Ching*. It's one of the books you saved from our house. There are lots of pertinent lines about yielding, compromising, seeing the world in shades of gray. There are also many lines with your name on them, talking about how a good fighter isn't angry or violent, how a passionate man will either kill or be killed, and how weapons should only be used when there's no choice."

Jakob put the toy pistol down and began punching the air. "If I'm going to read any old Chinese book, it'll be *The Art of War*, not a philosophy book written before modern warfare. A lot of stuff in the Bible seems silly today too, since it was written before the modern era. I didn't know you liked old Chinese books. I just dumped as many of your books into the suitcase as I could after I filled the others with clothes and more important stuff."

"I always believed one can find wisdom in many sources, not just one's own religion or culture. If the worst happens and you're expelled from gymnasium, you'll have no excuse to sit around playing soldier with yourself all day. I'll make you read the classics in what's left of my library."

"And if the worst happens and the future makes us long for the days when we were just shut up behind barbed wire, I'll make all three of you join me in fighting back. So far, we've been lucky in avoiding the fate some of our neighbors had."

2

On Saturday, while they were walking to synagogue, the peace and quiet was broken by the now-familiar sound of rumbling and goose-stepping. When a group of German soldiers armed with machine guns appeared about twenty feet in front of them, Jakob grabbed Luisa's hand and turned around, only to see another group of armed soldiers approaching in the other direction.

"Has there been another disturbance?" Kees asked. "I can assure you none of us has been involved with the resistance groups, and we don't have any weapons."

"Where's your identity card?" one of the Germans demanded, raising his machine gun. "Perhaps you'll be lucky enough to join your other friends whom we're rounding up."

Kees reached into his inner coat pocket and pulled out the requested card, his hands shaking. One of the Dutch policemen knocked it out of his hands and kicked it into a sewer.

"Now go and retrieve it. How clumsy, to drop your most important form of identification. It's too bad there's no law yet requiring you to have your race stamped on the card. But don't worry, that's coming soon enough."

"I can't reach into a sewer grate! Even a small child's hands and arms couldn't fit through there!"

"We can fix that for you." One of the Germans unbuttoned his coat and pulled a sledgehammer out of a toolbelt, then proceeded to smash the perimeter of the sewer grate.

"Aren't you going?" Another Dutch policeman pushed him towards it. "We're giving you one minute to produce your identity card."

Jakob couldn't hear anything going on around him. His heart was beating so strongly, his blood rushed and pounded in his ears. He only knew what he was seeing, Kees being forced to get on his hands and knees to reach into the sewer. Once he was on the ground, the soldiers and policemen took turns kicking him and hitting him with their guns. All around him, other men were being beaten as well. He saw Gusta's mouth opening wide and assumed she must be screaming. All he could do was tightly hold Luisa's hand and pray he wasn't the next to be beaten and humiliated.

Kees had sewage all over his arms and hands by the time he pulled himself out of the open sewer and stood up, handing over his identity card again. They began laughing at how violently he was shaking.

One of the German soldiers grabbed the card and turned his ugly fat mouth downwards in disgust, his eyes registering the same reaction. "You're too old for us. I thought you were younger than this. But don't rest easy, you dog. Your turn will come eventually, when we're not looking for younger men."

One of the Dutch policemen turned to Jakob. "You don't look old enough for us, but you need to give us your ID anyway. Your turn will also come soon. We'll get around to all of you in due time. Your time of troubles is only beginning. One day you'll long for these days and feel sorry you were ever born."

Jakob reached into his inner coat pocket for his passport and opened it, keeping a firm hold on it. No Nazi or NSB goons were going to knock this out of his hands and make him dive into an open sewer.

The German with the ugly mouth sneered again. "Not even fifteen yet. You're useless."

"May we continue on our way now?" Luisa asked, taking Jakob's hand after he put his passport away. "We don't mean you any trouble."

"Of course you can't continue on your merry way. Like we told you, your troubles are just beginning. You can go back to your house and stay there till we give you permission. Your days of ruling the world are over."

They turned around and headed back to their apartment, trying to avoid looking at the savagery going on all around them. It normally would've taken only fifteen minutes to get home, but they were all shaking so badly, it seemed to take at least five hours. It felt like forever between their dismissal and the moment they were finally in front of the familiar red building again, able to retreat into its safety for the time being.

Kees collapsed onto the stairs and had to be helped up by Gusta.

He hung onto her the entire way and collapsed onto the living room floor as soon as they were inside their apartment. Jakob began punching the davenport pillows after he threw off his coat and flung his boots across the room.

"What's the nearest neutral country?" Gusta asked. "As far as I know, our movements aren't that restricted. The Germans will probably be glad to be rid of us. Even if we have to leave with just the clothes on our backs, we can always rebuild our possessions. We can't get our lives back."

"We could try to find a boat going to England," Luisa suggested. "They're not neutral, but at least they're not occupied. It's a much quicker journey than to Switzerland or Sweden."

"We're not cowards like the Zealots!" Jakob shouted, ripping the weakest pillow in half. "We're going to stay and fight, even if we're not a real army!"

"They didn't even want to take you to prison, or wherever they were taking those other men. You're not old enough for anything but school."

"But this has to stop! Things are getting too bad for us to back down! I'd rather be killed in battle than wait to be arrested or murdered! If we run away, I'll lose the chance to revenge *Vader*'s murder."

"Thank God they didn't kick me in the head," Kees said as he slowly picked himself up. "It looks like we're safe so far. I'm too old and you're too young. Don't make them angry and decide to take us anyway."

"And let them continue making *me* angry? Why do they have the right to do whatever they want, while we have to bend over backwards to make them happy? That's not normal!"

"But it is the safest thing to do right now. Just be patient and wait this out. After things go back to normal, we won't be bothered so much anymore."

3

On Tuesday morning, Jakob found the gymnasium doors locked and all the lights out in the building. He was wondering if the teachers and administration had been arrested for anti-Nazi activity when a man in a red coat tapped him on the shoulder and handed him a pamphlet.

"The decent people of this city are on strike today, and hopefully the strike will spread to other areas soon. It was decided only yesterday, so your teachers probably didn't have enough time to inform you you'd have a day off school."

"Really? Everyone in Amsterdam is on strike?"

"Not everyone, but all the decent people with the guts to take a stand against the Nazis and NSB. If your parents haven't gotten the word yet, you should find a way to relay the news to them so they can join us in this noble cause."

"I only have my mother now. My father was coerced into suicide by three Nazis in October. I can't wait to track them down and serve them the same fate."

"All the more reason for you to encourage your mother and any friends to join us. Have a nice day."

Jakob read the pamphlet as he walked back home, smiling at how the uprising was really beginning.

Protest against the awful persecution of Jews!!!

Organize a protest strike in all enterprises!!!

Fight unanimously against this terror!!!

Require immediate freedom for the arrested Jews!!!

Require the dissolution of WA terror groups!!!

Organize self-defense in enterprises and neighborhoods!!!

Show your solidarity with the severely hurt Jewish part of the working people!!!

Protect Jewish children from the Nazi violence by taking them into your families!!!

"What are you doing here at this time of day?" Gusta demanded. "You're supposed to be at gymnasium, not strolling around the city!"

"My teachers are on strike," Jakob said proudly, holding up the pamphlet. "I guess *Moeder* and Kees didn't get the notice. They'll sure be surprised when they show up at work and no one's there."

"Striking? Isn't that what Communists and Socialists do?"

"It's what all decent people do when they're being mistreated. A labor union's as important as a strong military. This strike was thought up by the Communist Party. Good for them for not letting the Germans drive them out of town."

"You're lucky you're allowed to leave the neighborhood and still go to gymnasium! All that might be ruined after this strike! Do you really think the Germans will let this continue without punishment?"

"When enough people stand up against injustice, the evil people are overthrown. Finally, people are tired of being scared and doing something."

Gusta shook her head. "Your mother wouldn't be very happy to know you were wandering around all over the city just because you got a day off. Would you like to come with me? I've got a birth to attend, and babies don't always wait for the midwife to be born."

Jakob wrinkled his nose. "Why would I want to watch a baby being born? That's women's stuff. Even if I had a wife, I wouldn't want to watch our baby being born. I might be in the room, but not watching as it comes out."

Gusta smiled. "That's such a typical male attitude. No, you don't have to watch the baby coming out, but you can still be in the house with me. I'm sure Vrouw Rietveld won't mind you being there."

Jakob dragged his feet during the walk to Vrouw Rietveld's house. All the way there, no streetcars could be seen, and all the shops and market stalls were eerily quiet. Gusta grabbed his arm and dragged him along every time he stopped to gaze after groups of workers heading for various public squares and marketplaces.

"Here we are. You can listen to the radio or read some of their books to entertain yourself. We'll probably be here long enough to need lunch, so you're welcome to feed yourself, so long as you don't help yourself to their entire pantry."

He dragged his feet up the front stoop and stalked into the living room. He pulled down a Dutch translation of *The Art of War* and started reading while Gusta helped Vrouw Rietveld. At least he could put himself to some good use while the adults were out striking.

4

Just as the adults predicted, but to Jakob's great frustration, the strike was completely put down within several days. Even worse, now there was martial law in effect, as punishment. Still, at least more than a few people were brave enough to take a stand and risk punishment for standing up for their convictions. He didn't buy the claim the adults always made, that they were protesting by simply minding their own business and continuing to live normally. They weren't much better than the silent collaborators who weren't doing anything.

"You should be thankful we've avoided the worst," Luisa said as she stirred a pot of chicken soup on Saturday evening. "Kees wasn't one of the men taken during all those raids, and we only had our home broken into once. Many of your classmates don't have that kind of luck."

"The worst already happened! *Vader* is dead and Emilia's gone! Kees was beaten and humiliated by those goons! We need to step things up. You'll be so proud of me when I join the partisans and get a reputation as the best underage fighter ever."

"I'll be prouder of you when you finish the school year with high marks. Good always prevails over evil, no matter how long it takes. Eventually the tide of evil turns in favor of good. If you take matters into your own hands, you'll give me more gray hairs."

Jakob helped himself to chocolates sitting on a side table. "One day you'll realize I was right. The young generation's always smarter than the older one. That little glimmer of hope that was just crushed will keep me going for a long time. All I have to do is find a way to play my part at the right time."

Chapter 7: No Celebration of Freedom

Jakob was glad his family was Progressive, so he didn't have to observe Ta'anit Bechorot, the Fast of the Firstborn, on the day before Pesach. When he got home from school that Friday, he reached for a hunk of cheese and poured himself a glass of grape juice. As he had his snack, he started reading the library book he'd just checked out on physical fitness. Even if they had no exercise equipment besides old weights under Kees and Gusta's bed, he could always do simple exercises like pushups and sit-ups.

Kees came in and fixed him with the type of look usually only Luisa gave him. "Just what do you think you're doing?"

"Having a snack and reading. What does it look like I'm doing? Even if we're not as religious as the people in the East, it's still a long time between now and dinner. I wish the dinner part of the Seder came first, not in the middle of a long night!"

"Not that. I can see what you're doing. I mean what are you doing helping yourself to food without permission? It's getting harder to buy food under the occupation, and we shouldn't be greedy and have such large portions when there are three other people to think of. I was fired today, so from now on we only have two incomes, one of them part-time. As soon as you're old enough, you'll probably have to register for labor service."

"Not on your life. I'm not going to paint a target on my own back. How come you were fired?"

Kees gave him that look again. "Do you really have to ask that? I was lucky to hold onto my job longer than many other people. I knew my boss was in the NSB. Today he went public with his poorly-disguised secret and fired all his Jewish employees. What a way to wish us a happy holiday."

"If I got fired, I'd plant a bomb in the NSBer's office. Are you going to look for another job after the weekend?"

"I don't think most places will want to hire me. Even if they're in sympathy with us, the repercussions are too great. At least we have decent money and enough food to get by in the meantime. Gusta and I own this apartment instead of renting it, so we'll keep a roof over our heads. We only need to pay utilities every month."

Jakob put his empty glass in the sink and headed for the living room. He lay down on the floor and began doing pushups. Kees stood over him and inspected his form.

"You'll have to do better than that if you want to be taken seriously as a soldier, even in the partisans. That's how a woman does a pushup, or a man with no upper body strength."

"I have to start somewhere. If I keep doing this every day, I'll be a lot more muscular in no time. Not only will the other soldiers be jealous of my strength, but women will want to be with me too. Not that I'll let them, but it'll be nice to be admired by women."

Kees chuckled. "Aren't you a little too old to think like that about women? You'll be fifteen next month. I assumed the only reason you didn't have a sweetheart yet was because you had more important things to think about."

"I guess I'll have a wife someday, but she can't be just any woman. Only someone who's gone through this terrible time. The only woman I need to think about now is my mother." Jakob didn't feel like telling Kees he was too angry and bitter to let any girl get close to him emotionally. He couldn't risk getting hurt again after the heartache of losing his father and sister.

"That's a shame. Having a sweetheart might help take your mind off this time of troubles. Many a good woman has been known to reform a man."

"That sounds like something a silly women's magazine would say. I'm exactly the same as I'll be forever. Besides, if a woman is meant to be my wife, she'll be perfect for me and won't need to change anything either."

Kees laughed as he picked up the newspaper. "You've got a lot to learn about adult life in more ways than one. Get back to me on the topic of women when you've actually had a relationship with one."

Luisa came into the apartment and rushed towards the davenport. "My boss told me I could go home early for the holiday and never come back. I never suspected he was in league with the NSB."

"I was just fired too. I wish Jaap were old enough to work, because we're sure going to need extra money. There's no telling if soon Gusta won't be allowed to offer midwifery services to Christians. None of her Christian clients have fired her, but if it becomes illegal to work for Christians or associate with them in any capacity, they might have no choice."

Luisa looked down at her son. "Why are you doing pushups? If you want to exercise, you can join a club. A home isn't a place for that."

"Aren't you paying any attention, *Moeder*?" Jakob tried a pushup off of his knees and dug his hands into the floor for support. "Things are getting worse all the time. We might not be allowed to join clubs soon. Why pay money when I can do it for free here?"

"He thinks all the girls will love him once he's fit and muscular, but he doesn't actually want a girlfriend," Kees said. "One day, Jaap, you'll laugh at all your youthful ideas. Bram had ideas like yours once, but now that he's an adult, he realizes how little he actually knew. You'll be telling your son this someday, when he's the one insisting he knows better than the adults and sharing his idealistic theories about relationships and self-defense."

Jakob got up and headed into Kees's room. "Do you mind if I borrow your weights?"

"No, but you could've asked before you invited yourself into my room. I never go into your room without permission. Take care not to use the heaviest weights first. You'll injure yourself instead of getting more muscular quicker."

Jakob got on his knees and pulled out all the weights. "When was the last time you used these? They're kind of dusty."

"It's been awhile. I've had more important priorities since I've been a working man."

"Why don't we take turns? You could do well to bulk up too, so those goons don't beat you up again. A girl at my religious school was telling me how well I can punch with both hands, and I never had any strength training. Are you jealous of me?"

"Why would I be jealous of a fourteen-year-old boy with no idea how the real world works? You can use my weights out here. I don't like people in my room when I'm not there."

Jakob came out with a three-pound pair of weights. "These aren't as heavy as I'd like, but I have to start somewhere. How fast do you think I can graduate to the real weights?"

"Use your own judgment. You can tell when it's getting too easy to use light weights. It's about how many repetitions you can do, not a certain amount of time passing."

Luisa went into the kitchen and found some of the cheese missing and the bottle of grape juice almost empty. "Did you gentlemen help yourselves to a snack?"

"Only Jaap. I told him he has to start rationing his diet if he cares about the rest of us. He'd better not overeat tonight at the Antemas' house."

"Why can't we do it here?" Jakob asked. "What if our house is raided while we're gone?"

"Four people doesn't make a real Seder, and Bram and Floor live too far away to travel to us. I wish my children still lived in Amsterdam so Gusta and I could know how they're holding up. We haven't heard from them in awhile."

"The big cities are usually safer. Small towns are more dangerous, because people don't have modern ideas and aren't used to living with different kinds of people. Maybe you could write to them and make them come home."

"They're fine where they are. Gusta and I don't believe in interfering in our grown children's lives. Bram's in Eindhoven and Floor's in Groningen. Hardly backwater hamlets full of anti-Semites and people cut off from civilization and modern ideas."

"So far, things are worse here," Luisa said. "God willing, we'll soon be delivered just as our ancestors were."

"Our ancestors were only redeemed because they cried out and stopped accepting slavery as normal," Jakob said. "I hope it won't take four hundred years for us to get rid of these new enemies."

2

That evening, they arrived at the home of Rebekka Antema, who lost her husband Ludger and her sons Theodor and Jonas in one of the February raids. She, her remaining son Adriaan, and her daughter Elsje were hosting ten people.

Jakob looked around the house. It'd been awhile since he last visited, in much happier times. Without waiting for an invitation, he took a seat, choosing the nicest chair with the plumpest, fanciest pillows.

"Excuse me, Jaap," Vrouw Antema said as she headed into the kitchen for last-minute food preparation. "That's Adriaan's chair. It would've been my husband's seat if he hadn't been taken away to Mauthausen."

"You have assigned seating?"

"My family gets first pick on seats, and then you can be seated.

You can read a book while we're waiting to start."

Jakob headed into the living room and started doing sit-ups. "I'm not an atheist, but celebrating holidays now is a joke. How can we celebrate these things when we're under occupation? Are we supposed to pretend everything's just fine?"

Luisa took a seat on the davenport near him. "We'll continue to celebrate, occupation or no occupation. Our ancestors celebrated holidays and observed religious laws even in periods of severe persecution. You were just praising the Maccabees for fighting back against foreign rulers. They did these things in secret too. Be thankful we're still able to do these things openly."

Sixteen-year-old Elsje stood above him and carefully inspected him. "You've gotten pretty handsome since I last saw you. Do you have a girlfriend yet?"

"I don't need a stupid girlfriend. I wouldn't let anyone be my girlfriend even if someone wanted to be. Going out with a girl would be a big waste of my time. I'd rather spend my time learning to fire weapons and go on spying missions than waste money on taking a girl to restaurants and learning to dance."

"You might get more offers when you're more muscular," Kees said. "Try doing a sit-up with your hands above your chest instead of behind your head. You'd be laughed out of the Army if you exercised like that in basic training."

"That's why I'm practicing now. Are there any weapons in this house I can practice with outside?"

"Of course not!" Vrouw Antema shouted. "Our antique rifles were taken away during the raids, and I'm not going to risk trouble by acquiring new weapons. I wish our country had a junior military training program like the United States. That would probably keep you happy."

Jakob continued doing sit-ups till Vrouw Antema called everyone to the second-floor dining room table. He sat and looked at the illustrations in his Hagadah instead of paying attention to Adriaan's reading and the discussions the adults had every few pages. At least this wasn't like the Seder he'd been to a few years ago, where everyone was made to take turns reading a page or paragraph. When it came time to recite the various blessings, he mumbled them in a disinterested voice. He bit into his piece of parsley so hard everyone heard his teeth smacking together.

Luisa turned to him after the second cup of wine was poured. "Look at this, Jaapje. You're the youngest person here. Would you like to recite the Four Questions?"

"Emilia should be the one reciting them! If she's still alive, she's probably not at a Seder tonight! Maybe she's forgotten about us and thinks she's a Christian! I barely remember anything from when I was that young."

"Since Emilia isn't here, and there's nothing anyone can do about it, you're the youngest. Are you going to recite them, or should we do it as a group?"

Jakob's eyes gleamed. "Sure, I'll do it." He pushed his chair back and stood up, ignoring Vrouw Antema's grimace when he banged the chair against the glass door of the cupboard behind him. "Why is this night different from all other nights? On all other nights, we had complete families and lived in our own houses, but tonight many of our friends and family are dead, in prison, or in German camps, and some of us were forced to leave our houses."

"You're not doing it properly, and you know it," Elsje protested.

"Why is this night different from all other nights? On all other nights, we were a free people in a free land, but tonight we're living under German occupation, and our Queen is in exile with her family. Why is this night different from all other nights? On all other nights, our neighborhood was a free, peaceful place, but on this night, our neighborhood is cut off from most of the city and closed off by barbed wire. At least some of us are able to leave and enter at the police checkpoints."

"Jakob, that's enough," Luisa warned. "Think of what your father would've thought of this behavior."

"Why is this night different from all other nights? On all other nights, we had the same rights as all other Dutch citizens, but today we're living under more and more intolerable laws designed to set us apart for discrimination and violence. The religious freedom we enjoyed for so many hundreds of years is no more. But with the help of God, we'll rise up against these evil invaders and get our home back, and the Nazis and NSBers will be the ones thrown in jail, beaten, and humiliated. Amen."

"What is wrong with you?" Elsje asked. "If you set out to ruin a happy holiday and our entire night, you sure achieved it."

"Yes, he was definitely looking for shock," Adriaan said. "And he achieved it."

"This is why he was suspended from religious school," one of the guests said. "Little wonder he hasn't been allowed back yet."

"I'm better off without those people," Jakob said. "Most of them didn't realize the danger we're in. I wonder if they've changed their minds yet."

"Please don't embarrass me again," Luisa warned. "You're lucky you're my miracle baby and that I never believed in corporal punishment."

Jakob continued looking at the illustrations in his Hagadah till he saw they were up to Dayenu. Everyone groaned when they saw him standing up again. Vrouw Antema shrieked when the back of his chair left a crack in the glass cupboard door.

"If no one minds, I'd like to offer a different, modern, more relevant version of Dayenu."

"Everyone minds, and you know it!" Adriaan shouted. "This is supposed to be a celebration of freedom from slavery, not a time to rub it in our faces that we're not as free as we used to be!"

Jakob started counting the verses on his fingers. "If the Germans had only invaded our country, it would've been enough. If the Germans had only forced us to register our religion, it would've been enough. If the Germans had only had so many of our people kicked out of their jobs, it would've been enough. If the Germans had only murdered my father, it would've been enough. If the Germans had only gone on a rampage in our neighborhood once, it would've been enough. If the Germans had only turned our neighborhood into a ghetto, it would've been enough. If the Germans had only—"

"Jakob Eliezer DeJonghe, that's quite enough," Luisa said. "Now sit back down, and if you make another scene, you're going to sit in the living room and will have a small meal brought to you. I don't trust you to go home by yourself without getting into trouble."

He sat back down and reached for his Hagadah. "At least I got a chance to make my point before you interrupted me."

For the rest of the Seder, he sat looking at the illustrations, mumbling the required blessings, and chewing his food so violently everyone heard his teeth clacking together. He was very disappointed Vrouw Antema's food came up rather short of the usual Pesach feast he was used to. Just chicken, fish, chopped liver, some salads, carrot soup, and a vegetable kugel. Her dessert obviously didn't come from a bakery. It was a boring chocolate torte ringed by apple slices, as poorly-made as the rest of her food. Jakob was glad his mother was a much more accomplished, adventurous cook. If they'd hosted, even if they hadn't had a lot of money, Luisa would've given the guests at least three dessert options.

"Can we trust you to look for the afikomen, or should we make you stay seated?" Luisa asked. "You're the youngest."

"We don't have to give him a prize or money when he finds it, do we?" Elsje asked. "He might be intelligent and handsome, but he's got an awful attitude! And he broke our cupboard!"

"You'd have an awful attitude too if you saw your father coerced into suicide and lost your baby sister, while everyone around you acted like everything was so normal and we didn't need to fight back."

"I lost my father and two of my brothers, and saw all of them beaten in front of me. You don't see me giving angry speeches on happy holidays, beating up my classmates, or plotting revenge."

"You're a girl. A lot of girls think they're not supposed to do that."

"Are we really going to let him find the afikomen, *Moeder*?" Adriaan asked. "He's had an awful attitude all night. He doesn't deserve a prize or money."

"I deserve a hundred million guilders and the most expensive prize in the world after what I've been through. Someone has to find it, or we can't end."

"Don't you dare pretend you don't remember where I hid it, or we'll be here all night," Adriaan growled as Jakob got up. "If we're not done by midnight, you'll have to stay here overnight, and no one wants that."

"I don't know where you put it. And I am the youngest. I'm supposed to look for it."

Though he wanted nothing better than to stick it to the Antemas, Jakob was more eager to go home and eat real food. He went through all the rooms of the house, rifling through furniture, bedding, and closets, pulling books off of shelves, and rattling through the kitchen before it finally turned up in the nightstand in Elsje's room. Beaming triumphantly, he strode back into the dining room, holding it over his head.

"Where's my prize?"

"You haven't been a good sport all night," Elsje hissed. "You don't deserve a prize. Prizes are for children anyway. You're almost fifteen."

"He's been through a lot," Luisa said. "Perhaps he'll be back to normal in a few months. He's just grieving Ruud and Emilia in a different way than I am."

Vrouw Antema sighed deeply as she dug a few guilders out of her purse. "This is more than you deserve, but it is my obligation to give it to you."

Jakob pocketed the coins. "Thanks. Maybe I can use these to buy a rifle when I've saved up enough money."

"No weapons," Luisa warned. "I keep hoping you'll wake up one morning and be back to the sweet, loving boy you used to be."

3

That night, once he was back home, in his new room, Jakob chewed a large slice of his mother's delicious Pesach apple cake while he drew a picture of Ruud's three murderers being hanged, along with the thugs who beat and humiliated Kees in February. After he was satisfied with his artwork, he started a picture of the murderers begging an angel for forgiveness at the entrance gates to Paradise. Below the clouds of Paradise, he drew the flames of Hell and the beckoning Devil, as the angel pointed menacingly downward. It was a very Christocentric depiction of the afterlives, but he wanted something easy to draw, not something he'd have to think long and hard about how to depict. All he cared about was sending them off to Hell, even if it was only in a drawing.

"Are you still up?" Luisa demanded. "I see a light under your door."

"I'm just reading. You don't need to wait up for me to go to bed. I can't get into any trouble at home."

"I doubt you're really reading, but at least you don't have school tomorrow. I suppose it won't hurt if you stay up a little bit later. So far the midnight curfew only applies to outside, not inside."

Jakob pushed his red colored pencil across the page so hard he ripped it. His hand was starting to hurt from clutching the writing implements so tightly. Ruud had tried to tell him several times not to hold his pens and pencils so tightly and not to press them against the upper part of his index finger, but Jakob hadn't listened to him. Now he began to think his father might've been right when he'd said a writing callus didn't have to develop, if only more teachers taught correct writing methods early on.

"*Moeder*, if you have pain, is it okay to work through the pain, or should you find another way to do an activity till you don't hurt anymore?"

"What are you talking about? Can I come in there?"

"I'm fine. You don't need to find a doctor for me. I was just wondering."

"What are you doing in there that you'd hurt yourself? Dear God, don't tell me you're pleasuring yourself."

"If I was, I'd never tell you or anyone! I've never done that! Why would I do something like that? I don't even want a girlfriend!"

"You don't have to get so defensive about it. If you've hurt your hand drawing more pictures of God knows what, maybe that's a sign you should go to bed. It'll get better before you get married, at any rate."

Jakob waited for her footsteps to recede, then crept out to his door and peered out to see her turning her light off. After he was satisfied she was sound asleep, he turned off his light, climbed back onto his bed, turned on the small bedside lamp, and picked up his notebook again.

He turned to a clean page and picked up his favorite fountain pen to write his own version of the ending of the Hagadah. His hand started hurting again the moment he closed his grip on the pen. Determined not to postpone these final touches on his masterpiece, he shrugged and moved the pen to his left hand. Every once in awhile, he used his other hand to sketch, and practiced writing with it from time to time. Ambidexterity was a valuable life skill, particularly in a future soldier. He'd been very proud when Elma praised his skill at punching with both hands.

He looked on at what he'd written when he was finished and smiled, imagining the looks on the murderers' faces when he finally caught up to them and served them the fate he'd been dreaming about for the last six months.

This year we are slaves in The Netherlands and most of Europe, but next year we will be free in our own countries.

Have no mercy, God, on those soulless Nazi and NSB barbarians.

Rebuild Amsterdam, The Netherlands, and Europe, speedily in our days.

We thank you for our remaining limited freedoms, but most of all the gift of wisdom and bodily strength, the better to revenge ourselves with.

Send our Queen Wilhelmina, Princess Juliana, and Prince Bernhard safely back to our land, speedily in our days.

Guide our dispersed armed forces and brave partisans to victory and preserve as many of their lives as possible, speedily in our days.

NEXT YEAR IN AMSTERDAM!

Part II:
The Noose Tightens

(May-November 1942)

Chapter 8: A Cascade of Restrictions

Jakob swore he could hear every little prick the needles made in their clothes, every swish of the thread as it was pulled in and out of the fabric. The tiny magnified sounds made him nauseous. Instead of feeling happy about his upcoming sixteenth birthday, he was fuming about having to be publicly marked from now on. As though it weren't bad enough he'd been expelled from gymnasium in January.

"This is like something from out of the Middle Ages!" he protested, keeping his basket of clothes tightly in his arms. "We don't have to put up with this!"

"Your turn will come eventually, whether you like it or not," Luisa said gently. "Gusta and I are almost done with sewing stars onto all our clothes, and Kees will finish eventually. You might feel like a hero for defying the new rule, but the authorities will only see you as a criminal to be arrested."

"Why do we need these damn stars? We're not allowed to go almost anywhere anymore! Soon we'll only be allowed to sit around at home doing nothing! What good will these damned Medieval badges do then?"

"We must obey the law," Kees said as he threaded a needle. "It's too bad none of us knows how to work a sewing machine."

"I never liked sewing machines," Luisa said. "We should be grateful they were invented, but I always found it more relaxing to sew by hand. The worst you have to worry about with sewing by hand is a knot or ripped thread, not a machine jamming or breaking. Maybe I'd feel differently if I were a professional tailor or seamstress, or if I'd been blessed with a lot more than just two children."

"At least we're prolonging our public shame by sewing the stars on by hand," Gusta said. "We might already be done if we had a sewing machine."

Jakob twisted a sleeve of one of his shirts in his hands. "Where can we go anymore? I'm sure that by the end of next month, even more places will be off-limits. Will we have to wear those Medieval pointy hats next?"

"Whatever restrictions might come next, I'm sure you'll catalogue them in that depressing scrapbook of yours," Luisa said. "Why do you save all those clippings and notices? I'd be horrified if my parents or grandparents had shown me a scrapbook like that. If you're doing it for posterity, I'm very sure your children and grandchildren would much rather see an album full of happy pictures, greeting cards, post-cards, and graduation notices."

"I want the record for myself and no one else. And my teacher at that stupid new school likes to quiz us on dates and restrictions. I always get perfect marks on those quizzes."

"If that's your purpose, why not keep a diary?"

"That's for women, and if I did want to write a diary, I wouldn't want anyone snooping in it and reading my private thoughts."

Kees laughed. "We wouldn't be reading anything we don't already know, unless you're living a secret double life we've never suspected. You don't have a girlfriend or go on dates, and you don't go to your friends' houses anymore."

"Blame the Nazis and NSBers for how I barely go anywhere anymore. I'd love to get out more and see my friends outside of school. Do you think I like spending most of my time with three grownups?"

Luisa threw her final item of clothing into her large basket. "It's your turn, Jaap. Would you like me to show you how to thread the needle and tie a knot? Gusta can show you another way of fastening thread without making a knot, which she thinks is more secure."

"Do you know how big to make your stitches?" Gusta asked. "You shouldn't make them too tiny or too large. Those kinds of stitches are best in embroidery, not sewing patches on clothes."

Jakob didn't budge an inch from his chair. "I told you, I'm not doing it. I'll stay inside if I have to, or risk going out unmarked."

Luisa tried to pull his basket out of his iron grip. "You have to do it, even if it's unfair. You'll be sixteen in a few days, old enough for prison. Do you want to break your mother's heart? You're all I have left now. I'm fifty-six years old. My hands and fingers aren't so young anymore. I'm not going to sit and make all those stitches in a second batch of clothes when I don't have to."

"Can I attach them with pins so I can rip them off as soon as I get home? Or maybe I can wear a lightweight jacket over my shirts so I don't have to let everyone know I have a target on my chest."

"You know very well what the rules and regulations about the stars are. They're all in that silly scrapbook of yours. Now unless you'd like to try your hand at begging some of the neighbors for a sewing machine or their own manual labor, you'll have to sew them on yourself."

"Don't look at me to do it either," Gusta said. "I might be younger than your mother, but I'm not that much younger. At our ages, a ten-year age difference isn't the kind of big deal it is at your age."

"I only have to have a star on the shirt I'm wearing when I go out. What if I only wear one shirt for public? I could sew a star onto one shirt and leave the rest of my clothes be."

Luisa threw her head back. "Then everyone will think I'm a bad mother for letting you wear the same clothes over and over again! I take pride in regularly washing our clothes, repairing clothes, and getting you new clothes as our budget affords it! Even if they think it reflects only on you, you'll still get a bad reputation. Only tramps and poor people wear the same clothes all the time. They might think you smell bad and assume you're not washing this one shirt of yours."

"I don't give a damn what anyone thinks of me. I'll know the truth, even if they think the wrong things. That's their fault for assuming things without knowing all the information."

"Don't try to postpone it," Gusta said. "If you only sew stars on a few shirts each day, it'll be worse. Just get it over with all at once, like tearing off a bandage. It hurts more than doing it slowly, but you're not anticipating and dreading more pain when you do it all immediately."

"But I like my clothes. I don't want to ruin them with those ugly yellow stars. When we have to remove them after we chase these invaders out, there'll be lots of little holes in my shirts, maybe even an ugly yellow stain."

"You're not special," Luisa said. "You're just like everyone else. The rules say we all must do it. Even the traitors in the Joodenrat have to wear it."

"After this weekend's over, you'll have no choice but to leave the house," Kees said. "So far you haven't been expelled from the new religious school, and we'd like to keep it that way. You should be thankful there's no more barbed wire around our neighborhood. Didn't we tell you that situation would be resolved in enough time? Maybe the stars will also go away in a few months."

"Why does everyone keep telling me to be thankful for things no one would feel thankful for in peacetime?" Jakob stormed over to the nearest window with his basket.

"Are you going to throw all your clothes out the window? That's the petulant act of a little boy, not a young man who'll be sixteen next week."

"Would you prefer I rip all my shirts up instead so I have nothing to wear? Either way, it'll mean I don't have to wear a stupid yellow star on my shirts. It's nice weather, so I can go around without a shirt."

"No you won't!" Luisa shouted. "You have to buckle down and do it like all the rest of us. If this is how you want to act, perhaps I should reconsider giving you a present or having a celebration for your birthday. Naughty little boys act like this, not young men approaching the end of their tenth year of school."

"You'll be arrested if you don't wear a star," Gusta said. "We're so lucky all four of us are still together. After so many raids and mass arrests, you and Kees are still with us. A lot of your friends and classmates don't have any men left in their homes."

Jakob turned his basket upside-down and began kicking at his shirts and jackets. "I lost my father over a year and a half ago, and I still haven't seen the murderous bastards again! The only reason I'm living here and not in my real house is because I lost my father!"

"Throwing a tantrum or planning to break the law won't bring him back," Luisa said. "Now are you going to start sewing or not? I don't want to be arrested for truancy if you don't go to school on Monday, and I won't let you leave the house without a star. Education is so important. You should cherish it while it's still available. I hope we get rid of these criminals before you graduate secondary school."

"We won't get rid of them any faster if we constantly roll over and do whatever they demand."

"How much do you like the chocolate cake with strawberry filling I always make for your birthday?"

Jakob knelt down and began collecting his clothes, fuming as he tossed them into the basket. "Fine, I'll do it, but only because I don't want you to be arrested or get a bad reputation."

"Good boy. I'll give you a treat if you work fast enough and don't complain every ten minutes."

He reached into Luisa's sewing basket and rooted through it till he found a spool of dark blue thread. "If I have to do this, at least I can sew them on with an original color. And this is the color we're supposed to use in a tallit."

"Aren't you proud of who you are? Hiding inside is what you do when you're ashamed of yourself and afraid to let people know who you are. Now everyone has no doubt left you're a Jewish boy. You could blend in before because you only cover your head with a normal cap and don't wear a tallit katan, but now you have no choice."

"I'm going to burn these awful stars after we take back our country." He made a knot. "These stupid markings will give the Nazis no mistake when I get rid of the three *Bokkelulen* who murdered *Vader*. I bet they'll never expect to encounter a Jewish warrior who believes in fighting back and defending himself."

2

While riding his bicycle to school on Monday, feeling everyone's eyes on him once he crossed out of Jodenbuurt boundaries, Jakob noticed a tiny brown mouse nibbling on a rotten carrot that had fallen off the top of an overflowing garbage can next to a restaurant. Uncaring he might be late to school, he went over to the mouse and propped his bicycle against the brick wall.

Jakob took his lunchbox out of his bicycle basket and pulled out the apple, knowing full well Luisa would lecture him about not wasting her money and his lunch on feeding wild animals. "Come here, little friend. I've got something a lot nicer for you to eat. You don't have to be afraid of me. I like animals." He pushed his knife into the apple and cut out a little slice.

The mouse looked at him for several minutes before padding over and sniffing at the apple slice. Jakob smiled at the mouse when it jumped into his hand and began nibbling the apple.

"Do you know you're freer than I am, little one?" He stroked the top of its head with his thumb. "You can go wherever you want, whenever you want, and not have to follow anyone's orders. No one knows what mouse group you're from when you go out. You must be very brave to go outside in daylight. Most mice only show themselves when it's dark."

After the mouse ate about a quarter of the slice, it squeaked and stood up on its hind legs. Jakob smiled when it nuzzled against his nose, knowing Luisa would have even more of a fit if she knew he were touching wild animals who might have diseases.

"That's why I like animals so much. God didn't create you with the same prejudices he gave mankind. Most animals are happy with so little, and don't care what religion or ethnic group a person is from. All you care about is being loved, fed, sheltered, and protected by humans, not whether your owner or benefactor is Jewish, Christian, man, woman, child, in a wheelchair, blind, deaf, young, old, Dutch, Italian, French, or anything else. No one teaches you to blindly hate an entire group of people, and no one discriminates against you because of the way you were born." He gently set the mouse back on the ground and stuffed the remaining apple slice into his pocket. "If I see you again, I'll give you more of my apple."

***

When he arrived at school, Jakob didn't know whether to feel more heartened or depressed at being in a sea of people who all had an ugly yellow star sewn to their shirts. On the plus side, he fit in and wasn't a walking target, but on the minus side, he was just one in a sea of others. With the same marking as everyone else, he wasn't so different or special anymore. At least things weren't as worse as they were in Germany, and he didn't have to adopt a new middle name to set him apart even further. Eliezer was a bit old-fashioned, but he liked his first name just fine and couldn't imagine having any other identity. As Luisa often told him with an exasperated sigh, he certainly acted like his Biblical namesake, always getting into trouble, acting before thinking, and not having a mature enough mindset.

Heer Marquering, the first period history teacher, strode to the front of the room. "In light of recent events we're obviously all aware of, we're going to have a test on the various anti-Jewish measures and the dates they were passed. As usual, I'm sure Heer DeJonghe will score the highest. Many of you would do well to keep as up-to-date on these developments as he does. Scholarship has always been our strong suit, even in times of persecution."

Jakob smirked at his classmates as Heer Marquering distributed the tests. He smirked especially long and meaningfully at smug Luuk Klein, who was dressed rather like Little Lord Fauntleroy today. Vrouw Klein must've really wanted her annoying son to be a walking target on two fronts, unlike Luisa, who wanted Jakob to blend into the woodwork as best as possible instead of attracting attention and bringing trouble to either of them.

He picked up the fountain pen he'd gotten from Luisa for Chanukah and scrawled his name and the date, then began filling in the blanks as quickly as possible. Every so often, he lifted his eyes upwards and looked around the classroom to see how his classmates were faring. Most of them weren't working as quickly as he was, and many furrowed their brows, squinted their eyes, tapped their pens, scratched their heads, and looked up at the ceiling as they struggled to think of the right dates, or the nearest approximation. People might criticize him for being hot-headed, but no one could ever accuse him of being stupid or not caring about schoolwork. He thanked God for giving him such a voluminous, prolific memory as he looked back at his test and filled in the remaining few blanks.

When he'd filled everything in, he looked it over one last time to double-check for errors or missed questions. Out of the corners of his eyes, he could see many of his classmates were still struggling to get to the end. For a moment, he wondered if he'd know the information as well if he'd been presented with dates and been made to fill in the events, but then shrugged and went back to double-checking his work. He couldn't waste any time if he wanted to finish first and have a perfect score to show Luisa.

German conquest of The Netherlands complete, 15 May 1940

Jewish volunteers dismissed from air defense units, 1 July 1940

Non-Jewish government employees required to sign declaration of Aryan "purity," 5 October 1940 (five days before I lost my father)

Jewish businesses forced to report and register, 22 October 1940 (twelve days after my father was taken away from me)

All Jewish government employees fired, 21 November 1940

We are forced to register with the Town Register, 10 January 1941

Doctors, nurses, etc., forced to sign declaration of Aryan "purity," 5 February 1941

Amsterdam Joodenrat formed, 13 February 1941

Jewish businesses ordered to bring German representatives into their ranks, 12 March 1941

We are forced to give up our radios, 1 May 1941

We are not allowed to belong to non-Jewish organizations, 1 November 1941

Jewish-only marketplace formed in Amsterdam, 3 November 1941

We must have a permit to move or travel, 7 November 1941

We are not allowed to employ non-Jews as maids, cooks, etc., 1 January 1942

Gymnasium and other secondary school students no longer allowed to attend public school, 9 January 1942

We are no longer allowed to drive our own cars, and all identity cards must be stamped with the letter J, 23 January 1942

Intermarriage forbidden, 25 March 1942

Kosher slaughter outlawed, 24 April 1942

As of this date, we cannot appear in public without a star on our clothes, 2 May 1942

Jakob was wondering what restriction or law was next when he saw smug Luuk standing up. Determined not to be beaten to the punch, he leapt up and raced to Heer Marquering's desk, setting his paper down before Luuk had a chance to get that far.

"Look at this, class. Heer DeJonghe has once again finished first. Perhaps if more of you spent more time paying attention to current events and legislation that directly affects us, instead of caring more about topics like moviestars and the lives of the rich and famous, you'd be able to finish so quickly and accurately as well." Heer Marquering opened his answer key and took out a red pen. "Just as I expected. Heer DeJonghe has gotten a perfect score. For extra credit, would you like to provide the name and date of another piece of legislation not on the test?"

Jakob nodded and pulled himself up to his full height. "On the twenty-sixth of November of 1941, we were forbidden to go to non-Jewish swimming pools, hotels, theatres, and similar public places."

"Excellent work, Heer DeJonghe. I won't be surprised if you graduate in the top percent for this school in two years."

"Thank you, Heer Marquering. May I go back to my seat now?"

"Yes. You may read quietly while we're waiting for the other students to finish. Maybe they'll be quicker on the next test and learn to study harder. You're smart to keep a scrapbook documenting all these indignities."

Jakob smirked as he headed back to his seat and reached into his schoolbag for the Louis Couperus novel *The Hidden Force*. Ruud had inscribed it and given to him as a bar mitzvah present almost exactly three years ago, in much happier days. Now that his father was dead, Jakob felt slightly guilty he hadn't read the book yet, particularly since his father had always talked about how Couperus was the greatest Dutch novelist.

"Teacher's pet," Luuk sneered in a low whisper as he skulked back to his seat in shame.

"At least I pay attention to the news and study hard," Jakob whispered back. "And at least my heroes didn't commit mass suicide and kill women and children to avoid fighting back."

Chapter 9: The Noose Tightens

Though he hated walking around in public with the hideous marker on his clothing, Jakob felt it were his duty to accompany Luisa on her errands in the late afternoons and evenings just in case she might run into any trouble. Newly sixteen years old, he was now five feet eight inches tall, and confident he had at least a few more inches to go. After a bit over a year of daily exercising and weight-lifting, he was equally-confident of his physical strength. No one would dare harass or attack his mother if they saw her escort.

"I'd like to withdraw one hundred guilders, please." Luisa handed the teller the slip she'd filled out.

The teller looked at her name and then at the star on her blouse. "I'm very sorry, Vrouw Hartog, but as of today, you're not allowed to have a bank account. None of us at this bank wanted it, but it's the latest order from the Germans. Some of the other employees are wearing yellow stars in solidarity with you, but they can't let you deposit or withdraw money anymore if they want to keep their jobs."

"What? When was this decided? I would've appreciated some advance notice!"

"We just got the new order today. We've told all our Jewish customers the news when they came in."

"If we can't have bank accounts anymore, shouldn't that mean we can withdraw all our money?" Jakob asked. "I can go home for our suitcases so we can carry it."

"I'm sorry, but you're not allowed to have bank accounts in any capacity. Your money's being confiscated by those damn Germans. Believe me, if we'd known in advance, we would've sent out notices so you could've rescued your money from this gross theft."

"But that's not fair!" Luisa protested. "There's a fair amount of money in my account, and we need money to buy food!"

"I'm sorry, Vrouw Hartog, but orders are orders. Do you have enough money in cash to get by till your next paycheck?"

Luisa thought about this for a few moments. "Perhaps, if we budget strictly and don't buy anything we don't absolutely need. But if we can't deposit money anymore, we might be at greater risk of robbery. I don't want all our money to sit around in the apartment, even if we're there. My parents always told me never to have too much money in cash on me."

"I can think of some clever hiding places," Jakob said. "Those Nazis and NSBers have another think coming if they're trying to reduce us to poverty with this new rule."

Luisa turned around and walked out of the bank as quickly as possible, Jakob trailing behind her. As soon as they were back in Jodenbuurt, her unsteady gait gave out and she collapsed onto the nearest stairs, burying her face in her hands.

"They can't just take all our money away from us," Jakob ranted as he put his arm around her. "As soon as we drive out the Germans, we'll get all our money back, and get a full apology from the Queen. Don't cry, *Moeder*. We'll save up new money before you know it. I know a lot of clever places we can hide our money."

"We might not be allowed to spend money eventually! Or go shopping anywhere! I hate to admit this, but you were right all along. I didn't want to admit things could possibly get so bad so quickly. Just this once, you did know better than your elders."

"Does this mean you'll finally let me leave school and join the partisans?"

"No! I need you at home now more than ever! We're going to go home to collect all the coins and bills we can find, and then we're going to our marketplace to buy decent food. In the meantime, maybe you and Kees can go to the Amstel River for fish. Fish are always in the river, and they're free if you catch your own. We'll get by somehow, even if we have to do without."

2

Jakob burnt with fury as he rode his bicycle to the Amstel River with Kees after school on the last Friday of May. He still saw the pathetic Shavuot meals Luisa and Gusta prepared last week, without even a cheesecake. In spite of all the increasing restrictions, he'd always been somewhat happy at the holidays, made even better by his mother's wonderful cooking. Now Luisa hadn't been able to show off or compensate with a lavish feast. Four people couldn't survive or stay sane on fish, bread, bad cuts of meat, fruit on the verge of getting soft or moldy, and lower-quality vegetables. They'd generally only eaten kosher meat on holidays, so they weren't as affected by the recent ban on kosher slaughter.

"What kinds of fish do you suppose we'll catch today?" Kees asked as their usual fishing spot came into view.

"I don't care, so long as they're not pathetic little runts again. Next time, we should try coming here bright and early. Probably all the good, real fish are getting snapped up by other fishermen."

"We'll get a big one sooner or later. Don't worry. Good things always come to those who wait." Kees stopped his bicycle and walked it the remainder of the way to the waterfront. "At least we have rods and don't have to wade into the water or use a boat with nets."

Jakob fumed as he dismounted his bicycle. "I shouldn't have to be fishing for my food! Even my mother isn't such a good cook she can make the same food seem exciting or delicious when it's all we have every single day. Don't we have enough other foods to have a different meal?"

"Would you rather we overdose on potatoes and turnips? We only have to do this for a little while, before we break even with money. As soon as we've got enough cash, we'll be able to buy better, more varied food. There was a famine in the last war. You should feel lucky we haven't had that this time around."

Jakob selected his fishing rod and attached the hook. "Do you think it would be ruled an accident if I hooked a Nazi or NSBer instead?"

Kees grabbed the other rod. "What do you think? Sixteen years old now, and you're still hopped-up on these dangerous revenge fantasies!"

Jakob had just sat down and cast his reel as far out as he could when he felt a tap on his shoulder. He looked over his left shoulder and began to shake when he saw a fat, short Nazi. His heart raced as he struggled to get to his feet. Twenty feet to his right, Kees also noticed it and stood up to face the stranger.

"What do you want?" Jakob asked, trying not to sound too surly or accusatory. As much as he wished he could take that tone of voice, he didn't want to break his mother's heart by getting arrested for sassing a Nazi.

"You people aren't allowed to go fishing anymore. Our newest law concerning the Jewish problem says you can't fish. Nor can you obtain a fishing license. I'm sure you can find at least one notice about the new rules on your way home, vermin, or read about it in the newest edition of the paper. Would you like to hand your fishing rods over to me here, or surrender them at the police station?"

"I want to keep my fishing rod. I can always use it again after that rule's repealed."

The Nazi laughed long and hard, then began a disgusting deep, hacking cough. Jakob cringed and stepped back a little, repulsed at how he wasn't covering his mouth or turning away.

"You're an idiot if you think the new rule will ever be overturned," he finally managed to say in a normal voice. "If I catch either of you trying to fish again, you'll be punished with a lot more than just a warning. It doesn't matter too much how you get rid of your rods, since you won't have a choice soon anyway. Do you and your father understand all this?"

"He's not my father. My father was killed over a year and a half ago."

The Nazi sneered. "Like I care. Whatever the other man is to you, he needs to obey our orders too."

Jakob tied his fishing rod onto the back of his bicycle after the Nazi walked away, coughing that disgusting deep, hacking cough again. Kees tied his fishing rod to the back of his own bicycle, mumbling under his breath.

"What are we supposed to do now?" Jakob asked. "We don't have enough ready money to buy the kinds of food we used to!"

"Just before we were busted, you were complaining about how much fish we've been eating! Now you like it?"

"At least it was something. Now we don't even have fish."

"It was just an idea your mother came up with. We all knew it wasn't meant to be long-term, just till we got back on our feet with enough money. It's not like we're fighting to keep the wolf from the door just yet. You'll still go to bed with a full stomach every night, even if our meals won't be as big as you're used to." Kees hopped onto his bicycle. "Perhaps we can start selling things we don't need. Gusta and I don't use our camera very often, and we don't need a gramophone or telescope. Why do we need fur coats when we have regular coats too? Selling those things can easily get us enough money to last through at least three or four more months."

"I'm not selling any of my things. I don't want a stupid German reading my books or wearing my clothes, and my mother deserves to keep her jewelry. It shouldn't be given to a German bitch who won't appreciate it."

"You're lucky your mother isn't here. You know she doesn't like you using coarse language like that. Just because you're the man of your house doesn't mean you have to curse like a man. You'll learn soon enough being a real grownup doesn't mean cursing and fighting."

Jakob imagined the fat Nazi roasting on a spit the entire way home. He liked the image so much, he decided he'd draw a picture of it as soon as he was back in his room and had access to his notebook and colored pencils. At least no one had taken away his ability to draw and sketch. But before he could start his drawing, of course, he'd have to add the latest piece of anti-Jewish legislation to his scrapbook. First things first.

3

On 5 June, Friday, after school let out, Jakob went to the art supply store nearest his new all-Jewish school. He was glad the new school wasn't in one of Amsterdam's three Jewish neighborhoods, though he stood out among all these people with that yellow marker on his clothes. Since the star edict went into effect a month ago, he'd seen more than a few people he knew to be Christians also wearing stars. Certainly, the majority of Amsterdam hadn't started wearing stars out of solidarity, but it cheered him up to know there were still a fair number of good, decent people who weren't afraid to stand up and do the right thing.

Vrouw Daube, the co-owner, quickly turned around and busied herself with rearranging shelves when she saw Jakob coming in. She didn't respond when he called to her several times. A few other people came in after him and were quickly acknowledged and helped. Jakob was rather confused and upset to be treated like this. He regularly came to the store, and Vrouw Daube and her husband had always had friendly conversations with him and taken an interest in the art supplies he looked at. He'd always thought he were one of their best young customers.

When the store was empty expect for him and Vrouw Daube, he tried calling to her again. She looked around furtively several times, then rushed to lock the door and draw the blinds.

"Did I do something to make you mad last time I was here? If I accidentally broke something and didn't realize it, I can pay you back when I get enough money. I certainly don't remember stealing anything, except that time when I was five years old and too little to realize I'd walked out with an eraser in my pocket. You told me you forgave me for that and knew I didn't do it on purpose."

Vrouw Daube sighed. "I've always liked you, Jaap, but I can't let you patronize my store anymore. My husband and I enjoy having our little family business, and don't want to get arrested or fined. The newest order is that Jewish customers cannot buy things in non-Jewish stores. I suppose it could be alright to just come in and look around, but you can't buy anything. I'm not brave enough to risk it by not recording the transaction, putting down a fake name, or otherwise disguising it. These things are always found out."

Jakob let the sketchbook he was holding fall from his fingers. He dug his toes into the floor and repressed his urge to punch the wall or kick something. He knew better than to have a public tantrum at his age, and didn't want to leave Vrouw Daube with such an unflattering final memory of him. "I'm not as quick about learning these things as I used to be. I'll have to add this to my scrapbook when I go home. I'm sorry for disturbing you. You don't deserve to get arrested."

Vrouw Daube bent down and picked up the sketchbook. It had a bright red border on the cover, with a reproduction of Albrecht Dürer's woodcut *The Four Horsemen of the Apocalypse*. This was a much larger notebook or sketchpad than Jakob had ever purchased, with much higher-quality paper.

"Have you run out of room in your notebook?"

"Yes, Vrouw Daube. I wanted something with bigger paper and no lines, and separate from my schoolwork. Some of the pages of my last art notebook have class notes on them. I was thinking about buying professional-quality colored pencils or charcoal pencils, but I'll have to find a Jewish art store to get my stuff at from now on."

Vrouw Daube tiptoed to each window in turn and peered out through the blinds. Jakob could hear her heart beating and saw a scared look in her eyes. Finally, she headed over to the checkout desk, her hands shaking, and opened the cash register.

"Have you got enough money to purchase this?"

"But you just said it's against the law——"

"Do you or don't you have the money? I'll wrap it in brown butcher paper so no one will know what's inside. But after this, you can't come back here."

Jakob's eyes lit up. "Yes, I have enough money. I know I should be using my money to help my mother, but I really like drawing." He dug the guilders out of his pocket.

"Of course you do. You deserve to be happy and have something to take your mind off of what's happening. While I ring this up, you can pick out one of the drawing packages on that shelf." She indicated a shelf near the back of the store.

"But those are the expensive items! I don't have nearly enough money, and I don't think I'm the next Rembrandt or Vermeer. My mother always told me not to fool myself and think I'm a great art student just because I like doing it in my spare time. I took more than the basic art track at gymnasium, but I wasn't in the advanced track for the students planning to go to art school."

"I'll let you have it for free. My husband will understand and agree with me. You won't be able to come back here for probably a long time, so it's best to have a big stock of drawing tools. Each of those bundles has at least a hundred different colored pencils, paints, and charcoal pencils. When it's safe for you to come back, after the Germans are gone, I want to see your best professional-quality painting or drawing."

Jakob went to the back of the store and browsed the shelf he'd always fantasized buying something from. Luisa would probably be horrified to learn he'd been given something that expensive and professional-quality for free, and even more so because he wasn't a serious art student, but she wouldn't be able to do anything about it unless she wanted both him and Vrouw Daube to get in trouble for violating the newest law.

After fifteen minutes, he finally decided on a big wooden carrying case containing seventy-two colored pencils, a dozen charcoal pencils, twenty-four watercolors, five erasers, a dozen graphite pencils, three pencil sharpeners, ten paintbrushes, and five bottles of black ink for Oriental ink wash painting. There were also several wooden mannequins of various sizes and builds. If he were going to get something for free, and wouldn't be allowed in his favorite store for the foreseeable future, he wanted to make sure he'd make off with the best product in stock.

Vrouw Daube shook her head and laughed affectionately. "Okay, Jaap, you can have that for free. I did promise you could have whatever you wanted on that shelf for free. Perhaps you really will be the next Rembrandt by the time you come back here. If you're going to have something so well-stocked and professional, you'd better make good use of everything it has."

Jakob opened the case and took out two colored pencils, one red and one blue. "Can I write in the sketchpad? I'd like to show you something before I go."

"Sure. You've already paid for the sketchpad, and the drawing and painting kit is my treat."

He took the red pencil in his right hand and the blue pencil in his left hand, positioning them on the top of the inner cover. Beaming with pride, he wrote his name with each hand, going slowly and steadily so he wouldn't make a mistake with his less-practiced left hand. Both Ruud and Luisa had always thought he were a little crazy to want to teach himself to write with his other hand, but he persisted because it was a practical skill that'd come in handy if he ever broke his arm.

"Have you practiced that for a long time?" Vrouw Daube asked when he was finished. "I've heard of people who had to learn to write with the other hand because of injury, but never heard of someone who could write with both hands at the same time."

"The American president James Garfield knew how to do that, my father said. He didn't think I could ever do it well. I wish he were still here to see it. My father told me you need a lot of skill and dexterity for this, since you have to push the pencil with your left hand at the same time you're pulling it with your right hand, and form some letters in opposite directions. Maybe I can try drawing some pictures with both hands together too."

Vrouw Daube wrapped up the items in brown butcher paper and tied them shut with twine. "Will they fit in your bicycle basket?"

"I think so. I'll put them in with the short sides on the bottom and hope they don't fall out on the way home."

Vrouw Daube saw him to the door. "Remember, I didn't sell or give you these things, and I haven't let you in my store."

"I won't tell anyone. Thank you for giving me the drawing kit. I'll make good use of it over my summer vacation."

Jakob put the items into his bicycle basket and pedaled home, terrified the entire way he might be accosted by a Nazi or NSBer who'd seen him entering or exiting the store. He was relieved when he finally got home, no one following him or having looked at him suspiciously. He tucked his new belongings under his arm and dragged his bicycle up the steps. Luisa wished he'd store his bicycle outside like most people, but he loved his bicycle too much to leave it outside. A number of his friends over the years had had their bicycles stolen.

"What is that?" Luisa demanded. "Where did you get the money to pay for that, or is that stolen? At least it doesn't look like a stockpile of weapons."

"I bought a sketchpad at my favorite art store, and got a set of drawing and painting supplies as a courtesy gift." He pulled off the butcher paper and opened the case to show her.

Luisa gasped. "That's an extremely expensive gift to give to someone who's not a real artist! You could've gotten a regular deluxe set of colored pencils if you wanted more colors that badly! This is intended for serious artists, not boys who draw violent revenge pictures!"

"I draw other things too. You shouldn't judge my entire body of work on the only pictures you've seen. I draw animals, fruit, flowers, normal people, all sorts of stuff. I'll have lots of time over the summer to work on drawing."

Luisa sighed again. "At least this'll keep you out of trouble and give you something productive to do instead of plotting revenge or scheming to join the partisans. Go wash up, and I'll call you for dinner."

4

Jakob's new school ended classes the next Friday. Even if a lot of places were now off-limits to him, he was still thrilled to be done with school for the year, with only two more years left till he could go to university. He assumed by that time, the Nazis would be out of The Netherlands and he'd be free to go to any school he wanted once more. As he rode home, he was thinking about how he could fulfill his dream of joining the partisans or the real Royal Army of The Netherlands while completing his schooling and getting a university degree. He was so wrapped up in thinking these things through, he didn't notice a police officer yelling at him and several other students going his way.

"Didn't you idiots hear me the first time?" The policeman planted himself in front of them. "I've just told you several times you need to turn those things in this weekend."

"Turn what things in?" Sander Zeeger asked. "Our stars?"

The policeman snorted. "You wish. The newest anti-Jewish law passed today says you must turn in your cars and bicycles. Your plans for this weekend include a trip to the nearest police station or other collection point to turn in all the bicycles in your families."

"Why do we have to turn them in?" Elma Specht asked. "We're not adults. We're not using them for bad things."

"It's not up to you to decide the laws. If you don't turn them in over this weekend, you'll be arrested. Got that?"

Jakob sped the rest of the way home, his heart in his throat. All he knew was he wasn't going to hand over his bicycle to anyone, let alone a spoilt German or NSBer boy. No one else deserved to ride it except himself. His parents had given it to him for his twelfth birthday, when he got too big for his old child's bike, and he was very proud of it. A lot of the other boys in his class had boring, common-looking bikes, but only he had a bicycle with a beautiful dark blue color bordering on purple, with a basket his mother had woven and dyed to match the body. He also loved the bell he and Ruud had assembled and installed. It made a sound that wasn't as loud or obnoxious as some of the other bicycle bells he'd heard. If he had to, he'd hide it in the house or bury it.

"Did you hear the latest news?" Gusta asked. "You might as well leave that thing outside, since you can't have it anymore. As soon as Kees gets home, all of us are going to the police station to turn in our bicycles. Your mother wanted to do it on Saturday or Sunday, but I thought it were a better idea to surrender them as soon as possible instead of prolonging the inevitable."

"I'm not giving anyone my bicycle. It's been mine for four years, and I intend to keep it that way. Besides, everyone in The Netherlands has a bicycle."

"It's the law!" Luisa said. "We have to turn them in, or we could get arrested! When this is all over, I promise I'll buy you an even better bicycle. We even have to turn in Emilia's tricycle. It's obvious she's not coming back, even if she's still alive somewhere. Looking at that thing breaks my heart."

"No bicycle could be better than this one. If I ever get another bicycle, it'll be a bicycle I have in addition to my favorite one, like one specially made for mountain riding, if I go on a trip to a place with a different terrain."

"What do you intend to do with your bicycle?" Gusta asked. "Hide it under your bed and hope it's never discovered? You tried to fight the star edict too, and you gave in because you realized you couldn't risk doing your own thing."

"I can give it to Christian friends I know I can trust. *Moeder*, aren't you still good friends with Vrouw Zaal in Jordaan? I've seen her family wearing stars in sympathy with us, so we know which side they're on."

"What if they're arrested for hiding property that was supposed to be confiscated?"

"The new law only says we can't own bicycles. It doesn't say Christians aren't allowed to keep our bicycles for safekeeping. Come to think of it, it might be a good idea to give them some of our other things for safekeeping as well. We need to be prepared in case things get worse. What are the most important things we need to save in case we're arrested and sent away? I'd want important things to come home to, like family pictures. Not that I want us to be taken away. This would be for just in case."

Luisa rolled her eyes. "If you insist. It probably won't hurt to have some things stashed away. Get a suitcase, and I'll help you load it."

"Can I drive the things over in Kees's car? Since we're not allowed to have cars anymore, why not give it to friends for safekeeping too? It'll be a lot easier to bring a suitcase in a car than fastened to a bicycle."

"You're crazy. If we can't drive cars anymore, what makes you think you'll be allowed to drive it anywhere even to turn it in? The authorities will probably come around to all Jewish households with a registered car and take them away in person, or lock them up till arrangements are made for a mass collection in a large truck or what have you."

"I know how to get to Jordaan from here. It's not that far away. I'm sure the authorities have bigger concerns than catching people making a very short illegal trip."

Luisa stood up and went into her room. "One of these days, you're either going to kill someone or get killed yourself, the way you always act before you think and try to live so dangerously. I don't want to imagine what might become of you if I'm no longer around to hold you in check."

"Of course you'll always be around, till you're a very old woman. I won't let those damn barbarians kill you."

Luisa opened her wardrobe and pulled out her wedding dress, wrapped in tissue paper and on a fancy padded hanger. "I'm putting this into the suitcase for your future bride. Perhaps that'll give you something to live for beyond revenge and playing resistance fighter. I want to see my future daughter-in-law wearing my wedding gown, and that can't happen if you get yourself killed by being foolish."

An hour later, Jakob was on his way over to Vrouw Zaal's house, his bicycle tucked into the backseat of the Peugeot. In the trunk was a suitcase with the wedding dress, family pictures, a number of books, Luisa's best jewelry, an old doll Luisa had been given by her great-grandmother, the family Bible, their legal documents, and a teddybear Jakob had had as a little boy. The entire short drive, he kept his eyes peeled and tried not to drive too fast or slowly, so he wouldn't attract attention. The excitement of driving a real car for the first time was secondary to his mission to just go over there and then walk back as casually as possible, as though he weren't doing anything out of the ordinary.

Vrouw Zaal answered the door. "May I help you, Jaap? Is your mother not feeling well?"

"My mother is fine, Mevrouw. I came to give you my bicycle and some of our belongings for safekeeping. We were ordered to give up our bicycles and cars this weekend, and I won't let anyone steal my bicycle. Would you mind hiding these things? You don't have to unpack them, just keep the suitcase in a closet so you don't forget. I'd also like you to keep my bicycle inside so it won't get stolen."

Vrouw Zaal took the suitcase from him. "Sure I'll hide these things for you. Those damn Germans will be defeated sooner or later, and they shouldn't take everything away from you. My children feel the exact same way about their bicycles. I'll help you carry it out of the car." She looked around. "Who drove you here?"

"I drove myself," he announced proudly. "I did a very good job for someone who never drove before. You can keep the car too if you'd like. It's such a nice car, and I'm sure Kees will want his car back after the Germans are gone. It's not a fancy Duesenberg or Chrysler, but it's not a low-end American Ford either. It'll be nice to have a car to come back to after we're free, instead of saving up all that money for a new one or having to hunt all over for the old one."

Vrouw Zaal's eyes widened. "You're giving us a car? And you

risked God knows what to drive it here and leave it with us?"

"You've always been nice to my family, so we trust you to hide our things. I know you'll give them back to us after the Nazis are gone."

"Yes, we will. But for the love of God, please don't try anything like that ever again. Think of your mother. She doesn't deserve to have a nervous breakdown if her only child left is arrested or killed. I hope you're not still thinking about running away to join the partisans."

"I'd love to join the partisans. If I can't, I'm still very interested in taking out the three bastards who murdered my father." He tipped his cap. "Have a good day."

Chapter 10: Welcome to Westerbork

By August, things had gotten so bad, Jakob was actually looking forward to the new school year starting. It was hard to have a real summer vacation when he couldn't go to a public swimming pool, the movies, the park, a lot of stores, sporting clubs, or just about every place he'd always gone to in summers past. Now he was locked up inside the house from 8:00 at night onward, and couldn't venture out into the communal backyard, or even stand on the fire escape, an additional stringency Luisa insisted on just in case. He was glad they didn't have a phone, though the new ban on phones also meant he could no longer go to a Jewish hotel or drugstore to call his friends on the public phone.

But for now, they were still allowed outside during the daytime, and Jakob enjoyed looking at the wildlife in the backyard. He'd drawn a number of the flowers, trees, and animals in his new sketchpad over the summer, and when there were no other people around, he liked talking to the animals. Some of the rabbits, birds, and chipmunks were brave or tame enough to venture over to him and eat from his hand or let themselves be petted. He'd never live it down if a future partisan fighter, or any boy of his age, were caught doing that, so he always abruptly stopped whenever he saw or heard someone else coming into the yard.

"Maybe someday I'll have a pet rabbit," he said as he petted a young brown rabbit perched on his lap. "I'm not one of those people who eats bunnies or skins them for clothes. Maybe you were one of the baby bunnies I saved this spring when your nest was disturbed, and you remember me from that. Animals have special psychic feelings about people. You must know I'm one of the good guys and that I like animals. Animals only run from people they know want to hurt them." He leaned over to his left and picked up a brown colored pencil to continue his sketch of a bird with a broken wing whom he'd been helping.

The rabbit began squirming on his lap and making loud noises. In all the time he'd been around rabbits, Jakob had never heard one make any other noises besides happy purrs or squeaks every so often. Whatever the cause, it had to be very bad for a rabbit to scream.

"Are you upset I'm not paying all my attention to you?" He put down the pencil and began stroking the rabbit with both hands. "Once I went to a rabbit farm on a school trip, and I was so upset when I found out what was going to happen to the bunnies, I snuck off and released them." He picked the rabbit up and cuddled it against his chest. "There, now you're covering that ugly yellow star. Maybe you can be a good friend and rip it off. My mother might believe it was an accident."

As the rabbit continued squirming and making distress noises, Jakob looked over his shoulder and saw strange people standing at the third floor windows. When he heard his mother screaming, he set the rabbit on the ground, packed up his colored pencils, tucked the sketch-pad under his arm, took the carrying case of writing instruments in his hand, and dashed up the fire escape. Once at the third level, he hoisted himself up onto the balcony and pushed open the screen door.

His eyes filled with the sight of broken dishes, clothes, smashed records, ritual objects, books, and linens all over the floor. One of the Nazis standing in the apartment was the fat one he'd met at the water-front in May, the one with the gross hacking cough. Gusta and Kees knelt on the floor with their hands above their heads while Luisa was frisked by a tall, thin NSBer with a lecherous look in his eyes. Jakob wanted to murder all of them when he saw a welt across his mother's face, a large bruise under her left eye, and blood coming out of her nose. This was the woman who'd waited forty years to be blessed with a child, carried him inside of her for forty-two weeks, gone through sixty hours of labor to bring him into the world, given him her sable hair and eyes, and been his only parent for the last twenty-two months.

Everything inside of him wanted to scream at them to leave her alone, but his tongue had become like lead in his frozen mouth, and his arms and legs felt even heavier. He stood paralyzed by fear, and the same sensation he'd had last February returned, his blood rushing and pounding in his ears. He saw his mother's mouth moving, but couldn't hear a word coming out of it. Only when the fat Nazi with the disgust-ing cough came towards him and pulled him into the apartment did he start coming back to himself.

"So this is the fourth member of this household. Your mother said she didn't know where you were. At least you came back home instead of trying to hide or run away like some of the other pathetic vermin we've arrested."

The thin NSBer blew a whistle. "You're all going to pack your things in five minutes and then follow us to the police station. You'll be marched there with a group of other people in this neighborhood. I wouldn't pack too much if I were you, since you might not be around much longer to use your things. By the end of this year, if you're still alive, you'll wish you were never born."

Jakob rushed into his room, grateful some of their things were safe with Vrouw Zaal and that Emilia was gone, hopefully in a safe place and far, far away from this. He grabbed his new, much larger schoolbag and began stuffing things into it. His new sketchpad. The carrying case of paints and pencils. His previous notebooks and sketchpads, now filled up with drawings, notes, and plans for revenge. The Louis Couperus novels Ruud had given him. Family pictures. The scrapbook documenting the ordeal of Dutch Jewry under the occupation. All the money he could find. The Bible Ruud had given him for his twelfth birthday. As many clothes as he could fit in the remainder of the bag.

"Don't forget your coat and winter clothes, Jaap," Luisa called. "We don't know how long we'll be away, and you need to stay warm in the winter."

The fat Nazi started his repulsive laugh mixed with that hacking cough. "Even if you last till the winter, you won't need coats where you'll be going."

Jakob stuffed his scarf, boots, leather gloves, wool hat, and several heavy, long-sleeved shirts into the bag. He folded up his deep blue wool coat and fastened it into the carrying straps underneath the bag. When he was done packing his most important things, he headed into the kitchen and began throwing as much food as possible into the largest shopping bag they had.

"What is this?" A Nazi with a face full of liver spots held up a picture of Princess Juliana and her daughters Beatrix and Irene. "Don't you imbeciles know it's against the law to have these pictures?"

"We got that well before the edict," Kees sputtered. "We haven't bought any pictures of our Royal Family since."

Jakob's heart started beating even faster. He had a number of pictures of Queen Wilhelmina, her late Prince Hendrik, Princess Juliana, Prince Bernhard, and little Princesses Beatrix and Irene hidden among the pages of some of the notebooks in his bag. He was nauseated by the loud ripping of the picture, a sound that reverberated into his entire being. After the picture was ripped into shreds, the liver-spotted Nazi ground them into the floor with his dirty boot. This wasn't nearly as sacrilegious or an act of desecration as tearing up and stepping on a Torah or other holy book, but it still felt like a violation of something special. Queen Wilhelmina's only child and her two little girls were good princesses keeping the Dutch people's hope alive from exile in Canada. They weren't monsters who deserved to have their picture torn up and ground to a pulp.

"Can we lock up our home while you wait outside in the hall?" Kees asked.

The fat Nazi lit a cigarette and blew smoke into his face. "Everything you didn't pack is ours now. You're dreaming if you think you're going to lock up this apartment and come back to it someday. Forget about trying to contact Aryan traitors who might want to rescue your belongings. Now let's go to the public square. When we've got enough people, we're heading to the police station."

Jakob grabbed his mother's hand as they were marched out of the apartment and herded down the stairs and into the street. The entire walk to Jonas Daniël Meijerplein, the air was permeated by screams and shouts from many of the surrounding buildings. Once they were assembled in the square, Jakob looked around at the five bordering synagogues. His family had long been going to the Progressive synagogue some distance away, but he respected these other synagogues as holy houses of worship. Now he wondered if they'd be turned into stables and have their holy, priceless artwork, Torah scrolls, books, and architecture destroyed as though they'd never been.

Many of the people around him had been his neighbors for years, classmates, friends. Even people who weren't exactly his friends, like smug Luuk Klein, were now assembled around him. Jakob wished he'd packed the toy pistol and that it could shoot real bullets. Right about now, his desire to run away to join the partisans and join up with the Dutch Free Forces burnt stronger than ever. As soon as he had a chance, he'd run away and take Luisa with him. He wouldn't give her a choice. From now on, he'd have to play the role of the parent, and she'd be in the role of the child.

At a signal from a short, stout Nazi with a graying moustache and a pimpled forehead, the group started to march out of the square, past the boundaries of the neighborhood, and towards the central police station. The hot August air felt even thicker because of the eerie, dead silence. As they marched down the streets of Amsterdam, the lucky other people, the people judged Aryan enough to live in peace for now, were going about their normal daily routines. Some of the people in the streets and looking out of house and shop windows had pity in their eyes. Some had unmistakable hate and glee in their eyes. A few people looked away.

Jakob clutched his mother's hand even tighter as they were marched past a woman with three young children screaming curses and ill wishes. One of the girls looked to be about the age Emilia would be now, five years old. Jakob couldn't understand how anyone could teach an innocent child to hate an entire group of people. A baby came into the world so pure and innocent, not hating people from other religions or ethnic groups. Only two years ago, his own heart had been full of love for the entire world, before the Nazis and NSBers had turned it dark black with hate for everyone but his mother, Gusta and Kees, and his animal friends. As he walked on amidst the catcalls and rude gestures of the woman and her children, he wondered how he could have ever been so stupid as to think love could be enough to overpower hate and that anti-Semitic bullies might come around after they saw the people they occupied were no different than they were where it really counted.

The silence was broken when they reached the police station. The doors swung open and the crowd was pushed inside. Jakob stood between Luisa and Gusta, sweating more from fear now than the August heat. One by one, people were called in alphabetical order and made to come forward to confirm their information to an ugly bald Nazi sitting at a big oak desk and writing things in a bulging ledger. The few people who didn't cooperate or who actively resisted were dragged off or beaten. After they were done giving their information, they were pushed into another room. Jakob's heart rang in his ears again when he realized he'd have to go first in their group, according to their alphabetical order. Luisa would be left alone in that huge room with hostile people, even if it were only for a few minutes.

"Jakob Eliezer DeJonghe?"

He stepped forward, casting backwards glances at Luisa, Kees, and Gusta. When he was in front of the registrar, he pulled himself up as tall as he could make himself appear.

"Date of birth the ninth of May, 1926?"

"Yes, Meneer." He chaffed at having to use that term of respect with a Nazi, but knew the consequences of doing otherwise.

"You were born in Amsterdam?"

"Yes, Meneer."

The Nazi took a strange tool out of his desk drawer. Jakob stood mutely as the cold metal instrument was positioned around his head and the ends poked his skin. After the strange instrument was put away, the Nazi wrote some numbers in the ledger.

"That's odd. Your skull size isn't as small as it's supposed to be. Maybe you have a big Aryan-sized skull but a tiny brain." He scanned a fat finger down the list. "Luisa Mirjam DeJonghe, legal surname Hartog?"

Jakob was pushed towards the door to the other room as his mother came forward. Once the door was closed, he stood as close to it as possible so he could hear what was going on in the main room. If the worst Luisa had to go through was having her skull measured, they were relatively safe for the moment.

"Date of birth the tenth of March, 1886?"

"Yes, Meneer."

"Place of birth Utrecht?"

"Yes, Meneer."

Jakob thought his mother was about to come through the door after a period of silence, then heard a new, more menacing line of questioning starting.

"We already processed your son, and our records show your husband Rudolf DeJonghe died in October 1940. But according to our records, you also have a daughter named Emilia, who was born in 1937. How repulsive, a member of an inferior race thinking she deserved to have another baby past the age of fifty. There's no record of her death in here, and you obviously don't have a little girl with you now."

"I don't know where Emilia is, Meneer. She disappeared the day my husband was coerced into suicide. No one has seen her since."

"Liar. Where the hell is Emilia, you stupid Jewish bitch? If you don't tell us where your other brat is this moment, I'll smash your head against the wall in front of all these people!"

Jakob bit down on his lower lip very hard to keep himself from bursting into tears in front of all these people, both friend and foe. He also had to resist the urge to vomit when he heard what sounded like

Luisa being beaten again. In his mind, he began spinning a fantasy of bursting back into the processing room, rushing the bald Nazi, and strangling him with that damned craniometer. Of course, he knew he'd be shot or beaten himself if he dared try anything like that.

"I swear I don't know where my daughter is! My son and I were forced to relocate that day, and Emilia never came home. She was playing with other children in Oude Pijp. My son and our friend Cornelius ter Avest over there went to see the family a few days later, and they were gone. A neighbor and one of the new residents of their house both said the same thing, that they moved extremely suddenly and no one had any idea where they were going. They didn't notice my Emilia with them either."

"If this story is true, you'd better tell me the names of these people who were last seen with your worthless younger offspring. We'll find these people and take care of all of them."

"Willem Krusen and Alida Peerenboom. But my son and our friend were told they left the city. Perhaps they left the country or changed their names."

"Oh, believe me, we'll find all of them. We're smarter than you. We always find a way to take care of the Jewish menace."

Jakob rushed to his mother when she stumbled into the other room. He tore off the bottom of his right pant leg and wrapped it around her bleeding head, then tightly wrapped his arms around her from the side and rocked her back and forth like a small child.

"You're safe now, Mama. I'll take care of you and protect you the way you used to do for me. From now on, I'm the parent and you're the child. I won't let anyone hurt you again. I'm sorry I was drawing and playing with animals in the backyard instead of in the house to defend you when they broke in this afternoon. Please don't hate me for leaving you alone." Her sobs felt like daggers through his heart. "This was exactly what I was always afraid of. But don't you worry, I'll think of a way to get us out of this situation. You lost Emilia and *Vader*, but you won't lose me."

Luisa reached up and smoothed his hair back. "I wish you hadn't come back into the house," she managed to choke out. "The *kankerhonden* didn't know where you were. You could've made a run for it when you heard the commotion. It was your perfect chance to join the partisans or get involved in the underground. No boy should have to see or hear his own mother being beaten." She buried her face in his sea green shirt and starting sobbing again, even harder.

Jakob's heart burnt with anger as he felt his shirt becoming wet with the blood still coming out of his mother's head. "If they wanted to beat someone, they should've picked me. I'm tall and strong. You're not supposed to beat women and children."

A nearby woman came up to them. "Would you like real bandages for that wound? I'm a nurse, and I have some supplies in my suitcase."

Luisa nodded, a dazed look in her eyes.

"Hold my hands," Jakob ordered when he saw the nurse uncapping a bottle of iodine. "Just squeeze my hands if you feel pain. You'll get abused again if you scream. I'm sure iodine can't be more painful than childbirth."

Many of the women in the room started laughing, and his ears burnt in shame. After Luisa had a proper dressing over her wound and it had been disinfected, Jakob helped her over to one of the few chairs in the bleak, foreboding room. He knelt by her, holding her hands and telling her a story about being reunited with Emilia and having a lavish banquet in an Irish castle, till Gusta and Kees came into the room. It seemed as though a thousand years had passed till they saw their friends finally being admitted to the room.

Gusta rushed over to Luisa and put her arm around her. "Are you okay, *liefje*? I mean, physically."

"I think I'll be fine," Luisa murmured lifelessly. "Thank God I have such a good son. God was good to me when he decided to give me my boy first, and to leave me with my boy. If I had to lose one of my babies, I'm glad Jaapje was the one I got to keep."

Kees pointed to his left eye. "That bald bully with his skull-measuring toy knocked me around too. At least I'm closer to his size than you."

"We're going to get out of here soon," Jakob promised, rubbing his mother's hands. "I'll make sure of it. You'll live with me in my bunker in the woods, and I'll always bring you back nice food from my foraging and stealing missions. You'll be so proud of me when I'm a hero of the Dutch Resistance."

The room filled with at least thirty more people over the next hour, and then they were given the order to march out the back door of the holding room. Jakob kept his arm around his mother as they were led back onto the street and paraded past the people who didn't have to have their lives disrupted and restricted. A stone's throw away from the police station, an inordinate number of large, open-roofed vans started pulling up.

When their turn came, Jakob climbed into the van first, followed by Kees. They helped pull Luisa up, while Gusta was able to climb up by herself. They found seats somewhere in the middle of the hard bench on the left-hand side. Jakob immediately wrapped his arms around Luisa again and began stroking her hair and rocking her like a small child. At this point, all he cared about was protecting his fifty-six-year-old mother, not feeling grateful his belovèd bicycle was safe or that he'd taken his artwork with him. He made a mental note to also take down the cretins who beat and humiliated Luisa today, after dealing with the three goons who murdered Ruud.

It was very dusky, and stars twinkled, when the vans stopped. Jakob forced himself to stay very alert in spite of the darkness, the emotionally exhausting day, and the long journey. He patiently waited his turn to unboard, and once again helped Luisa to step down. He looked all around at his new surroundings, his eyes adjusting to the dark, as he helped Luisa walk through the thick mud. The most important thing was to pay attention to the orders being barked at them and not to get in the way of the guards he saw everywhere.

"Welcome to Westerbork," the man behind the registration desk said in a high-pitched voice that sounded like splinters of ice jabbing at Jakob's soul. "You are to give me your names, dates of birth, places of origin, and professions. Perhaps some of you may be put to good use before you have to relocate."

This time Gusta and Kees were in front of Jakob and Luisa. Jakob gently massaged the gauze over Luisa's head, by now caked in dried blood. He was promising her, in the most soothing voice he could manage, that they'd soon change the dressing and put more iodine on it, when he heard Gusta telling a bold-faced lie after stating her profession.

"That woman behind me, Luisa Hartog, is my assistant. She's attended at leave five hundred of my births and caught at least one hundred of my babies. She's even assisted me in some of my multiple births. I assure you she'll be a very valuable addition to this camp's maternity ward."

The registrar looked Luisa up and down. "What's a midwife's assistant doing with that repulsive wound on her head? Why should we let a useless, injured case like that anywhere near our hospital as anything other than a patient?"

"The client I delivered just before we were brought here was in so much pain, she kicked my assistant in the head. Some women don't handle labor pain as well as others, and they do and say things they'd never normally do. Let me handle any complications like forceps deliveries or turning breeches, and she'll do the rest. Ask any woman in Amsterdam, and she'll tell you we did an excellent job."

The registrar grunted and waved Gusta and Kees on. When he got to Luisa, he asked for her basic information and didn't inquire any further into her credentials or training as a supposed midwife's assistant. Then Jakob gave his information and said he was a student.

The registrar looked back over his information. "Too bad. You're two years too old for the school here. You'll have to get a job like all the other grown men."

They were herded out of the registration office and towards the barracks, the bright lights from the watchtowers constantly circling around. Jakob was glad when they finally got out of that thick muddy road and were ushered into their sleeping quarters. He mentally breathed a sigh of relief when he saw clean sheets and plump pillows on the bunks, even if they weren't private. He couldn't afford to be too picky about what kind of bed he slept in when he was lucky to have a bed and not be in prison. Best of all, he was still in his own country. If he broke out of captivity in Germany or Poland, he'd never know the landscape so intimately, and wouldn't be among his own people.

As soon as they were as alone as they could be, Jakob went over to a nearby man who hadn't arrived with his group. "Say, do you happen to know of any resistance groups in this place?" he whispered. "And where are the weapon stashes and escape route maps?"

The man stared at him. "Are you insane? We'll all be severely punished if anyone tries to escape! We have it pretty good here. No one in his right mind wants to jeopardize this relative peace and freedom by starting a terror cell or hatching an escape."

The woman next to him nodded. "The only thing my husband and I, or anyone else, needs to worry about is keeping our names off the weekly list. Be a good worker and don't make any trouble, and you'll stay safe."

Kees looked up from unpacking his things. "What weekly list? Do you mean to say there are regular raids and roundups here too?"

"Not really. But once or twice a week, there's a list made up, and the people on the list are taken to the train station in town. Some of the inmates are working on a main rail track going straight out from the camp, so soon the weekly departures won't need a middle step."

Jakob felt his hair standing on end. "Where are these people going, Germany? I've heard rumors about people being taken to Poland too, but I have no idea what exactly is in Poland."

"Beats me. But remember, in the meantime, just work hard and enjoy how nice things are here. You don't want to jinx anything."

Jakob got under the covers of his new bed, maneuvered his day clothes off, and pulled on his pajamas. In the morning, he'd see what kind of work he could do and try to find out more information about these weekly trains, but for now, all he wanted to do was sleep. After the nurse who'd travelled with them changed Luisa's dressing, Jakob softly padded over to her bed and tucked her in. He was relieved she still carried the same regal, dignified look as she always did, even after being beaten twice that day. He gently touched the welt on her face and the bruise under her eye, then kissed her hands.

"Sweet dreams, *Moeder*. Remember, I promised I'd take care of you like you're my child and I'm your parent. I love you more than anyone else in this world, and I'll never let anyone hurt you again."

She squeezed his hands. "I love you most of all too, my darling little Jaapje. Please don't put our lives in danger because you wanted to play a hero so badly. If you're meant to be a partisan or resistance fighter, God will open up a way for you to do that. But don't force Fate if it's not meant to happen."

He patted her hands. "I'll do what I must. You've been the parent for sixteen years. Now it's my turn to take care of you, and I'll do whatever it takes to make sure our family isn't split in half again. I'll make sure I carry out my plans safely."

Luisa propped herself up on her elbow when he was back under the covers of his new bed. "Remember what I told you, Jaap. A passionate man will either kill or be killed, and a wise man only engages in warfare when he has no choice. You're lucky one of the books I packed is *The Tao Te Ching*. Perhaps you can read it when you're not working. I can see you rolling your eyes in the dark. Just because you're taking on a parental role to me doesn't mean I've stopped really being your mother and you've stopped being my child."

Chapter 11: Jakob's Leap of Faith

As much as he hated having to trudge through the mud and fight off the incessant flies, Jakob was enjoying his stay at Westerbork so far, if a stay in a transit camp could indeed be considered enjoyable, even comparatively so. While Kees was forced to work on the camp's railroad, and Gusta and Luisa worked in the maternity ward of the makeshift hospital, Jakob had landed the cake job of a cook in the restaurant. Not just the ordinary kitchen, but the actual restaurant. He would've preferred working in a munitions factory or a related enterprise, so he could smuggle ammunition and weapons, but being around food all day was a very close second. Every day, he smuggled out food for Luisa, and snuck morsels into his mouth when his supervisors weren't looking. All those years he'd been made to help his parents in the kitchen had paid off. Meanwhile, Zealot-worshipping Luuk had been assigned work on the farm, and spent his days digging for potatoes. Luuk probably wasn't smart enough to figure out he could escape because he had one of the off-grounds work details.

But best of all, so far all four of them had kept their names off the deportation lists. Jakob's heart was in his throat every time the *Blockältester* read the newest list of names, sometimes twice a week, and every time the list was concluded without their names, he rejoiced. He felt badly for the people whose names were called, but he had to look out for himself and his mother. Getting emotionally attached to anyone else would do far more harm than good. He didn't know if he still had the capacity for normal human feelings and the development of love for anyone but Luisa. Not after what happened to Ruud and Emilia. He just couldn't do that to himself.

"I like your new haircut, *Moeder*," he smiled as they ate breakfast one day in October. "It takes at least ten years off you. Now you look like a young, beautiful woman again, not a woman who's forty years older than her son. It was good how the hairdresser took away those hideous gray hairs. Maybe they'll never come back after they were dyed so well."

"I thought I'd never go to a hairdresser again after the new law in July." Luisa tore off a hunk of bread. "The camp hairdresser is a lot better than the one back home. She was in the NSB."

"I didn't like her either," Gusta said. "The rule about not letting us visit non-Jewish salons couldn't come soon enough for her. I'm sure she would've turned us away long before July if it'd been outlawed sooner."

Jakob was very pleased with how well his mother's injuries were healing. The serious bruise under her eye and the welt across her face had faded, and her head wound also appeared to be healing on schedule. He was glad she was safe in the maternity ward and not out in the open, subject to the Nazi overseers. They'd been through several *Sturmbannführer* since their arrival in August, and the worst one had recently been forcibly retired. Now that that whip-happy alcoholic was gone, Jakob had one less thing to worry about in regards to his mother's welfare.

"Perhaps we can go to the orchestra tonight." Luisa smiled. "Now that I look like a younger woman again, I should show myself off. Or maybe we can go to the cabaret."

Jakob pursed his mouth tightly. "We shouldn't have anything to do with that damned cabaret. We should only listen to performances in our native language, not that repulsive German. I can't wait till I never have to hear another word of German spoken ever again."

"It's not their fault," Gusta protested. "They're being forced to perform in German. I'm sure they'd love to perform in Dutch for us, but it's not allowed. They'd be punished if they broke the rules and sang in Dutch as a protest. It's better to be safe than sorry when we've got it so good."

"Dutch and German are cousins," Kees said. "You can understand it better than you would if your native language were Polish or Italian."

Jakob spooned strawberry jelly onto his bread and began violently moving it around with his knife. He glared at the people giving him funny looks for using his knife in his left hand. While he'd taught himself to write and draw left-handed, using a knife in that hand had always come naturally to him. His parents had tried to make him use a knife in his right hand several times, but it always felt strange and unnatural, and he hadn't been able to cut well.

"To celebrate the end of the war, perhaps we can go out to a theatre or cabaret performance in Dutch," Luisa said. "I'm sure we'll spend more years of our lives in freedom than under German occupation."

"Dutch is a much prettier language than German," Jakob asserted. "It looks and sounds so much more refined and elegant. German looks and sounds ugly and harsh. Dutch has a special something German doesn't have."

Kees looked at his watch. "It'll be time for me to get to work soon. I can't believe I'm saying this, but I wish I'd come here sooner. I feel so much more useful and productive with a good job to go to, without worrying I'll soon be fired or arrested on my way to work."

Jakob rolled his eyes. "You're probably just saying that because you're still feeling spiritual after the High Holy Days. When the holidays are just a memory, you'll feel a lot differently. I like my job here too, but it's not what any of us wanted. We should have jobs in freedom, not behind barbed wire."

"Always the rebel, even here. Would you rather be like some of your old school friends and forced to work on the farm? You have nice indoor work. I wish I could work indoors like you."

"I wouldn't trade my job for anything, but it'd be nice to work in the fields. I'd have a better chance to escape."

Luisa sighed softly. "You're not going to escape if you want to protect me. The sooner you get it through your head that our chances of surviving and staying together will increase if you don't rock the boat, the better."

2

On the evening of 18 October, Monday, while Jakob sat on his bed drawing pictures of the Westerbork environs, his legs crossed like an Indian Yogi, the *Blockältester* strode into the middle of the barracks. He quickly stuffed his sketchpad and art supplies back into his schoolbag and moved to Luisa's bed, gripping her hand tightly. This was the moment everyone dreaded every week, the announcement of the list of people who'd make the trip to the East tomorrow morning.

He held his breath until the *Blockältester* got past his place in the alphabet, then loudly exhaled. It was always an agonizing wait for the *Blockältester* to get from the Ds to the Ts. Though legally Luisa was a Hartog and Gusta was a Kikkert, they'd registered with their so-called "married names" under the hope of staying together more easily. Jakob wished the ter Avests' names were closer to theirs in the alphabet, so they wouldn't have to wait for those petrified, terror-stricken moments once or twice a week. All he wanted was for the list to leave their names off every time, so they could get on with their relatively well-off existence in this transit camp.

"Cornelius ter Avest."

Gusta screamed as though she were going mad. Jakob had seen her mouth making the movements of a scream last February when Kees was beaten, but he hadn't been able to hear her because of the blood ringing in his ears. Now he could see as well as hear her uttering a series of maddened, panicked, hysterical screams. Kees had gone as gray as the lumpy porridge they sometimes ate for breakfast, and his whole body violently shook, his breath coming in ragged, frantic gasps. Meanwhile, the *Blockältester* continued to read the names off his list, indifferent to the emotional reactions of the people around him. That damned traitor was a member of the Joodenrat and didn't care he was ripping apart families and sending people off to an unknown fate.

"Start packing," he barked at the conclusion of the list. "You know the drill. The train leaves at eleven tomorrow morning, and there'll be consequences for anyone who isn't at the depot."

"But I'm a railroad worker," Kees protested when he finally found his voice. "I perform necessary labor."

The *Blockältester* sneered at him. "Everyone in this camp is a guilder a dozen. We can easily replace anyone. Soon we'll be done with the camp railroad, so you won't have to walk all the way into town to start your relocation journey. If you're not packed and ready by tomorrow at eleven, you'll regret it."

After the *Blockältester* walked away, Jakob got off his bed and went over to Kees. "Do you want me to help you pack? I couldn't pack very well if my name had just been read."

"No, I'll be fine. It's not fair, but I'll manage."

"Make sure to pack your coat," Gusta said, her voice shaking. "You'll be there over the winter, and you don't want to freeze to death. I don't know if you should sew a star onto your coat or if you'll get one there."

Kees began folding up his clothes and slowly putting them into his suitcase. All around him, other people were starting to pack as well. Jakob wondered if they'd need personal belongings in Germany or Poland, but knew enough by now not to voice such sentiments in an already panicked, heartbroken crowd. Instead he raised the subject in a different way.

"Would you like to give me some of your things for safekeeping, in case they're taken away or lost at the new place?"

Kees looked at him suspiciously. "What are you planning? Eventually you'll have to leave too. If the worst is going to happen to me, at least I can have my things with me. If your plan is still to escape and join the resistance, you probably won't have room or use for most of your own things. After I leave, you'll be the only man left. You have to look after Gusta and your mother, and you know that doesn't involve dangerous stunts."

Jakob couldn't sleep the entire night because of Gusta's incessant weeping and Kees's tossing and turning. Every time he thought he was finally asleep, he was jerked awake again by one of their noises or movements. Even the noises from other people bothered him this night, and he'd learnt early on to tune out things like footsteps, snoring, creaking bedsprings, and people shouting in their nightmares. The last time he'd been kept up all night was Yom Kippur, when Elma Specht, five beds down, wept the entire night because her parents' names were called. Instead of going to the camp's synagogue services for the holiest day of the year, her parents were taken to the train station. Absolutely nothing was holy to these cretins who'd reversed the normal order of the universe.

In the morning, the lucky ones were locked into the barracks while the new deportees were herded out of the camp and to the train station. Jakob stood at the window and watched Kees trudging along through the mud, a suitcase in either hand. Gusta's eyes were red from crying as she strained her eyes to follow her husband till he became a dot in a mass of people. She fell onto the floor sobbing even harder when he finally disappeared from view. Luisa helped her back up.

"We'll be okay," Jakob promised. He pictured the newest drawing he'd make that evening, the train station being hit by a bomb as he and other resistance fighters sprayed machine gun fire at the Nazis and NSBers. "I'll figure out a way out of this. There have to be some weapons around here somewhere we can steal."

"You're an idiot," Luuk proclaimed. "Even if you had a weapon, you couldn't take two older women with you. They'd give away your group in the woods, or wherever you're planning to set up your operation."

"Maybe your heroes the Zealots believed in murdering women and children, but I don't." Jakob stormed over to Luuk and dismissively looked down at him. "You're short for a guy our age. You'd be of no use to any partisan band. You don't even make up for your puny height with muscle. Would you like to feel mine? While you were sitting around being a mama's boy, I was exercising and coming up with all sorts of plans for revenge. And I paid attention in school. So I'm smart in addition to strong and tall. No wonder you were picked for farm labor instead of restaurant work."

"Jaap, stop that," Luisa ordered. "Now isn't the time to start a petty fight. You shouldn't act like this right after we've lost a dear friend."

Gusta dabbed at her eyes. "When do you think Kees will come back? I don't know what I want more, to join him soon or to have the war end right now so he can come home."

"We're all doomed anyway," Luuk said. "Maybe we should imitate the Zealots so we won't be taken alive all the time."

"Or maybe we should stand and fight back like the Maccabees," Jakob growled. "Show our enemies we're warriors who aren't afraid to defend themselves. Maybe I can sneak aboard the next transport. I can see what's going on in the East and then come back with a full report. Maybe I can smuggle weapons to our friends over there so they can fight back too."

"That's not happening," Luisa said firmly. "You're needed here. You can't protect me if you run away to play hero or detective."

3

Now that November was well underway, Jakob had to go to work bundled up in his blue wool coat, a dark green scarf, his leather gloves, boots, his wool hat, and the heavy winter clothes he'd packed back in August. He hated the sight of the yellow star sewn onto his beautiful coat, but even a restaurant worker couldn't appear without it. As he made his way to work in the snow, he stopped to stare at a column of people arriving at the camp. Every time new people arrived, he asked them if they knew anything about Emilia, or what happened to his father's body. He always scanned their ranks for Emilia, and didn't know whether to be more relieved or agonized when she never appeared. No news didn't always mean good news.

As the column proceeded, his eyes caught on a tall woman with light brown hair and blue eyes, wearing a gray camel's hair coat and a matching gray hat with a feather in it. She held her head high and carried herself with the type of quiet dignity, elegance, and refinement

Luisa always had. He stepped back when he recognized the woman as Vrouw Antema, who'd hosted their Seder during the first year of the occupation. Elsje was on her right, and Adriaan was on her left. Her two remaining children also held their heads high, and briefly turned to look at Jakob. Their eyes met only for a few moments, but he could tell they recognized him. He wondered if their luggage contained the china in the cupboard he'd broken, or if they still were upset at him for using their Seder as a bully pulpit.

"Isn't it sad?"

Jakob looked to his right and saw Elma at his elbow. Elma worked in the restaurant as a waitress, and Jakob often swore he saw her giving him little looks and smiles every time she came into the kitchen to drop off or pick up an order. Sometimes she asked to walk back to their barracks together, but he always kept his hands in his pockets and walked ahead of her. On the occasions where they walked next to one another, he didn't make any eye contact and barely said a word. Even if he'd always liked her as a friend since their school days, he couldn't risk becoming close to anyone here. He had to protect himself and Luisa only, without any distractions.

"I wonder if everyone in Amsterdam has come here by now, and how long the rest of us have. Do you think we'll still be here by the time 1943 starts?"

"It's best not to worry about that," he muttered as he shoved his hands into his pockets. "We have to get to work, not stand around chatting."

"Chanukah's coming up soon," Elma continued as they trudged towards the restaurant. "If we're still here by then, do you think we'll have a party? I hope my parents are able to celebrate wherever they are now."

"We'll see if we're still here." He quickly looked her up and down. "You don't look like most other girls. You look like you could be a good fighter. A lot of the girls here are delicate things who think beauty's more important than brains. Have you ever fired a gun or used weapons? Maybe we could start a resistance group, and inspire the other young people to join. I'll teach you how to punch."

"That's a nice offer, but I care more about keeping my name off the lists than learning to shoot and punch. Of course, there are other things I'd like to learn too." She gave him a sideways glance he could've sworn was flirtatious. "Maybe you can teach me about other things."

"If you want. I don't have time for anything else besides working, eating, making sure my mother's taken care of, and drawing."

"Are you still drawing revenge pictures?"

"Sometimes. Now I mostly draw the camp buildings, the residents, and the outdoors. I haven't had a chance to use all those beautiful paints that came with my art set. The paint wouldn't dry fast enough for me to get back to work or go to sleep on time."

"That's good you're making a record of this place. I hope your sketchpad isn't destroyed. If you're taken away someday, you can leave it behind as evidence. Your sketchpad and that scrapbook might do more for our cause than you could as a resistance fighter."

4

On Sunday, 29 November, the *Blockältester* came into the middle of the barracks. No matter how many times these evening terrors took place, Jakob had never gotten used to them. All he could do was hope and pray he and Luisa were passed over yet again.

"Adriaan Antema, Elisabeth Antema, Rebekka Antema."

Elsje began weeping loudly and rubbing her fists across her eyes, oblivious to her brother's wheezing, hyperventilating breaths and her mother's hysterical screams. Jakob watched the scene with as much sympathy as he could scrape up until he heard his own name being announced, followed by Luisa's name. He stopped breathing for moments that seemed to stretch on to eternity. By the time he came back to himself, the *Blockältester* was continuing to read names, and Luisa sat like a stone, no expression on her face, not even shock or sadness.

"Luuk Klein."

At this point, Jakob didn't care his old school enemy was going to the East. His whole body felt hollow, while his spirit hovered somewhere between his physical shell and the other world. The entire barracks spun before his eyes, and he struggled to contain his urge to vomit.

"Anselma Specht."

Five beds down, Elma screamed and began punching at her pillow and pulling at her sheets.

"Augusta ter Avest."

Gusta turned white and put her arms around Luisa.

"Debora Tholberg."

Jakob cast a glance at his old classmate, still feeling hollow and like he were floating outside of his body. Everyone he cast his eyes upon seemed as if he or she were a kaleidoscopic vision of a Hindu deity with many heads and limbs, constantly spinning, rotating, and changing.

"Alexander Zeeger."

Sander fainted.

"You all know the rules. Pack your things, and be ready to board the train tomorrow at eleven. Everyone on this list must get on the train, no exceptions allowed. You're lucky we now have our own railroad going right through the camp. You won't have to walk into the town's depot in this cold weather."

Jakob felt himself coming back to his senses when he heard Luisa coughing. This wasn't as deep or hacking as the fat Nazi's cough, but it wasn't a regular cough either.

"How long have you felt sick, *Moeder*?"

"I'll be fine," she said in a deadened monotone that scared him to death. "I have warm clothes, and I can probably get medicine in the hospital before we leave tomorrow. I have special privileges, since I work there."

"I'm worried about your health. You're fifty-six, not the type of person who'd be first to be picked for a good job in a labor camp. You've only been so safe and protected these past three months because you've been in the maternity ward."

"There'll be another maternity ward at the new place," Gusta said, in a similar deadened monotone. "Women are always having babies, even in wartime. For some reason, most of the babies I've delivered who were conceived after the occupation were girls. Maybe women are stronger than men, and God knows this."

"You really think there'll be any hospital where we're going?" Elsje howled. "We're all going to die!"

"That's nonsense," Jakob said. "Don't you dare try to scare my mother. If they wanted to kill us and be done with it, they could do it right here. Why waste so much time and money shipping us to the East when we could be butchered here? It's probably just a worse version of Westerbork, with harder labor. Don't worry, *Moeder*, you'll get to rest on the train, and I'll see to it you get the best job available at the new place. Maybe we can escape *en route*, and find a group of partisans in the woods."

"You're still talking about escaping and becoming a soldier!" Luuk shouted. "Just accept the truth! We're going to go to our deaths tomorrow!"

Jakob looked him square in the eye. "Oh, so now you're going to go along with it? You're not going to follow in your heroes' footsteps? Go on, try to murder all of us. I'll murder you first."

"If I do decide to kill myself to avoid being killed by our enemies, I'll be remembered as a hero and die on my own terms."

Jakob turned his back on Luuk and grabbed his schoolbag. Still reeling from shock, he began stuffing all his things into it. First he packed his sketchpad, scrapbook, and case of art supplies, then rolled up all his clothes and stuffed them in. At least now it was winter, so he didn't have so much of his bag taken up by bulky winter clothes. He'd dress in layers tomorrow.

After packing his clothes, he put in his books and his other notebooks and sketchpads. Then he safely tucked in the family pictures and whatever money he still had left.

Luisa tugged on his sleeve. "I'm sorry to ask this of you, Jaapje, but would you mind letting me put some of my things in your bag? I don't know if I'm strong enough to carry all my things."

"Of course, *Moeder*. You can put in whatever fits. I think I'm going for a little walk around the barracks for some fresh air."

Jakob left his schoolbag lying on his bed and stalked outside. He barely felt the cold late November winds blowing on his face. Right now, his biggest concern was coming up with a good last-minute plan for escape. After what Luisa told him, and what he'd observed, he was very worried for her health. There was no question she'd have to come with him, whether she wanted to or not. He'd grown another inch since coming to Westerbork, and now stood five feet nine inches tall, in addition to all the muscle mass he'd picked up over the last year and a half of exercising and lifting weights. He could easily protect her from their enemies.

His train of thought was interrupted when he felt a slight touch on his arm. He wasn't entirely surprised to see Elma.

"Do you really think we'll be killed, Jaap?"

"I know I won't be, and neither will my mother. I'll save Gusta too, though it'll probably be hard to have two extra people with me. She did a really good thing by taking us in when she didn't have to, and I was born into her hands. It'd be really cold to desert her."

Elma eased herself onto the ground. "Would you like to sit next to me?"

He shrugged and got down on the ground, shielding his eyes from the bright lights of the watchtowers. "I'm sure you'll be given a nice job at the new labor camp. Your parents aren't as old as mine. You'll probably see them there. And a bunch of our friends are going. You can try to escape too, but I can't promise I'll keep you in my group. It'll be every man for himself."

"I'm not as brave as you." Her voice sounded very far away. "Tonight could be our last night of freedom. There are so many things I'll never get a chance to experience if I'm going to die in a few days. I want to have memories of some of those things in my final moments. I don't want to leave this life not having done certain things I'd looked forward to doing."

He lifted his eyebrow. "What things are you talking about? How do you intend to fit an entire lifetime of moments and experiences into only one night and morning?"

"I never had a boyfriend." She curled her fingers around his arms. "If I should die this week, I want to know I had that experience just once. I don't want to die never knowing what it feels like to kiss a boy."

He edged away from her. "What are you talking about? I like you as a friend, but not a girlfriend! Even if I were interested in a girlfriend, I wouldn't do something so personal with someone I don't love!"

"I know you don't love me. I don't love you either, though I really like you. Please tell me you'll grant my dying wish? I'll think of you in my final moments and remember how you were the first and only boy I kissed."

"Aren't there any other guys you can pester for that? I don't know how to do that. I never had a girlfriend or even took a girl on a date. You're a nice girl, smarter and more progressive than other girls, but I don't love you. I want my first experience of that to be with a woman I really love, not someone I picked just to say I did it."

"I'm not suggesting we get married, if I'm meant to live. Only very old-fashioned types still think you can only kiss people you love. My mother told me people who don't marry their first and only love have two first kisses. The first one is their first, and the second one is their first kiss of true love. You can still give that first kiss to your future wife. Won't you be nice to me and give me that beautiful memory? I'll carry it with me all the way to the East and to my death. If I'm going to live, the memory will keep my spirit alive when I'm enslaved behind barbed wire."

Jakob pulled at his collar. "I just told you, I don't know how to do that. If you want that just for a memory, you can go to a guy who knows what he's doing. It'd be the blind leading the blind, and it'd feel wrong if I did that with someone I don't love."

"Come on, you don't even have to put your arms around me. And I know you don't love me. It's not like you're a rake leading me on, or I'm a tease leading you on. If I'm going to die at only sixteen, at least I can go to my death knowing what it feels like to kiss a boy."

He stared up at the Moon and twinkling stars. "Do you know everything we see up there has been there longer than the Earth has existed? My father used to look at the stars with me, and tell me the names of all the stars and constellations. He showed me my constellation, Taurus, and told me all the stories behind the stars. I always liked knowing we're literally looking back in time when we look at the stars. It takes so long for their light to reach the Earth. Perhaps some of the stars we see now died long ago, but their light still lives on, just like very important people's names live on long after they've gone to the other world."

"You're smart. After the war, I bet you'll go to a good university and make a name for yourself. I bet you'll be a great fighter too, but it's not what you were made to do. You're not the type of guy I could see as a professional soldier. Just the type who fights for a few years in a just battle. Someday you'll be a good husband and father too. You treat your mother so well, and you treated Emilia really well too. I'm almost sorry I don't love you and that I'm probably going to die soon." She pushed her sandy blonde hair out of her face.

"If it'll make you feel better, I'll hold your hand on our way to the train tomorrow. Your parents probably would've wanted someone to help you."

Elma leaned over and kissed him faster than he could react. He smiled faintly at her as she giggled.

"Well, you weren't going to do it, so I had to take the initiative. Did you like it?"

"It was a pleasant sensation, I guess."

"You only guess? It felt a little funny, but it was more than just pleasant. You've got a very soft mouth for a boy. Would you like to try reciprocating? Now I'll have a final memory of kissing a boy, but not of being kissed in return. What if some hideous Nazi kisses me against my will? I won't have any memories of doing that with a nice guy when I wanted to. No girl's first kiss, of true love or not, should be forced on her by a bully."

He reached for a handful of snow and threw it towards the nearest building. "Damn you for appealing to my chivalrous side." He leaned his neck to the left, positioned his face in front of hers, and softly kissed her. "Now are you happy?"

"More than you'll ever know. Now I'll have that lovely, beautiful memory to comfort me in my final moments." She picked herself up and brushed the snow off her clothes.

5

The next morning, Jakob wasn't among the inmates locked into the barracks. This time, he was among the crowd of people marching to the new camp railway station. The snow-covered roads were cordoned off to prevent escape or attempted contact with other inmates. Jakob held his mother's left hand and Elma's right hand, as Gusta walked in front of them. Anyone who didn't appear to be walking fast enough was kicked, whipped, or beaten with a cudgel. Jakob was glad his group was keeping a good pace and that so far Luisa hadn't coughed.

Jakob stood back in horror, shock, revulsion, and disbelief at the sight of the train that awaited them. This wasn't a passenger train, or even the vans that took them to Westerbork. These were wooden railcars meant for transporting cattle. There were no benches, chairs, windows, or latrines. A bucket stood in the middle of the car, which he realized in horror was meant to be the outhouse for however many people were in each car. The only semblance of a window was a long open panel along the back, with barbed wire placed at regular intervals. Now he was even more worried about Luisa's health, and his mind began working even faster to try to figure out a realistic escape plan.

"I'm not riding in that," Luuk announced. He tapped the nearest guard on the back. "Officer, may I have your side arm? I'd like to kill myself."

The guard began laughing, and his ample midsection shook with mirth. "Your misery is only beginning, little boy. By the time you reach your destination, you'll wish you were never born."

"Then kill me now. I don't want to go through such a fate."

The guard laughed even harder. "Suffer you will, boy. I'm not stupid. Killing you is exactly what you want. You don't get to decide your own fate. Leave that to us."

"There's no heat in here?" Elma whispered. "And no kitchen?"

Debora was crying. "My friend is visiting me. My clothes will be all ruined by the time we arrive, and everyone will laugh at me because I'll smell awful and have blood-stained clothes."

Jakob was glad he wasn't a girl, and even gladder he'd thought to dress in several layers. After he pulled himself up into the railcar, he knelt down and helped first Luisa up, then Gusta, then Elma. He helped Luisa into a corner and eased her into a sitting position. Gusta took a seat to Luisa's left, against the shorter portion of the car, and Elma sat on Jakob's other side.

After the car was filled with several score of people and the entire train was loaded, the door was pushed shut. Jakob cradled his mother in his arms and stroked her hair as they were suddenly bathed in pitch black. The echo of the slamming door and metal bar of the lock sent nauseating reverberations through his stomach.

"Can someone stand at the window to read road signs?" Adriaan asked. "Maybe we're going to the coast and will be sent to England in exchange for prisoners."

"That's a dream if there ever were one," an older woman scoffed. "If we were being exchanged, we'd never travel like this. Even cattle have more dignity."

"Thank you for giving me that lovely memory last night, Jaapje," Elma whispered as the train began to move. "Now I'll go to my death knowing I got to have that experience. Maybe I'll die a virgin, but at least I won't die unkissed."

"It was nothing doing. It was probably the right thing to do. It's not like I suddenly fell in love with you when I did that. And I guess it's good I have a little practice. My future wife probably won't be an innocent maiden who's never done anything with anyone. She might laugh at me if I tell her I never kissed a girl."

"Who here is familiar with Dutch geography?" Adriaan asked. "We'll have some idea of where we're going if we see the names of cities we're passing through. We can figure out if we're going to the coast, to the south, or to the East."

A man who looked to be about forty stood up and pushed his way through the terrified crowd. "I'm very familiar with the map of The Netherlands, as well as the bigger cities in the surrounding countries. Not only that, but I have something we might be able to use before we leave our country."

Luuk's eyes lit up. "Please tell me you've got suicide pills! I won't be taken alive. I want to die a hero like the Zealots instead of waiting for a gruesome fate as a slave, or killed in a horrible way."

The man laughed as hard as the guard Luuk had begged for a pistol. "Someone clearly doesn't live in the real world or value his freedom very much. I intend to jump off this train before it gets to the German border, and I have just the tool to do it."

Jakob saw sunlight glinting off a piece of metal the man pulled out of his roll of bedding. He couldn't see much in the unnatural darkness, but he could tell from the general shape and size that this wasn't a pair of pliers that could cut away the barbed wire. As he squinted at it further, he realized this was an axe.

"How did you smuggle that all the way here?" he asked. "All our weapons were taken away from us long ago."

The man looked in his direction as he pushed his way towards the excuse of a window. "You don't quite live in the real world either. Now isn't the time to ask such questions. First you act, and then you ask. We're not too far from the German border, and can't waste any time with inane questions." He pulled his arm back and began hacking at the boards under the window.

Jakob squeezed Luisa's hands. "You see, *Moeder*, we'll be fine. God sent us an angel to rescue us. After he makes a big enough space for us, we'll jump. I'll go first, so I can catch you. Gusta, you can jump next."

"I'm not jumping off a moving train," Gusta said. "What if I broke my neck or smashed my skull?"

"Jump feet-first," Luisa said. "You always want to land on your feet when you jump, like a cat. Exit with your legs and then squeeze your body out. Or you can lead with your hands, if you can't put your legs out first."

"Won't we get in trouble if an axe is found in the car?" Luuk asked. "Even if you take it with you, there'll still be a big hole in the train. There'll be a punishment for that."

"Once again, you don't understand the art of refraining from unneeded questions and that it's every man for himself." The man continued to hack away at the boards.

"Not all of us are going to jump," Elsje said, rubbing her hands together. "We'll be left with a big hole. I don't want all that snow and cold air blowing in when we don't have any heat."

"We'll all be punished, even if only a few people escape," Debora said.

"You think the Nazis will notice the hole while you're being unloaded God knows where? You might not all be registered, if you know what I mean."

"There are probably guards looking back at us," Elsje went on. "You could be shot if you jump off. Where will you hide, if you're successful? At least we know we'll be given food and housing at the new labor camp."

"I wouldn't be too sure of that if I were you." He continued pushing his way against the back panel of the train and hacking away. "Some of us have a chance to escape and tell the tale."

"Do you intend to take down the entire back wall so we can all escape?" Jakob asked. "I'm not sure such a big group could make a safe getaway. We can't sacrifice a lot of people for the sake of the strongest few."

"Whoever wants to escape can jump, but it has to be very soon, or it probably won't succeed. Look. We're coming up to a woods, and I see a sign saying there are only ten kilometers to the German border."

"Germany!" Luisa gasped. "So we really are leaving home for a labor camp!"

The man with the axe ripped off the remaining pieces of wood by the careful space he'd made under the barbed wire. Without saying another word, he stuffed his axe back into his bedroll and jumped. The train was moving so fast, Jakob couldn't see where he landed or was rolling, and couldn't hear if anyone were shooting at him. Over the next several minutes, a few other people shoved their way over to the space and jumped.

"Are you ready, *Moeder*?" he whispered. "If we escape while we're still on our own soil, we'll be much safer. And there's a forest right there. If we make it to the woods, we'll be safe. I'll find a safe place for us to hide, build a fire to keep you warm, and forage the healthiest food I can. I'm sure there are partisans in the woods. I'll stay right where I am so I can catch you."

"That's too dangerous!" Sander shouted. "If you're going to escape, you jump off, run, and don't look back! Anyone else can follow you."

Jakob stood up, making sure his schoolbag was still safely on his shoulders. He didn't want to lose his artwork or the scrapbook. "Remember, Mama, you'll follow me. I'll take care of you until we find a safe place to stay. Gusta, you go after my mother." He squeezed Elma's hands before turning all his attention to finding a way off this slave ship of the land.

"I love you, Jaapje," Luisa whispered. "Don't ever forget I love you."

When he pulled himself up to the thin, precarious ledge under the barbed wire, he saw the woods in front of him and quickly estimated it'd only take about a minute to get there if he ran as fast as possible. The snow in this area was very thin to nonexistent, so he wouldn't have to worry about leaving tracks. It would've been nice if a thick blanket of snow could break his fall, but getting away without leaving a trail of evidence was more important.

Remembering Luisa's advice, he pulled himself into a very uncomfortable squatting position, still holding onto the ledge with a death grip. Then, knowing it was now or never, he propelled himself off the ledge and let himself drop, landing very hard on his right foot. It all happened so fast, he had no time to be scared.

Wasting no time, he began running towards the forest, but a sharp pain in his right ankle slowed him down. He was forced to hop and shuffle along, without turning back to look at the train. Finally the pain caught up with him, and he fell backwards just after he reached the woods. The next thing he knew, four young men with guns were standing over him, and his mother was nowhere in sight.

Part III:
Welcome Danger

(November 1942–May 1945)

Chapter 12: An Unexpected Twist

Jakob looked around at the four men standing over him as his heart thumped almost out of his chest. He was starting to feel the same sensation he had last night, where everything around him spun like a kaleidoscopic haze. He tried to speak, but his tongue was frozen in his mouth. The pain in his ankle was agonizing. If he'd broken his foot, he'd be useless as a fighter, if he ever got away from these strangers. He wished he were back on the train, that damned travelling coffin, so he could at least have the comfort of his mother. Maybe she could protect him from these strange men with guns.

"You don't have to make up a story about what you're doing here," one of them told him in Dutch. "We all know the story behind those trains. Don't worry, we're your friends. We're partisans hoping to join the Dutch Free Forces when they come home. We'll get you to the nearest safe house, where we'll all be more at liberty to talk."

Jakob tried to get up, but the pain in his ankle was so intense he was unable to stand. Feeling like a helpless invalid at just sixteen years old, he was held up by two of the men as he hopped along on his left foot. Without any questions, they were admitted into the back door of a house just outside the woods and shown into the basement, where Jakob collapsed onto a bed.

"This is Vrouw Heleen Visser, and I'm Dries Quackenboss. My three friends are Govert Vrooman, Leendert van den Hoff, and Jeronymus Schermerhorn. In the underground, we're known by our names backwards, so you might want to get used to calling us Vrouw Ressiv, Seird, Trevog, Tredneel, and Sumynorej. Vrouw Visser lives here alone, though many of us live here on and off. It's a way station for the underground."

Jakob propped himself up on the bed and looked around at the four men and the woman of the house. They had friendly, sincere faces, and he could tell Dries was speaking real Dutch, not German-accented Dutch. Slowly, he eased himself into a sitting position, took off his gloves, hat, and scarf, and slipped off his schoolbag.

"What have you got in there?" Govert asked. "Anything useful?"

"You can look if you want. It's not much. Clothes, a Bible, Louis Couperus novels, art supplies, a big sketchbook, a scrapbook I've been making to document the occupation, some money, family pictures, and some of my old notebooks and sketchpads. And some of my mother's things, but I didn't look to see what she put in my bag last night." His mind raced back to Luisa alone on that foul railcar, now right against that hole in the wall and exposed to snow and cold air. "Is there any way someone can run after that train and get my mother? I'm worried about her health. The plan was for her to jump with me."

Leendert shook his head. "I'm very sorry, Comrade, but that's not one of the things we do. The train's probably too far away by now for us to catch it anyway. Just think, if you join our ranks, you can do it for her sake."

"What's your name?" Govert asked. "It feels wrong to talk so personally to someone when I don't know his name."

"My name's Jakob DeJonghe, and I demand you admit me to your ranks as soon as possible. I might be young, but I promise to make a damn good soldier."

Dries smiled faintly. "We'd love to have you, but judging from how you were limping all the way here, you're in no position to join any fighting forces. You can wait out the winter here. Vrouw Visser will be more than willing to hide you. She's hidden a number of other people before this. Hopefully by the spring, your foot will recover and we'll be able to begin training you. But first, you've got some learning to do. You should've removed this before you jumped. If you'd been found by anyone else, they would've known who you were instantly." Dries reached over and pulled the yellow star off of Jakob's coat. "I understand you were thinking of more important things, but such a simple mistake could've been very costly."

Jakob put his hands around his ankle and massaged it, but the intense pain continued. "Do you have any morphine, or whatever drugs they use for severe pain?"

"We have alcohol to numb the pain," Vrouw Visser volunteered.

"What about a doctor?" Dries asked. "Somehow I think you've got more than just a sprained ankle or torn ligament."

"We know a very good doctor in the underground," Leendert said. "We can arrange to have him brought over here to set your break. He won't be able to dispense drugs outside of a hospital, but he can perform a basic procedure."

Jakob felt faint. "No pain relief? What is this, the Middle Ages?"

"He's not a primitive quack, if that's what you're afraid of. Normal women give birth all the time without drugs. Are you saying you're not as tough as a woman in childbirth? Surely a guy who wants to be a soldier can handle a little pain without medicine."

"You're safe here," Dries said. "You must know you'd be at greater risk if we smuggled you into a hospital for a real operation. I never believed in that stupid Nazi idea about 'looking Jewish,' but you do have very dark hair and eyes. A lot of people would assume you're not a real Dutchman because of that. And you generally have to undress for surgery and wear a loose hospital gown. Not to bring up such an indelicate subject in front of a lady, but I assume you're circumcised. That would give you away even more than dark hair and eyes."

Vrouw Visser fluffed his pillow. "Why don't you try to get some sleep while we arrange for the doctor to come over? You're welcome to drink as much of my alcohol as you want. If you drink enough of the right kind, you might fall asleep."

Dries slowly pulled off his right boot and sock. "I don't see any blood, and there are no bones poking out, though it is very swollen. At least you got away with minimal injury."

"My foot is screaming in agony! That's not minimal!"

"How much is your pain on a scale of one to ten?"

"Five thousand!"

Jeronymus pulled a small bottle out of his pocket. "Maybe you can have some sleeping pills. After what you must've gone through, you need sleep. Vrouw Visser, please make tea for our new friend. Do you have any favorite flavors?"

"I don't care about flavors! Just knock me out!"

Jakob clutched at the sheets and breathed the way he remembered Luisa breathing when she'd been in labor with Emilia. As much pain as he was in, he couldn't bring himself to cry or scream in front of these partisans. They might think he weren't manly enough to join their ranks. He tried to distract himself by thinking about happier days, before the occupation, but still felt that intense throbbing, shooting pain in his ankle. The thought of becoming an amputee left him cold with horror.

"Here you go," Vrouw Visser announced after what felt like forever. "Peppermint tea with honey and two sleeping pills. I hope it's enough to make you sleep till we get a doctor."

"Thank you, Mevrouw. If my foot heals, I'll help you around the house to repay you for your good deed."

"Just focus on healing yourself. I'm just doing what any decent person would do."

Jakob popped the sleeping pills into his mouth and took a big gulp of tea, barely feeling the hot liquid burning his tongue. That paled in comparison to the pain in his ankle. After another miniature eternity, he finally fell asleep.

2

"That poor young man. I can't imagine what he must've been through. Thank God he only hurt his foot instead of being sent off to the slaughter."

Jakob fluttered his eyes open and saw a strange man in the basement bedroom he'd been put up in. Vrouw Visser stood next to him, and two of the four partisans who'd rescued him were in chairs. He'd been in such a haze of pain, he didn't remember who was who, except for Dries, the one who'd done most of the talking. He didn't remember the names of the other three partisans.

"Oh, our houseguest is finally up," Vrouw Visser said. "Bokaj, this is Dr. Gustaaf Xylander. He'll set the bones in your foot and put a splint on you. Unfortunately, I have no crutches or wheelchair, and it would arouse too much suspicion to have them snuck in here."

He became aware of the sharp pain in his ankle again, and instinctively put his hands around it. "What did you just call me?"

"Bokaj. It's your name backwards. Don't you remember Seird—Dries—telling you we go by our names backwards in the underground? Your given name isn't too obviously Jewish to require a false name. Plenty of Christian Dutchmen are also named Jakob."

"Would you care to put these on?" Dr. Xylander held up a very baggy pair of pants. "Once you've got a splint on, it'll be harder to take normal pants on and off. It looks like you've got layers on. Vrouw Visser will be happy to fold, iron, and launder your clothes."

"With everyone watching?"

"We'll leave you alone for a few minutes. Call us when you're ready."

Jakob unbuttoned his shirts and pulled off his sweaters, leaving them in a heap on the floor. Luisa had always lectured him about not throwing his dirty clothes on the floor, but even if she were here now, she'd probably understand he couldn't stand up or walk around. He saw his winter clothes lying across the foot of the bed, next to his schoolbag. Vrouw Visser had neatly folded them up the way Luisa had, and his heart ached for his mother when he saw this.

His heartache gave way to frustration when he tried to pull off his first pair of pants and found himself unable to maneuver them off from his position. He tried kneeling on his left leg and pulling his right leg behind him, but quickly realized he wasn't enough of an acrobat to undress like that without putting any pressure on his right foot or falling flat on his face. Finally he decided to swing his legs over the side of the bed and let the pants fall off of him onto the floor. When he had difficulty maneuvering them down, he stood up on his left foot and dug his toes into the floor as hard as possible. As a boy, he'd often ridden the streetcar with Ruud, and Ruud had taught him to dig his toes in to avoid falling when they had to stand. Finally, he pulled on the pants that looked like they'd come from a clown's closet. He was proud of himself for not having to call for any help. Even without modesty concerns, it was embarrassing to need anyone's help for anything at his age.

"I'm ready, Doctor!"

Dr. Xylander came back with Dries and the other partisan. Jakob let him touch his foot, which throbbed in pain at every little touch. He desperately wished Luisa were there to hold his hand.

"Stop asking where it hurts! It hurts everywhere!"

"I can see that, my good fellow. Why don't you tell me where it hurts most."

"Everywhere! I can't distinguish different types of pain!"

Dr. Xylander began poking and probing it even more aggressively. When he finally determined what parts were most severely twisted and broken, he opened his black bag and started taking out strange instruments, bottles, and things Jakob guessed were for making a splint.

"This is for you," Dries said. "Drink as much as you want. Vrouw Visser won't charge you for using all her good liquor."

Jakob grabbed the bottle of vodka and chugged down as much of it as he could, ignoring the strong taste. If this were as close to anesthesia as they had, he wanted to get as much of it into his system as possible.

"Easy there, Comrade," Dries laughed. "You don't want to die of alcohol poisoning before you have a chance to join the partisans.

That's probably enough for you. Even seasoned drunks don't gulp that much vodka at one sitting."

Dr. Xylander finished taking things out of the bag. "Leendert—Tredneel—will put a blindfold on you and stuff a cloth in your mouth, so you won't scream or be frightened by what I'm doing. It'll all be over before you know it. At any rate, it'll get better before you get married."

Jakob's heart raced as the other partisan came towards him with the blindfold and washcloth. He was relieved to be spared the embarrassment of having to ask the other fellow his name. He made a mental note that Dries had thick brown hair and deep blue eyes, and Leendert had sandy blonde hair and hazel eyes. With his photographic memory, he was sure he could remember those details the same way he still remembered the faces of Ruud's assassins.

"Remember what Dr. Xylander said," Leendert said soothingly as he tied the blindfold and wadded up the washcloth. "This will all be over sooner than you think."

"You might want to tie him down too, just to be safe," Dr. Xylander said. "I've had patients who thrash around very violently during procedures without pain relief."

Jakob felt helpless with a blindfold on. He flashed back to the ride inside that foul cattlecar, bathed in sickening, unnatural darkness, as someone tied his hands and good ankle to the bedposts. The horrific images in his head increased a thousandfold when Dr. Xylander began pulling on his foot and ankle. He bit down on the washcloth as hard as he could, praying he wasn't breaking any teeth and necessitating dental work as well. He'd always been proud of having good teeth, while boys like Luuk hadn't been made to brush their teeth or regularly see a dentist.

"You're sweating like a pig," Dries commented. "Would you like a cold water compress?"

He nodded, glad he wasn't choking on the huge mass in his mouth. When Dries put the cold washcloth on his forehead, he didn't feel any distraction from the intense pain in his foot. Even after Dr. Xylander stopped pulling and pushing on his foot and started putting it in a splint, the pain continued. If he didn't know any better, he'd think he were caught by the enemy when he jumped, or that he'd died and gone to Hell.

"There, it's all over now," Leendert said as he removed the blindfold. "All you need to do is ice it and keep it elevated, and you'll heal on schedule."

Jakob sat up as soon as the restraints were off. He cringed at the sight of the big ugly splint encasing and pressing against his leg. He felt like a monster in a science fiction movie, or one of the strange creatures in the old German Expressionist silent films Ruud had sometimes taken him to see at film festivals.

"How come my whole leg has to be wrapped up? I only hurt my foot."

"That's how it has to be when a foot or ankle is broken. You broke yours very badly. It's a miracle you still have a foot. Your break is so bad, I'd ordinarily send you to surgery, but this is the best I can do under the occupation. Don't worry, I think your bones will heal well on their own. Perhaps they'll grow back together a little funny, but they'll heal if you give yourself plenty of rest. Given the chance, the body wants to heal itself."

"Do you have any pain relief?"

Dr. Xylander pulled out a prescription pad and scribbled something. "My secretary can drop this off with my pharmacist. They're all in the underground too and know what's really going on. I'll give you these pills in a day or two. In the meantime, there's always alcohol or sleeping pills. Just don't take them together."

3

Over the next few weeks, Jakob alternated between alcohol, sleeping pills, and the prescription medication Dr. Xylander dropped off. He spent most of the day sleeping and having bizarre dreams and the worst nightmares of his life. He didn't know if they were the result of the pain, the drugs, the alcohol, or the stress of being hidden and not knowing what had happened to Luisa and Gusta. During the brief periods he was awake, he nibbled at the food Vrouw Visser left on a tray on the table next to the bed. He couldn't find much of an appetite, as much as Vrouw Visser and the four partisans kept encouraging him to eat so he'd heal faster.

In spite of his delirium and scant waking hours, he still had enough cognizance to be utterly, completely humiliated by the bedpan he was forced to use. Even a convenience chair on the left side of the bed would've been more dignified and adult than this. He'd figured out how to maneuver himself onto and off of it without spilling, and was able to lean out of bed to set it on the floor for retrieval, but could never feel as proud of that as he had about undressing himself without help before getting the splint. He never looked Vrouw Visser in the eyes when she came to collect it or to bring a new one.

Sometimes Vrouw Visser had friends or neighbors over. When Jakob was awake for these visits, he strained his ears to listen to their conversations. To his relief, they were always normal people, not people who might suspect something and blab to the authorities. Vrouw Visser's house was never searched by the authorities, to his even greater relief. He burnt with rage every time one of the people in the underground stopped by to relay news of what was happening on the outside. The hatred in his heart burnt darker than ever, and the iron wall he'd put up around it became even thicker and higher. Now that he'd lost everyone, he had no more love left. If Elma had approached him now for a kiss, he not only would refuse, but would also tell her in no uncertain terms what a stupid, flighty, selfish request that was when there were so many more important things to worry about.

Near the end of December, the pain finally began to decrease a little bit. Before long, Vrouw Visser noticed he was no longer sleeping so much, and went down to visit with him on one of the coldest evenings of the month. When she came into the room, she found him propped up on all the pillows, painting in his sketchpad, a wistful, faraway look in his eyes. She blinked when she saw him switching his paintbrush back and forth between his hands.

"I'm figuring out which hand I like best for painting. I haven't gotten a chance to paint for a long time. Right now I'm working on turning my scrapbook about the occupation into a series of paintings. I'm starting with the invasion, and writing the date in small print on each painting."

Vrouw Visser took a seat next to him. "Are you an artist?"

"I wish. I just like drawing and painting in my spare time. You're welcome to look at the stuff I drew in my old notebooks and sketchpads. A lot of the drawings are me getting revenge on the *kankerhonden* who murdered my father. I have a lot of time now to work on my art."

She put the scrapbook on her lap and started turning the pages. "You've certainly put a lot of effort into this. If you'd like, I can bring you old newspapers and flyers so you can fill in the blanks. Your scrapbook only goes up to August."

"That's because I was taken to Westerbork that month. I had to make do with drawing pictures of the camp and its people during the last few months."

"This is a very thorough record. You should be proud of yourself for taking the time to do this. What a miracle you were able to take it with you and save it when you escaped. It would've been a tragedy if such a valuable record were lost or destroyed."

He dipped his paintbrush into his cup of water to get rid of the red paint and rubbed it into the yellow palette. "Will you keep my artwork and scrapbook safe when I'm well enough to fight in the partisans? I won't need to lug them around when I'm a soldier."

"Of course. So far you seem like a very nice young man." She reached into his bag, pulled out a random notebook, and opened it.

A picture fell onto her lap. Jakob looked away when he saw his family when it was complete. Vrouw Visser turned the page, and an official photograph of Queen Wilhelmina with Princess Juliana fell out. He shoved his sketchpad off his lap with the wet brush still on it, sick to his stomach over the memory of his arrest. When he closed his eyes, the flashback of the Nazi tearing and grinding up the photograph of Princesses Juliana, Beatrix, and Irene became even more intense, and he started gasping for air.

"Have you taken ill? I can't open the window in this cold, but I can see if I have any medicine. If you want, I can help you walk around a little bit so you can get some air."

He pressed his hands against his eyes, determined to force away any tears. It would be downright humiliating to cry in front of a woman, or to cry at all at his age.

Vrouw Visser rubbed his back. "What are you thinking about, Jaap? I can't begin to imagine the sorts of things you've gone through. Thank God you escaped the worst. My heart breaks for you every time I hear you calling for your mother in your sleep. I assume this is your mother in the other picture."

"What do you mean, I've called for her in my sleep? I've never talked in my sleep!"

"I hear you screaming and calling in your sleep all the time. Often you call for your mother. I hope for your sake that she survives whatever you escaped from."

"She's fifty-six. Not a spring chicken. She was with my midwife—I mean, my mother's midwife. They worked together at Westerbork. Gusta, the midwife, lied that my mother was her assistant. I hope they were taken to another labor camp and not their deaths. Like a few people on our transport said, it made no sense to spend all that time and money sending people to the East when we could easily be murdered right here at home."

Vrouw Visser looked around the room. "There's enough room in here for another bookcase. How would you like it if I moved a smaller bookcase down here so you can read while you're recovering? You can't draw and paint all day long. I've got a lot of underground publications, including international newspapers, and a fair number of military magazines and books. You said you wanted to be a partisan, so here's your chance. By the time you're well enough, you'll already know a lot about warfare, weapons, fighting techniques, everything a good partisan needs to know. It won't be a substitute for training, but you'll know the basics."

"Yes, thank you very much. I'd love to read every military book or magazine I can get my hands on. I used to play soldier with myself, with a toy pistol, and imagine how I'd get revenge on the barbarians who murdered my father. And I've done lots of exercises and weight-lifting. The partisans have to accept me into their ranks. I'll be their best fighter ever."

"Good. I'll have one of my partisan friends help me carry the bookcase downstairs, and we'll fill it up with all the reading material your heart desires. In the meantime, now that you seem to be more cognizant, why don't you finish unpacking your bag? I want you to feel like this place is home as long as you're here. A house isn't a home if all your belongings are in a suitcase."

4

That evening, Vrouw Visser came back and helped Jakob out of bed. Since there were no crutches on hand, he had to hold onto her arm on his left side. As she explained, she was serving as a human crutch, and if there were only one crutch available, it was most important it be on the stronger side. Trying to ignore the feeling of helplessness and unmanliness, he dutifully held onto her right arm and hopped along on his left foot, keeping his right foot up at an angle.

When they reached the large bookcase, already largely filled, he hung onto the closest shelf as Vrouw Visser slid the schoolbag off his back. He held onto the shelf with his right hand, and used his left hand to arrange his books, notebooks, and sketchpads on the empty space she showed him. It was nothing like the library he'd once had, but it was something.

"I take it you're a big fan of Louis Couperus?"

"I didn't start reading him till this May. My father gave me *The Hidden Force* as a bar mitzvah present and told me Couperus was our greatest novelist, but I never read it. He got me *The Mountain of Light, The Books of the Small Souls* cycle, *Of Old People and the Things That Pass, World Peace, Majesty,* and *Eline Vere* for various holidays and birthdays after that. I politely smiled and accepted them. Now I feel bad I never read them. I took them with me because my father gave them to me. He gave me that Bible too."

"If you finish all these novels and like him enough to want more, I've got all the rest of his books upstairs. Just ask, and I'll lend them to you. I can bring them down when I put the other bookshelf in here."

"Can I keep my current sketchpad and art supplies next to my bed? I don't want to inconvenience you every time I want to use them. I'll need my scrapbook there too, so I can continue working on it and using it for my new series of paintings."

"Of course you may." Vrouw Visser pulled out two more books. "You also enjoy poetry and Chinese philosophy?"

Jakob stared down at the books in her hands, an anthology of Dutch poetry and *The Tao Te Ching*. "So that's what my mother put in my bag. She asked me if she could put some of her things in my bag because she didn't feel strong enough to carry everything in her own suitcase, and I agreed. I was outside talking with a friend while she was packing, so I didn't know what she put in there. My mother was after me to read *The Tao Te Ching* for some time. Maybe that was her way of finally forcing me to read it."

Vrouw Visser reached into the bag again and pulled out a stack of papers. "Is this your mother's handwriting?"

He nodded. "Can you please leave those papers on the bed? I'd like to read them in private."

"I can do that. Since your mother wanted you to read this Chinese book so much, I'll leave that on the bed too." She went over to the bed and deposited them, then pulled out the clothes he hadn't unpacked yet. "I'll wash, iron, and fold all your clothes as soon as I can. I can only guess you weren't able to wash them very well at the labor camp."

"How far are we from Westerbork? I know we're very close to the German border, but not the name of the city. Westerbork's near Hooghalen."

"Winschoten. We had a nice Jewish community before the occupation. Some of the people in this town speak a Gronings dialect with a Jewish influence. I'm one of the relative few locals who speaks real Dutch. Don't worry, no one suspects anything of me. There have been plenty of raids, arrests, and roundups, but no one ever searched my house. As Dries told you, I've hidden a number of other people before, and we were never caught or suspected."

"Can I go back to bed now? I'm tired of standing on only one foot and holding onto this shelf."

Vrouw Visser helped him back to bed. As soon as he was lying back down, she elevated his foot and put the icepack back on. "Try to get some sleep. You've probably had more activity than you should for one day."

"Is there anything more in the bag? It's a really big bag. I bought it for my eleventh year of school, but I'm glad it got good use as my suitcase. My old schoolbag never could've held nearly so much."

She reached into it and pulled out an atlas, a small photo album, and Pieter Corneliszoon Hooft's seventeenth century *History of The Netherlands*. "Your family certainly valued the written word. I've never heard of any other family taking so many books with them when they were forced to leave their home or possibly be taken to their deaths. I'd pack mostly clothes, linens, medicine, personal supplies, those sorts of things." She turned the bag upside-down and shook it, and several pieces of jewelry and a rolled-up piece of tissue paper fell out. "I suppose your mother took her clothes and other necessary items in her suitcase. Perhaps she knew you'd escape, and so gave her most important things to you for safekeeping."

After Vrouw Visser bade him goodnight and left the table lamp on for a little more reading or drawing, he reached for Luisa's papers. He forced himself not to cry when he saw most of the pages were her recipes, and that the final page was a note she'd written, dated 30 November 1942, the very day they'd been taken away. She must've found time to write it that morning, before they came face-to-face with that foul travelling coffin, that slave ship of the land they'd never dreamt existed.

My darling little boy Jaapje, the light of my life, my reason for still living,

I love you so much, and my love for you has only increased over these past 25 months. Until you hold a child of your own in your arms, you'll never understand how much a parent loves a child and will do anything for that child. You've always been even more special to me because I was unable to have a child for so long, and was finally blessed with motherhood at age forty. Now that you're my only child left, I love you even more and am even more determined to do anything for your sake.

I know you'll survive, and I'll survive too, in my own way. We just won't survive together. After this is all over, I know we'll find each other again. You have the intelligence, desire, and strength to escape and survive on your own or with a band of partisans or resistance fighters. I, however, am not a young woman. I'd be a liability to you. It'll be easier for you to escape and survive on your own. Don't be sad because I won't follow you when you escape. Know my maternal love for you will keep me alive and see me safely back to you. I cannot let myself die and leave you without a living parent. Just imagine if your future wife lost both her parents to the Nazis and NSBers. My future grandchildren deserve at least one grandparent to love and spoil them. No child should grow up without any grandparents.

By the time you read this, we'll be separated. You'll escape, and I'll go on to the new labor camp. I'll do whatever it takes to get along and survive. If I have to, I'll escape myself, should I be faced with certain death. I'm sorry I didn't take you seriously when you spoke about how much trouble we were in and that things would only get worse. You now have my full blessing, permission, approval, and orders to join the partisans or resistance. Make me proud, and make our homeland proud.

Here are some of my things for you to take care of till we meet again. I wasn't lying when I said I didn't feel strong enough to carry all my things, but these things in particular I wanted you to have. Now you have no more excuses not to read The Tao Te Ching, *and you'll find the atlas very useful as a partisan. The history book will help to ground you and remind you of where we come from. I've given you my recipes so you can make them when you're on your own. When you're old enough, you can give them to your wife, so she knows how to make all the foods you love so much. I've memorized them, so don't think I'll ask for them back. Maybe I'm only saying this because I'm your mother, but I know you'll make a very good, nurturing, protective husband and father someday. I shouldn't have to be the most important woman in your life forever. I want your destined one, the other half of your soul, to take over that role before you get too old. A grown man's first loyalty and greatest love should always be for his wife, not his mother. I hope you don't have to wait as long as I did to be blessed with children. After what's happened to our people in the last two years, it's extremely important to replace those who were lost.*

I've also given you your caul, to keep you safe. Gusta says you were one of only thirty caulbearers she delivered, out of the several thousand births she's attended over the last 25 years of her career. You were always such a sweet, sensitive, inquisitive, easily-wounded little boy, and I know you're still like that deep down in spite of how angry and withdrawn you've been the last two years. Someday you'll go back to your true nature. All caulbearers have such a sensitive, deep nature. You also must know no harm will come to you so long as you always have your preserved caul with you. I'm not suggesting you'll never get hurt, but you won't meet your death or find yourself in severe danger.

I hope you're not too upset at me for not following you. We've gone as far as we can together, and now it's your time to be on your own and prove yourself as a man. I always taught you the value of independence and not being dependent on your parents forever. And you always bragged you were better than a spoilt mama's boy like Luuk Klein. Here's your chance to prove it. I wouldn't be doing my job as a mother if I let you stay safe under my wing forever and never forced you to go out into the world and fend for yourself. I've always been deeply embarrassed for mothers who treat their children, particularly their sons, like that. If you always unquestioningly do everything for your child, no matter how old he is, he'll never learn to stand on his own two feet and become a real grownup who can function on his own.

Remember, Jaap, you're going to be fine. I wouldn't have decided to go without you if I believed you couldn't make it on your own. I love you so very, very, very much and already miss my darling boy. It'll be forever until the war is over and we can see one another again.

Your loving mother,
Luisa Mirjam Hartog

5

The next morning, when Vrouw Visser came to bring him a tray of hard-boiled eggs, smoked fish, toast with strawberry jam, and chamomile tea, he asked if he could have some paper to write a letter to his mother. She crept up to the windows, stood up as high as she could on her toes, and looked for any movement.

"How'd you like to come upstairs after you finish breakfast? I'll let you have a look around my house. You can write your letter there if you want. It must be lonely and boring to be in this little downstairs room all the time."

"Oh, no, Mevrouw, I could never endanger you like that. You're doing such a righteous thing by hiding me when you don't have to and when you didn't plan on having me. I can't risk your arrest just because I might be curious about the rest of your home."

"I live alone, and I'm not expecting any visitors. The area's been pretty quiet recently, probably because of the winter. I still see the trains coming through, but there haven't been any raids or arrests on a large scale. It's such a pity what's happened to your people. If the Nazis and NSBers continue much longer, there might not be anything to show soon for what a large Jewish community we had not so long ago."

He reached for the cup of tea. "Are you sure it's safe to come up? Sometimes the biggest danger is when you don't expect any trouble."

"I assure you, this is a safe time. After you have your splint off, I'll let you come up more often, so you have more room to practice walking. Only at very specific safe times will you be allowed upstairs. Would I suggest this unless I were absolutely certain there were no danger? You can call for me after you're done eating, and I'll help you up the stairs. If there's any danger, I'll stall for time while I help you back down the stairs. If there's not enough time for that, I'll hide you in a secret room."

After he finished breakfast, he maneuvered his pajamas off and put on his favorite red shirt and the hideous clown-sized pants he wore day in and day out. He longed for the day he could wear normal pants again, and get dressed without going through a whole ridiculous routine that took four times longer than it had to get dressed only a month ago. And he hated how he could only put a sock and shoe on one foot. It looked so bizarre, even if he had a splint preventing it. At least he wasn't a woman and didn't have to worry about menstruation. He could only imagine how horrible that must be for a girl with a broken leg.

Vrouw Visser once again served as a human crutch on his left side as he hopped over to the stairs. When they got to the first step, she helped him turn around, and he grabbed the banister with his left hand. As she helped him into a sitting position, he flashed back to how he'd helped Luisa into a sitting position in the corner of the railcar. He wondered if he'd ever be really normal again, or if his mind would always be called back to these haunting memories at any and all times.

"Keep your splinted leg up in the air, and push yourself up the stairs with your right hand on the steps and your left hand on the banister. With your good foot, of course. When you get to the top, I'll help you stand up, and you'll get a little tour."

"Can you get my fountain pen on the table? My mother got it for me last Chanukah, and it's been my favorite pen ever since. I won't be able to give her my letter for probably a long time, but at least I'll have it ready to give to her. She'll know I was thinking of her this whole time."

Vrouw Visser went to get the pen and waited for him at the top of the stairs. It took at least fifteen minutes to navigate his way up the stairs backwards, though there were only ten steps. He never thought so few steps would seem so terrifying and daunting. When he got to the top, Vrouw Visser helped to pull him up and helped him hop over to the nearest chair.

"Just think, when you're all better, your left leg will be about ten times stronger than your right leg. You can rest for awhile, and then I'll help you around this floor. I won't ask you to tax yourself by going up another flight of stairs to the other two floors."

He looked around at the living room. Vrouw Visser's walls were lined with books, framed old maps, paintings, old photographs, upscale posters, and cupboards full of miniatures, fancy silverware, crystal, and china. She was the kind of woman Luisa would've been good friends with. His parents tended to associate only with people as literate and culturally aware as they were.

"I used to have antique firearms and pictures of the Royal Family on display too, but I had to hide them in the basement. They're in a locked room a short way from yours." Vrouw Visser jumped up at a knock on the door. "Who's there?"

"It's us, Seird, Tredneel, Trevog, and Sumynorej. We're alone, and no one followed us."

"Should I hide just in case?" Jakob whispered.

"Oh, believe me, if they weren't alone, I'm sure there'd be more than just a polite knock on the door."

He pulled on her sleeve as she passed him. "This is really embarrassing, but I don't remember all their names. I only remember Dries and Leendert and what they look like."

"Don't worry, I'll address them so you won't have to embarrass yourself by asking for their names. Perhaps they'll address one another before I have a chance to."

Jakob observed them coming in. The third one had dark blonde hair that was almost brown, with brown eyes and a small nose, and the fourth one had chestnut-colored hair brushing his shoulders and large green eyes, the darkest green eyes he'd ever seen. The latter looked rather like a man from a Renaissance painting, or an artist himself. A real artist, not someone who drew and painted in a sketchbook in his spare time.

"We brought some food for our injured friend," the small-nosed partisan said. "We got it from an NSBer's store we raided. Justice was dealt accordingly to the owner and his wife."

"Thank you, Govert." Vrouw Visser took the bag from him and put it on Jakob's lap.

Jakob smiled with relief. Now he only had one more partisan to learn the name of. He vaguely remembered the one who looked like an artist had a long, somewhat old-fashioned-sounding name.

"How's your leg coming along?" Leendert asked. "You must feel at least a little better if you're up to leaving the basement. Vrouw Ressiv, I trust you won't make it a habit. We can never be too careful, and if Bokaj wants to join us so badly, he needs to stay alive and in a safe place."

"My leg doesn't hurt quite as badly, but there's still some pain. I think it's a four or five on a scale of one to ten. I can't wait to start reading all the military books and magazines in the house."

"Jaap is also an artist," Vrouw Visser said. "Would you fellows like to look at some of his paintings and drawings? He knows how to paint with both hands."

"You can?" Dries asked. "Can you do anything else with both hands?"

"I can throw, draw, write, punch, and use tools. My left-handed writing isn't anything I'd enter in a calligraphy competition, but it's not chicken-scratching either. I've worked hard on getting it as legible as it is now."

"However lacking you might think it is, I'm sure it's better than any of us could do if we tried to write with the other hand! Do you know what a valuable asset you'd be to us in the partisans? Someone who can throw, punch, or shoot with the other hand can launch a very effective sneak attack and throw the enemy off-guard, since he didn't expect it from that direction. I hope your leg gets better soon, because

I'd give my right arm to have a man with two right arms in my company."

"When do you think I can get my splint off?"

"Given how badly you broke your foot and ankle? I'd say in another two months. At least you didn't break your leg. Those bones are bigger and thicker, and take a lot longer to heal."

"Jeronymus broke his toe last year," Govert said. "It only took him a couple of weeks to heal, and a few months before he was completely back to normal."

Jakob nodded, happy he now knew the names of all four of the partisans. He wondered why the long-haired partisan's parents had given him such an old-fashioned name instead of the modern form Jeroen, but supposed it could help him stand out in a crowd. After all, his own name usually had a C in Dutch, but his parents felt the K gave him more personality.

"Would you like to eat some of the treats we brought you?" Leendert asked. "We won't think you're rude if you eat when we're not eating. You deserve treats more than we do. While you're still in a splint, you should milk this time for all it's worth. Once you're out of the splint, you won't have any excuses to sit around in bed all day reading and painting, eating as many sweets as you want, or sleeping all day."

Jakob reached into the bag and popped a handful of chocolate-covered raisins into his mouth. He wished Luisa were safe here with him, but the sentiments in her letter were right. A boy of sixteen and a half didn't need his mother to survive, and he'd look like a baby to his new friends if his mother cooked for him, did his laundry, and hovered over him like a helpless invalid. Vrouw Visser only did those things because he was recovering from an injury, and wouldn't continue doing so much for him indefinitely. Perhaps Luisa was right, and it was finally time to prove himself as a man, not a young boy playing soldier with himself and planning revenge with no means to achieve it.

6

That night, after he was helped back into the basement, Jakob sat propped up on the bed, his fountain pen in his hand and a portable walnut desk across his lap. He hadn't been able to write his letter earlier, for fear of being looked down on by his new friends.

30 December 1942, Wednesday,

To my beautiful, compassionate, righteous, self-sacrificing mother, Luisa Hartog,

I know you won't get this letter for awhile, and we'll both have been through awful things by the time you can read it. I just want you to know I've been thinking of you the entire time and never forgot about you.

I'm safe. I broke my foot and ankle very badly when I jumped, and probably broke them even worse because I was trying to run, but the broken bones are being treated. With any luck, they'll be back to normal in a few months, and I can join the partisans. At least I didn't break my neck or crush my skull, and I still have one good leg left. I don't know what I'd do if I'd injured both legs, or if I should injure my remaining strong leg in the future. I'm very impatient to be healed already, and angry because I thought I'd get away without any broken bones in my life, but I can't just wish this away.

I'm being hidden by a very nice woman, and I've made friends with four guys in the partisans. They found me and took me to this house, and would like me to join them when I recover. I'll be the best partisan I can be. When the Dutch Free Forces come home, maybe we can join them, and then I'll be a real soldier. My greatest day as a soldier will come when I find the barbarians who murdered Vader *and serve them the same fate. But I won't be a soldier who delights in killing, like you warned me about. A good fighter only kills when he has no choice, not because he wants to shed the blood of someone who was created in the image of God just as he was.*

I love you very much and will think of you the entire time we're apart. If I find a wife after we're together again, I'll do as you said and live only with her. I doubt I can ever find the love in my heart to give to anyone else after what happened to me, but if I do find a woman I like that much, she'll be the only woman of my house. I don't want my future wife to have to compete with my mother or tiptoe around you. We'll live in different houses, though we'll always be close.

Your loving son,
Jakob Eliezer DeJonghe

Chapter 13: A Flicker of Joy, A Heaping of Anguish

The year had now turned to 1943. Jakob spent most of his time drawing, painting, and reading. His favorite reading materials were the military books and magazines Vrouw Visser and the partisans had brought into the basement when they'd taken down the promised bookshelf and loaded it up with reading material. He dreamt of the day when he'd handle and fire real weapons, particularly when those weapons were pointed at the three monsters who'd coerced his father into suicide. He might not wear a uniform, but he'd still be serving his country. Resistance fighters were fighting the same good fight as official soldiers. Their means and organization might be different, but the desired result was the same.

On the third of March, he thought his dreams had come true when Vrouw Visser came into the basement with Dr. Xylander, Dries, and Leendert. Jakob had started to grow very anxious about still having a splint. The worst part was being unable to itch himself, flex his ankle, or wiggle his toes. In his worst nightmares, his entire leg had atrophied, and he'd never be able to use it again. Vrouw Visser had given him a hairdryer to aim above his leg if it itched, but the air penetrating the splint to cool his skin wasn't the same as having a good scratch, feeling his own skin, and itching it in all the right places. He also hated having to take sponge baths. As soon as the splint was off, he wanted to run upstairs into the bathtub and take a five-hour bath to scrub off everything impure and get himself cleaner than he'd been since he couldn't remember when.

"I'm sorry if I've been a bit too conservative in how long I've kept you in a splint, but I didn't want to chance anything," Dr. Xylander said in a comforting voice as he sat down on the foot of the bed and took a pair of scissors out of his bag. "Your break was mighty severe, and in several different places. It's been a bit over thirteen weeks since your break, and you weren't able to have it set immediately. God willing, your bones have healed as well as they can on their own, though I wish I'd been able to take you to surgery."

Jakob watched Dr. Xylander cutting off the layers of off-pink bandages on top of the splint. His leg immediately felt a bit lighter as soon as the top layers were off. Next, the cotton padding was pulled and cut off. Finally, the stiff piece of fabric at the bottom was taken off, and the rope holding it in place was cut off.

Jakob savored the feeling of the air hitting his skin and finally being able to look at his leg for the first time in over three months. He was horrified at how shrunken and wrinkled it was, but it was still there and hadn't shriveled to a toothpick.

"Can you wiggle your toes for us?"

He elatedly wiggled his toes as he stroked his shrunken leg, feeling as though he were a baby just discovering his body and taking an innocent, newborn delight in realizing this was all his.

"Will my leg grow back to its normal shape soon?"

"In time. I brought a book about physical therapy. Many of the exercises you can do lying in bed or sitting in a chair. Your left leg shouldn't be ten times stronger than the right leg. That creates an unhealthy imbalance, and could lead to another injury if you rely too much on the stronger leg."

"Can I try walking now?"

"I'm not sure it's a wise idea to do too much walking, but you can try to walk a little to see how it feels. You never want to go right back to normal activities immediately after healing from an injury. It can injure you even more."

Jakob swung his legs over the side of the bed and held onto Dries and Leendert on either side. After he stood on his left leg, his courage failed him. After not bearing weight on his right leg in several months, he was suddenly afraid he might break it all over again, that it might not be fully, properly healed yet. He hadn't had an X-ray. Gingerly, he moved his right foot toward the floor at the rate of a millionth of a centimeter per second. His heart beat faster the closer his foot got to the floor. When his foot finally reached the floor, he just barely brushed it against the cold wood and didn't bear any weight through it.

"Very good. Now why don't you try walking. Seird and Tredneel will hold onto you at first, just to let you get used to the sensation."

Jakob held onto each with a death grip as he tried to walk. The entire ten steps he took, he bore all his weight through his left foot and continued only brushing his right foot against the ground. He wasn't so sure anymore if he remembered how to walk properly. Even babies just learning to walk could move more naturally than that.

He panicked when Dries and Leendert let go of him and stood off to the side. Uncaring how he looked in front of the doctor and two partisans he hoped to fight with, he began screaming uncontrollably for help, his heart crazily skipping beats and pounding out of his chest. He hopped to his left and grabbed onto Dries for support, struggling for breath.

"That's probably enough walking practice for one day," Dr. Xylander said. "You're not the first patient I've had who was scared to try walking right after he healed from a broken leg or foot. Just try a few steps at a time, and you'll grow more confident and dexterous with enough consistent practice. I wouldn't have taken off the splint if I thought your foot were still broken or that you'd immediately break it again."

"Don't worry, it takes time to start walking normally again," Leendert reassured him. "You'll relearn how to walk properly. You just haven't done it in so long, your body doesn't quite remember the correct motions."

Jakob hopped back over to the bed and lay down, putting his hand over his heart. He practiced bending his knee, moving his leg up and down, rolling his foot around, and wiggling his toes. After he was confident enough the bones and muscles still worked, and his heartrate was returning to normal, he pushed himself up into a standing position to try again.

"Remember, go slowly," Dr. Xylander said. "No one here is judging you based on how slowly or awkwardly you walk. This is perfectly normal for a person in your condition. I wish I could give you an orthopedic walking boot for a transition between the splint and full walking, but I don't want to arouse suspicions if I'm seen bringing it to the house."

Determined to prove to everyone and himself he wasn't a weakling or coward, he held onto Dries and Leendert less forcefully than before, and put a little more weight through his foot. He was still terrified at the idea of breaking it all over again, but he wanted to believe the doctor was right and he was the victim of his own overactive imagination. When they let go of him after ten steps, he held his arms out for balance and tried to bend his knee a little more. The gait that resulted was a mixture of hopping on his left foot and shuffling on his right. Try as he might, he just couldn't get himself to bear full weight through his right foot.

"That's probably enough excitement for one day," Dr. Xylander said. "Everything will become more natural and less frightening to you the longer you practice. If you feel the need, I'll come back in another few months to check on your progress. Free of charge, of course. I don't seek any monetary gain from helping people in need. Don't even think of repaying me after the war is over and you have a job."

Jakob felt as though everyone were staring at his bizarre gait as he navigated his way back to the bed. He took some comfort in the fact that he was able to walk by himself, even if he didn't walk like a normal person. This meant he'd finally be able to bathe normally and could stop using that hideous bedpan. As soon as he was back on the bed, Vrouw Visser fluffed his pillows and pulled a heavy blanket over him. Exhausted from his walking practice, he almost immediately fell into a deep sleep.

2

As the month wore on, Jakob still found himself hopping and shuffling along, in spite of his constant walking practice around the basement and how he sincerely tried his hardest to walk normally. He began to panic when it slowly started to dawn on him that his injury had been so severe, the trauma so sudden and sharp, he might never walk normally again.

Jakob felt useless. The more he tried to walk properly, the more he seemed to have problems. Risking being smuggled to surgery wasn't worth it. How would he pay for it, and why would he want to spend even longer recuperating? He burnt with desire to take up arms right now, limp or no limp.

"Who wants a soldier with a limp?" he grumbled. "Noncombatants perform valuable services in their own way, but that's not why I want to join the partisans! Only if I can kill the bad guys do I want to join. Even after the war, everyone will stare at me. 'Oh, there goes the man with the limp.' I'll be seen as a pathetic charity case. People will feel sorry for me. Old people have difficulties walking, not young people. Name me one important person with a limp."

"Oedipus Rex had a limp, though he was a fictional character," Dries volunteered.

"He married his mother and killed his father! That's hardly a role model I want to have, fictional or not!"

"Tamerlane the Great, one of the Mongol Khans."

"Most normal people aren't fans of Genghis Khan and his descendants!"

"The Greek god Hephaestus was born crippled."

"He's just as fictional as Oedipus Rex!" Jakob reached for several chocolates in Vrouw Visser's fanciest candy dish.

Govert lit a cigarette and passed his lighter to Jeronymus, who was fumbling for his own cigarette. "Care for a smoke, Jaap? Vrouw Visser doesn't mind us smoking in her house. Dries and Leendert don't smoke as much as we do, but they do it from time to time."

Jakob shook his head. "I don't care I'm underage, but my parents always told me smoking was a bad habit. Even if they hadn't said that so many times, I think I'd be uninterested anyway. No offense. I'd still like to be your comrade-in-arms someday."

"What a pity. There's nothing quite like the taste of a good cigarette. Maybe you like alcohol better, after all the alcohol you've been drinking for pain relief." Govert blew a smoke ring toward the ceiling.

Jakob forced a smile. He didn't want to offend his friends by telling them the real truth, that besides his parents' moral warnings, he'd always thought cigarettes smelled terrible. If he ever married or had a girlfriend, he'd never want someone who smoked. Kissing a smoker must feel like licking an ashtray.

"Would you like to demonstrate walking for us?" Leendert asked. "Maybe we can still use you in some way. I'm sure our commander will be very impressed to find out how much you know about military tactics and firearms. Pretend you're a member of a pacifist church. Some pacifists don't mind being soldiers, so long as they don't use weapons. Many of them are still damn good soldiers in their own way."

"But I'm not a pacifist! I want to kill as many Nazis and NSBers as possible, particularly the *kankerhonden* who murdered my father and beat my mother!"

"Maybe that'll give you extra inspiration to get better at walking."

Jakob stood up and commenced his hoppy, shuffling walk up and down the length of the living room. By now he no longer held his arms up for balance, and he was a little more confident and steady about bending his knee and bearing weight through his leg. Sometimes he picked his bad foot up and moved it by bending his knee forward, without letting it touch the ground, instead of letting his leg form a natural slope.

"You've done worse," Dries said. "Practice makes perfect."

Jakob returned to his chair, burning with shame. Absolutely nothing had gone his way for a very long time. Even his escape from that death train hadn't turned out the way he'd planned it. In his dreams, he'd pictured himself immediately joining the partisans, and killing and capturing scores of Nazis and NSBers by now. Instead, he was holed up in a basement in a house by a forest, and learning to walk worse than a baby. At least a baby could figure out how to make the correct, natural movements of locomotion. The only thing that gave him any semblance of hope in all this was that he was still alive, and not an amputee or prisoner.

Chapter 14: Rekindling the Flames of Hope

Vrouw Visser had made several pieces of matzah for Jakob, according to Luisa's recipe. He'd tried to tell her he didn't want her to get in trouble if she were caught baking it, but she insisted he should have a semblance of a Pesach celebration. Tonight, 19 April, Monday, he sat in bed chewing on the matzah after quickly swallowing the smallest piece of maror possible. He'd told Vrouw Visser the five basic halachic requirements for a Seder were eating matzah and maror, drinking four cups of wine, telling the story of the Exodus, and reciting Hallel. Earlier in the evening, he'd briefly had a discussion with her about the Exodus, and recalled the few lines of Hallel he remembered. Now he was left alone to eat and drink.

As he ate the matzah, he flipped through the Bible Ruud had given him. Instead of reading about the Exodus, as he should've, he preferred to read the stories about his namesake. When he got to Genesis 32:25-33, he sat up at attention, and grabbed a blue colored pencil to underline the passage.

Jakob was left alone. There a man wrestled with him until the break of dawn. When he saw he hadn't prevailed against him, he wrenched Jakob's hip at its socket, so the socket of his hip was strained as he wrestled with him. And he said, "Let me go, for dawn is breaking." Jakob answered, "I will not let you go, unless you bless me." The other asked, "What is your name?" And he replied, "Jakob." The other said, "Your name shall no longer be Jakob, but Yisrael, for you have wrestled with beings Divine and human, and have prevailed." Jakob asked, "Pray tell me your name." The other said, "You must not ask my name!" And he took leave of him there. Jakob named the place Peniel, meaning, "I have seen a Divine being face to face, yet my life has been preserved." And the sun rose upon him as he passed Peniel, limping on his hip. That is why the children of Israel to this day do not eat the thigh muscle that is on the socket of the hip, since Jakob's hip socket was wrenched at the thigh muscle.

Knowing no less of a person than his namesake had had a limp, he suddenly felt stronger, at least emotionally. His mother had always teased him about acting so much like his namesake, the way he could be impulsive, sneaky, and not always so forward-thinking. Now he was like his namesake physically as well. One of his religious school teachers had tried to say there was no historical or archaeological evidence to support the existence of the majority of Biblical characters, but

Jakob had insisted they'd existed, simply because he believed they had. Absence of evidence wasn't evidence of absence. It seemed absurd, a committed member of the Progressive Movement arguing for things most people in his denomination eschewed or actively mocked, but he couldn't imagine those larger than life figures and the amazing stories about them were mere fiction. It was comforting to believe there'd been people by those names, in that place, in that era.

And now he'd been reminded of that fact that his own namesake was a limper. Not only that, but he'd earned his limp as a battle mark of sorts. Only after he'd gone through so many trials of faith, so many difficulties in his life, wrestled with both God and men, had he been given that limp. It wasn't a liability or punishment. It meant he'd finally won his battles, conquered his demons, proved himself as a man. That was what Luisa had urged him to do in her letter. He smiled as he began thinking about how proud of him she'd be when they met again and she found out he'd passed his own trial.

2

Jakob's four partisan friends came to visit during the week of Pesach. He eyed them curiously when he saw how much they were smiling. He suspected these smiles were about more than just wishing him a happy holiday.

"Is the war over?"

Govert smiled. "We wish. It's still going strong. We came by to tell you a piece of good news. Dries, would you like to tell Jaap the latest information?"

Dries sat in an overstuffed red velvet chair and ran his fingers through his thick brown hair. Jakob was a bit envious of him for having such thick hair. He'd always wished his own hair were thicker, since the boys at gymnasium who got the most female attention had hair like that. Not necessarily longer hair like Jeronymus, but thicker hair nonetheless. Then he chided himself for thinking about such a subject, since he couldn't fathom letting any girl into his heart. Even going on just one date would be asking too much of him emotionally. That was a chance he refused to take.

"We'll start training you next month, after you've had a little more time to develop a somewhat normal gait."

Jakob's eyes lit up. "What! Is this a late April Fool?"

"Not at all. Why would we lie to you about something you want so badly?"

"But why? I'm useless with a limp. What made you decide to take me?"

"Most people aren't fans of the Mongols, but you can't deny Tamerlane was a brilliant military commander. It takes more than a limp to keep a good soldier down. The official Army might disqualify you on health reasons, but we spoke to our commander, and he can't wait to have you with us. It's not as though you're in a wheelchair, and you want this badly enough you could make up for it. Considering what might've happened to you, having a limp is the least of your worries. It was a small price to pay for escaping an even worse fate."

Govert smiled. "I used to go a theatre that showed American movies. Some of the short comedies featured a group with a bald fat man who got a lot of laughs. I believe he was one of your people. He walked with a limp. It's something I noticed, but it wasn't part of the big picture. I'm sure you'll find something to do that draws similar attention away from your own limp, so people will notice and pay attention to you for your own skills and talents."

"Do you mean De Drie Stooges? My parents used to take me to see American comedy movies too. It seems so long ago I last saw a movie." Jakob reached for a huge strawberry on the tray of fruit on the table. "I was reading my Bible a few nights ago, and I remembered my namesake had a limp."

Leendert smiled. "Yes, now that you mention it, I do remember that. And he only got that limp after he won an important test of his character."

"I daresay the Nazis and NSBers are more disabled than you," Dries said. "They may not be physically disabled, but their hearts and souls are diseased, crippled, blind, deaf, limping, cancerous. The whole reason you want to join us is to start killing some of those evil creatures, particularly those thugs who killed your father."

"That's damn right," Jakob said. "And kill them I will, as soon as I can."

3

Jakob's seventeenth birthday, 9 May, was a Sunday. He stood and watched at the basement windows at the time Vrouw Visser usually got back from church. No one could see into the basement from the way the windows were situated, but he could see through the windows if he stood at the right position. Once in awhile, Vrouw Visser returned from church with friends, and he had to stay extra-quiet during these visits. He hoped today she'd return alone, so no one would question why there was a cake on a cooling rack in her kitchen when she lived alone and wouldn't have been home when the cake would've been pulled out. Before she left for church, Vrouw Visser had made the birthday cake Luisa had always made, chocolate with strawberry filling, and thrown it into the oven. Jakob had gone upstairs, backwards and hopping on his left foot, at the appointed time to remove it. He no longer had a problem going downstairs normally, but he still felt safer going upstairs backwards.

Jakob saw five other pairs of feet streaming past the windows, in male shoes. Had there only been four pairs of shoes, he would've assumed his friends were visiting, but the fifth pair threw him off. He quickly retreated to the bed and grabbed the military magazine he was reading.

"Jaap, would you like to come upstairs?" Vrouw Visser called. "I've got a visitor who really wants to meet you."

"Don't worry, it's not a trick," Leendert said. "Come on up and meet a very important man."

Jakob slid off the bed and limped over to the bottom of the stairs. He liked to think he'd gotten pretty good at navigating stairs, but he still didn't ascend stairs as quickly as normal people. Vrouw Visser told him he usually took about five minutes to go up the basement stairs, and ten minutes to climb the stairs leading up to the second and third floors, but it felt like much longer. Particularly when there was a supposedly important person waiting for him.

"Happy birthday," the stranger said, extending his hand. "I'm Jurriaan van der Beek, and I'm the commander of these four fine young men. Hopefully, I'll soon be your commander as well."

Jakob grabbed his hand and shook it. "I'm very pleased to meet you. Thank you so much for this opportunity. When can I begin?" He scanned the commander's shirt for any indication of a decoration that would indicate his rank, so he'd know what title to address him by.

"I'm not an official soldier. None of the men in my unit are," he said when he noticed what Jakob was doing. "When the Dutch Free Forces come home, hopefully they'll accept us into their ranks and give us ranks commensurate with our experience."

"I'll frost your cake while you discuss things," Vrouw Visser said. "When would you like to eat?"

"Can we have it after lunch?" Jakob asked. "I hope you made the cake as good as my mother. It wouldn't feel like my birthday without that cake."

"Of course we can have it then. You can do whatever you want on your birthday."

He walked as well as he could to the table, trying to impress the commander with his gait. Maybe this was a test, and the commander wanted to vet him before accepting him into their ranks. He felt like he had in his gymnasium days, when people came to inspect his teachers and he and his classmates had been on their best behavior. Not that he'd act undesirably in the partisans once he were accepted, of course. But for now, it was important to do everything exactly right so he didn't take any chances.

"Have you ever fired a gun?" Commander van der Beek asked.

"No, Meneer, but I've read a lot about weapons of all kinds, and I know how to fight pretty well. I can punch well with both fists, and once gave a bloody, swollen eye to a little *Bokkelul* who insulted my father. I wonder if that little idiot killed himself yet. His heroes were the Zealots."

"We'll teach you everything you need to know," Govert said. "How to make bombs, be a sniper, organize a raid, go on spying missions, make a camp in the woods, you name it. There are other safe houses around the country we go to besides this one. We usually walk or get around in vehicles we've appropriated. Can you drive?"

"Yes, I sure can. I drove a Peugeot to a friend's house so the owners wouldn't have their car stolen after the order to turn in cars and bicycles. I was very careful the whole way."

"Sometimes we hitch rides or make a cab driver take us somewhere," Leendert said. "Our group mainly does unofficial fighting. We work with another group who specializes in sabotage. And, of course, we're connected with those in the business of hiding people. Assassinations and interrogations give me such a rush. Once you start, you'll want to do it all the time."

"I can't wait to fire a gun. I'd love to use a knife too."

"You'd be one of the youngest members of my group," Commander van der Beek said. "I have one fellow who's sixteen, and two others who are seventeen. Most of my fighters are between twenty-five and forty, but we have a fair number of younger fellows. They're our lifeblood. Sometimes a young fighter is more valuable than an experienced veteran. My young fighters have soaked up everything like a sponge."

"How many people are in the group?"

"At any given time, probably forty. Your friends have been members since almost the beginning of the occupation. They just missed the boat to England. Once the Dutch Free Forces are home, I'm sure they'll let all of us join them."

"We'd be in a lot of trouble if the Nazis caught us," Jeronymus smirked. "Guys our age are supposed to be doing forced labor in Germany. I'm not going to let some Nazi order me around in his enemy factory or farm. I'm staying in my own country and working for the good of my own people."

"How old are you guys?" Jakob asked. "I don't think I ever asked, though I assumed you're not much older than I am."

"I'm nineteen," Dries said. "Govert's twenty, and Jeronymus is twenty-two. Leendert is the baby at eighteen."

"Where will we be staying?"

"It depends. Sometimes in a safe house, sometimes a camp in the woods or in one the houses carved out of the hills. We're not always so close to the Winschoten area. We've worked in Amsterdam, Utrecht, Groningen, Apeldoorn, Eindhoven, you name it. Sometimes we find the time to have female companionship. Of course, never for very long. That would distract us from our duties. But if you want us to find you a girl, just let us know."

"That won't be necessary. I want to fight, not go around with girls."

"I like your attitude," Commander van der Beek smiled. "A good soldier is single-minded. You'll have plenty of time after the war to enjoy the company of women."

Vrouw Visser brought the cake to the table. "Before I start making lunch, would you like to open your present?"

"You bought me a present?"

"Of course. You've been through too much to not deserve a birthday present." She stood on a footstool to open a high cupboard door and pulled out a package in orange tissue paper.

Jakob carefully pulled off the wrapping and found a book, a thin metal box, and a very small stuffed brown rabbit. He opened the box and found a multicolored array of Conté crayons. As he flipped open the book, Jean-Jacques Rousseau's *Confessions*, he wondered what Luisa would've gotten him, and if she had a calendar where she was now. Perhaps she was helping Gusta to deliver a baby right this very moment and reflecting back on how she'd finally become a mother seventeen years ago this very day.

"I saw in your sketchbook that you like drawing rabbits, so I thought you'd like a little stuffed rabbit to keep in your pocket for luck. Maybe when you have some free time, you can draw in the forest. You seem to like drawing animals."

"Yes, Mevrouw. Thank you very much for thinking of me. You've been almost as good as my mother. One day I'll repay you for your kindness."

"For now, all you need to worry about is having a happy birthday. After you become a partisan, you'll never again have back this time when you were so well-taken care of and didn't have to do much in return."

4

Near the end of May, Commander van der Beek came back to the house and beckoned to Jakob. He left his sketchbook on the bed and hobbled up the stairs backwards, then hesitated when he saw the commander opening the door and motioning for him to come outside. As much as he longed to go outside again and breathe fresh air, he'd gotten used to hiding in the basement. And it was broad daylight. He expected he'd be taken to training and eventually the partisans under cover of darkness. As isolated as Vrouw Visser's house was, one could never be too sure.

"We've got you covered, my good fellow. Some of my men, whom you haven't met yet, staked out the area for a few days to make sure this was safe. I've got a few more men posted as snipers. Nothing bad will happen to you."

Jakob slowly edged toward the door, secretly glad his limp slowed him down. He was suddenly as terrified as when he'd first borne weight through his right foot again. This was an unknown. It was easy to think everything would go perfectly when it only existed in his mind as a fantasy.

"Do you want us to come in there and carry you out?" Govert called. "You'll get used to doing this over the next month. Most of our members haven't needed much more than a month to get trained and master all the basics. The ones who haven't been able to hack it with us are always referred to other branches of the resistance, like the underground presses or the people preparing for the return of our Queen."

Jakob gradually made the journey to the back door and covered his eyes the moment he crossed the threshold. The bright sunlight was almost blinding after six months in hiding. He barely remembered what it felt like to be outside and feel the fresh air and sunlight. Everything around him looked so foreign, even the birds, chipmunks, and rabbits he'd once so loved drawing, talking to, feeding, and petting. At least they were in the forest and not really out in the open. The sunlight would be even brighter outside the forest.

"Here you go." Dries handed him a pistol and a knife. "Let's see how well you can attack that dummy." He indicated a life-sized, faceless ragdoll tied to a small tree. "Don't hold anything back."

"You're letting me use real bullets?" Jakob asked, still blinking in the intense light. "Won't that be wasteful?"

"We can always make more. We have our ways of getting weapons and ammunition." Govert lit a cigarette and leaned against a tree. "Does the name Walraven van Hall ring a bell? He's a very important banker who's a national hero for all the scams he's pulling to keep the Resistance well-supplied with money."

"We've got our ways of getting food too," Leendert added. "You'll never starve with us. Maybe you can help us steal ration coupons or raid NSB stores. Or perhaps you'd prefer to assassinate NSBers instead of taking their food."

"Here. You'll need this too." Dries reached into a bag and pulled out a belt. "It's the special kind that lets you keep weapons by your side."

Jakob fastened the belt around his waist, putting the knife on his left side and the pistol on his right. "I'm afraid I can't use a knife with both hands. That was just about the only thing I was never able to teach myself to do both ways."

"Even better. I told you that's a very valuable asset. The enemy won't expect an attack from the other side."

"Now run at the dummy and pretend it's one of the goons who

murdered your father," Commander van der Beek instructed. "Just don't make too much of a mess. It's too dangerous to clean up all that spilled stuffing and lug it back to the house. We set it up at night so no one would catch us."

"How close do I have to get to it? In real life, I probably won't be able to get very up-close and personal."

"I suggest about an arm's length away."

Jakob broke into his version of a run, heavily dragging his gimpy leg behind him. He hadn't had any running practice, and now realized that was something he needed to work on. But at least he was able to run again.

Halfway towards the dummy, he squeezed his eyes shut and fell onto his knees, gasping for breath. The horrific memories were floating through his mind again, appearing before his eyes as though they were unfolding right now. This time he saw himself leaping from the train and running as fast as he could for the forest. He felt phantom pain in his foot and ankle.

"Have you hurt yourself?" Leendert asked. "I didn't notice any rocks or branches in your way."

"I'm sorry," he gasped. "I'll just need a minute to collect myself." He could never tell his friends what was really happening to him. As sympathetic as they were, they weren't there. They could never fully understand the sights and sounds that would be a part of him as long as he drew breath. He wondered if he'd ever be a real, full part of the human race again, or if he'd forever exist in a special category of people with a gigantic chasm separating them from normal people. Even if he'd probably escaped the worst, he still didn't feel like a normal human being anymore. A limp was the least of his worries.

After twenty minutes, with all eyes on him, he picked himself up and limped back to his starting place. He tried his best to block everything out and concentrated only on running towards the dummy and stabbing it. As soon as he was an arm's length away from it, he pulled out the knife and maniacally stabbed it in the areas designated as the stomach, heart, and lungs.

"That's more than a bit unrealistic, but you've got good form," Commander van der Beek said. "Try to remember you're supposed to be stabbing a real person, not playing make-believe and doing whatever you want."

"Can I practice shooting now?"

"Sure, let's see how well you shoot the first time. Next week we'll let you practice with a rifle."

Jakob went back to the starting place, putting the knife back in the holster. He reached for the gun and brought it up to his face, shutting his right eye to focus with his preferred eye.

"Careful!" Jeronymus said. "You never hold a gun that close to your face unless you're trying to injure yourself with too much kickback. That's a good way to break your nose, fall on your back, or get gunpowder all over yourself."

Dries pulled out his gun and demonstrated. "Always hold it like that. You never want to hold it either too far or too close. And don't just keep shooting in one spot or as you're walking. In real life, you might be getting shot at in return, so you'll have to duck and move around a lot."

Jakob tried to do as they said, varying his position and ducking as he walked. He was overcome with joy at finally being able to handle and fire a real weapon. With a gun in his hand, and real bullets coming out of it, he felt so powerful and adult. No one would push him around now or mock him as belonging to a people who didn't fight back.

"You shoot well with both hands," Commander van der Beek observed. "That's a good skill for a soldier to have. You can use your own judgment as to which hand you shoot with in actual combat, but if you're going to be in a group operation, I'd prefer you to shoot with your left hand. Just to throw the enemy off."

"Now you can practice throwing a grenade," Leendert said. "Pretend these rocks are grenades, and throw them with everything you've got. We'll see which hand you can throw farther with."

Jakob reluctantly put the pistol back into the holster and picked up a rock. First he threw with his right hand, then picked up another rock and tried with his left. He imagined they were grenades he was lobbing into Nazi headquarters in Germany, or NSB headquarters in Amsterdam.

"You threw much better with your left," Dries called as he investigated where the rocks had landed. "Are you absolutely sure you only taught yourself to do things left-handed and weren't really born *linkshandig*?"

"As far as I know, I wasn't. I have no memory of anyone switching me, and most people are old enough to remember by the time they start writing and eating by themselves."

"Who knows, perhaps you copied the adults around you, or you were gently nudged when you were too young to remember. I've never seen anything like this. You can teach yourself how to write with the other hand with enough practice, but some things you can't really teach yourself well. That kind of dexterity and strength usually only comes naturally. The American baseball player Babe Ruth is *linkshandig*, but he writes with his right hand. Parents and teachers usually only switch the main tasks, and leave kids alone for minor stuff like throwing and playing sports."

"Whatever the reason, a fighter like this is a goldmine!" Commander van der Beek said. "I have high hopes for you. After you pass our basic training, I expect you to become one of my most valuable fighters. After enough time, perhaps you can one day train new recruits too."

"Thank you. So what's next?"

"You can practice with the knife a little more if you'd like, but we don't want you to have too much excitement in one day. You're still recovering from an injury, and we want you in the best shape possible when we make you a member. Don't force yourself beyond your limits just to try to impress us."

"Yes, Meneer. Thank you again for this opportunity."

As he headed back to Vrouw Visser's house after finishing his first day of training, Jakob smiled when he imagined the surprise his enemies would soon be in for. They'd never see it coming, particularly not from a limper. Those bastard Nazis and NSBers would only be laughing at his limp until he got up-close and personal and blew their brains out.

Chapter 15: Trading in His Shelter for Danger

On the final day of June, when Dries, Govert, and Commander van der Beek came to visit, they looked happier than Jakob had ever seen them. He began smiling too, imagining what they were about to tell him.

"It's official. You're joining our group." Commander van der Beek extended a holster belt in one hand and a pistol in the other. "They're yours to keep. We'll give you a knife and a rifle when we get to our current headquarters. Probably we won't stay much longer in this area, but we'll be back from time to time."

"Thank you very much. Do I get a uniform?"

"We all wear what we have. You probably have enough clothes to last for at least a year. Why don't you pack your necessary items, and then join us."

"Yes, Meneer. Do I need to sign a contract?"

"We're not the real Army. You know you won't get paid with us. We'll see what happens when the Dutch Free Forces are home. We might need to sign contracts then."

"Remember not to pack things you don't need," Vrouw Visser called as Jakob hopped down the stairs. "Particularly now that it's summer. You won't need extra weight dragging you down and making you more exhausted. I'll take care of whatever you leave behind."

Jakob tossed his bag on the bed and began rolling up his clothes. Many years ago, Ruud had taught him clothes took up less space when they were rolled instead of folded. He gently stroked the pair of pants Luisa had sewn a patch on, and the shirt she'd sewn up a tear in. He was glad none of his shirts had any noticeable holes or yellow stains from having those hideous yellow stars sewn on for almost seven months.

After loading his bag with clothes and stuffing his coat into the carrying straps on the bottom, he put in the little stuffed rabbit, his sketchpad, the Conté crayons, his carrying case of art supplies, *The Tao Te Ching*, and a few family pictures. He wished he could take the scrapbook, but it was awfully heavy, and he could always catch it up when he came back to visit Vrouw Visser.

He put the bag on and went upstairs backwards, feeling slightly more confident about ascending stairs than he had a few months ago. At least there wouldn't be any stairs to navigate in the partisans.

"I've got some food for you before you leave," Vrouw Visser said. "Did you remember to pack your caul?"

"It's in the drawer of the nightstand, Mevrouw. My mother would want me to take it with me, though I never really believed in all the superstitions about caulbearers."

"You're a caulbearer?" Dries asked. "A real caulbearer?"

"Don't tell me you believe all those superstitions too."

"Not really, but I think the basic idea is right, that caulbearers are lucky. You'd better keep that thing in your possession at all times. Who knows, maybe you'll bring good luck to the rest of us."

Vrouw Visser went downstairs for the caul and stuffed it into his bag, then went into the kitchen and brought out a bag of food. "This should be enough to last you for a few days. Hard-boiled eggs, chocolate bars, raisins, apples, strawberries, bread, smoked fish, and hard cheese. I won't hear of you going off hungry. Maybe you'll meet my husband when our Army comes home, and you'll get to fight with him."

"Your husband's a soldier? But why have you been left alone—"

"The Nazis and NSBers around here are stupid. They believe I'm a widow, and don't know my husband's in the Dutch Free Forces. My children went with him to England and are hopefully with a nice foster family. I had to stay to help people in need and maintain a home for my husband and children to come back to."

He shook her hand. "Now I know why you were so good to me. I'll never forget your righteousness. There are special rewards for those who perform acts of charity and lovingkindness without ulterior motive or trying to get a reward."

"Are you ready to go?" Govert asked. "We'd like to be back at our current headquarters by the evening."

Jakob took the bag of food and followed them to the door. By now he was more used to going outside, but the sunlight still hurt his eyes. He shielded his eyes as he limped over to the blue Citroën Traction Avant waiting for them. A man he didn't recognize was in the driver's seat.

"This is yours," the chauffeur said, extending a tin box. "All the supplies you'll need to get by as a partisan. A roll of gauze, scissors, rubbing alcohol, a jackknife, shaving razor, shaving brush, iodine, aspirin, soap, a washcloth, a deck of cards, and a cigarette lighter. And here's your canteen. Since it's summer, you won't need to worry about rationing your water. I hope forest living agrees with you. We don't spend too much time in houses or other buildings, to avoid danger."

"Thank you, but I don't smoke. I guess I could use the lighter to start a fire. And I'm a good cook. I'll help with cooking duty as much as possible. After the war is over, I'll make some of my mother's recipes for you guys. Vrouw Visser's holding on to the recipes for safekeeping."

"You're smart," Commander van der Beek said. "You know how to make yourself useful. So far, you don't seem like the type of guy I sometimes remove from the group."

"This is also yours." Dries extended a passport and ID card. "In case anyone questions you, or if you're captured, your name is Maarten Theodor van der Zee, and you were born the eleventh of June, 1924. We figured you could pass for two years older because of how tall you are."

Jakob sat in the backseat, watching the landscape going by as the Citroën drove down dirt roads over the next few hours. He was too excited over the prospect of starting life as a partisan to think about the last two times he'd ridden in a vehicle. Already he was imagining himself as the group's youngest hero, and the pictures he'd draw of his successful missions and raids. In the meantime, he stroked the new pistol in his holster.

Late in the afternoon, they arrived at an encampment in the woods. Jakob got out of the car last, still not entirely sure of himself out in the open. Most Nazis and NSBers thought they all looked alike, but there could always be a few with a voluminous, photographic memory matching his. Then he remembered he was armed, and among a group of men who were also armed and trained to fight. This time he'd be able to raise his pistol and shoot, or pull out his knife. No one would ever get away with measuring his skull, ransacking his home, destroying his possessions, or beating his mother again.

He felt like a minor celebrity as Commander van der Beek led him around the encampment and introduced him to all the other partisans. Most of them were as old as he'd been told, but there were others around his age. They seemed impressed to be told about how he'd jumped off a train and had a scrapbook documenting the occupation.

Most seventeen-year-old partisans couldn't boast either of those things.

"Even though it's summer, we don't want to take any chances," Commander van der Beek said as he showed him the makeshift huts. "There could always be a raid in the night, and we want to be relatively protected. There's enough room in this hut for you. You'll stay with Leendert, Dries, and two of the more senior members."

Jakob looked inside and saw blankets, pillows, candles, clandestine radios, and a few small tables for personal effects. "How do you keep warm in the winter at night? I assume a campfire would alert the enemy."

"We dig bunkers. Maybe you'll be able to predict the weather for us. I've heard stories about people with bone injuries and sensitivities being able to feel bad weather."

"You don't have any foxholes dug now?"

"We don't need them. There's no front here. God willing, the British and Americans will send troops into the continent sooner rather than later, and we can join the fight officially. Till then, you'll have to be satisfied with this."

"Yes, Meneer. I don't mind spending days or weeks sitting around playing cards and spying, so long as I still get to kill Nazis and NSBers. Quality counts more than quantity."

2

A month after Jakob joined the partisans, he was taken on his first real mission. Someone had gotten word that a number of Nazis and NSBers would be attending a party at a hotel near Amsterdam, and Commander van der Beek wanted five of his fighters to ambush them. Jakob was thrilled to be among the group chosen. He, Dries, and Leendert joined two of the older partisans several hours before the party's start time, while five other partisans were posted around the area as snipers. Another group had built a bomb that would be planted in one of the hotel rooms.

Dries looked through his binoculars as they lurked in a small forest a short distance from the main road. "There's the car. A blue Duesenberg. Those *Bokkelulen* wouldn't dream of going around in normal cars. All we have to do is find out if they're already inside or if the driver's on his way to pick them up."

"They can't all fit in that car," Jakob said. "Do you know what other cars they're using?"

"Probably only the most important ones are being chauffeured like damn princes. The more common *kankerhonden* are walking or taking normal taxis."

Jakob called to mind the ugly, evil faces of Ruud's three assassins as they walked towards the road as though nothing were amiss. In spite of the hot weather, they wore long lightweight jackets to cover the weapons in their holsters. If one of Ruud's assassins were among the enemies in the car or at the hotel, all he'd have to do would be to reach under the jacket, aim, and shoot.

The oldest partisan in their group jumped in front of the Duesenberg and waved his hands. When the driver stopped, he pulled open the door and looked inside before the others climbed in.

"Are you on your way to pick up some Nazi and NSB guests for a party tonight?"

"What does that have to do with anything? Unless you intend to take a ride yourself and have money, you can get out. I have clients to pick up."

The other older partisan, who was on the driver's side of the back-seat, pulled his knife out and pressed it against the chauffeur's throat. "Perhaps this will make you talk. What are the names of the people you're picking up?"

Dries, in the passenger seat, held his pistol to the chauffeur's head. "This should make you want to talk even more. You wouldn't want to end up like your traitorous buddies, would you?"

"I'm just a chauffeur! I don't know who my clients are!"

"Now we know you're lying," Dries sneered. "Just a moment ago you said you had clients to pick up. Now you claim you don't know anything about your clients. Which is it?"

"I know I'm picking up clients, but not who they are!"

"Then would you care to drive us to pick these mystery men up? If you're such an innocent chauffeur just picking up ordinary people, you should be able to prove to us your clients are good guys."

"We don't have all day!" Leendert barked. "Either you'll drive us to your clients to prove your supposed innocence, or you'll start talking now!"

"You're a fellow Dutchman," the oldest partisan said. "You should know better than to collaborate with our enemies. You'll be in for a special punishment after the war. Traitors deserve a fate worse than a few years in jail."

"I say we should make him show us his identification," the other older partisan said. "If he won't surrender the card, we'll search him."

The driver pulled his ID card out of his pocket, trembling. Dries grabbed it with his free hand and sneered when he saw it was an NSB card, not a normal ID card.

"I guess someone was lying to us all along. Imagine that. They do say people show their true colors when they're under stress. Now drive us to your clients, and we'll take care of things. Are they waiting in one group, or are you picking them up one by one?"

He gulped. "I was going to pick up four people a few kilometers away. Not together."

"Good boy. Drive us there, and don't you dare make a sound on the way, or your head will be on display in the center of town tonight."

Jakob took all this in delightedly, making mental notes about what to say and how to act. These people made it look so natural. He hoped he'd one day be just as good about interrogating people and prying out answers, and could hold his weapons without shaking.

"Just continue to watch us, and don't do or say anything," Leendert whispered as the NSBer began driving, his palms sweating and his hands crazily shaking. "When we get to the hotel, you'll help us take out the rest of them. Right now, you just need to learn by observation."

True to the chauffeur's word, the car stopped four times, each time a short distance from a house. Jakob peered out of the window at each stop, and was disappointed to see ordinary NSBers, not Ruud's assassins or the vile specimens who'd beaten Luisa. Each time, the oldest partisan got out, asked a few questions, drew his pistol, and shot. Jakob was impressed at how coldly and matter-of-factly he carried out these hits, as though he were counting out change or serving breakfast.

"So I get to kill real Nazis at the hotel?" he whispered.

"If all goes according to plan," Dries said. "There'll be ten more at the hotel. By the time we arrive, our friends will have already planted the bomb in one of the rooms, but there'll be at least four more to take out where they came from."

"Remember, it's not real murder," Leendert said. "Only real murder is forbidden by the Ten Commandments. Killing in time of war or in self-defense is allowed in the Bible. God doesn't want us to be pansies who don't defend ourselves."

Jakob's mind drifted back to Luuk. He wondered if Luuk had changed his tune yet, or if he'd found a way to commit suicide either on the train or soon after their arrival at the new labor camp. Maybe he hadn't survived the winter because he wasn't used to such harsh working and living conditions. Jakob supposed Sander had probably secured a decent position at the new place. But about the others, he wasn't sure. Elma had been speaking so fatalistically that last night, and he'd never pegged any of the Antemas as hearty stock. They were used to sitting around looking attractive at social gatherings and house parties, not working in fields or factories.

Leendert gently tapped him on the shoulder. "Aren't you paying attention, Jaap? We're here."

"Oh." Jakob looked around and saw the car was stopped. "Where did the driver go?"

"Our older friends took him behind a bush to pry out some final answers before killing him. He already told them more information was in the trunk."

Jakob nodded and got out of the car. As he limped across the threshold of the hotel, he was a little scared. He was breaking the law by entering a hotel and walking around without a star on his clothes. And he wasn't supposed to have weapons. If anyone found out his real identity, he might be sent back to Westerbork or dealt an even worse fate. He cast his gaze downward and stayed very close to his friends.

"We should celebrate the end of the war in a hotel like this," Dries said. "Of course, we'll probably have to fumigate it first."

Jakob carefully looked around and took in the crystal chandelier, exotic animal skin rugs, dark wood paneling, and beautiful, thick carpeting. He could only imagine how lavish the banquet room must be, and the ballroom. Even the restrooms must be fit for a king.

"Are we staying overnight?"

"We can't. We have to get in and get out. But before we take out these people, we have to go through their rooms. Just stay in the lobby with us, watching people. We'll get a signal when our targets have all entered. The party's at eight, so we'll have ample time to go through their rooms. At the end of the evening, they'll be dead men."

Jakob was suddenly a little scared at the idea of really killing people. Soldiers and partisans weren't murderers, since they had to kill as part of their duties, but he still felt a numbness and cold horror at knowing he'd take at least one life before the night was over. Killing on a battlefield seemed so less personal. Now he had to look the other person in the eyes and spill his blood, even if he were an evil monster. The words of Debora in religious school came back to him, how her mother had told her everything was perfect in a fantasy, but one often started to change one's mind when the fantasy became a reality. Now the real and the ideal were conflicting at the very moment he'd thought he'd be on top of the world. He hoped he wasn't losing his nerve about taking revenge on Ruud's assassins.

The oldest member of their group tapped him on the hand. "They're all here. We'll continue to look casual while they check in and freshen up. I give them about twenty minutes before they're all in the ballroom. With any luck, at least one of them might retire to his room midway through and never return to the party."

Jakob nodded, doing his best to look confident and normal. He reached for one of the Nazi propaganda rags on the coffeetable by their chairs, and flipped through the pages of racist rot as his mind was far away. Every so often, the older partisans made conversation with other guests, so as not to draw suspicions.

"You're sweating," Leendert whispered. "I was a little nervous my first mission too. The more times I did it, the more natural it got. You're being a good Dutch patriot, and a good human being. The God I believe in doesn't send people to Hell for killing in the defense of their country and helping to rid the world of an evil menace."

"You're taller than some of the *Bokkelulen* we're taking out," Dries added. "You can intimidate them with your size."

Jakob had to smile when he thought about his height. Before he'd left Vrouw Visser's house, he'd measured at five feet eleven inches tall. Dries was right. He'd easily tower over some of these targets. While they'd been stuffing their faces with creampuffs and chocolates, he'd been lifting weights and exercising. Not to mention how much strength he now had in his left leg, and the strength he'd built up in his arms and hands when he'd had to use them in place of crutches. A case of cold feet wouldn't bring him down.

"We're ready," the oldest partisan whispered. "You go with Leendert. I'll lead the way, and you each follow me. Not too closely, so no one suspects anything. The rooms are all on the fifth floor, all in a row. I know how to pick locks, so we won't have to shoot the doors down."

Jakob slowly rose when his turn came. He could feel everyone's eyes on him as he headed for the stairwell, staring at the limper in their midst. His eyes widened when he reached the stairwell, realizing he'd have to ascend it as normally as possible. He didn't trust himself to go up the stairs facing forward yet. His limp was still too heavy, and he wasn't used to bearing so much weight on his right foot.

Leendert noticed his discomfort and linked his arm through Jakob's. "I'll be your crutch on the right side, and you hold onto the banister with your left hand," he whispered. "Just hop up on your good foot. You can do this. After we're through here, you won't have to navigate stairs for a long time, probably."

"All those flights of stairs," he whispered in fright. "Can't we take an elevator?"

"This hotel has none. You'll be fine. The sooner you start, the sooner you'll be on the fifth floor."

Jakob closed his eyes to block out the neverending staircase and held onto Leendert's arm with a death grip. It seemed as though ten thousand years had passed before he heard Leendert announcing they'd reached the fifth floor. By this point, all he wanted to do was to collapse onto a bed and sleep away his exhaustion. Only someone with a limp or leg injury could ever understand how frightening something like that was, what a big accomplishment it was to get through it, how something that generally only took five to ten minutes stretched into at least twenty minutes for him. Even a great military genius like Tamerlane probably hadn't had to deal with gigantic staircases.

Jakob was limping more heavily than usual as he and Leendert entered the room that had been pointed out to them. He sank into the nearest chair while Leendert locked the door and began going through the papers in the briefcases and on the desks.

Leendert put a stack of papers on his lap. "Have a look at these, Jaap. Is there any chance the DeJonghes or Hartogs on this list are your relatives?"

Jakob sat up at attention and began scanning the list of people recently arrested by whomever had this room. His insides twisted with rage when he recognized the names of his grandparents, aunts, uncles, cousins, great-aunts, and great-uncles, who'd lived outside Amsterdam. He hadn't heard from them in a long time, but he'd wanted to believe they were safer than he'd been in the capital. The list had dates from

May through July, so it was entirely possible some of them had already left Westerbork for the East.

Several pages in, as he was still reeling from shock, his eyes fell on two more familiar names. Bram and Floor ter Avest, Kees and Gusta's adult children. He didn't know whether it were a blessing in disguise that they were listed as single. In the grand scheme of things, it didn't much matter if they didn't have to worry about children or spouses. They'd still been arrested for the non-crime of how they'd been born.

"This one's mine," he announced with a steely look in his eyes. "Whoever's staying in this room is living on borrowed time."

"There are two people in this room. One for each of us. Even if you need practice, it's a bit much to assassinate two people your first time."

"Well, whoever wrote this list and made the arrests is mine. We can pry that out of him when he comes back, can't we?"

Jakob froze when he heard footsteps coming down the hall. Then he heard a disgusting deep, hacking cough going along with the footsteps. He pushed his hands over his eyes to try to drive away the flashback to the ransacked apartment and the sight of his brutalized mother, but the images remained in his mind. In his panicked state, he realized he didn't know for sure if the fat Nazi with the hideous cough had been the one who'd beaten Luisa. He hadn't been alone, and Jakob had only come upon the scene after Luisa was beaten.

The doorknob began rattling, and two voices began shouting in German. Leendert pulled out his gun as he got the door. Jakob got up and lunged towards the fat one, squeezing his hands around his neck, pushing him onto a bed, and holding his knife against his throat. With his other hand, he patted him down and felt no weapons.

"Did you or did you not arrest, beat, and humiliate a woman named Luisa Hartog last August? And who's the butcher who arrested all these people, you or your friend?"

"Look at him," Leendert said in disgust. "He's too fat to beat anyone. Probably his lily-livered friend did it. Very fitting that he's covered in liver spots. He's such a villain, his liver and skin changed places."

Jakob looked up and saw Leendert had the other resident backed up into a corner at gunpoint. This was sure enough the liver-spotted Nazi who'd ripped up the picture of Princesses Juliana, Beatrix, and Irene. The richness of the choice overwhelmed him. Should he choose the easier target, the fat cougher, or make a name for himself by choosing the liver-spotted Nazi?

"Hand over your weapons," Leendert barked. "Leave them on the bed."

"We have no weapons on us," the liver-spotted one stammered. "We left them in our room to go to the party. We didn't think we'd need them there."

Leendert smirked. "You people are really a lot stupider than you'd like the world to believe. Where might we find these weapons?"

"In the top drawer of the bureau on each side of the room."

Leendert turned his head and saw Jakob raising his knife above the fat one, a maniacal look in his eyes. "Take it easy, Bokaj. A good soldier never kills in anger. It's something he does like any other job. He doesn't take delight in it. Let me take that one for the team, and you can have this one as your first kill. But before we dispose of them, they need to give us some answers about their activities."

Jakob put his knife away and replaced it with his pistol. "Would either of you care to answer my question? Last August, did you arrest, beat, and humiliate a woman named Luisa Hartog? You were with a tall, thin NSBer who was frisking her, but any of you could've beaten her. Perhaps this might ring a bell." He reached into his jacket pocket and held out a photograph that had been taken of him and Luisa in the spring of 1941. "She was fifty-six years old at the time and lived on Jodenbreestraat with Cornelius ter Avest, Augusta Kikkert, and myself. Did you or did you not lay hands on my mother?"

"How should I remember every criminal I've arrested or beaten? And if you were arrested with them, what are you doing walking around a free man? That makes you a wanted criminal, and my friend and I have every right to report you!"

Leendert turned around and shot the fat Nazi. Jakob stared at the blood gushing out after he slumped to the floor. With any luck, he'd be able to do the exact same thing to the liver-spotted creep, without either losing his nerve or going berserk. He tried to remember the words of the thirty-first chapter of *The Tao Te Ching*, which spoke about how war must be conducted like a funeral and that a man who delights in killing cannot fulfill himself.

"Your turn, Jaap. It doesn't matter whether or not he confesses while he still wastes oxygen, because you know he was involved in some way. We'll take the papers and weapons and get out of here. I'll help you go back downstairs."

Jakob was heartened by Leendert's voice, which always sounded so comforting and soothing even when he was talking about things that were anything but rainbows and kittens. And it was pure luck they'd been assigned to such a stupid pair, people who left their weapons behind for a party and hadn't attempted to scream for security or fight back. This kind of opportunity might not come again soon. Keeping his eyes as wide as he could open them, he aimed for the liver-spotted Nazi and pulled the trigger.

"That's for what you did to my mother, you piece of sewage." He put the smoking pistol back in his holster and limped towards the dying body to kick it in the head and kidneys several times. "I bet you never thought you'd someday meet your death at the hands of one of your intended victims."

"Very good form," Leendert said. "Just the way we like our fighters to take out traitors and enemies. Calm, cold, and collected. Like I told you, you'll do even better next time, and keep improving till it feels like second nature."

Jakob stuffed the papers back into the briefcases while Leendert pocketed the pistols and ammunition in the drawers. He was proud of himself, and regretted he only had one witness. It would've been nice to prove himself in front of his entire partisan group.

"We're leaving by the fire escape," Leendert said. "It'd look too suspicious if we leave the way we came upstairs, carrying things we didn't have when we went up. And you already drew attention to yourself with your limp."

Jakob went onto the balcony and straddled it backwards to get onto the fire escape. He was glad it wasn't a big drop between the balcony and the fire escape, and that this fire escape wasn't connected to each and every balcony. Once he was on it, he had to keep going down instead of straddling each new story or going through a door on the bottom. He eased himself into a sitting position and propelled himself downward with his hands and good foot. By the time they got to the ground, he was exhausted and just wanted to curl up to sleep.

Leendert hailed a cab and gave the driver an address a few kilometers away from their current encampment. Jakob slumped against the seat during the drive and had to be helped out when they arrived.

As soon as he finished limping back to their hut, he threw himself onto his pallet, breathing heavily and sweating even more than usual in the late July heat.

"Good work," Leendert said as Jakob took off his holster and maneuvered out of his day clothes and into pajamas under the covers. "Your mother would be very proud of you. Keep this up, and perhaps one day you'll run into your father's assassins and can do the same to them."

3

Jakob was sent on his next mission in early September. This time he was going to go through an NSBer's house after a bomb detonated. He lurked in the bushes with Dries, Govert, and two other partisans in the growing twilight, waiting for the bomb to go off. The bomb had been assembled and planted in large part by Jeronymus, whom Jakob had discovered was well-respected and sought-after for his skill in bomb-making and -planting. Commander van der Beek liked to joke it was his greatest skill only after seducing women. In the few months he'd been a partisan, Jakob had seen at least ten different women going into the hut Jeronymus shared with Govert, and heard the accompanying noises. He wasn't surprised to find out Jeronymus was such a ladies' man, given how he looked like a Renaissance painting model. No part of him was jealous, though. He had no desire to collect a string of lovers when he could be concentrating on becoming a good scout and assassin.

He heard screams simultaneously to seeing the targeted house shake before exploding in a grand show. He smiled and rubbed his hands together in glee as people ran through the street in confusion and fear. It was a good thing Jeronymus had made this an ordinary shrapnel and cast iron weight bomb, instead of an incendiary bomb. All they'd have to do would be to wait till the chaos died down and then enter the house, instead of waiting for a fire to be put out.

At a signal from the oldest partisan, he limped away from their hiding place and across the road, keeping a firm hold on his lantern. The first thing he noticed when he got to the remains of the house was how beautiful the tiny shards of glass looked as they glittered in the twilight. After he got back to camp, he'd start a painting inspired by that.

"If anybody's alive, surrender yourselves now or await the fate all traitors deserve!" the leader shouted as he stormed through the hole that now stood in place of a door.

The only response was moaning. The leader went to the top floor and sent the other older partisan to the second floor with Govert, while Dries and Jakob were assigned to the first floor. Jakob was thankful he didn't have to navigate any stairs, which he was surprised had survived the explosion.

"Look at all these ration coupons!" Dries opened his knapsack and swept in the vast supply. "We'll eat like kings for a long time!"

Jakob helped himself to the chocolates in a candy bowl decorated with swastikas before pocketing the rest of the chocolates and smashing the bowl. Then he moved into the main room and began going through the papers that littered the floor like snow. He could hear shots from the upper floors.

"May I have a suicide pill or my pistol?"

Jakob saw a tall, thin man with a maimed stomach, stuck against the wall and with a desk crushing his legs. He swung his lantern towards the NSBer's face and instantly recognized the cretin who'd frisked Luisa.

"You're not going to get the honor of ending your own life, you traitor. Not after how you abused my mother and betrayed our country. I hope you know I killed your liver-spotted friend, and one of my friends killed your fat friend with the disgusting cough. Now it's your turn to face punishment for your crimes." He pulled out his pistol, which he'd become accustomed to wearing on his left side, per Commander van der Beek's wishes. "Any final words before I send you to Hell?"

"I help with the arrests of enemies of the people. I've done nothing wrong." He put his hands over his disfigured stomach.

Jakob shot him in the chest, and was pleased at the blood spurting out in two different places. Trying to ignore the fresh corpse in front of him, he went through the desk for any papers or weapons.

"Look at what I found!" Dries shouted. "Just what our company could use!"

Jakob looked over and saw a squirming orange and white Kooikerhondje puppy in Dries's arms. For years, he'd begged his parents to let him have a dog or cat, but they always insisted he was too young to properly care for a pet. He'd had to make do with befriending wild animals, but he'd never stopped longing for the day when he'd be a grownup and able to have a pet.

"It's not the most ideal breed for a war dog or guard dog, but it's not like he's a tiny Pomeranian. Maybe by the time our troops come home, they'll have a Dutch Shepherd for us. In the meantime, this little guy can keep us company. When he gets big enough, maybe he can go on missions and raids with us. A duck-hunting dog is a better war dog than a pampered lapdog."

Jakob took the puppy and cuddled it against his chest. "Hey, buddy. We've just rescued you from a very evil person who might've turned you into a very evil dog. You're going to live in the woods with us, help us hunt for small game, help us with fishing, and guard us against enemies." He looked on the collar for the tags. "We'll change your name to something much nicer. Your name isn't Adolf anymore, it's Bernhard, after our exiled Princess Juliana's prince, the leader of the Dutch Free Forces. We'll call you Ben for short."

"I think he likes you," Dries smiled as the dog licked Jakob's face. "I'm not much into superstition, but I think it's probably true animals have a sixth sense and know when they're around someone who loves animals."

"Of course he likes me. Animals always loved me. I got rabbits, birds, chipmunks, and mice to sit on my hand or lap so I could feed and pet them." Jakob slid off his schoolbag with his free hand and slipped his new friend inside. "You stay in there, buddy, so we don't lose you. You'll love your new home. The best part will be that it's outside. Lots of room for you to play." He moved back toward the dead NSBer and kicked him in the head, admiring his handiwork. "Looks like I stole not only your undeserved life, but your little dog too. Now who wants to claim we don't fight back?"

4

Jakob's third mission was the second weekend in October, scouting the area near their fall encampment and if need be serving as a sniper. Govert trailed behind him, and one of the older partisans went in front. After this, Commander van der Beek had promised he'd be allowed to go on missions all by himself when the opportunity arose. Jakob was beside himself with pride when he thought of how far he'd come already, how he'd proven himself as a good partisan and calculating assassin. He could bear waiting for the Dutch Free Forces to come home if it meant he'd continue to enjoy this respect and recognition among both peers and elders.

Little Ben, the puppy, tried to keep pace with him. Ever since the puppy came back with them last month, he'd been extremely attached to Jakob, and appointed himself his personal guard dog. Several of the partisans suggested he'd noticed Jakob's limp, and was trying to protect him. Luisa had told him animals could feel a person's pain and often stayed with an injured person for comfort.

As he limped his way along the route on his map, he stopped in his tracks. There, by the banks of a creek, he heard a woman's voice speaking some very familiar words, and in the vernacular, not the original Hebrew.

"'….who shall live and who shall die, who in the fullness of years and who before, who shall perish by water and who by fire, who by sword and who by beast, who by famine and who by thirst, who by earthquake and who by plague, who by strangulation and who by stoning, who shall have rest and who shall wander, who shall be at peace and who shall be pursued, who shall be at rest and who shall be tormented, who shall be exalted and who shall be brought low, who shall become rich and who shall be impoverished.'"

"Someone's watching us," he heard another woman whisper.

"Oh, nonsense, Juli. You act paranoid every Yom Kippur. Let me enjoy leading what I can remember of the service."

As he came closer, Ben ran ahead of him and began barking. Jakob saw a young woman with very dark hair running away, frantically tying up her hair under a dark pink scarf as she ran. Five other people, three men and two women, were hot on her heels. A young woman with long curly blonde hair, glistening like cornsilk in the autumn sunshine, translucent blue orbs dangling from her ears, and very dark green eyes turned around to face him. He disinterestedly took note of how beautiful she was. A part of him wondered if she would've gone off with him had he been like Jeronymus. Then he remembered he had to have a one-track mind and that even using a woman as a plaything for one night would be an inexcusable breach of the thick, high iron wall he'd put up around his heart.

"Would you care to explain what this is all about?" he asked, trying to sound gruff. "It seems at least seven people are hiding in these parts."

"My friends are scared of dogs. I can't wait to tell my friend Juli she was scared by a little puppy. That girl is so shy and timid, she's practically scared of her own shadow."

"You expect me to believe this story? Six out of seven people are so scared of dogs they run away, and one of them covers her hair as she's running? I noticed you're the only one with blonde hair. That must be why you stayed. You assumed you'd be safe and could pass for an Aryan. And I know what you were saying. It's called U'Netaneh Tokef, though I'd never heard a woman reciting it before."

She knelt down and picked Ben up, scratching him behind the ears. "That's a detail a supposed Aryan Dutchman wouldn't know. Your secret is safe with me. I don't venture out very often anyway. You're probably freer than I am. Sometimes Juli and I gather mushrooms or bathe in the river, but we're mostly stuck inside. Our other friends never go out, except sometimes our friend Solomon, who's old enough to be our father. He's arranging things with someone on the outside for us to go to Liechtenstein next month."

"You assume I'm of the same persuasion as you. Never assume anything, Juffrouw. Under the occupation, you never know who's a real friend and who's an enemy about to stab you in the back."

She laughed as she set Ben down. "You talk a very good game, but I don't believe your bluff. Would you like me to pull down your pants so we can both see who's telling the truth?"

He stood in silent horror as she skipped off laughing, her long blonde curls dancing in the breeze. Whoever this girl was, she had no sense of social etiquette, manners, or decency. He was humiliated to be beaten at his own attempted game by a girl, as much as he'd always believed men and women to be equal. So much for having a successful third mission.

5

Tuesday, 30 November, was the year-anniversary of Jakob's escape. He felt the cold in every bone in his right foot, even a little up into his lower leg. He sat by the campfire that night with Ben huddled up against his foot, as he and his friends played Mahjong with an old set Dries had. As he thought about how it had now been a year since he'd last seen his mother, Gusta, and his old friends, he found himself also thinking about the people he'd caught by the riverbank. He wondered how long they'd been hiding there and how they'd managed to get away for so long. True to the blonde's word, he'd glimpsed her and the dark-haired girl gathering mushrooms a few times before it started getting cold. One time he'd spied on her bathing in the river, and thought she was even more beautiful without any clothes on. He'd never seen a naked woman before, and hadn't been disappointed at his first sight of one.

"Have a look at this." Govert came up panting, back from the mission he'd been on for the last week. "Do you happen to know the names of any of those people you found hiding nearby?"

"The pretty blonde never told me her name. The only names she provided were Juli, her scaredy-cat dark-haired friend, and an older man named Solomon. Why, did you find out something about them?"

"Five people were recently arrested and sent to Westerbork, according to this diary I absconded with from one of my targets. Since so many people have been captured in hiding, and this happened in the vicinity, I tend to believe he's bragging about arresting those people you stumbled upon."

Jakob took the diary and opened it to the bookmarked page. He saw the names Julia van Acker, Zipporah Schrijver, Margaretha Nissenbaum, Daniël Zuckerman, and Rachel Roggenfelder. Solomon and the other young man must've escaped.

"You look like someone just stepped on your heart," Leendert gently teased. "More than from being upset as a human being over what happened. Did you have a crush on the blonde or what?"

"No I didn't! I don't need any stupid girlfriend or even a one-time lover! Only fools waste their time with women when they're supposed to be working or fighting. I'll have to take a woman someday, so I can have kids, but I won't be some pansy groveling at a woman's feet and writing her sappy love letters."

Jeronymus laughed. "Methinks the gentleman protests too much. We won't think you're less of a man if you admit you liked the girl. I'd actually think less of you if you'd never liked a girl by your age. Did you ever have a sweetheart or do anything with a girl?"

Jakob slammed the diary and threw it on the ground. "I never wanted a girlfriend because I had more important priorities. The night before I escaped, a girl I was friends with ambushed me when I went outside to be alone. She gave me this ridiculous sappy speech about how we might all be going to our deaths tomorrow, and she didn't want to die without ever doing anything with a boy. She wanted to be comforted by that memory in her final moments. Then she forced a kiss on me, and somehow convinced me to kiss her back. I was stupid to do that. If she came to me now and tried that stupid song and dance, I'd tell her where to get off."

"That's all you've done with a girl?" Govert asked. "You're seventeen and a half. You don't know what you're missing."

"I did spy on the mystery blonde bathing one morning. So I do know what a woman looks like naked in person. I must admit, she was gorgeous. I mean, in the way I'd find any beautiful woman gorgeous. She's not special just because she's the first girl I saw naked."

"Which one do you think your object of admiration was? We already know it's not Julia. Rachel, Margaretha, or Zipporah?"

"I don't care! I'll probably never see her again anyway. She was a beautiful girl, but I don't have time to waste with that junk." Jakob clenched a Mahjong piece in each hand. "If I do decide I want a lover, I'll let you all know."

"Excellent," Jeronymus beamed. "I'll gladly teach you all my secrets of how to please a woman. Just don't make the mistake of bedding experienced women the first few times. Some of them are nice about it, but others laugh guys out of bed once they realize they're being had by a newcomer. Oh, and just a quick note for future reference, most women don't reach ecstasy the same way we do, if you know what I mean. You have to use other parts of your body. What most guys consider an appetizer is the main course to most women. Trust me, they'll love you for knowing this and not just focusing on your own selfish pleasure."

"Are you done embarrassing me yet? It's embarrassing enough I overhear you doing that with women all the time."

"It's not meant to be embarrassing. I'm trying to educate you. God knows you'll need it when you decide to become a man in the other way. You should be thankful someone more experienced than you wants to impart all his worldly wisdom for free, out of the goodness of his own heart. Every guy deserves a mentor."

Jakob rolled his eyes. "I'm going to bed. My ankle hurts from the cold air, and I'm feeling overwhelmed because it's the year-anniversary of my injury."

"Goodnight, Jaap," Leendert smirked. "Don't neglect to let us know if you have any dreams about the mystery girl. You have fertile ground for dreams, since you've seen her naked as well as clothed."

Jakob limped to his hut with Ben, glad to be alone, and pulled out his sketchbook and art supplies. By the light of his lantern, he began drawing a picture of the beautiful blonde girl. He told himself it was just to capture her likeness for memory's sake. To reassure himself he really was only drawing her for that reason, he also drew a picture of Juli. After he was satisfied with his artwork, he put away his sketchbook and curled up to sleep with Ben by his gimpy foot. As far as he was concerned, part of the danger he'd traded in his shelter for didn't include becoming emotionally attached to women. He had a war to help win, and the only woman allowed in his heart was Luisa, whom he prayed he'd be reunited with soon. Time would tell what time would tell.

Chapter 16: Showtime

By June of 1944, Jakob had gone on missions all over the country and in time had been allowed to begin training new recruits himself. He no longer really cared he had to walk by hopping and shuffling, and the limp had become less painfully obvious and pronounced. Besides, he was too busy fighting to liberate The Netherlands, in his small way, to care about minor things like that. He now limped with more pride, remembering his namesake had earned his own limp as a reward of sorts for prevailing in his struggles with both God and men.

For Jakob's eighteenth birthday last month, he'd been taken back to Vrouw Visser's house in Winschoten. He was relieved all his things were exactly where he'd left them in the basement. Commander van der Beek thought he deserved a furlough of sorts, and had given him permission to rest from his birthday till the middle of June. This time, hiding in the basement wasn't so bad, knowing he had a job to get back to and had already done a lot in the service of the Resistance. And he had Ben to keep him company. Right now, he was working on catching up his scrapbook when Dries came into the basement, looking very excited and about ready to pop. Vrouw Visser was right behind him, also looking very excited.

"It's finally happened!" Dries enthused. "The Americans are here! The war might be over by the end of the year!"

"Here? In The Netherlands? Did they just land?"

"No, but they are on the continent. A huge group of the Allies just launched a surprise invasion in Normandy, and they're going to fight their way through France on their way to us. We're going to be saved!"

"Not a moment too soon," Vrouw Visser said. "I wish they'd opened three fronts instead of concentrating on the Pacific and North Africa, but it is what it is." She sat on the bed and reached for the sketchbook, now almost full. "Do you mind if I look at what you've done since you've been away? None of the people I've hidden between then and now were artistic or as intellectual and literary as you. They were good people, but not big on literature, philosophy, and art. I had no one to have intellectual conversations with."

"I'm glad you think so highly of me. Some of my old classmates derided me for studying so much and memorizing stuff they thought was boring."

"Those words are always spoken by people who won't amount to much in life. While they're making fun of scholarship, you'll be using your brain to get ahead." She flipped through all the pages and took in Jakob's renditions of the various encampments he'd stayed at, the men in his group, the missions and raids he'd gone on, forest animals, little Ben, firearms, and a girl with brilliant green eyes and long blonde curls. "Jaap, did you get yourself a sweetheart and not tell me? I've seen at least five pictures of the same girl so far!"

Dries looked over her shoulder. "Oh, Jaap can tell you all about her. He even spied on her naked one morning. We don't know her name, but we know she and four of her friends were arrested in November and sent to Westerbork. If Jaap is this obsessed with his secret crush long after their few brief encounters, I'm surprised he hasn't snuck off to glimpse her through the barbed wire, or to try to liberate the camp single-handedly. For all you know, your lady friend could still be there."

Jakob twisted uncomfortably. "I barely knew her. I talked to her once, and that was it. She was too forward and unladylike. The other times I saw her, we never exchanged words. She didn't know I was looking most of those times. All she is is an interesting subject for drawing, since she's so beautiful."

Dries laughed. "You can't call her out for being forward and unladylike when you were the one who was so ungentlemanly he spied on her naked. You might not've expected to see her bathing, but you didn't look away or turn around once you got an eyeful!"

Vrouw Visser smiled knowingly. "It's okay to admit you liked a girl, Jaap. I'd be shocked if a fellow your age had no impure thoughts and never had any romantic feelings for a girl. How romantic and mysterious, not knowing her name."

"We know three names she could have. Govert found her arrester's diary, and in it were the names of five of the people in her group of seven. She already told Jaap one of her friends, whom he's also drawn, is named Julia. The other three female names listed were Zipporah, Rachel, and Margaretha. Women are supposed to have a sixth sense about these types of things. Based on her appearance, what do you think her name could be?"

Vrouw Visser studied the pictures. "Zipporah seems like a name for a girl with dark hair, and Margaretha seems like an awfully heavy name for someone who looks like this, even if she probably goes by Greet or Marga. It would be very fitting if this girl's name actually were Rachel. It matches your name."

Jakob rolled his eyes. "Can we please get back to discussing the news you came down here with? I don't care to think about a girl I barely knew. She's been gone for seven months, and I'll probably never see her again. How many times do I have to say I don't want a stupid girlfriend or even a one-time lover?"

"Of course," Dries said. "On the sixth of June, a huge mass of Americans, British, and Canadians landed on the beaches of Normandy by parachutes and boats. The Germans didn't expect them to land that soon. I think all the branches of their militaries are in on this. If they fight their way across France according to plan, some of them might be here by the autumn...."

As Dries talked, Jakob found his mind drifting back to the blonde with beautiful dark green eyes. In addition to drawing her a number of times, he'd also had more than a few dreams about her over the last seven months. It was the oddest thing. He'd never before been so strangely attached to someone he'd only had a few brief encounters with. But now he had more important things to think about, not an overly brash, beautiful girl. The liberation of Europe was finally at hand, and he ought to turn his mind to counting the days till the Allies reached The Netherlands.

2

The news that continued trickling in via the underground newspapers and radio broadcasts painted a rosy picture of hope, in spite of the fact that there was still tough work ahead to win the war. In August, the Dutch Free Forces landed in Normandy and served with the Canadian 1st Army, then moved forward with the British 2nd Army. On 20 September, after the crushing Allied defeat in Operation Market Garden, they crossed into The Netherlands and began fighting the SS Grenadier Brigade Landstrom Nederland. Knowing their army was finally home was a huge morale-booster to Jakob and his friends. All they had to do now was wait for Commander van der Beek to make the first move towards contacting them and presenting themselves for service. Jakob was secretly relieved he was still a partisan and not fighting an SS unit, though he was also extremely impatient at not being allowed to do real fighting even after their troops were on their native soil.

"You ought to cherish this time," Leendert said, trying to cheer him up. "After we join the Army, you'll never be as relatively free as you are now. Once we're wearing uniforms and obliged to answer to a real commander with military training, you won't have much time to draw, paint, read, or think about women. You'd probably get in trouble for doing your own assassinations and scouting missions. Some of us might not make it once we're on a real battlefield. At most, we've had to worry about Nazis and NSBers catching us. Once we're real soldiers, we'll have to worry about a bullet on the battlefield catching us."

"But we'll eat like kings. No one can even get butter anymore. I'm worried about our food supplies running out during the winter. In the real Army, food is guaranteed."

"It's just a temporary, unfortunate side effect of the Allied defeat," Dries said. "I'm sure we'll have food lines opened again as soon as possible. The Allies were a bit too eager to push forward, and didn't think their strategy out enough in advance. But rest assured, by this time next year, our homeland will be liberated, and we'll be heroes for helping to save the Dutch people."

"Why don't you go on a scouting mission around the neighborhood?" Govert suggested. "Commander van der Beek wants someone to scout around to see what our new environs are like. Since we're moving closer to the action, it's important to know what's going on, if we're in a town of enemies or people rolling out the carpets for the Allies."

Jakob stood up, remembering to step onto his left foot first. "Sure I'll do it. Just show me where to go and what to do."

"It's only a scouting mission," Jeronymus said. "I know how much you like assassinations, but it's not what you're supposed to be doing. Don't go falling for any mysterious women either. Just do what you're supposed to do and report back to us."

After receiving details and an okay from Commander van der Beek, Jakob set off to scout the neighborhood, Ben running at his heels. The dog was probably a bit over a year old by now and no longer a little puppy, but he wasn't a gigantic breed. His size was a good compromise between a huge guard dog and a tiny lapdog. He could intimidate enemies at his full size, but he was small enough to sit on Jakob's lap.

Twelve blocks into the neighborhood, in a quiet alley, he saw three men coming out of a bookstore and laughing. Jakob felt everything spinning around him the instant he recognized the evil faces of the men who'd forced his father to commit suicide. They were just as he'd written in his pretend Book of Life the day after Ruud's murder four years ago:

Murderer with cigarette, average height, light brown hair, pale blue eyes, eyebrows too thick and close together, moustache, thick mouth, nose oddly shaped on the right side.

Second murderer, a little short for a man, blonde hair, dark green eyes, big Adam's apple, scar on the forehead, thin mouth, bullfrog voice.

Third murderer, average height, brown hair, hazel eyes, short beard, very feminine eyelashes, reddish skin, high-pitched voice, slightly chubby, face full of ugly measles or chickenpox scars.

He was supposed to be on a scouting mission only, but if he didn't take this excellent opportunity for revenge right here and now, it might never come again, and these sick excuses for life would get to go on living, never brought to justice because they weren't as important as thugs like Eichmann or Goebbels. Trying to control himself, he limped up to them and planted himself squarely in their path. He looked them in the eyes with a hateful, steely look consuming his large sable eyes.

"Hello, murderers. Do you remember coercing Rudolf DeJonghe into suicide four years ago almost to this very day? He was begging and pleading with you to stop, but you threatened him with an even worse fate if he didn't point that gun at his head and pull the trigger. He was only fifty-five. He still had many years ahead of him, while sick thugs like you got to go on living your happy undeserved lives. But rest assured, you won't live to see a single day more."

The ringleader stood staring at him stupidly, while the other two looked at one another and back at Jakob, not quite sure what to make of this speech.

"What are you talking about?" the ringleader finally asked, taking out his cigarette. "We can't remember the names of every undesirable we've disposed of. If you're one of those undesirables who's gone on the lam, you can bet your worthless life you'll soon have the same fate as that man you think we killed."

"I can barely understand a word he's saying!" the pockmarked one said in his high-pitched voice.

Jakob sneered. "Please don't look at me like that. You stupid bastards might not have bothered to take the time to learn Dutch, even though it's the language of the country you're illegally occupying, but you know as well as I do that German and Dutch are mutually intelligible. Don't pretend you can't understand what I'm saying, monsters. There are about to be three less Nazis in the world, and I couldn't be more glad about it." His heart seething with hatred, Jakob raised the pistol concealed in the left-hand pocket of his long coat.

"Help! Police!" the pock-marked one screamed.

Jakob shot him first, and smiled at the sight of the body falling to the ground as blood spurted out. "Do you two have any questions? Care to beg and plead for your lives just as you made my father beg and plead?"

"I have a wife and five children back in Germany!" the bullfrog-voiced murderer croaked. "No child should grow up without a father! And I'm only forty!"

"That's too bad. My father had two children and a wife, and waited a long time to have me and my sister, who went missing that day because of the murder. Look how short you are. I'm now taller than you are, you murderer." Jakob, who now stood at six feet one inch, estimated the froggy-voiced murderer was at least six inches shorter than he was. "Doesn't your kind believe in killing people with undesirable characteristics?" He pulled the trigger and once again relished the sight of the murderer falling to the ground and dying before his eyes. He also took great pride in how he'd begged and pleaded just as Ruud had.

The ringleader had a dazed look in his eyes as he looked around stupidly. Jakob shoved him onto the ground, pulled the cigarette out of his mouth, and extinguished it in his right eye, smiling at his yelps of pain. While he was still in that state of disorientation, Jakob shot the final murderer. He brutally kicked the limp bodies with his left foot before quickly hopping away. Finally. Justice, a dish best served cold. Three less Nazis in the world.

As he limped away as quickly as possible, the voice of the mysterious blonde came back to him, reciting the words of U'Netaneh Tokef from memory in Dutch. He didn't know whether it were because of his continuing strange attraction to her, or because he'd just personally fulfilled the responsibility of choosing "Who shall live and who shall die." Trying to push her out of his mind, he imagined himself writing an updated U'Netaneh Tokef, including lines such as, "Who by resistance fighter and who by avenging son."

Chapter 17: *Hongerwinter*

Jakob's sense of triumph at avenging his father's murder was short-lived. Not long afterwards, the winter began much earlier than usual, and with much colder than usual temperatures. He'd always enjoyed serving as the partisans' cook, but now he dreaded having to make suitable food with the scant rations and foraged food available, and dredging out much smaller than usual portions to his friends. Right now, he was stirring a pot of the most repulsive dish he'd ever tasted or cooked, tulip bulb purée. He could hardly believe the Dutch people were starving so badly they'd resorted to eating their beloved tulip bulbs. Not only that, but they were freezing as well, since the Nazis had cut off fuel shipments along with food, to punish the Dutch people for staging a railway strike to try to help the Allies' efforts. But as far as Jakob was concerned, they were heroes for standing up to these evil occupiers.

The Dutch Free Forces were spending the winter on the islands of Walcheren and North Beveland. Even if they were soldiers, they were probably just as starving and freezing as everyone else. Commander van der Beek had planned to join up with them and present their group for service, but now he figured they didn't need any further strains on their resources. For now, they'd have to starve and freeze separately.

"What was your favorite dish in the old days?" Govert asked, rubbing his hands together in front of a campfire fueled by wood taken from an abandoned house. "My favorites were my grandmother's stuffed mushrooms, cherry pudding, creamed beef, and carrot and tomato salad. Those were the days."

"I was always partial to my aunt's stewed apples stuffed with candied raisins, beef roast, raspberry jam on fresh homemade bread with rosemary, and as much soft goat cheese as my stomach could hold." Dries rubbed his stomach in remembrance.

"How about our wonderful cook?" Leendert called. "What was your favorite, Jaap? There are a lot of pages in that recipe collection your mother gave you."

"Anything but sugar beet pancakes and mashed tulip bulbs." Jakob gave the next man in line a sickeningly small dollop of the repulsive-looking purée.

"Oh, come on, you can do better than that," Jeronymus said. "You like cooking more than some women. Don't be a spoil-sport and think you don't have to play along."

"Remembering our favorite dishes won't do anything to help allay our hunger now! It'll only make you even more upset and hungry, knowing you can't have them!"

"Oh, come on. When you're thinking about food in such detail, you won't have any room to focus on your hunger. Let's hear what Chef DeJonghe misses most from his mother's kitchen."

"Everything." He ladled out another tiny portion for the next customer.

"Do you suppose your Rachel, Zipporah, or Margaretha will cook your mother's recipes as well as she did?" Leendert smirked. "They do say the way to a man's heart is through his stomach. Perhaps she's run into your mother by now. Do you think you'll find her again after the war?"

Jakob fumed as he served the last man in line. "Does everyone have to keep razzing me about that stupid girl with no manners? Even if, for the sake of argument, I did have a crush on her, she's long gone. Plenty of you have had women you've never seen again, and you're not being teased about it long after the fact."

"That's because the rest of us don't paint pictures of those women or dream about them. You've got to get a woman soon, Jaap. Any woman will do. She'll help keep you warm on these freezing winter nights, and distract you from being hungry. Unless, of course, you're being old-fashioned by saving yourself for this mystery girl?"

"It's nobody's business but my own what I plan to do in my private life."

"Didn't you feel tempted to touch her when you spied on her naked?" Govert asked. "I haven't had nearly as many lovers as Jeronymus, but I can tell you a woman's body is a work of art. If you thought she was gorgeous when you only looked at her, imagine how much more heavenly it feels to actually touch her flesh."

"Once you get a woman in bed, you'll wonder why you ever hesitated so long," Jeronymus said. "Remember, I'd love to teach you all the ropes anytime you want. Just give me the word, and I'll tell you everything you need to know to send a woman into the best rapture of her life."

Jakob put the remaining tulip bulb purée into his own bowl and limped towards the campfire his friends were warming themselves by. "All I care about is staying as full as can be. And I'm not going to sleep with any old girl just to get it over with."

Jeronymus sighed. "Well, if you're not going to admit you liked that girl, you can at least share with us your favorite dishes. What did the talented young assassin enjoy eating before the occupation?"

He eased himself down onto the upturned log and shoved a spoonful of the hideous concoction into his mouth. "If you really want to know, I loved my mother's apple cake, chicken soup, chocolate strawberry pie, Sabbath stew, which we call cholent, salads of all kinds, jams, poached eggs, and most of all the chocolate birthday cake with strawberry filling she always made for me."

Dries finished his purée and set his bowl on the ground. "Sounds to me like your future wife will have a lot of work to do to prove herself a cook worthy of your approval."

"So tonight when we're freezing all our extremities off in our bunkers, will you keep yourself warm by imagining your mother's cooking or your mystery girl?" Leendert asked.

"Neither. I'll keep myself warm with the help of my furry little buddy." Jakob pulled Ben onto his lap. "Isn't that right, Bentje? Just us guys, without any women to bother us."

"You're lucky your mystery girl liked him too," Govert said. "Some dogs won't let their owners take a spouse or lover."

"Is that really all you want to talk to me about, something that happened a year ago? I thought I was joining a resistance group of real men, not guys who gossip as much as women."

"We just like your predictable reactions. I guarantee when you finally admit you've fallen for someone, anyone, it'll hit you harder than a ton of bricks, and you won't be able to believe you avoided love and women for so long."

2

With the remaining fuel in the company's Citroën Traction Avant, Jakob went to visit Vrouw Visser on the final weekend of the year, which coincided with New Year's Eve. While Govert and several other partisans scouted the area and collected firewood and food, Jakob enjoyed his mini-furlough.

"It's just like old days." Vrouw Visser tried to smile as they ate sugar beet pancakes and watery cabbage soup in the basement. "Even when I was a child, it was common to have a wood-burning stove and not derive heat from gas. I'd prefer coal, but we can't be picky when we only have one type of fuel."

"Bentje doesn't seem to mind much." Jakob scratched Ben behind the ears. "He's such a trooper. All he cares about is getting enough to eat, staying warm, and being played with. He was adopted by us so young, he probably doesn't know to miss the better material life he had when that foul NSBer owned him and his name was Adolf."

"You'll both have that kind of life again within the new year. I'm positive. The Nazis' end must be near, in spite of this final retribution they've unleashed. Things always get worse before they can get better."

Jakob looked around the basement bedroom that now seemed like a home away from home. "I'm glad you never burnt any of my books or papers to stay warm. I'd understand if you had, but I'm glad you saved them."

"I could never burn the written word. I was brought up just like you, to respect and revere the written word. Even burning books for warmth instead of censorship is a horrific sacrilege. So much love, time, and thought went into writing them, and you put the same effort into your drawings and scrapbook."

"Right now I'm too cold and hungry to want to draw anything. It's just as well, since I ran out of pages in my sketchbook. That was the best sketchbook I ever had. It lasted about two and a half years." He pulled some bills out of his pocket. "I'd like to pay you for how you hid me on so many occasions, and how you hid so many other people. I always wanted to repay you in some way, but I thought it could wait till after the war. Now that we're all starving and freezing, you need this money."

She tried to push his hand away. "I can't take money away from you. You're the one freezing in a bunker in the woods while I live in a real house."

"The resistance never lacks for money. You're in the underground too, so you know about all the bank and tax scams Walraven van Hall orchestrates to keep our coffers full. I almost wish I were a banker."

"I have enough money. I have my own ways of securing money for my activities and enough left over for personal things. I used some of that money to buy you a New Year's present. Would you prefer I give it to you on Sunday night or Monday?"

"You've been too good to me when you didn't have any obligation to help me." Jakob stuffed the bills back into his pocket and began stabbing at the sugar beet pancakes with his knife. "It's been a bit over two years since I last saw my mother. I'm sure she'll want to pay you back when she comes home. You've been a really good stand-in for my mother. She'll think you did a really good job."

"I've treated you the way I've treated all the people I've hidden. A lot of the people in this town are traitors, but I'm lucky to be in a decent neighborhood. I'm not one of those people who's cut apart former Jewish houses or stolen their furniture for firewood. Those thieves surely have a punishment in their future."

"I wonder if my old house, or Kees and Gusta's apartment, was torn apart for firewood. I doubt anyone still lives in my old neighborhood, at least not the original residents. There'll probably be strangers living in our house after the war. I wish there were more people like you, not afraid to do the right thing."

"There are many people doing the right thing, but when one's country is under occupation by such an evil, dangerous menace, it's hard to take a stand. In times like these, it's easier to blend into the woodwork instead of taking a public stand and risking one's life."

He swallowed the last of the almost inedible sugar beet pancakes. "It looks like the war will be over in the new year. It's hard to believe it's been going on for so many years now."

"Everything has to come to an end, even if it takes a long time. Even our planet will come to an end someday, unless our descendants figure out a way to stop it. Only God has no end. But rebirth and change for the better can also go along with endings. An ending doesn't always have to be bad."

Jakob nodded, a wistful look in his eyes. "My mother told me something like that shortly after my father's murder. She reminded me our autumn holiday of Simchat Torah is a simultaneous ending and beginning, and we're celebrating both. We even celebrate what's really a sad ending, the death of Moses, because his death was merely the beginning of something new, different, and greater."

3

1945 dawned with a beautiful full Moon in the starry sky. Jakob intensely felt the freezing air in every bone, muscle, sinew, vein, and skin cell of his foot and lower leg. At only eighteen, he was just like an arthritic old man who could predict and feel the weather in his bones.

"I remember the first time you came in this door," Vrouw Visser said as they stood by the back door, watching a small display of fireworks. "I can't believe how tall you've gotten. It's like you've done a lifetime of growing up in the two years I've known you."

"I've only grown a bit over ten centimeters. It's not like you've seen me growing from a little boy to a man. My mother will be the one who'll be really surprised to see how tall I've gotten. She hasn't seen me in so long, she probably forgets how tall I was last time we were together."

Vrouw Visser sighed, and her breath formed a dark, thick white mist in the frozen air. "Do you really believe she's still alive? If we're suffering so much in relative freedom, I can only imagine how much people are suffering in German or Polish labor camps. They might not even have the kind of meager rations we do."

"Of course my mother's still alive. How could she not be? We shouldn't be fatalistic just because the end is so near. My mother will return to Amsterdam on a train with Gusta and my old school friends. Well, except that little milksop Luuk Klein, not that he was ever a friend of mine. I'd bet money on him offing himself either on his way to the labor camp or shortly after he got there. He thought I was an idiot for wanting to emulate the Maccabees instead of those suicidal cowards the Zealots."

"I can't argue with you there. People's true colors always come out in situations like this. You did the right thing by taking action against our occupiers instead of rolling over and refusing to fight back. I've never thought you were a murderer because you've killed so many people. Nazis and NSBers aren't real people. They're evil spirits masquerading as humans. They don't have real souls."

"I wouldn't have killed them if I felt I were committing real murder. I'm sure my mother will understand that." He shifted his weight onto his left foot. "Can we go inside? I can't take the cold anymore."

"Of course. You can warm yourself by my stove till it's time for bed."

He limped back inside and stretched out by the stove. The few minutes it took for Vrouw Visser to start a fire with the salvaged scraps of wood seemed to stretch on forever. He pulled his dark blue coat tighter around himself, trying to drive out as much cold as possible. The black market champagne Vrouw Visser offered him didn't do much to warm him from the inside. He found himself longing for the weeks right after his injury, when he had an unlimited supply of alcohol to pour down his throat.

"Sleep will come soon enough," Vrouw Visser said as he headed for the basement. "I'll be right along to tuck you in. At least you won't feel the cold when you're deep in sleep."

Jakob knew she was giving him the thickest, toastiest blankets, but said nothing. She'd insist it was her duty, but he felt awful for being much warmer than she was. Before sleep overtook him, he nibbled on some of the precious chocolates she'd left on the nightstand. As he slept, he dreamt of the blonde girl yet again, and saw her riding a bicycle with him down a beach boardwalk. He was on his beloved dark blue bicycle, and she was on a deep green bicycle matching her stunning eyes. Then the scene shifted and he was in bed with her. In his dream, he knew exactly what he was doing, as though he'd been with as many women as Jeronymus. Even in sleep, under those heavy, warm covers, his body suddenly became a lot warmer.

4

He woke to a plate of tulip bulb purée on the nightstand and a wrapped package on the foot of the bed. He was a little disappointed to find he was alone and the beautiful blonde wasn't next to him. After eating the disgusting excuse for breakfast as quickly as possible and washing it down with water that had started to turn into ice, he reached for the New Year's present. He carefully pulled the medium pink tissue paper off and found a new sketchpad. It had the same high-quality paper as the one he'd just finished, and was roughly the same size. The main differences were that the edges of the pages were tinted with gold leaf, and the front cover had a blue border and depicted Vermeer's *The Little Street*.

Though his hands were already cold, he leaned over the side of the bed for his case of art supplies. The first picture in this new sketchbook, his first drawing of 1945, was of the nameless blonde standing on the beach, wearing a dark green dress that matched her eyes. She could just as easily be anyone else. For all he cared, he could be drawing one of his partisan friends on the beach instead. She was no one special.

In the evening, Vrouw Visser walked him to the back door and saw him off in the Citroën. As Jakob waved goodbye to her, he prayed the next time he saw her, it would be in peacetime and they'd be celebrating their homeland's liberation. Best of all, the next time he saw her, it wouldn't be winter anymore and the Dutch people would no longer be starving. Sometimes dreams did come true.

Chapter 18: A Real Soldier

Even after the merciful lifting of the winter's bitter cold, food was still very hard to come by in the area Jakob and his friends were camping out in. Much of the Southern Netherlands had been liberated over the course of the fall, and other parts of the country were slowly being liberated as well, but unfortunately for him, his company wasn't in one of those places. Part of him was scared of moving towards the areas that had become battlezones, but the other part of him was angry and jealous he was missing all the action. If only Commander van der Beek weren't so insistent on not taking resources away from the official military during this time of national starvation.

It was now late February, and Jakob had been sent on a mission with Leendert and Govert to throw grenades into confirmed NSB houses and shoot anyone they caught with swastika armbands or other Nazi or NSB insignia. Though spring hadn't officially begun, Jakob savored the feeling of the dying winter air. After the frigid cold temperatures he'd lived through, this felt like paradise by comparison. If these temperatures were as warm as he'd get for the rest of his life, he'd be very happy.

Jakob raised his left arm and lobbed a grenade into a blue house across the road. He smiled when he saw it going in an open third floor window. Everyone in the company praised his throwing arm and how far he could throw grenades. And to think that before he'd become a partisan, he hadn't seriously considered the possibility of being predominantly left-handed. Perhaps handedness wasn't entirely determined by the primary writing hand after all.

He ducked into one of the houses set against the hills to wait out the explosion. Sometimes he and his comrades stayed in these houses built out of hills, or built into the hills. They were a marvellous natural resource he was sure the Germans couldn't boast of. And who would ever suspect an ordinary hill housed resistance fighters?

His eyes fell upon a bunch of papers strewn over the floor, and several books tossed into a corner. A ragdoll rested on top of one of the books. When he lifted the doll up, he saw the complete works of Shakespeare in Dutch. Several bookmarks stuck out of the pages. Since he didn't have to go into the grenaded house for awhile, he sat down to look through the book. He'd always enjoyed Shakespeare back at gymnasium, though most of his friends found the language too stuffy and hard to understand. The appeal for him was the timelessness of the themes, which transcended language, culture, and era.

As he opened the heavy volume, he stopped breathing for a minute. There, staring back at him, were the beautiful blonde and her friend Juli. The girls were standing on the beach, wearing rather modest bathing suits, smiling, their arms linked around one another. When he turned the picture over, he saw the inscription, "September 1939, Scheveningen, Rachel and Juli, best friends forever." So her name really was Rachel, not Zipporah or Margaretha.

Under the picture was an inscription dated 1 April 1938. He smiled when he realized she must be his age, if she'd turned twelve in 1938.

To our dear daughter Rachel,

This is a gift from us to you on the special occasion of your reaching the age of bat mitzvah. Perhaps by the time you have your own daughter, the bat mitzvah ceremony will be equal to the bar mitzvah ceremony, and we'll be able to witness our granddaughter reading from the Torah and leading services. But right now, we're very proud of the fact that our only child has come of age and been recognized in some way for all her learning. If you were a boy, just think how much further you could go with all your learning and intelligence. Even our Progressive Movement still has a ways to go.

We hope you enjoy this volume. Perhaps you won't read it all the way through at your age, or read it for pleasure for a very long time, but it's here for you when you're old enough to appreciate Shakespeare. It's never too early to start adding to your personal library of great world literature. Shakespeare was the greatest writer of the English language, the same way Louis Couperus was the greatest writer of our Dutch language. If the language of his plays is too intimidating for you, you can always start with his sonnets. There are some writers all educated people should be familiar with, and Shakespeare is one of them.

We hope you enjoy your very special weekend and carry these memories with you for a long time to come. Happy memories have a way of keeping your spirits up even in unhappy times.

Your loving parents,

Felix van der Meer and Tirzah Roggenfelder

He put the picture back in the book and tucked it into his bag along with the doll, then gathered up all the papers on the floor. Before leaving the hiding place, he picked up the other books, the only things left there. He smiled when he saw they were Dutch translations of *The Divine Comedy*, *The Decameron*, *The Iliad*, *The Odyssey*, and *The Bhagavad Gita*. It pleased him to know she came from parents who taught her to revere the written word and classic literature the same way he'd been, and that she'd cared enough to bring books into hiding in lieu of necessity items only. And she'd been raised Progressive and taken her mother's surname. Not that he thought he'd run into her again, but it would be nice to have these reminders of his mystery girl to look back on in old age.

2

Jakob was gazing at the picture of Rachel and Juli a few days later when one of the older partisans came running into their current encampment. He quickly put the picture away and stood up at attention.

"Commander van der Beek just had a meeting with some very important people in the Princess Irene Brigade of the Dutch Free Forces. He gave them our names and brief résumés, and a representative will come back here with Commander van der Beek to let us know which of us will be joining the brigade."

"We'll be real soldiers?" Jakob asked. "Today?"

"The brigade is in the middle of figuring out reorganization of its ranks, and they need new blood to fill the soon-to-be-empty slots. They're mostly taking replacements who've been trained by real military officers, but willing to consider taking on guys who've been active in resistance groups like ours. The guys that are chosen will be given ranks commensurate with our experience and skill abilities."

"Do you think Commander van der Beek will become a general?" Govert asked. "I'd like to be a major, at least."

The partisan laughed. "It's not up to us to decide our own ranks. They probably won't be able to take all of us, but they can use as many as they can get. Just so long as they select experienced, qualified guys."

Jakob was on pins and needles while waiting for Commander van der Beek to return to camp. When he finally returned, he had three other men with him. Jakob respectfully took in the camouflage, caps, and insignia the real soldiers wore. He cast his eyes upward and began praying he'd be selected and given a good rank. Anything but private. Even if he'd be a newcomer to the Army, he'd served in an unofficial combatant capacity for two and a half years. If anything, that should count as time already served.

"Comrades, these are Sergeants Pieter van Donk, Stefan van Rossem, and Lodewijk van Willigen. They're here to convey their commanding officer's decision regarding who'll be let into the Princess Irene Brigade and commence official fighting."

Jakob kept his eyes closed as they read the list of names. He heard a buzzing around him as he blocked out all sensations in his intense concentration. Only when he felt someone jabbing him in the ribs did he come out of his trance-like state.

"Didn't you hear, Jaap?" Dries asked. "You're in."

His eyes widened and he started laughing, partly from shock, partly from joy, partly from the release of some of his long-repressed feelings. Within the week, he'd be a real soldier, acting in an official fighting capacity instead of going around taking justice into his own hands and constantly having to evade discovery. Even if he were trading in his tenuous shelter for another kind of danger, it was a danger he welcomed.

"Congratulations, Lieutenant DeJonghe." Sgt. van Donk extended his hand.

Jakob grabbed his hand and shook it heartily. "Thank you very much. How many steps above private is a lieutenant?"

Sgt. van Donk smiled. "It's certainly not within spitting distance of being a general, but it's a fair bit above private. After private, the ranks are corporal, sergeant, second lieutenant, and lieutenant. From what your commander told us about you, we thought that rank was an appropriate one for you. Most eighteen-year-olds aren't as experienced or skillful as you."

"Can I take my dog with me? He's been our company's dog for almost a year and a half. His old name was Adolf, but I renamed him Bernhard, after our prince. We call him Ben for short."

Sgt. van Donk peered down at Ben. "He's a handsome fellow. I don't see why not. It's never a bad thing for a company to have a dog, and even better if there's more than one canine soldier."

Jakob kept grinning stupidly long after Sgt. van Donk moved on down the line and continued selecting partisans and assigning them ranks. He felt as though he were in the best dream of his life, his dream finally coming true. Luisa would be so proud of him when she came home and discovered he'd become a real soldier in her absence. He was so caught up in his own happiness, he had to force himself to smile and congratulate his friends when their names were read.

"Tonight we're moving you fellows into Walcheren, where you'll be given uniforms and briefed on your new duties. You can all start packing up, and we'll come back in a few hours to transport you."

Jakob felt as though he were floating on Cloud Nine as he limped back to his bunker with Ben running at his heels. He continued in a trance-like state as he put all his books and personal effects into his bag. Over the next few hours, he tried to distract himself and allay his nervousness by reading *The Tao Te Ching* and Rachel's *Bhagavad Gita*. He'd never read the latter before, but knew it was a sermon delivered to a soldier who got cold feet on the eve of a major war, meant to raise his spirits and inspire him to fight. In the middle of reading the ancient words Krishna had imparted to Arjuna, a picture fell out.

"Lucky you. Now you have two pictures of your mystery woman." Dries blew a smoke ring.

Jakob picked it up and took in a sepia-tinted picture of Rachel with a rather handsome young man with dark hair and eyes. The boy's arm was around her, and she was holding his other hand. Both of them gazed lovingly at one another. He hoped Dries and Leendert hadn't seen him wince.

"Oh, look, she already has a fellow and you're out of luck," Leendert smirked. "Maybe she's waiting for him to rescue her. Do you think this boyfriend was one of the guys you caught hiding by the river?"

"It's dated 1938 on the back. That was a long time ago. Maybe they ended their courtship, or God forbid the guy died."

"If she's your age, she would've been only twelve in '38," Dries said. "Your Rachel is one mighty precocious girl. I still thought girls were too silly to bother with at twelve. If she already had at least one fellow by twelve, perhaps she's had several others since."

Jakob waved his hand at them dismissively and stuffed the picture back into the book. He spent the rest of their waiting time reading, glad no further pictures fell out. By the time the Princess Irene Brigade soldiers came back, he felt almost ready to explode.

"Let's go, Bentje. We're going to a place called Walcheren, where we'll live among real soldiers and do real fighting." He lifted his bag onto his shoulders and limped towards the waiting trucks.

Ben jumped up first when their turn in line came. As Jakob was being helped into the truck by Dries and Govert, he flashed back to boarding the vans that took them to Westerbork on that hot, sticky August day. He could see it all as though it were yesterday, that long ride full of fear and uncertainty, as he cradled his wounded mother in his arms like she were the child and he were the parent. One of the happiest moments of his life, and those damned memories had to pop up again and remind him he wasn't really a normal member of the human race, would forever exist in a separate class of people. He could only hope his mother hadn't been through even worse things after their separation, and that she hadn't been put in an even more alien class of people.

Ben curled up on his lap during the ride to Walcheren. Jakob absentmindedly petted him, glad he had the comfort of his furry companion and four dear friends on this truck ride. When they arrived at their new headquarters, they'd be taken care of as well as possible, in spite of the continuing food and fuel shortages. They wouldn't live in constant terror of being put on a list of new deportation victims, even if they'd be without a restaurant, orchestra, cabaret, and salon. Now that he thought back on it, those things had probably only been put in Westerbork to lull the transitory residents into a state of false security and make them believe everything were normal.

Jakob was helped off of the truck by Govert and Leendert. He remembered to jump onto his left foot only. As he walked into the headquarters the brigade had appropriated for themselves, he held his head up and tried to limp as little as possible. His limp was still there, but it wasn't as heavy and pronounced as it'd been a few years ago, years that now seemed like an eternity ago.

"Your new uniforms are in this crate," someone announced. "We didn't have time to get them in all your specific sizes, but most of you will probably find they're a good fit. If not, you can switch with someone else or hem them out."

"Can we keep them?" Jakob breathed as he lifted out a long pair of pants and a big shirt he estimated would work on someone of his height.

"Of course you can keep them, my good fellow. I'm sure the vast majority of you won't be staying to become career soldiers, but it's your right to retain your uniform after your term of service. I hope you fellows will be proud of your service, proud enough to wear your uniforms on parade and celebration days. Even if you never attend an anniversary or memorial parade, it'll be something nice for your children and grandchildren to look at in a memory chest someday."

"Can we try them on now?"

"Our friend is very eager to get into uniform," Jeronymus said. "He wanted to join the partisans right after he broke his foot and ankle, that's how badly he's wanted this for a long time."

"For now, all you need to do is get a good night's sleep, so you can greet your first full day as official soldiers bright-eyed and bushy-tailed. Before you get to bed, you can sign the contracts we've made out for you. Though the end of the war is probably very near, a normal term of service is still one year. There are many things a soldier can do in peacetime, and perhaps some of you will want to serve in the Dutch East Indies after this front is liberated. This brigade will probably be disbanded by the end of the year, but you'll continue as part of the Royal Army of The Netherlands. Does everyone understand that?"

Jakob held his new uniform up to his body to check it wasn't too short or long, then folded it up and left it on the bed he'd claimed. It wasn't the bed in Vrouw Visser's basement, but it was a fair sight better than the pallet he'd slept on in huts and bunkers. Before heading over to the desk where the contracts were, he tried on his cap and almost salivated at the thought of wearing a helmet soon.

"Why don't you show our new friends how well you've taught yourself how to write with the other hand?" Dries suggested. "The young Lt. DeJonghe is very talented and can punch, write, paint, draw, shoot, and throw with both hands. We've made him throw and shoot left-handed because he shows more strength and dexterity with those tasks with that hand. He claims he taught himself, but I refuse to believe that kind of skill didn't come naturally."

Jakob shrugged, transferred the pen to his other hand, and signed his name. After he was done, he put down the pen and pushed the paper away to admire his handiwork. Not bad for someone who'd only picked up a pen in his left hand three or four years into knowing how to write, and having to practice on the sly in fits and starts.

He fell asleep almost as soon as his head hit the pillow, and dreamt of leading a heroic charge against the Germans. In his dream, he killed at least fifty Nazis and won twenty different medals and citations for bravery. Afterwards, he was held high on the shoulders of his comrades as he was taken through the streets of Amsterdam in a victory parade.

The Royal Family was back, and they all shook his hand, gave him flowers, and congratulated him. When morning broke, he felt an intense disappointment at realizing he was just a brand-new lieutenant and not a glorious war hero.

"It's time to put on that uniform you were itching so badly to get into," Leendert called from the bed on his right. "I bet you'll beat all of us to getting dressed first."

Jakob threw off the covers and took the uniform behind the changing curtain he was relieved for the presence of. The boots and cap fit, and the pants and shirt felt comfortable, but there was only one way to tell for sure if it were a perfect fit.

As he adjusted his shirt and admired himself in the full-length mirror propped up against the wall, he froze. He blinked several times to make sure he wasn't seeing things. There, in the reflection, he saw Rachel standing next to him, her arms around his neck, a playful smile on her face. He looked behind him and only saw other men. His heart beat rapidly as he ambled towards the breakfast table with Ben at his heels. If he were seeing visions in mirrors, it could either mean he were going crazy or had some sort of unfinished business with that girl. He almost hoped it were the former.

3

Jakob crouched below a fourth story window of an abandoned building overlooking a dead-end street, his rifle balanced on the windowsill, when he heard footsteps coming up the steps behind him. He dropped to the floor and pulled his rifle alongside him, making sure his helmet was securely fastened, and aimed his rifle at the door.

"What are you doing pointing a gun at me?" Jeronymus asked. "You know our guys staked out this street before you came up here. It could only have been one of us."

"How was I supposed to know that! The Germans are masters of deception, and I can never be too careful."

"I was sent to tell you there's going to be a very important visitor coming to see us later today. I wasn't told who, but I got the gist this is a very important person we don't want to miss seeing."

Jakob sat up and pulled himself into a corner. "Could it be General Eisenhower? Or General Patton? That would be amazing!"

"Sorry, I don't know anything further than you do. If this mystery visitor is so important, we ought to be at the head of the line so we can see him up-close and get a handshake."

"So I have permission to leave my sniping duties?"

"I wouldn't have come up here if it weren't okay."

Jakob followed Jeronymus back to headquarters, trying not to limp too badly as he ran. All the way there, visions of heroes like General Eisenhower and General Patton danced through his head.

When they got back, Jakob pushed and shoved his way to the head of the line to see who the visitor might be. During the time he stood waiting, he shifted his weight onto his left foot countless times. He still didn't like standing for too long, and preferred to either sit or be on the move. As soon as the war was over and his term of service was complete, he hoped he could get a desk job, or something that involved minimal standing. Perhaps an art history professor.

Jakob held his breath as the car pulled up and the door opened. He turned into one gigantic smile when he recognized the woman getting out of the car and walking along the line of soldiers. Everyone began cheering Queen Wilhelmina and singing *Wilhelmus van Nassouwe*. He hoped those Nazi and NSB bastards could see them now. The Dutch people had their Queen back, and she was exactly where she belonged, greeting her loyal troops. As the Queen moved down the line, he prayed his stomach wouldn't rumble and offend her. Even now that he was a real soldier, he still had to put up with food shortages.

He put out his shaking hand, hoping it wasn't too sweaty. "Hello, Your Majesty. I'm so honored to meet you. I've kept your and your family's pictures hidden even after it became illegal. My name is Lieutenant Jakob Eliezer DeJonghe, and I've been in the Dutch Resistance for almost two years, and joined the Princess Irene Brigade a few weeks ago. This is my canine comrade Ben, named after your son-in-law Prince Bernhard. God bless you, Your Majesty."

She smiled at him, and Jakob thought she looked so regal and dignified without even trying, the same way Luisa had. "I'm very pleased to meet you too, Lt. DeJonghe. Your service to The Netherlands is very much appreciated."

Jakob's hand tingled long after the Queen had moved on down the line and greeted the other soldiers. He didn't want to wash it ever again. Never in his life had he ever imagined he'd one day stand in the presence of the Queen, shake her hand, speak to her, and be spoken to in return. This was an even prouder moment of his life than joining the Princess Irene Brigade, and he wouldn't soon forget it. This was the type of thing he'd tell his children, grandchildren, and great-grandchildren about. And, of course, brag about it to Luisa when she came home. His mother would be home soon. He was sure of it. As Vrouw Visser had said, the Nazis' end had to be at hand soon.

4

During April, Jakob finally got his chance to take part in a real battle. The Princess Irene Brigade was sent to Hedel on the River Maas to join up with the Royal Marine Commandos of the 116th Infantry Brigade Royal Marines at Kerkdriel. The plan was to liberate the Bommelerwaard district, but the Royal Marines gave up under intense Nazi fighting. Now the Princess Irene Brigade stood alone at the bridgehead of Hedel.

Jakob kept his caul, the little stuffed rabbit, Luisa's letter, and the picture of Rachel and Juli in his knapsack for good luck, along with all the required gear he now had to carry. His days of being able to peacefully draw and paint in the evenings were a thing of the past. Now he constantly worried he'd be attacked or shot in the night.

Bullets whizzed around his head and body as he ran across the battlefield, a pistol and knife on both sides of his holster and a rifle on his back. Every time he saw the earth explode or a comrade fall, he gave thanks he hadn't stepped on the bomb or been shot. The sky was constantly lit up with orange and yellow, a sight he would've found worthy of inspiration for a painting in another lifetime. Half the time he had to crawl or wiggle through the ground to avoid getting hit or exposing himself to danger. There was no time to wonder why he'd been spared when he saw a soldier next to him or in front of him shot down.

Both of his hands had grown numb from shooting so much, and he felt as though he'd thrown his left arm out from how many grenades he'd lobbed. Every time he was in a safe position to see Germans falling, he rejoiced. These damned occupiers might be putting up one final stand, but they weren't going to hold his homeland hostage much longer.

He wished he could shave his head or fight without a uniform. He constantly sweated buckets under his helmet, the weight on his back, his socks and boots, and the uniform, which now seemed like a prison instead of paradise. Much of the sweat came from fear and terror as well. He was sure the entire brigade could hear his heart beating as loudly as the dismembered heart in "The Tell-Tale Heart." When he looked around at his comrades, he saw the fear in their faces as well. At least they wouldn't make fun of him for being unmanly. Even the toughest guy would be scared in an intense battlezone.

The bridgehead was captured on 23 April, but the heavy attacks continued. Jakob wondered how many years had been taken off his life from all the stress and terror he'd been under, and felt grateful to be alive every time he came back from a charge or getting too close to enemy fire. Every time he took shelter in, fired a gun, or launched a grenade from an abandoned house or barn, he was constantly on edge, wondering if there were Germans lurking just behind him. He was shocked his hair was still sable, with no gray or white hairs sprouting up overnight.

Late at night on 25 April, they received an order to withdraw from the bridgehead. Jakob thought his nightmare was over when the brigade withdrew and crossed the River Maas, but it just began all over again. No one had realized how numerous their opposition still was, and now he found the nightmare starting all over again, but even worse this time. These damned barbarians weren't about to go down without one final fight.

Jakob kept his left hand on his knife and his right hand on his pistol, constantly on alert as the brigade made the treacherous river crossing. All around him, his comrades were being attacked hand-to-hand. He could barely see from the haze of gunsmoke and the sickening images of blood and maimed bodies. Every time he saw a German approaching, he shot blindly, not giving himself time to line up his target. In a situation of kill or be killed, he had to act first and not even think. He was barely grateful Ben had made it through the fighting unscathed. His life mattered more than a dog's life, and part of him would be relieved if Ben and not he took an enemy grenade, shot, or bayonet.

Jakob wondered if he was avoiding being hit because he'd had to become such an acrobat after his accident. He knew how to rely on other parts of his body, how to maneuver himself into and out of different positions, how to get around without walking. The river seemed endless, but at least the harsh winter had lifted and the water wasn't freezing. He felt the cold in every bone of his right foot, but that was only a distraction now.

"Watch out!" he heard someone scream.

He looked to his right and saw three approaching Germans. He pulled out his right-hand pistol and shot one of them, and grabbed the bayonet the second one aimed at him. While he was struggling to commandeer the bayonet and turn it on the enemy, he heard a loud splash to his left.

Everything around him began spinning like the visions of a crazed kaleidoscope, the same sensation he'd had the night before he was deported. Everyone transmogrified into nightmarish Hindu deities with a thousand heads and arms. All he knew was Dries had just been wounded, and he hadn't seen who did it. The fact that the German with the bayonet had also mysteriously just fallen wasn't a concern.

"Medic!" he screamed as he dropped into the water. "We need a medic right now!"

He heard splashing behind him. The instant he saw it was another German, he lunged up and shot him with the last bullet in his right-hand gun. Like a man possessed, he ran the rest of the way across the river, shooting blindly with the gun on his left side. When he ran out of bullets in his pistol, he used his rifle. For the first time, he wasn't afraid of all the bullets whizzing around him, the flying grenades, or the up-close and personal faces of the enemy. After all his ammunition was used up, he pulled the bayonet off his rifle and charged at any Germans he could find. He wasn't keeping track of how many people had been added to his impressive body count.

"Take it easy, Jaap," he heard Leendert saying in his soothing voice. "It's over. We crossed the river. The remaining Germans are surrendering."

Jakob looked down at the German he was sitting on top of and maniacally bayoneting. He had the face of a child, looking easily several years his junior. For a fleeting second, Jakob felt sorry for him, then remembered this boy soldier was brought up to hate and was serving in the army of the country who'd committed so many human rights violations and caused darkness to fall for so many years. Jakob looked at him with disgust and gave one final stab, relishing the sight of the blood coming out of his mouth and from his chest.

"*Mutti,*" the boy soldier whispered.

Jakob rolled his eyes and punched him. "You don't deserve to go home to your mother. Your Nazi mother is sitting safe at home, while my mother is God knows where, subject to all sorts of indignities your monstrous race approved of. I hope your mother cries rivers of blood when she finds out about your death. How does it feel for a big, strong, mighty Aryan to meet his death at the hands of a Jewish soldier? Now who's going to claim we never fight back?"

Jakob got up when he saw some of the higher-ranking officers approaching. He stood at attention, letting his bayonet fall into the water next to the maimed, bloodied body of his most recent kill.

"What *was* that?"

His heart suddenly went into his throat again. Visions of being punished for going on a rampage ran through his head. Maybe he'd be demoted to private or removed from the brigade.

"You're only eighteen, Lt. DeJonghe?"

"Yes, Meneer. I'll be nineteen next month, in less than two weeks."

"And you've only been in the brigade since February?"

"Yes, but I've been in the assassination and sabotage wing of the Dutch Resistance since June '43. I started training for combat and related duties a month before that, but I read a lot of military magazines and books before then."

The officer shook his head. "I've never seen anything like that in anyone your age. I would've been too scared to lead my own charge at that age. You didn't seem afraid, and kept going like it were the most normal thing in the world."

"I had no choice. Some *Bokkelul* shot my buddy Dries, and I had to get even with the entire lot of them. It's not the first time I've taken revenge on Nazis and NSBers who hurt people close to me."

"How do the Bronze Lion, the Order of Orange–Nassau, and the Order of Willem sound, Lieutenant?"

"Are you kidding? Of course I'd love to be decorated!"

"Excellent. I'll include your name in the list of men I'm recommending for these honors."

"Thank you very much. That means so much to me after everything I've been through, you can't even imagine." Jakob looked behind him, suddenly remembering what caused him to snap. "What happened to Dries? My friend, Andries Quackenboss. Did the medic come for him after I took off?"

"Our medic has tried to tend to all the injured men, but we can only do so much at once. The ones whose injuries aren't fatal will be removed to the nearest hospital."

Jakob watched the sickening parade of his injured comrades being carried on the shoulders of other soldiers, by their shoulders and legs, and on makeshift stretchers. Some of them had their faces covered by cloths, many of which were blood-soaked. He was newly-glad he'd killed the boy soldier when he saw what these monsters had done to his friends. Normal people surrendered when it became clear they were losing a war. They didn't unleash barbaric attacks so close to the end and murder brave soldiers who fought fairly. These people didn't function according to the normal rules of society. They wanted to take down as many people as possible till the last second possible.

He was somewhat relieved when he finally saw Dries being carried out. His deep blue eyes were open, in spite of the blood seeping out of his chest. He faintly smiled at Jakob.

"You owe me big-time for the second time, Jaap. That's the second time I've saved your hide. First I rescued you after you jumped from the train, and now I shot that guy who probably would've bayoneted you."

"Don't try to talk," one of the soldiers carrying the stretcher cautioned. "You need all your strength to recover."

"May I go with him to the hospital?" Jakob asked. "I can't believe he was able to shoot anyone after he was wounded."

"All good soldiers protect their comrades. I'm sure you would've made every effort to shoot someone attacking one of your closest friends if you'd been the one shot down."

Jakob got on the truck taking the most severely wounded to the nearest hospital. He barely cared about Ben panting at his side and just held Dries's hand, trying not to look at how bloodied his friend was.

One of the higher-ranking officers stormed into the hospital and pushed aside the nurses in his way. "We need beds for wounded soldiers right now. Get wheelchairs or stretchers for these men, or we'll go through the hospital and do it ourselves."

"I'm afraid we're all out of beds. In case you didn't know, there's a war—"

The officer pulled out his pistol. "Does this make you want to empty some beds? I'm sure we can find plenty of people who don't deserve beds if we look hard enough."

"You're losing the war," Jakob sneered. "I can tell you're in the NSB. A real Dutch patriot would immediately provide care to her wounded heroes, not act like we're breaking your precious rules."

The nurses and receptionist stood by as the wounded of the Princess Irene Brigade were taken into the hospital and a number of German soldiers, Nazis, and NSBers were pushed out of their beds. Jakob pushed out a big fat NSBer and helped set Dries onto the bed.

"My friend is a brave soldier, you piece of pig lard." He planted his left foot on the evicted patient's neck. "He's a Dutch patriot, unlike other people we might think of. You've violated everything our home-land ever stood for." His eyes lit up when he saw a lit cigarette in a garish green ashtray on the side table. Ignoring the NSBer's screams, he extinguished it in his right eye.

"Our friends will be taken care of," the officer promised. "Justice will be dealt accordingly to all the traitors at this hospital. In the mean-time, we have to get back to the brigade."

"Do you think we'll have to fight many more battles?"

"Hopefully, what we just experienced was the last trial. The Germans are fools if they intend to sacrifice the last man in a suicidal cause. Going down with a fight when you're in a losing battle isn't heroic or smart. God willing, by the summer, we'll be a free people again, and the Germans will go home in shame. What a pity such a cultured, intelligent people devolved so much in the last twelve years. This is the kind of legacy you can't undo overnight."

Chapter 19: The Best Birthday Present Ever

Jakob proudly sat on top of a tank rolling into The Hague on his nineteenth birthday, 9 May 1945, wearing his new dress uniform with his beautiful new decorations. Leendert was to his left and Govert was to his right, with Jeronymus next to Govert. The Princess Irene Brigade was the first Allied unit to enter The Hague after the liberation, which once seemed so far away.

He felt a personal victory every time one of the enthusiastically cheering townspeople smiled or waved at him. This was better than a trillion birthdays. Besides the tanks, there were also trucks, motorcycles, bicycles, horses, and a brass band coming down the streets. Best of all, the Nazis and NSBers were now the ones being rounded up and paraded down the streets in shame, as people shouted at and pushed them. Their pathetic propaganda rags were also being burnt, the same way they'd tried to consume so much knowledge and family history in flames.

"God bless you, soldier," a woman told him as she handed him flowers.

"Thank you very much, Mevrouw. We fought very hard to liberate our country, and couldn't have done it without your support."

Jeronymus nudged him. "How about it, Jaap? We're conquering heroes. After this victory parade and any additional duties, we'll have our pick of women to sleep with. I'll give you an intense crash-course beforehand, so you don't embarrass yourself."

"I'm not interested. I have more important things to do."

"Come on, this opportunity probably won't present itself again," Govert pestered. "You could bed five women in the same night if you really wanted to. Look how these women love us. Your birthday will be even better if you become a man. Your future wife probably won't mind, if she's a modern woman. She'll understand soldiers have to do certain things. Why would you want to live like a monk when these women are practically throwing themselves on us?"

"Suit yourself," Leendert sighed. "I'm going to have fun with any willing women I can find. Probably half the female population of The Hague wants to sleep with us right now. Don't disappoint them by withholding your services. Any woman will be very excited and honored to get the task of making a man of you."

Jakob continued smiling and waving at the jubilant townspeople, feeling as though his heart would burst of joy and happiness. He was very sorry Dries had to miss the victory parade, but sure his wounded friend would receive lots of flowers, cards, chocolates, candies, and presents at the hospital. One of the anti-Semitic pieces of legislation had expelled Jewish patients, and now the Nazis and NSBers were the ones thrown out of the hospitals. He relished the sight of the traitors and occupiers being pushed, shoved, screamed at, and publicly humiliated. Turnaround was fair play.

After the victory parade was over, the liberators were treated to a celebratory banquet. While Jakob's friends made eyes at all the pretty young women, he only thought about filling his stomach and waiting for his mother to come home. He missed his usual chocolate cake with strawberry filling, but the feast he was served was even better. After spending the entire fall, winter, and most of the spring starving, this was a feast fit for a king.

"Just let us know when you see a girl you like," Jeronymus whispered as they walked through the streets on their way to their first post-liberation assignment that evening. "Remember, I've got as much experience with women as I've got with making bombs."

"Don't you ever worry about getting a girl in trouble? Or venereal disease?"

"There are ways to take care of those problems. Mostly it's the woman's responsibility. If a woman is so paranoid about that she refuses to sleep with me, she's not the type of lover I'm after. I want someone I can have a good time with, not someone too worried to enjoy herself. The kinds of women I've bedded aren't the disreputable types anyway. Only dirty streetwalkers and camp prostitutes carry diseases."

Their group was led into a prison guarded by some of the Canadian soldiers. The Nazi and NSB jailers and interrogators had been forced to kneel and remove most of their clothes, while locals screamed at them. The newly-freed prisoners looked to be in a state of shock.

"Here you go." One of the Canadians handed them electric razors and a bucket of orange paint. "These criminals are going to be publicly marked. In daylight hours, we'll do it again in the streets. There are lots of Nazis and collaborators we're snuffing out. Now it's their turn to suffer."

"They're unarmed," another Canadian said. "They know there'll be serious consequences if they attempt to kill or lay hands on an Allied soldier."

Jakob shoved the nearest NSBer onto the ground and held him in place, digging his nails into the NSBer's flabby arms. Leendert turned on the razor and dug it into his scalp as close to the skin as possible. His traitorous head glowed with razor burn after the shave was over. Over his protestations and yelps of pain, Govert painted his freshly-shaved, raw, red head orange. After he was done, they shoved him aside and started in on the next traitor.

"We're doing this to the women too," one of the Canadians said, puffing on a cigarette. "Some of these broads are just as bad as the men, and sometimes worse. Show them no mercy, even if they are women."

Jakob had been taught never to lay his hands on a woman, but orders were orders. He grabbed the closest woman and pushed her onto the ground. Her eyes were empty, reflecting nothingness. It didn't look like she had a soul behind her eyes.

"I can't go out in public without any hair! Everyone will make fun of me!"

"Exactly the point, bitch." Govert shaved her honey-blonde hair and kicked it across the room. "Everyone needs to know you're a traitor. Do you realize how many innocent people died over the last six years because of your foul ideology?"

She began squealling when the paint dripped into her eyes. Leendert ignored her and laid it on even heavier. Jakob didn't feel sorry for these women anymore. He'd been brought up to believe in the equality of the sexes, and that had to mean a woman could be just as mean and evil as a man.

"Jaap, is that you?"

Jakob looked to his right and saw Vrouw Visser among the group of newly-freed prisoners. "What are you doing here, and so far from Winschoten?"

Jeronymus grabbed the next NSBer in line and kicked him onto the ground. "Would you care to explain why one of our friends in the underground is in prison? Do you remember processing this woman?"

"I can't remember the name and story of every criminal!"

Jakob turned his razor up to the highest setting and dug it in so deeply he drew blood. "That woman has been like a mother to me for the last two and a half years! If you can't explain why she's here, we'll either pry answers out of you or find someone who can answer."

"That woman?" someone farther back in line asked. "She was caught hiding Jews in early January. She was supposed to go to the prison in Amsterdam, but it was impossible to cross that route with all the bombs and battles."

"I could've been in that house! I stayed with her over the New Year's weekend and many times before then! This woman risks her life to save innocent people, and you reward her with prison?"

"I was about to be executed," Vrouw Visser said lifelessly. "Then the Allies came into the prison and freed us. I never named any names, Jaap. Your things are still all safe in the basement. You know how well-hidden that bedroom is. Even most of my regular visitors don't know my basement has that room."

Jakob ruthlessly went through the rest of the traitors and enemies in line, always digging in the razor deep enough to cause injury, putting the paint on thickly over the wounds, holding the perpetrators down roughly enough to cause bruises, and shoving them onto the ground hard enough to break something. He couldn't wait to do this to the entire collaborating population of The Netherlands, and was very disappointed when the line ended.

"Tomorrow we'll do this to some of the whores who fornicated with the Germans," one of the Canadians said. "As well as some Nazis and NSBers."

Govert turned to Vrouw Visser. "Do you have a place to stay for the night? We'll give you money for a hotel, until you can go home."

"I wish we could take you to our headquarters," Jakob said. "Can we send you home with a military escort?"

"Yes, the roads probably won't be passable for regular people for some time," Leendert said. "You've been really good to us, and you don't deserve to be stuck so far away from home."

One of the higher-ranking officers of the Princess Irene Brigade looked at Jakob. "You're one of the Jewish fellows in our brigade, correct?"

"Yes, Meneer." He glared at the bald goons with orange heads. "Thought you'd never live to see the day when one of your former victims turned you into victims, did you?"

"And you said this woman is from Winschoten?"

"Yes, Meneer."

"How would you feel about a short-term assignment in that area? The transit camp was liberated by the Canadians last month, but many survivors are still recovering and transitioning to the outside. I'm sure they'd love nothing better than to see a real Dutch Jewish soldier among their rescuers. We also discovered a lot of NSBers, pro-German sympathizers, and other collaborators hiding there with their families, and we need to question everyone to determine who's guilty. The camp now doubles as a prison and recovery center. Perhaps two weeks you could spend there helping out? You can accompany your benefactor back to her home, and then go to the nearby camp. But not right away, of course. You'll need to spend at least a few more days here helping to clean up the Germans' mess. Someone will notify you when it's the appropriate time for you to be transferred on that assignment."

"Yes, Meneer, that would make me very happy. Would you mind travelling with me, Vrouw Visser? We won't let any bandits attack you on the way. You should've seen me when we crossed the River Maas. I led my own charge and killed so many Nazis, it was incredible. It's part of the reason I got these beautiful decorations. My entire brigade got the Order of Willem, but I probably would've gotten it on my own anyway."

Vrouw Visser smiled faintly. "You've certainly earned the right to be proud of yourself, but I hope you don't let it get to your head. Have you met my husband in your brigade? His name's Norbert Haas."

"The name's not familiar, sorry. But I'll ask tonight."

Govert pushed some bills into her hand. "Stay at any hotel on us, and come to our headquarters when you're ready to go home. Maybe sometime this summer, we'll be able to have a celebratory meal there."

"Would you like someone to take you to a hotel so you're not accosted in the street?" Leendert asked.

"Yes, let me escort you there," Jakob said. "I'll be right back at headquarters after I see you inside."

Vrouw Visser nodded. "Can you promise me something, Jaap? If it turns out you no longer have a mother, will you let me act as your mother? You're too old to need a mother in the way a small child needs one, but it's always nice to have a house to come home to. Surely you've heard the stories that have trickled in, about the things that went on in Germany and Poland. I'm not so sure your mother survived."

He looked up at the ceiling to avoid giving away his pained expression. "I'm sure my mother's alive somewhere, but if the worst happened, I couldn't think of anyone else I'd like to be my surrogate mother."

"Good." Vrouw Visser gave him her arm. "Didn't I tell you things would get better after we went through the worst trials? No matter how long it took, the most important thing is that we're finally celebrating liberation."

As he walked with her through the streets of The Hague to the nicest hotel he could find, Jakob thought back to his old notebook. When he'd been writing and drawing on the first night of Pesach in 1941, he thought he really would be free next year in Amsterdam. Even if it had taken five years for his homeland to conquer their oppressors, at least it finally happened.

He shivered as he thought about the assignment he'd just agreed to take on. Even if he'd be entering a liberated Westerbork as a free man, it'd force him to relive things he didn't want to. He sat down on a bench to take off his knapsack and collect himself for a few moments.

Vrouw Visser leaned down to pick up the picture that slipped out of the knapsack. "Is this your sweetheart, Jaap? Did you finally get a girl before you became a soldier?"

He grabbed it and stuffed it back in the bag. "No, those are two of the women I found by the river. By chance, I went into their hiding place in February, and found some pictures, books, papers, and a ragdoll. Her name really is, or was, Rachel."

"You thought enough of her to take her things?"

"They're just pictures, and I like the books. For some odd reason, I keep dreaming about her, drawing her, and even seeing her in the mirror. I hope I return to normal soon."

"There's usually a reason for someone to have recurring dreams, thoughts, and visions, particularly when they're of someone you only met briefly a few times. I think you have unfinished business with this girl, even if you don't realize it."

"She was probably deported to the East. She might be dead. I shouldn't feel a strange attraction to any girl after what happened to me. There's only room in my heart for one woman, and that's my mother. When I have to take a woman someday, I won't let her have all of my heart. I can't bear getting hurt again."

She rubbed his shoulders. "Maybe this is just the opposite. Perhaps God sent her into your path so she could help with healing you. Closing off your heart to love and only wanting to hate or be suspicious of everyone isn't good for you. Nothing ever happens by accident. If God tosses this woman into your path again, don't resist anything. Love is the most beautiful thing in the world, and after what you've been through, you deserve it more than anyone."

Part IV:

And Jakob Loved Rachel

(May 1945-May 1946)

Chapter 20: Heat Beneath His Winter

There it was. Westerbork, after two and a half years. The watchtowers, barbed wire, mud, and searchlights were all still there, but this time, the guards and overseers were in Allied custody, the residents were free, and the camp's train service was suspended forever. Best of all, this time Jakob was greeted with cheers from the survivors when he and his comrades were announced as Dutch soldiers.

His sense of euphoria and equilibrium broke when, quicker than he could react, a woman with long blonde curly hair flung herself on him and began crying onto his shoulder. He understood why he was being greeted like a conquering hero, but the camp had been liberated for a bit over a month. Surely the time for excessive emotional displays had been when the Canadians arrived.

"You have no idea what I've lived through! Thank God some of our own are finally here!"

"I was here too. I was deported in late November '42, but I jumped from the train." All he wanted was for this strange woman to pry herself off of him and go bother someone else. He'd come here to help the survivors and possibly find out what happened to Emilia, not to get accosted by strange women.

"You're a real Dutch Jewish soldier? Now I'm even gladder to see you! I've been here since November '43. It's such a tragic story of how my friends and I were captured in hiding. Thank God, two of them got away. I don't want to live here a single moment longer. I'm going to America as soon as I can. I have friends there, and I'm sure they'll vouch for me and say they'll support me till I find employment and enroll in university."

"Are you always this forward with strange men you've just met?"

"I'm forward with everyone. My parents taught me to always speak my mind no matter what the consequences."

Jakob looked down at her and felt a shortness of breath. This was the same girl he'd found by the river, the girl he'd drawn so many pictures of, spied on naked, and had numerous dreams about. He saw from the look in her eyes that she recognized him too. He was numb with embarrassment upon remembering how she spoke to him the one previous time they'd exchanged words. Decent girls never threatened to pull a respectable man's pants down to see what religion he was, and they certainly never laughed about such a scandalous thing.

"Rachel Roggenfelder?" he breathed.

"How do you know my name?"

"That's a long story. What kind of joker is God, to send me here and have me bump into you all over again? You have no idea how much annoyance you've caused me when you weren't even there. Now get out of my way. I have work to do."

Jakob pushed past her and walked through the rest of the camp grounds. Thousands upon thousands of people had been interned in this camp, yet now under a thousand remained. Most of the deportees were never coming back. In spite of a strong resistance, most of the Dutch Jewish community was no more. Hundreds of years of history and community, all but obliterated in the blink of an eye.

Most of the people he spoke to told him the same thing, over and over again. He'd heard the reports, but somehow he'd hoped it hadn't been so bad. So long as he hadn't known exactly what he'd escaped from, he couldn't know for sure things really would've been that bad. He remembered how terrifying it'd been. Every day was spent dreading and fearing the next deportation list. And still, as much as some people might very well resent him for his relatively good fortune, there could be no denying he'd suffered mightily too. How could they hate or blame him for escaping? As Rousseau said, no one calls the person who leaps out of a burning building a suicide.

Though he'd been there himself, nothing compared to the experiences of those who'd been there far longer than three months. Already he couldn't wait to get back to The Hague or Amsterdam so he could get his hands on more Nazis to kill. It would save the hangman a job.

For the first time, the enormity of what he'd escaped hit him. He'd heard the radio reports and read the newspapers, but didn't want to believe the rumors were true. What happened here was nothing next to what he'd heard about in Germany and Poland. Before he'd come on this assignment and taken Vrouw Visser home, he and his men had watched newsreels of the most horrific sights imaginable, the kinds of things that made the images of Hell in *The Divine Comedy* seem like the work of an amateur. Living beings resembling walking skeletons; gigantic ovens for burning bodies; piles of skeletal, diseased corpses; mountains of human hair and confiscated shoes, clothes, glasses, suitcases, crutches, gold teeth. If the reports going along with the images were to be believed, very few children and people over the age of forty or so were allowed to live more than a few hours past their arrival at these gigantic factories of Death.

Luisa had never looked her age, perhaps because she'd only had two children and hadn't had them till well into her reproductive lifetime, but she hadn't looked like a young woman either. Even with that smashing new haircut that had taken away any gray hairs, she couldn't completely disguise her true age. If anyone should've jumped from that train, it should've been Luisa. Jakob stood a fighting chance at being selected for labor, maybe even another cushy job in a kitchen.

The worst part was that he hadn't told her he loved her before he jumped. Luisa told him she loved him, but he hadn't told her. Now he'd never get back those final moments with his mother. When she wrote that letter in the morning, she hadn't known about the foul, evil kingdom of Auschwitz–Birkenau, where the natural laws of the universe were turned on their head and evil reigned over righteousness. And that was assuming she'd been on a train to Auschwitz. Some of those trains had been headed to Sobibór, where 99% of all deportees were immediately butchered. He thought of Elma, and wondered if that memory of their non-love first kiss had indeed kept her spirits alive in her final moments.

Emotionally overwhelmed, he sank down onto an outdoor bench that night and began sobbing. For the past four and a half years, since Ruud's murder, he'd kept everything bottled up so tightly inside, and made a wall not only outside his heart, but inside his entire being as well, so no one could get too close to him and reach him. Even the deep friendships he shared with Dries, Leendert, Govert, Jeronymus, and Vrouw Visser had their limits. He'd never let himself get so close to them he'd completely surrendered himself and made himself vulnerable. Now all these pent-up emotions came pouring out, until his whole body was violently shaking and his whole face, his neck, his hands were drenched with his salty tears.

He was mortified to see Rachel Roggenfelder appear beside him.

"Can't you find some other soldier to bother?" he choked out, tears still flowing copiously down his face. "Please don't tell any of my comrades you saw me like this."

"I won't tell them, though I don't think you're acting unmanly for crying. My parents taught me a woman can do anything a man can do, and vice versa. How could anyone not shed tears over what happened? Here, put your head on my shoulder." She took him into her arms. "Just let it all out, and you'll feel better, for the time being, at least."

He stiffened when she tried to take his hands to put his arms around her. "I wasn't raised Orthodox, but I've never made it a habit of embracing strange women."

"The shared experience of war and occupation has made everyone instant friends. People who've come together under such horrible circumstances feel drawn to one another. In normal time, it'd take years for such close friendships and romances to take hold, but these aren't normal times. And I'm not a complete stranger. You know my name's Rachel Roggenfelder, although I don't know your name."

"Lt. Jakob DeJonghe. I don't care about unusual circumstances; proper decorum should still be observed. My parents would've never approved of me taking a strange woman in my arms, and I don't think your parents would've either."

"Would you feel better sitting here alone all night, no one to comfort you in a moment of grief? I'm not family or even a friend, but wouldn't you rather have someone there to comfort you instead of mourning all alone? Will you grieve alone for the rest of your life?"

Too emotional to counter anything she said, he mutely submitted and put his arms around her in return. Deep down, he realized she was right. With one's entire family gone, one had to reach out to the nearest person for comfort and understanding. And he was somewhat flattered he'd been the soldier she'd flung herself at. Absentmindedly, he took in how nice and soft her body was.

Jakob woke up in the morning to find himself lying on the bench, a blanket draped over him and a pillow under his head. When he went to stand up, he momentarily forgot about his gimpy foot and began to push off with his right foot. He sat back down again quickly to massage it, then set off hopping for the hospital. The face of every young child was that of Emilia; the face of every older man was his father; and the face of every woman was his mother. Once again overwhelmed by emotions, he had to step outside for some air and to get away from this nonstop reminder of his recent past and everything that had been lost. He almost leapt out of his skin to find Rachel Roggenfelder walking towards him.

"Did you sleep well? You wore yourself out from sobbing and fell right asleep, so I put you into a sleeping position and got you a blanket and a pillow."

"I'm going to ask to be transferred back to my brigade as soon as possible. I can't handle this. I must go back to The Hague, and as soon as I've been given my honorable discharge, I'm leaving this country. I love The Netherlands and will always be proud of how I served our country, but this is no longer really home after so many people were murdered. I'll always wonder who was in the Resistance, who was in the NSB, and who was a silent collaborator. Is there anywhere I can just sit down and be alone?"

"I feel the same way. The sooner I leave this foul place, the better. Hopefully I won't have to spend years on a waiting list. I don't want to be on Dutch soil a moment longer than I have to either." She began to lead the way, but when she saw he was lagging behind because of his limpy gait, she slipped her arm through his to help to steady him. "May I ask why you're limping? Were you wounded in battle?"

He cast his eyes in the direction of the train tracks. "I jumped off of a train heading East and landed very, very hard on my right foot. Thank God, I was found by four partisans. They took me to a nearby safe house, and a doctor in the underground was brought into the house to set the bones. It was too risky to go to a hospital. Who knows, perhaps if I'd had surgery, I might be walking normally today."

She helped him down onto her mattress. "Think of it as a battle wound. It gives you character. You're not like everyone else. It's like being *linkshandig* or mute. Some might think such a person is a freak or deserving of mockery, but you know you're special and in very select company. My parents taught me being different is something great, no matter how many ordinary people might be afraid of differences." She sighed. "I went into hiding almost immediately after the invasion, and don't know what happened to my parents. I was told they were deported a few months before I came here. So were my other relatives. Now I have nobody."

"What about friends?"

She sank down next to him and leaned against him. "I don't know what happened to them. Juli, Zippi, and Dani were deported last February, and Greetje left two months later. I was too busy avoiding the weekly list to relax enough to get to know anyone. But I have friends in America. They immigrated in 1938 and live in Atlantic City. They'll be glad to hear I'm alive, but they'll never understand, since they didn't go through it."

He let her talk on aimlessly about her life before the war, her experiences in hiding, the shock and fear of being captured, the fear and indignity of Westerbork, never being able to fully let down her guard, and the slow, sick realization that everyone she'd ever cared about was gone and would never be coming back. True to what he'd surmised from her parents' inscription in the Shakespeare volume, she came from a family very similar to his, parents who taught her progressive ideas, who embraced progressive politics and affiliated with the Progressive Movement. She'd wanted to help her fellow inmates after the liberation, but quickly got depressed and overwhelmed because the suffering was everywhere, and she couldn't get away from it unless she left The Netherlands. Without really meaning to or knowing what he was doing, he put his arm around her as she emotionally babbled on. When he was summoned back to the hospital late in the afternoon, he patted her on the head before leaving.

2

The next morning, he showed up, unasked, at her barracks. "I came to tell you I'm very sorry for how rude I was to you." He smiled shyly, then assumed a stoneface. It was still too early to let his guard completely down.

"I understand why you acted and spoke that way. Some of these people are even angrier and more distant."

"It wouldn't be fair for you to tell me so much about yourself if I didn't return the favor. I've told my comrades something about what I went through, but they weren't here. They could never understand or relate to it."

He sat down, and the words began pouring out, years of pent-up pain, frustration, heartache, fear, and rage. He told her about his own prewar life; the terrible first two years of the occupation; the murder of his father; his escape from the train; his time hiding in Vrouw Visser's house; his early frustration over not being able to walk normally; his proud days as a partisan; how he'd taken his revenge on Ruud's murderers; his even prouder days as a member of the Princess Irene Brigade, an officially-recognized soldier, in uniform, with an official rank, no longer just a resistance fighter; and his hopes for rebuilding a life after the war.

As he took his leave of her, Jakob felt a strange sensation he'd never felt before. If he didn't know any better, he had butterflies in his stomach. When he looked back at her, his heart skipped a beat, and he felt a gnawing, aching yearning to immediately go back there and sit with her. He stuffed his hands into his pockets to hide his sweating palms. It really was true that after being left alone in the world, he had no choice but to reach out to the nearest person. All he cared about was she'd been through the same thing he had, and understood where he was coming from.

In normal time, these friendships and romances he'd witnessed so many of would never have begun after a matter of days, but with such heightened emotions, niceties were no longer required. People needed to create new families and circles of friends as soon as possible. They were lonely. Interpersonal relationships developed at lightning speed. People no longer took years, even months, before feeling comfortable intimately opening up to people who were little more than strangers. Human life had to carry on one way or another, and everyone felt extraordinarily close to one another because of such an intense, painful shared experience.

When he was back at his headquarters that evening, he realized he had to give her back her things. And he had to tell her he'd constantly been thinking of her ever since he'd found her by the riverbank. Maybe he should man up and tell her about how he spied on her naked. But in spite of the abnormally fast rate at which these friendships and romances were blossoming, he still had to consider propriety. Any decent man who wanted a respectable woman to be his lady had to spend a little time courting her first.

3

During his lunch break the next day, he took a walk outside the camp. He smiled every time he saw someone with a bald orange head. These cowardly collaborators were publicly marked even more humiliatingly than he'd been marked. At least he could take off that damned star. They couldn't grow their hair back and wash out the orange paint overnight. The sight of the women in particular repulsed him. What was so wrong with native Dutchmen they'd bedded down with Germans?

He tried to concentrate on his purpose for taking this walk. He was picking crocuses, purple heather, and colored daisies. Those seemed like flowers Rachel would like. He didn't have the heart to pick any tulips. After the heartbreaking massacres of tulip bulbs over the *Hongerwinter*, they deserved to grow free and beautiful all over The Netherlands and never be picked or eaten ever again.

Rachel looked up from reading the newspaper when she saw Jakob standing in front of her, holding a bouquet. He tried not to smile, though he wanted with everything in him to smile at her the way he'd smiled at the people of The Hague during the victory parade.

"Did you pick those flowers for me?"

"I hope you like them, Mejuffrouw. Consider them a goodwill offering."

She stood up to take them, but he held onto them. "If they're such a goodwill offering, why won't you let me have them? And please don't call me Mejuffrouw. It makes me feel like a first grade teacher or old maid. We're both nineteen, and last time I checked, peers address each other by name, not titles."

"I was just trying to be polite. And I have a confession to make first. If I confessed when you were holding the flowers, you might hit me with them."

"What in the world do you need to confess after only a few days? You didn't have anything to do with my capture, did you?"

"Oh, no, Mejuffrouw." He blushed slightly when he realized he'd used the honorific again. "I was very upset when one of my buddies found a diary from the jerk who arrested you and your friends. It's just that I sort of saw you when you were bathing in the river, and I didn't look away." He ducked and held his arms over his head.

Rachel began laughing. "I know you spied on me naked. I saw you. I figured it was probably the first time a guy like you ever saw that sight, and I wanted you to enjoy it. So what did you think?"

"So you routinely exhibit yourself to strangers?"

"Only to you. Did you like my body? Not even my one serious boyfriend Pietje saw me naked."

"I don't think there's a right answer to that question. If I say yes, you'll be offended I was lusting after you with my eyes, but if I say no, you'll be offended I didn't think you were attractive."

She pulled the flowers out of his hands. "Smart boy. Maybe while you're still here, I'll have a chance to spy on you naked." She laughed as he limped away in mortification.

4

The next evening, Jakob showed up at her barracks with his schoolbag and a tissue paper parcel. He felt himself melting when Rachel gave him a little smile, and the butterflies in his stomach were more intense than ever. He wanted so badly to touch her, but it wasn't respectable yet. First he had to win her affections and make sure she had feelings for him too.

"I made you something in the restaurant. I used to work there, and I was the cook for my partisan group. My mother made this all the time. It'll cure what ails you."

Rachel unwrapped the parcel and found a stack of cookies. "That was very thoughtful of you."

"They're honey and cinnamon. I would've made you chocolate, but that's not available. Here, I have some other things for you. They're not really presents, since they're already yours. I'm just giving them back to you."

She set the cookies down and burst into tears when she saw the ragdoll he pulled out of the bag. A surge of electricity went through his body when she flung her arms around him and kissed him on the cheek. He felt his face tingling, and definitely not the way he felt his hand tingling after Queen Wilhelmina shook it.

"How in the world did you find this? I lost everything when I was picked up, and wasn't allowed to go back to my hiding place to pack! I never thought I'd see my old doll ever again, and that some spoilt German child was playing with her! You're an angel, Jaapje!"

He smiled to hear her calling him by a diminutive. It must mean she felt very comfortable with him already. "I found a place to hide while waiting for one of my grenades to go off in February. I saw these books and papers, and when I lifted the doll off one of the books, I saw a picture of you and Juli inside. That's how I knew your name, from the inscription on the back. The fellow in the other picture, was he one of the guys you were hiding with?"

Rachel hugged the doll very tightly. "I assume you mean Pietje. His real name's Otto, but he goes by Barry in America now. I always wondered why his parents insisted on giving their kids new names every time they changed countries. Everyone always mispronounces his American name. They assume it's pronounced with a short A. He was my first and only serious boyfriend, my first and only love, and I was very upset when he immigrated. We kept in touch, but we agreed it'd be stupid, at only twelve years old, to continue our relationship long-distance. I dated some other guys in the next two years, but none of them for very long. Pietje wasn't the first boy I kissed, but he was the only guy to touch my breasts. My parents would've been scandalized, even as modern as they were, had they known I was doing that with a boy at twelve years old."

He felt twinges of jealously. "Is this Otto person, or Pieter, or whatever his name is now, one of those American friends you mentioned?"

She nodded. "When I get permission to immigrate, I'll stay with his family. I assume he has a new girlfriend by now. Perhaps he's married. I'm certainly not in love with him after seven years apart."

"What if he's been pining away for you all this time? My namesake waited fourteen years to marry the love of his life."

"This is the twentieth century. Why, are you jealous of him?"

"No, just curious." He pulled the books out of his bag one by one, then set the stack of papers on the mattress. "I didn't read your letters, or diary, or whatever's in these papers."

"Those are mostly Juli's. She was always writing love letters to her long-distance boyfriend, Pietje's older brother. That's how we became friends, because we were dating brothers. Juli's two years my senior."

"Oh. Maybe you should reunite with your boyfriend, so you and your best friend can become sisters-in-law." He stood up and put the bag back over his shoulders. "Enjoy the rest of your day, Mejuffrouw."

5

Over the next two days, Jakob found excuses to bump into Rachel or walk by her while acting like he hadn't noticed her. Every time he saw her, his heartrate quickened, and he felt that strange gnawing in the pit of his stomach. He went to nearby shops on his breaks and bought her chocolates, candied fruit slices, silk stockings, perfume, and scented lotion, under the guise of giving her things to make her feel better. When they took walks at night, he kept his hands in his pockets. As badly as he wanted to hold her hand, he'd be given away by his shaking, sweating hand.

Every night since he'd been back at Westerbork, he'd had nightmares about the jump from the train, and seeing the bluish dead bodies of his mother, Gusta, Kees, Elma, the Antemas, Juli, Debora, Sander, even Luuk, their mouths frozen in horrific screams. Even in dreams, he couldn't bring himself to picture his mother or any of his friends naked. He always awoke sweating bullets and screaming at the moment his mother's body was loaded into the oven. He wondered if she hated him from the other world for not telling her he loved her in their final moments.

"If I really like a girl, how long should I wait to tell her?" he asked one of his brigade friends as they took a walk after lunch. It was now the fifth day after he became friends with Rachel.

"The blonde with green eyes?"

"You *know*?"

"She probably does too, the way you look at her like a lovesick puppy. And what man gets a woman presents all the time and finds excuses to see her if he doesn't like her?"

"But it's only been about a week, not counting the times we met before. I won't be here forever, and she wants to go to America. She didn't wait for her previous boyfriend. Besides, this is probably just lust."

"No one ever starts out really loving a person. It's always lust in the beginning. Real love only develops over years, but most people don't wait that long to declare their love or get married. If you like her that much, you'll mark her as yours before you go your separate ways. It's nice to have someone to get letters from when you're away at war. I'm going to the Dutch East Indies after this, and my tour of duty will be so much more bearable with my wife writing to me."

Jakob's heart began racing at the thought of being put on another frontline. It couldn't take until February to adequately clean up the mess left by the Nazis. Perhaps he too would find himself deployed again, only this time facing off against the Japanese. He pictured himself dying on the battlefield, in agony not over his wounds but because he never told either his mother or the girl of his dreams he loved her when he still had the chance.

It was now or never. That night, as they were counting stars, Jakob slipped his violently shaking arm around her and pulled her towards him, then wrapped his other arm around her, leaned down to her height, and kissed her. Rachel seemed to sense he didn't really know what he was doing, and he gratefully let her take over and teach him. He let his mouth become soft, pliant, and passive against hers as she demonstrated the techniques she liked. After awhile, he became emboldened enough to try imitating her, while still letting her lead. His only active role was running his hands through her hair and along her face. He was burning with desire to touch a lot more than just her hair and face, but respectable people never went from nothing to everything overnight.

His whole body was shaking when he finally released her and gazed into her eyes. "I love you," he blurted out.

Before Rachel had time to respond, he pulled her back into his arms and began kissing her again. Once more he let her dominate him, glad at least one of them knew how to kiss properly. There were so many different factors that had to come together in just the right way, but there was no time to think them all through in the heat of the moment. As jealous as he was of her prior boyfriends, he was glad she had experience.

"I love you too, my beautiful Jaap," she whispered after he released her the second time. "I've had feelings for you almost since I saw you last week, and maybe even since our first meeting when we didn't know each other's names. Something deep inside of me told me I'd be able to break down those walls you'd put around your heart. I looked through your sketchpad the other day, and saw so many drawings of me. You must've had a funny feeling about me too."

He squeezed her hands. "I've been constantly dreaming about you, thinking about you, having visions of you in the mirror, and drawing you. My previous sketchbook had pictures of you too. I just couldn't admit to myself till this week I was in love with you."

"You don't have to be afraid anymore. Your beautiful heart is safe in my hands, now, forever, and always. And you're the most beautiful man I've ever seen. I love dark hair and eyes."

"You really think I have a beautiful heart? After how gruff and distant I've been to you?"

"Of course I do. Maybe there really is such a thing as woman's intuition. I can tell you're a very sweet person when you feel safe letting your guard down. A lot of soldiers like to present themselves as tough guys, men's men, but you have a gentle soul. And you kiss in a very sweet, innocent way. Maybe tomorrow, if you're a good boy, I'll teach you how to use your tongue."

Jakob hoped she couldn't see him blushing in the dark. Part of him was excited she wanted to give him a lesson on more advanced techniques, but the other half of him still couldn't believe how forward she was, almost like a man trapped in a woman's body. He walked her back to her barracks and said goodbye at the door. As he walked back to headquarters, he had a spring in his step and couldn't stop smiling.

6

The next afternoon, he came to her barracks with a fancy leather suitcase he'd just bought. Her name was embossed in gold, and it had dark green velvet trim matching her eyes. He smiled at her and watched her face for approval as he presented it.

"So your idea of romance is buying a girl a suitcase the day after you first profess your love."

His face fell and he shoved his hands into his pockets. "I'm sorry, Mejuffrouw, if I offended you. Please accept my apologies. I just wanted you to have something nice for your trip to America, since you didn't come here with any luggage."

Rachel jumped up and hugged him. "Come sit with me, Jaapetje. I was only joking with you. I guess you don't understand sarcastic humor. Boy, are you a sensitive one. If only your Army buddies knew how soft you really are."

He took a seat. "So you do like it?"

"It's beautiful. I can't wait to put my things in it." She leaned over and kissed him. "Does that make you feel better?"

He smiled shyly and caressed her hands. "Your hands are so soft, like silk. They're so gentle and kind."

"Wait'll you touch other parts of my body." She smiled devilishly. "You probably never touched a girl's breasts, did you?"

He shook his head, hoping he didn't look too happy at the prospect. He didn't want Rachel to think he were a crazed sex fiend who just wanted to have his way with the first woman he'd had a chance with in a long time.

"Maybe I'll let you touch mine eventually. Don't worry, I'll teach you what I like. I can even teach you how I like to be touched—"

"I think that's enough graphic talk for now. And I thought you hadn't gone that far with that one guy."

"I guess you're not familiar with self-gratification either. You'll probably be like a kid in a candy store if you're my fellow long enough to do those things."

He shifted in his seat, very uncomfortable with the direction this conversation was taking. "I really came here to recite poetry to you. Do you think Shakespeare would turn over in his grave if I recited one of his sonnets with the sexes and pronouns mixed up?"

"I don't see why not. Popular songs switch them all the time, like if a man sings a song originally sung by a woman. The beauty of Shakespeare is how timeless and universal he was."

He took a deep breath and closed his eyes, picturing the words of Sonnet 145 on the gold-leafed page of Rachel's book. His voice trembled as he haltingly recalled the words written several centuries ago, making sure to put in the correct substituted words.

"Those lips that Love's own hand did make
"Breathed forth the sound that said 'I hate'
"To you that languished for my sake.
"But when I saw your woeful state,
"Straight in my heart did mercy come,
"Chiding that tongue that, ever sweet,
"Was used in giving gentle doom,
"And taught it thus anew to greet:
"'I hate' I altered with an end
"That followed it as gentle day
"Doth follow night, who like a fiend
"From heaven to hell is flown away.
"'I hate' from hate away I threw,
"And saved my life, saying 'not you.'"

Rachel caressed his face. "I can see why that sonnet spoke to you. You really think I saved your life?"

"In a way. I don't know how much longer I could've gone living only for myself and not letting anyone into my heart. If someone had told me a year ago that the next time I met you, I would've fallen so quickly for you, I would've laughed in his face. But maybe I already loved you, and was too proud or scared to admit it. Can you please forgive me for being too proud to give myself to you sooner? I wish I'd approached you while you were still safe in hiding. Maybe you could've joined my partisan band and been spared all this. Thank God you avoided every deportation list for a year and a half."

"Ten months," she corrected him. "The last train left in September."

"However long you had to live in fear, it was too long. God must really want us to be together if we crossed paths by chance twice. I promise you, my sweet Gepje, I'll make up for all that lost time, and make the remainder of my time here worth your while."

7

The next afternoon on his break, Jakob hitched a ride into Hooghalen and walked around the town till he found a jewelry store. He'd already told his superior his plans, and had gotten permission to be out longer than usual on break.

His heart beat a little faster as he walked into the store and looked around. Buying an engagement ring was serious business, and perhaps foolhardy after less than two weeks of being properly acquainted. Even if Rachel understood the need to bond and pair off at lightning-speed in these abnormal times, she might not be warmed-up to the idea of getting engaged so soon. A modern woman like that might insist on at least a few months of courtship, even if she saw the need to skip a lengthy prologue to couplehood.

"May I help you, soldier?" the manager asked. "Take as much time as you like to make your purchase. Everyone is so grateful to our soldiers for how they helped to save us from those damned Nazis. We can't thank you enough for your service. Were you one of the ones who fled to England, or did you join after our Army came back to the continent?"

"I'm glad you appreciate what I did. I officially joined the Resistance in June '43, and my friends and I were accepted into the Princess Irene Brigade in February. You should've seen me when we crossed the River Maas at the end of last month. I was like an animal, shooting and bayoneting Nazis right and left."

The manager inspected his insignia. "I'm sorry, but I'm not good with what decorations stand for which ranks. At most, I'm guessing you're a little higher than a private with all those decorations."

"I'm a lieutenant," Jakob said proudly. "And I got the Bronze Lion, the Order of Orange–Nassau, and the Order of Willem. Well, my whole brigade got the Order of Willem, but I reckon I would've gotten it on my own anyway."

The manager looked at him in awe. "You're a national hero, Lieutenant. How old are you? You look rather young to have that rank already."

"I just turned nineteen the day after V-E Day. My comrades and I rode into The Hague on my birthday. That was the greatest birthday present I ever got."

"You're welcome to have whatever you want for practically free. Consider it my gift for your service to our country. I'd be honored to let a member of the Orders of Willem and Orange–Nassau patronize my business, and I'd never dream of making such a national hero pay full-price or even half-price. You deserve only the best after all the sacrifices you made for us."

"Please, let me pay full-price. A lot of merchants have given me things for deeply discounted prices, and I feel bad taking so much away from them. You all deserve as much money as you can make after how you suffered."

"But you're the national hero who put his life on the line to save us. I insist. What are you in the market for, by the way, and who is it for?"

He blushed slightly. "It's sort of an engagement ring. I met this girl a year and a half ago and couldn't stop thinking about her, and then I met her again not even two weeks ago. She's such a perfect match for me, it's unbelievable. I never thought I'd want to marry anyone who was little more than a stranger, but we don't have time for long courtships after what happened. She's at Westerbork, and I was a former prisoner there myself. We have no one left, at least not that we know of. We have to make our own new family as soon as my year of service is up. God in heaven, I can't wait to make her my bride or for her to bring my child into this world." He abruptly stopped talking. "I'm sorry, I'm just babbling. You probably don't care about all that."

"If you're both survivors of that damned transit camp, you doubly-deserve to pay almost nothing. What kind of stone do you think she'd like, and what kind of band?"

He browsed the rings in the glass display cases. "I don't know anything about bands, but I think yellow gold might look better on her. She's a blonde. And her eyes are such a beautiful dark green. She might like an emerald, to match her eyes."

"What's her birthstone?"

"I don't know anything about birthstones, but her birthday's in March."

"Perfect. The aquamarine. That can be green, though it's usually a lighter shade. The usual color is blue. What size would you like, and what shape?"

He pondered this for a few moments. "She's not the type of girl who'd want a big gaudy stone, but she's not the type who'd be happy with something really delicate and tiny. And she probably would like something in a circle or oval. I don't mind blue, if I like that color more than the green."

The manager looked through the rings on display and finally went into the inventory room. Jakob browsed the fancy watches, diamond rings, bracelets, and necklaces while waiting. During this time, several people entered the store and thanked him for his service. As proud as he was of serving, this seemed a little overkill. He'd done the right thing because it was the right thing, not because he wanted total strangers to treat him like a superhuman hero.

"Here you go," the manager announced after he returned. "Our only green aquamarine in stock. It's probably the darkest green specimen you can find without paying thousands of guilders. It's not real green, but blue-green seems close enough."

Jakob's eyes lit up. "It's beautiful! I'm sure she'll love it! How much is the asking price?"

"The pricetag was for five thousand guilders, but for a brave soldier like you, I'll let you have it for ten."

"Ten! That's a huge loss you're taking! I don't have nearly that much money, but I have more than ten guilders. Can I buy it on credit or IOU? I promise I'll pay for it in full within a year."

"I insist. Our soldiers deserve deep discounts. I'll put it in a nice box and wrap it in pretty paper, and you can give me ten guilders. You both deserve every nice thing in the world after what you've gone through. I wish you a good, long, happy life with your intended, and good luck on the rest of your military service."

8

The next afternoon, Jakob received a telegram. He felt waves of sadness as he read it. Now three more people who were dear to him were far away, and he wasn't so sure he wanted to join them.

Dear Jaap,

We (Leendert, Jeronymus, and Govert) have asked to be transferred to the Dutch East Indies so we can see more combat during our term of service. There's nothing disreputable about serving our country in a noncombatant peacetime posi-

tion, but we joined so late, we have a lot of battles to make up for. When you get done with your assignment, we'd love for you to join us. Dries is still in the hospital and probably won't be able to join us anytime soon. You can take Ben with you too if you'd like. We could always use a good war dog.

Best regards,
Your brothers-in-arms

"Did you hear?" one of the other soldiers asked. "There's a ship leaving from Terneuzen in a few days. Priority is being given to wives and children of Allied soldiers. A few refugees are also going, if they can prove their connection to people in America. Maybe your new girlfriend would like to go. You said she has American friends."

"Her former boyfriend's family. I wish she knew other people."

"That doesn't sound like a good idea, but maybe nothing funny will happen. Perhaps her old boyfriend has gone away to university or gotten married."

"Did you give her the ring yet?" another soldier asked. "She'll have higher priority if she's your real wife, not just a fiancée or friend of Americans."

"She'll get benefits for being your legal wife," a third soldier said. "If God forbid the worst happened to you, she'd get a widow's pension. She has no family left. This is an excellent way to ensure she's taken care of when you're away from her."

"I can't do that. Who gets married within days of engagement unless the woman's in trouble? And it's not right to make a bride be apart from her husband for so long."

"You can always do a more formal ceremony later. Everyone does it that way. First you get married civilly, and then you have a religious ceremony. She can wear a real gown then, and you can have a fancy party afterwards. Best of all, you'll have someone to write you letters and make you feel wanted."

Jakob scratched Ben behind the ears. "Couldn't she just stay here waiting for me instead of in a foreign country?"

"You said she's desperate to immigrate, and I don't say I blame her. Do the right thing, and we'll see to it she gets on that ship."

9

That evening, just before the light started fading from the sky, Jakob took Rachel on one of their walks outside the camp. It always felt good to get away from the atmosphere of Westerbork, even after liberation. This time, Ben went along on their walk. During Jakob's assignment, he hadn't spent much personal time with his dog, and had let Ben cheer up the survivors and help to heal them with his special animal energy.

Jakob stuffed his hands in his pockets and dragged his feet. Right now, he was more terrified than when he'd fought at Hedel or crossed the River Maas. He almost wished he could dive back into his combat fatigues and helmet and go back to the battle for the bridgehead.

"Gepje, is it okay if I discuss something serious with you?"

"Since when do we discuss things that aren't serious? Have you forgotten ours isn't a normal courtship?"

"I think my assignment here is ending soon, and you want to go to America. I found out there's a ship leaving from Terneuzen soon, and you can get on it with my help. Would you like to go and wait for me while I'm still in service? I'll write you letters if you write me letters."

"Sure I'll keep in touch with you. I like you enough to be your long-distance sweetheart. I wasn't old or serious enough to do that when Pietje moved away. That is, if you don't cavort around with women while I'm thousands of kilometers away."

"Of course not! I'd never sleep with a woman I wasn't really serious about!"

"You're an uncommon soldier. I hope you stay true to your ideals when you're back in action. If you couldn't stop thinking about me before you even really knew me, you'll think about me even more after we've gotten to know each other."

He struggled against his tied tongue, trying desperately to push out coherent words and speech. "You know, when I was little, I built the most beautiful snowman with my parents. I was so proud of my work, I never wanted to give it up. When the snow melted, I was so sad and couldn't believe my lovely friend was gone forever. Now all my friends and relatives are like my snowman, lost forever. Even if a few come back, it won't be like it was before. I don't want you to be like the snowman. I've lost so many people, and you're the only one who knows what I've gone through. Can you please, please promise me you'll be faithful to me after we're apart? I'd just about want to die if I were alone again and lost my dream girl twice."

"What's gotten into you? You never make speeches like this. Is this a preview of the kind of love letters you're going to send me?"

Jakob fell onto his knees and hugged Rachel's legs, resting his head against her soft midsection, the way he remembered Rudolph Valentino doing it in one of the silent films Ruud had taken him to see at the film festivals they used to frequent. He felt like a happy little boy when Rachel gently stroked his hair.

"Please, Gepje, *mijn liefje*, you're the only woman I ever want to kiss, hold, touch, or be with for the rest of my life. Will you please, please, please, please, please, please, please take away my loneliness and be my wife?"

"Did you just ask me to marry you?"

"I can't imagine any other woman I'd want to be with for the rest of my life. Please, please, please take away my sorrow and be my beautiful bride."

The seconds seemed to drag on for years as Rachel remained quiet. He felt like his heart was about to tear out of his chest when he finally heard her start to speak.

"I love you more than I've ever loved a man, my sweet Jaapetje. I'd love to marry you, but only on one condition. You have to promise to respect this condition instead of only pretending to because you're so desperate to marry me."

"What is it, *mijn liefje*? I'll promise you anything if it means you'll be my beautiful bride, the mother of my children, and my partner in life!"

"As you know, I'm from a very progressive family. And as you know from my parents' inscription in the Shakespeare book, I have my mother's name. I was born a Roggenfelder, I survived as a Roggenfelder, and I'll die a Roggenfelder. Even if the Dutch custom is for women to keep their names, unlike American women, it's not necessarily the custom for couples to favor the wife's name for their children. You have to promise me any children of ours will be Roggenfelders, not DeJonghes."

"Of course! They'll be Roggenfelders no matter what! It's no fun having the most common Dutch surname, even if my family spells it a little differently. Is that all you wanted me to agree to?"

"Stand up. A brave soldier like you shouldn't be groveling on his knees like a child or a royal subject. If I'm going to be your wife, I want to be your equal, not your master. Even if women are superior to men, you shouldn't grovel before me."

"Did you just say—"

"God made man before woman, since you always make the rough draft first. Men and women might be equals in most ways, but in other ways, women are superior. Do you still want to marry me after you know my feelings on the matter?"

He nodded. "Yes, Gepje. I'll let you be my boss, as long as you're a nice boss." He reached into his pocket and extended the wrapped box. "This is for you. I hope you like it."

Rachel pulled off the tissue paper and put it in her pocket. Her eyes sparkled in the twilight when she saw the uncommon green aquamarine. "This is beautiful! It's just the kind of gemstone and ring I like! Not too plain and not too fancy, and best of all an original stone. Is it peridot? I know this isn't emerald."

"Aquamarine, your birthstone." He gently took the box out of her hands, pulled the ring out, and slipped it onto her finger. "Now everyone will know you're my woman and no one else's."

Rachel grabbed his face in her hands, pulled him down to her level, and kissed him. His whole body tingled when she slithered her tongue into his mouth, and he felt emboldened to slip his hands under her blouse. Even better, she didn't pull away from him or slap him. If they'd been in their own house, he would've seriously considered carrying her to the nearest bed or sofa to purge himself of all his pent-up sexual energy.

"That's enough for one day," he heard her murmuring. "Save the rest of me to unwrap later. If you do everything at once, you don't have any anticipation, and you won't appreciate it as much. I'm a good girl, even if I am a modern woman."

He nodded, his whole body still shaking with desire. "It'll be forever till you're my bride and I can make love to you."

"Oh, you probably won't have to wait that long." She smiled as she slipped her arm through his and started walking back to her barracks. "Just because I'm a good girl doesn't mean I want to be a wedding-night virgin. I already broke my hymen through self-gratification, so you don't have to worry you'll hurt me."

He turned bright red. "Is this the kind of talk I have to get used to?"

"You know I talk about lots of other things. You still want to marry me, don't you? The way you were just pawing at me, I'd think you'd been wanting to do that since you first saw me."

"Did I ever."

She paused in front of her doorway. "Goodnight, my brave soldier. I'll see you tomorrow, when we can make more plans about a wedding date and where we'll live till that ship leaves and your assignment ends."

"I love you, my beautiful Gepje. Now, always, and forever."

"I love you too, my darling Jaapje."

10

Jakob stood quaking in front of the marriage registrar at the Winschoten registry office. After being informed Rachel couldn't get on that ship unless she were his legal wife, he'd broken the news to her, and she'd nervously agreed to immediately get married. The officials had agreed to expedite the marriage process under their circumstances, and understood why Rachel only had her passport and Jakob only had military identification to prove their identities. Now, only two days after they'd gotten engaged, they were already getting married. Vrouw Visser and three of Jakob's army buddies on the Westerbork assignment were the witnesses. There was a huge lump in his throat knowing his mother wasn't there, nor Dries, Leendert, Govert, or Jeronymus.

Rachel gently nudged him. "Jaap, you're being asked if you'll take me as your wife."

He swallowed, trying to get rid of the lump in his throat, but it was still there. "Yes, I take Rachel Susanna Roggenfelder to be my legal wife, in sickness and health, in riches and poverty, and forsake all others for her sake, so long as I'm alive."

His mind was far away as Rachel made her vow and the marriage registrar presented the rings. He had to be nudged again when it was time to take the ring, put it on Rachel's finger, and say the words of the ring vow. All he could think about was that he was marrying someone he barely knew, and hoped this impulsive decision was worth it. He jumped a little when he felt cold metal being pushed onto his finger. The last time he'd had cold metal on his skin had been when the balding Nazi measured his skull.

"Congratulations, Lt. DeJonghe, Vrouw Roggenfelder. I now pronounce you husband and wife."

Jakob quickly kissed Rachel, a little embarrassed to do something so personal with an audience. Afterwards, he shook everyone's hands and let Vrouw Visser hug him. Then they posed for a few pictures on the steps of the registry office, and it was over. No chupah, no ketubah, no seven blessings, no broken glass, no wedding dress, no circling seven times, nothing to mark this as a Jewish wedding. All they had were a marriage certificate and some pictures that would be rushed through development.

Jakob felt like he were arriving at his funeral when they checked into a hotel that evening. In the morning, he was being sent to Amsterdam, and Rachel would be going to Terneuzen. He wanted with every fiber of his being to set upon her like a raging tiger, but he couldn't bear the thought of creating a child who might be half-orphaned. The prospect of being sent to the Dutch East Indies was very real, as evidenced by the telegram. And without a ketubah, it seemed wrong to consummate a marriage.

He looked away guiltily when Rachel emerged from the bathroom and let her towel fall to the floor. He longed to devour her with his eyes, but had to withstand temptation for a noble cause.

"What's wrong? You act like you've never seen me naked before." She climbed onto his lap and pulled on the sash of his robe. "I know you know what happens on a wedding night. You're not that sweet and innocent."

"I can't do this. Not now. There's a chance I could be asked to go to the Indies, and what if I were killed? I don't want to create an orphan. Maybe if I were more experienced and not a virgin, I'd know how to, you know, have enough knowledge and self-control to, uh, abruptly end things before they get to that point. I don't think you have a diaphragm, and I probably wouldn't know how to use prophylactics even if I had them."

"Not everyone gets pregnant the first time, or any given time. I want to know all of you, the way a woman knows a man. There's no sin if you love each other, even if there's no religious marriage."

"I wish I could, but I can't. Even if you didn't become pregnant, we'd have that experience. If we remain virgins, we might long for it, but we won't know exactly what we're missing. We might be driven crazy by wanting something we can't have. I swear to you I'll be a very good boy while we're apart, just like I trust you'll be a good girl and not do anything with that former boyfriend in America." He tried to push her hands away. "So, how are you getting to Terneuzen, *mijn liefje?* I don't think there are that many trains running in this area."

"I'll go on foot until I can find a train that is running, and if I find no trains, I can always hitch rides, particularly with soldiers."

Jakob held her close. "Don't you know how some soldiers behave? You can go with Vrouw Visser in a cab. She'll take care of you. I don't want any other man putting his hands on you. If anyone does, he'll meet the same fate as the three degenerates who murdered my father."

"Fine, if you insist. In the meantime, would you like to put your hands on me?"

"Yes, but I just told you why I can't. I don't think I could control myself if I started. I'd want to touch all of you, and then you might find yourself a mother."

"Give yourself more credit. If you want to know, there are other ways to have a sexual experience." She grabbed his hand and guided it along her body. "Go on, try to bring me to ecstasy with other parts of your body."

"I don't know how!"

"That's how you learn. Don't forget I'm a virgin too, even if I've touched myself. Look what I've got for you to play with, my handsome soldier."

Jakob turned into a gigantic smile at the sight of her hidden treasure. "Do all women have that?"

"Of course. That's how God wanted to make us. You look like a kid in a candy store. Come on, show me you know how to please a woman in ways that don't involve intercourse."

"I get to do whatever I want to you?"

"Within reason. Now let's have some semblance of a real wedding night. Afterwards, I'll give you your own treat, if you know what I mean."

"Your wish is my command!"

11

In the morning, Jakob put his robe back on and went into the bathroom to wash up. He wished he could invite Rachel for a bubble-bath, but that would make both of them late. When he came out, he found her already dressed and sitting at the little table.

"Do you still respect me, after you saw and touched all of me?" she whispered, lowering her eyes. "I don't consider myself a virgin anymore, even if we didn't actually couple."

"Of course I still respect my beautiful bride. I'd never do that with anyone I didn't respect." He sat down and caressed her hands. "I knew from overhearing my buddies, but I never realized I could produce that reaction in a woman. I wish we could do that all over again right now."

"At least you overheard people. I didn't know I'd move around like that or make those noises. I wish I didn't have to go back to touching myself so soon after being touched by a man. Did you realize you sounded like a panting wolf in heat when I was pleasuring you?"

"You sounded like a drunken money in heat," he teased. "I'll remember those noises for a long time to come."

"Will you remember anything else?"

"Yeah. Your elixir tastes like ambrosia."

She blushed. "I'm glad we'll be out of here before the maid comes. She'll know what we did when she sees the sheets."

"So? Newlyweds are supposed to do that. Damn, if it was that much fun without coupling, I can only imagine how much fun our real wedding night will be. I'll come to you fresh as a knight entering the battlefield."

"Sixth story of the third day of *The Decameron*," she smiled. "There are so many great dirty puns and double entendres in there. Next time we're together, I can't wait to put the Devil back into Hell."

They ate in silence, not exchanging looks. After breakfast, Jakob dumped the dishes in the sink and packed up his things, avoiding any looks at Rachel's body. It was against halacha to make newlyweds separate when the husband was in the military, but they lived under Dutch law, not Jewish Law.

"Here." He handed her a stack of papers. "These are my mother's recipes. I'd like you to learn them to perfection while we're apart. If you can cook them as good as my mother, you'll be even more of a perfect wife."

"Am I allowed to cook my own recipes?"

"Sure, as long as you don't forget to feed me my favorites. Every year on my birthday, I have a chocolate cake with strawberry filling. This year was the first time I never had it. And remember to leave out onions. I hate onions and always pick them out. Don't worry, I'll help you in the kitchen. I love cooking."

Jakob felt like he were losing his dream girl for the second time as they vacated their room and checked out. They silently walked the short distance to Vrouw Visser's house and then waited twenty minutes for a taxi. The entire drive to Amsterdam, they just held hands and exchanged longing looks.

"Lieutenant, this is your stop," the driver said. "I've been parked outside your headquarters for the last ten minutes. Do you feel okay?"

"I'm fine. I'm just missing my bride already."

Rachel left her suitcase in the car and got out with Jakob and Ben. They held one another and kissed for the next fifteen minutes, till the driver came out to see what was taking so long for the other passenger to come back. Jakob almost wished he could continue riding to Terneuzen, even knowing he'd be considered a deserter and would probably be stripped of all his military honors.

"I love you, Gepje," he called as she got back in the cab. "Never forget I love you."

"I love you too, Jaapje. I can't wait to see you again next year and marry you all over again."

Jakob watched the taxi driving away with his heart. The last time he'd said goodbye to someone he loved had been right before he hurt his foot. This new goodbye was even more painful, even knowing he'd see Rachel again next year. At least this time he'd remembered to say "I love you" before parting ways.

Chapter 21: Back to Amsterdam

"Aren't you Rudolf DeJonghe's boy?"

Jakob looked up. It was now mid-June, and he'd been assigned guard duties at a luxury hotel near his old neighborhood. Sometimes he was still called upon to shave heads and paint them orange. This was the first time he'd run into anyone from the old days.

"Yes, I am. Were you friends with him?"

"He was one of my co-workers. I'll never forget the day I went to visit him and found him with half his face blown away. Thank God those damned Nazis are gone. I assumed you, your mother, and your sister were murdered too, or imprisoned, since you never came back."

"My sister's still missing, but my mother and I only moved a short distance away. I personally took revenge on the murderers last autumn. I'd never be able to rest if they still walked the Earth."

"You've gotten very tall and handsome. How old are you now, eighteen?"

"I turned nineteen last month, shortly after the liberation. As you can see, I'm a soldier now, a lieutenant. And I'm married, though my wife's on her way to America and not where she belongs."

"I know nothing can ever make up for what you had to go through, but I think you'll like to know some of us smuggled him away and had him buried. I'll show you where we put him."

Jakob went in search of his commanding officer and explained the purpose of his errand, and got full permission to take leave of his duties. He nervously went back to Ruud's friend and followed him to a cemetery behind a Dutch Reformed church.

There, towards the back, stood a small stone marking the spot. Jakob fell onto his knees and put his hands on the stone. "Would anyone mind if I had him moved to our cemetery and reburied? I can't imagine how difficult and risky this must've been, but it'd just seem right if he were transferred to his own people."

"We'd be more than happy to do it. Ruud was a very good man, and his son has become the same type of man. May you, your children, and your children's children be eternally blessed for what you've done. Everyone is so proud of all of the boys who defended our country."

2

A few days later, the coffin was exhumed and brought to the large

Jewish cemetery where Jakob's ancestors had been buried since the late seventeenth century. The neighbors insisted on paying for the tombstone. He wrote down the inscription he wanted:

Rudolf Jozua DeJonghe
1 Augustus 1885–10 October 1940
Geliefde echgenoot, zoon, broeder, en vader.

Then he wrote the Hebrew inscription, giving the Hebrew dates of his birth and murder, along with his Hebrew name, Reuven Yehoshua ben Menachem Yoav v'Elisheva Dvorah.

"Now you can sleep with your ancestors, *Vader*," Jakob whispered as the copper coffin was briefly opened so he could see Ruud's perfectly-preserved face one last time. "The mortician did a really nice job on you. I can't even tell you were shot in the head." He patted his father's hand and kissed his forehead. "Sweet dreams. I hope I've made you proud of me from the other world."

"The headstone will probably be ready in a few months," one of the neighbors said as the coffin was closed. "Do you have a preference for color or shape?"

"Sure. We sometimes went for cemetery walks, and we both liked the really old stones with curlicues on the sides. I always know I'm approaching a very old stone when I see curlicues. Nothing too fancy or gaudy, though he deserves the best."

"I think that can be arranged. We'll order a stone in the old style, and make sure it's thick and sturdy enough to withstand the elements."

"Thank you very much. I'll never forget what you did for my father at great risk to your lives."

"The pleasure is ours." One of the neighbors reached into his pocket. "I almost forgot about this. Your father would've wanted you to have this. He was wearing this watch when he was murdered, and it still runs."

Jakob took the watch and fastened it on his right wrist. "This means a lot to me. Now I have a way to tell time when I'm on assignments. Speaking of, I have to get back to headquarters soon. Thank you again for what you did for my father."

3

Over the next weekend, Jakob went to visit Vrouw Zaal, whom he'd left some of his and Luisa's things with. His heart was heavy when he opened the suitcase and saw all the things still packed exactly as they'd been that day in 1942. He didn't care some of those things were very important, like his legal documents and the family Bible. They were a dent in the number of possessions his family once had. And all the religious articles were gone. He'd have to slowly accumulate new Judaica for his and Rachel's future home, while his family's heirlooms were in the garbage or destroyed.

"You can keep my bicycle for now," he muttered as he closed the suitcase. "I won't have a chance to ride it anywhere for awhile. I'll come back to get it before I immigrate. You can keep the car too."

"Don't you want to ride your bicycle around the neighborhood to make sure it still runs smoothly?" Vrouw Zaal pestered. "It's been lonely waiting for you for three years."

"I'm not sure I still remember how to ride a bicycle. And with my gimpy foot, I might fall off and hurt myself again."

"You won't know till you try. I'll help you push off if you'd like. Just a few blocks from our house is a list of survivors. You might like to read it and see if you recognize any names. You should have your name put on the list too. People might be looking for you."

"I'm sure my mother's dead, but I could register myself. Maybe I'll find other friends or relatives."

"I'm truly sorry about your mother. Luisa was a very good woman. At least you have her old doll to give to your daughter someday. I can't believe you're married."

"I don't really believe it either. Hopefully soon my Gepje's first letter will come in, as soon as her ship lands and she makes her way to those friends. I can't wait to start writing to her every single day." He pulled the bicycle over to the door. "Does it need greasing or anything?"

"Probably, after three years of stagnation. I'll get some, and you can go for a short ride."

Jakob watched Vrouw Zaal bringing out bicycle maintenance tools and pumping up the tires, greasing the chain, and checking the brakes. After she was done, he propped the bicycle up and mounted it from the left side. He gripped the handlebars tightly as he pushed off with his left foot and began pedaling down the street. Every few minutes, he abruptly stopped because he was so scared of crashing or falling off. He didn't care if he looked like a fool. Bystanders couldn't understand he hadn't ridden in three years or that he'd sustained a permanent injury to his right ankle.

Finally, he was able to go for more than ten minutes. As he pedaled down the street, starting to feel like it were old times again, he saw an older man bent over an open garbage can, grabbing stale and rotting food and stuffing it in his pockets and under his shirt. Several people were gathered nearby, laughing and pointing. Jakob stopped the bicycle and started towards them to tell them, under the authority of his uniform, to leave the crazy man alone, when he recognized the lunatic.

"Kees! What in the world are you doing? Stop that and come say hello to me!"

"Who are you?"

"It's me, Jaap! Don't you remember me? I can't believe you're still alive! Why are you scavenging from a garbage can? Can't you afford food?"

He looked Jakob up and down. "What are you doing in uniform? Are those the kinds of clothes your liberators gave you?"

"I'm a real soldier! My dream came true after I escaped. So, why are you scavenging food? I'll give you money." He turned around when he heard a noise and ran after a young boy riding off on his bicycle. "Hey, don't you know I'm a lieutenant? Is this how you thank me for putting my life on the line to liberate you, you dirty thief?"

The boy jumped off the bicycle when Jakob pulled out his side arm. Jakob grabbed his bicycle and pulled it back towards Kees. This time he propped it against the wall and stood in front of it.

"I've been so hungry. I have to take extra food in case I run out. I've been staying with Bram since we recovered and were sent home, and he's always yelling at me about how I hoard food, sleep with it under my pillow, and go through garbage cans."

"Bram's alive too? What about Gusta and Floortje?"

"I don't know. All I care about is that I'm alive."

Jakob held out his arms, and Kees mutely stepped into his embrace and began weeping. "I'll help take care of you. If you really don't have enough food, I'll arrange for someone to help you, and I'll come to see you when I have free time. But you have to promise not to scavenge for food again. Maybe you were reduced to an animal not too long ago, but you're better than that now. One day we'll all feel more normal and won't be so tormented by all these bad memories."

"You got really tall."

"Did I ever. I'm almost two meters tall, or six feet three inches, as the Americans told me. My height sounds more impressive with American measurements. I think I've probably stopped growing at my age, unfortunately."

Kees reluctantly threw the bad food on the ground. "Are you really sure I'll never go hungry again? Bram hasn't made enough money yet to afford a big pantry, so we don't have much food. It never feels like enough."

"I'm a soldier. I'll see to it you don't starve again. I killed so many Nazis and NSBers, I lost count. Would you like to visit my father's grave? He was just reburied in our old cemetery. Some very nice neighbors had him in their church cemetery. He'll have a real stone in a few months." Jakob remembered why he'd gone out. "I heard there's a list of survivors nearby. Could you show me where it is?"

"Sure, but I can't promise you'll find anyone. People are just starting to come back, and not everyone back in Germany has registered yet. I'm sorry if I didn't take you seriously when you said things would get so much worse. Maybe older people don't always know best."

"I wish you hadn't had to find out the hard way. I can only imagine what you went through." Jakob dragged his bicycle behind him as they went up the street.

When they reached the list nailed to a crammed public bulletin board, he started reading from the bottom, not wanting to have his hopes dashed too soon.

"You'll find out soon enough not to get your hopes up," Kees said. "Bram and I always walk away disappointed from the newest lists. The people who perished outnumber the survivors."

"Some of the trains leaving Westerbork went to Bergen-Belsen and Terezín. My mother might be alive if that was where our train was going. At least, I can imagine that."

"You can't keep imagining it forever."

Jakob's eyes briefly lit up when he recognized Sander's name near the bottom of the list. "There's one person, at least." He scanned farther up and smiled when he saw Elma's name. "And there's another. Maybe more people than we think survived."

"Only the strong survived. You know that. Sometimes I wonder why I still believe in God after what happened."

Jakob went up the rest of the list and didn't recognize any further names. "Well, it's still early. How often do the lists get updated?"

"It depends. I don't think there'll be that many changes between now and the end of the year. And I'm sure many people didn't bother to register because they're too busy trying to get the hell off this continent that betrayed us so badly. Europe is a gigantic graveyard now." Kees looked at Jakob's hands. "Why are you wearing a ring? Is that part of your uniform too?"

"I'm married, but not religiously. My wife's on her way to America. We didn't technically consummate our marriage, since I didn't want to create an orphan. I'm worried I'll have to join my buddies in the Indies. At least she'll be taken care of with a widow's pension if the worst happens to me."

"Wow. I'm away from you for two and a half years, and I come back to find you a lieutenant and a husband."

"Would you like me to take you back home? Or maybe you'd like to drive back in your car?"

"What car? You know I lost my car three years ago, and I haven't had time to acquire a new one!"

"Vrouw Zaal down the street has your car. It's yours for the taking, if you'd like it back. Would you?"

"She really still has my car?"

"She and her family are good people, unlike certain other people in this city. This is my old bicycle they kept for me. I was going to go back there anyway to pick up the suitcase with my belongings. I bet they'll be glad to see you."

Kees followed Jakob to the house as Jakob rode his bicycle a bit more steadily and confidently. Everyone always said riding a bicycle was something one never forgot, no matter how long it'd been. Maybe returning to the human race was a similar skill, and it just needed a little practice to get used to doing it again.

4

Jakob's newest assignment involved going to the depot to keep order when repatriated survivors arrived. But for the fact that he didn't want to appear like a poor, unmanly excuse for a soldier, nor for the survivors to lose control themselves, he contained his emotions whenever he saw these frightening-looking people unboarding. Many of them were quite skinny, and were only just starting to grow their hair back. He couldn't tell the men from the women. The sight of the children was even more heartbreaking. After awhile, he stopped asking if they'd ever seen or heard of a little girl named Emilia DeJonghe, who'd now be almost eight years old.

"Jaap, is that you?"

Jakob looked to his left and saw a young man of above average height with sandy blonde hair and hazel eyes. He looked at him for several minutes, trying to place him.

"It's me, Sander Zeeger! Are you a real soldier?"

"Yes I am," he said proudly as he hugged Sander. "Welcome home, old friend. I saw your name on one of the lists. Thank God some people survived."

"I wish I'd jumped with you. I wasn't prepared for the Hell that was waiting for us. Thank God our train wasn't going to Sobibór, or I'd probably be a dead man."

"It wasn't? So this means there's a tiny chance my mother might be alive?"

"I don't know about any women besides Elma, who came on the train with me. She should be getting off with her fiancé any minute now. Do you have the heart to hear what happened to some of the others?"

He looked around for his commanding officer, who'd give him a talking-to if he were discovered fraternizing. "I have to hear it sometime."

Sander got a very faraway, wistful look in his eyes. "Debora is no more. She froze to death on the train. She would've given anything to be embarrassed for menstruating all over her clothes instead of dying at sixteen."

Jakob felt a twinge of pain. "My mother was right next to that hole I jumped from. Did she freeze to death too?"

"Elma kept her warm and helped plug up the hole with bedrolls. She was still alive when we unboarded in Hell. All three of the Antemas were sent right to the gas. The Nazis could tell they didn't look like workers or sturdy stock. They never knew anything but sitting around in parlors at teas and socials, as healthy and beautiful as they looked."

Jakob felt an even stronger gnawing ache. "If I'd known what was going to happen to them, I never would've acted up at their Seder or broken their cabinet."

"I'm sure they forgive you from the other world. I wish I'd been as forward-thinking as you and done something to be the master of my destiny. Luuk was supposed to be sent to the gas too, but he ran away and threw himself on the fence. I'd never seen that little coward run that fast before. They couldn't catch him till it was too late."

"What does that mean? He impaled himself on a fence? Even if I did emulate the suicidal Zealots, I could think of better suicide methods than impaling myself with a fence!"

"There was a double electric fence at Auschwitz. It was so strong we could see it moving and hear the electricity. All the other camps I was at had them too. A lot of people threw themselves on the fence rather than live another day. I don't want to imagine what kind of death is worse, being trampled and suffocating in a gas chamber or having my body jolted with thousands of volts. One of the prisoners unloading us was being pestered by Luuk for information on how he could kill himself, and he told him the fence was lethal."

Jakob shook his head. "That's an awful end for anyone. I almost feel sorry he couldn't take a pill or shoot himself."

"I don't think he would've survived anyway. He wasn't strong, tall, or resilient enough. All he wanted to do was kill himself instead of finding ways to survive."

"Sander, who are you talking to?"

"This is our old buddy Jakob DeJonghe! Look how tall he got! He's a real soldier now!"

Elma rushed over and hugged him. "I knew you'd escape! And your dream of becoming a soldier finally came true!"

"I'm a lieutenant, and I've got the Orders of Willem and Orange–Nassau, plus a Bronze Lion. And look at this." He held up his hand. "I'm married now too."

"You *are*? And here I thought it was a big deal for me to be engaged!" Elma indicated a tall young man coming up behind her. "That's Willem Brinkerhoff. We met shortly after Bergen-Belsen was liberated, and we became engaged about a month in. He's not a bit jealous of you for being the first guy to kiss me. That memory made me so happy while I was in Hell."

"Can we meet your wife?" Sander asked. "Did you meet her in the partisans?"

"I met her while I was a partisan, on Yom Kippur 1943, and then I met her again during a relief assignment at Westerbork last month. She's on her way to America, or maybe is already there. I can't wait to get her first letter. I can't wait to see my beautiful wife again and start our marriage properly."

"I feel sorry for her," Elma said. "I'd hate to marry Willem and then have to be away from him for a long time."

"We did what needed doing. You can come to our religious wedding if you'd like. I have to get back to my official duties, but I'd love to visit with you when I've got free time."

"Sure thing," Sander said. "We're going to try to stay at the Grand Hotel Amrath. You know where that is?"

"Yeah, it's not too far from the station. I'll stop by this weekend and ask for you."

Jakob turned back to watching and escorting the people debarking the trains. As he resumed his duties, he kicked himself for forgetting to ask his friends what had happened to Luisa and Gusta. Not that he expected to hear a miraculous story. The short hair on the survivors, their gaunt frames, the way they carried themselves, the haunted looks in their eyes, and the numbers on their arms told him everything he needed to know.

5

Jakob was looking forward to visiting his friends at the luxury hotel over the weekend as he oversaw the arrival of the survivors' trains late on Friday afternoon. He tried to smile at the pitiful children and gave little pieces of chocolate and candy to some of them. A few of the young women gave him flirtatious smiles, which was somewhat flattering. It was so good to see these people slowly returning to life and re-learning how to do normal things.

As he was returning the smile to a dark-haired girl in a blue dress, his eyes caught on an older woman walking very slowly, but with her head held high. She had the same intense dark eyes he did, and the same beautiful black hair. He stopped breathing when his heart recognized her before his eyes did.

"Mama!" he screamed as broke into a run. "Mama!"

She halted in her tracks and stared at the tall soldier racing towards her with tears streaming down his face. She shrieked when she recognized him.

"Jaap! My baby boy is alive!"

Jakob flung himself into her arms, his chest heavily heaving from sobs as they embraced. "I love you, Mama, I love you so much. I've thought of you every single day for the last two and a half years. I'll never abandon you again. You're the best mother I ever could've asked for. Please, please, please forgive me for not telling you I love you before I escaped. I've had so many nightmares about what happened to you ever since. I screamed for you in my sleep sometimes. Oh, God, I love you so much, Mama. I promise I'll tell you I love you every single day for the rest of your life. I can't believe I still have a mother."

She gently released him and dried her eyes. "You didn't know where that train was going. How could anyone? I knew you loved me, even if you didn't tell me. Didn't I promise you I'd survive for my beautiful baby boy? You deserve at least one living parent, and your future children deserve at least one grandparent to love them."

Jakob reached into his bag. "This is for you. I wrote you this letter a little while after I escaped, when I was recovering from a broken foot and ankle. Please don't feel like you have to read it now. Did you come home with anyone else?"

"Gusta and Floor travelled with me. Poor Gusta isn't the same as you remember her. The poor woman lost much of her mind after what she went through."

Jakob turned around and saw Gusta on her daughter Floor's arm. Gusta was rolling her head around, a frightening, vacant look in her eyes.

"What happened to her?"

Luisa closed her eyes. "The worst thing a midwife could ever be made to do, over and over again. I lived because I kept up the farce of being her assistant, and your friend Elma claimed she was Gusta's assistant in training. We tried to tell Gusta over and over again she'd make up for it after the war, but she won't listen to us."

Jakob stood back in fear as Gusta approached him.

"Look, *Moeder*, this is our old friend Jakob, Luisa's boy," Floor said patiently. "It looks like he's a soldier now. He'll be able to help us get housing and money. Maybe he can get you a job delivering soldiers' wives' babies."

"Yes, Gusta, I'll be happy to help you. Kees and Bram are alive and in the city. They'll be so happy to learn you and Floortje survived." He looked away from her, too scared to look in those vacant eyes. His eyes fell upon the number on his mother's arm, and he started sobbing again.

"Do you understand what I had to do?" Gusta demanded. "I had to kill babies! I had to kill babies! I'll never work as a midwife again! Who would want a midwife who killed babies and performed abortions with her bare hands! And I'm almost fifty years old! I'm too old to start a new career! What I am supposed to do with myself for the rest of my life! I should've died along with the first baby I had to murder!"

"You saved their mothers' lives," Floor said. "Because of what you did, they stood a chance of surviving and being able to have many more babies. Any compassionate, realistic person will understand why you did what you did. Preserving a life takes precedence over all else. What we lived through required doing things we never would've considered in normal times."

Jakob stood at attention as his commanding officer approached, quickly drying his eyes and struggling to compose himself.

"Lt. DeJonghe, aren't you forgetting your duties?"

"My apologies, Colonel Onderdonk, but this is my mother. I haven't seen her in two and a half years. Thank God she's alive."

Colonel Onderdonk smiled and extended his hand. "I'm very pleased to meet you, Vrouw DeJonghe. You must be a very special woman if you produced a brave soldier like Jakob. We've all heard about what the Nazis did to you. What a miracle anyone survived."

"Yes, what a miracle. I'll be using my salary to set her up in an apartment. This is the midwife who delivered me, and her daughter. I think they'll be moving in with her husband and son."

"Gusta needs a sanitarium," Luisa said. "God willing, she'll recover her mind and stop hating herself with enough treatment and love."

Jakob had a huge smile on his face the rest of the day as he ushered people to and fro, gave children candy, greeted survivors, and reluctantly accepted blessings for his service. As soon as he was off-duty, he went to get Luisa and walked her to the hotel where Sander and Elma were staying. He wouldn't let go of her hand until he'd seen her into her room with Floor and Gusta.

"I love you, Mama," he proclaimed before he left. "Since tomorrow's Saturday, I'll be able to visit you. I'll take you to *Vader*'s grave, and we can say Kaddish for him. Thank God I only have to say it for one parent."

"Now, Jaap," she said gently. "Remember how your father and I told you, after you became bar mitzvah, that you were too old to still call us Mama and Papa? I don't mind you calling me Mama once in awhile under emotional circumstances, but I don't want you to get back into that childish habit. Is that understood? You couldn't have survived if you'd been a mama's boy."

He twisted his cap in his hands. "I'm sorry, but I just can't help myself. I'm so happy to have you back, I feel like a little boy who's gotten lost in a big department store and thought he'd never see his mother again."

"I understand why you're doing it, but I expect you'll start to regularly call me *Moeder* again within a few months."

He hugged and kissed her one final time before going to the door. "Goodnight, *Moeder*. May you have only the sweetest of dreams. I'll see you tomorrow after breakfast."

6

Jakob had gotten used to not going to synagogue or praying since his escape from the train, though he tried to read from his Bible at least once a week. He thought nothing of going to the hotel instead of one of the synagogues still left on Saturday morning. His family had long been Progressive, and hadn't held to Orthodox prohibitions against things like streetcar travel, carrying in the public domain, and writing on the Sabbath and holidays.

He rushed towards Luisa as soon as the door was open and hugged her tightly. "Good morning, *Moeder*. I hope you had wonderful dreams and a very sound sleep. Would you like to go for a walk first, or to see *Vader*'s grave?"

"I want to see my father and brother," Floor said from the back of the room. "We can all go over together afterwards. Are they still at our old apartment?"

"They live in Jordaan. I don't think many people had the heart to go back to the old neighborhood. I looked at some of the streets, and a lot of the buildings were destroyed. A lot of the Jewish houses were ripped apart for firewood last winter."

"I read your letter last night, Jaapje," Luisa said. "It was very heartfelt and mature. It's a good thing I didn't know what happened to you after you jumped. I would've died of worry if I'd known about your injury. Thank God you were found by the right people."

Jakob looked over at Gusta. "Are we all going? I'll understand if Gusta can't do much."

"We're all going," Floor said. "My mother needs to get out. It'll help her recover her mind faster."

Jakob shied away from Gusta as she ambled towards him. He held Luisa's hand tightly as he went down the hall for Sander, Elma, and Willem, and didn't look back at Gusta on Floor's arm. He felt blessed he wasn't the one whose mother had lost her mind.

"You've gotten so tall and handsome," Luisa said as they walked to the graveyard. "As soon as you get an honorable discharge, I'm sure you'll have no problems finding a wife."

"Jaap doesn't need to worry about finding a wife after the service," Sander said. "He already has one."

"What! You picked up a real wife since I last saw you? When in the world did this happen?" Luisa released his hand and saw the gold band. "Dear God, when were you planning to tell me you had a wife? Where is this woman? Is she unable to join us because of injury? For the love of God, don't tell me she's in a maternity hospital having my grandchild."

"She's probably in America by now. We got married last month, after about two weeks of officially knowing each other. We met two years ago on Yom Kippur, and had a few brief encounters after that. The next month, she was arrested. I couldn't stop thinking about her that whole time. I'll show you all my drawings of her, and our wedding picture. It wasn't a religious wedding, so you can be there for the real ceremony next year in America. I assume you'll want to follow me to America."

Luisa was struggling to process all this information. "You married a woman you barely know, on some kind of whim? And you're not living together as husband and wife and won't see her until next year?"

He felt a gnawing ache in his heart for his beautiful bride, now so far away and depriving him of her sweet, loving touch, adoring looks, and soothing voice until God knew when. "This was no whim. When you know in your heart, you just know. I know this isn't a very mature love, but that never comes right away. You and *Vader* probably didn't love each other in that way until you'd been married for a long time. Absence makes the heart grow fonder."

"But you weren't even courting her for six months! Not even one month! This wasn't an arranged marriage. What if she's expecting your child and takes it away from you when you come to America? You might come to see her and find her with another husband! Do you know where she's living?"

Jakob hesitated. "Her American friends are sort of the family of her former boyfriend. But she stopped loving him long ago, and he might be away at university or married. There's no chance of pregnancy, since we didn't technically consummate the marriage."

"So you not only agreed to marry a stranger, but also thought nothing of letting her live with a former beau? At least you knew enough not to consummate this marriage. I hate to be the one to tell you this, but it seems like she just used you for her visa. I'm sure you're in love with her, but you deserve better. Did you give her any of my jewelry or books?"

"No, only your recipes."

"Those are our family's recipes! I wanted you to have them, not for you to give them to a stranger you might never see again!"

"You don't understand, *Moeder*, I was obsessed by this girl from the first time I saw her! I denied it to everyone and even myself, but I obviously kept thinking about her for a reason! And then I stumbled upon her former hiding place and saw some of her books, an old doll, and pictures, and it was like I were sent there because we're meant to be together. Why would I cross paths with her, become obsessed with her, be led to her old home, and meet her again if she's not my soulmate? I didn't want to get married and immediately part, but it was the only way she could get on that ship. She'll be taken care of with a widow's pension if the worst happens to me."

"Give Jaap some credit," Sander interjected. "He's not stupid. Maybe this really is on the level, and you'll love your daughter-in-law."

Luisa started walking again. "I don't like any of this, though you obviously had no way of consulting me. Don't worry, I'll take care of you and help you find a real wife after the inevitable annulment. Thank God you didn't sleep with this woman."

Jakob let go of her hand and walked ahead, fighting back tears. "You never met my wife. My Gepje is the most perfect match for me, and she'll become my wife all over again as soon as I'm in America. Do you know how much it kills me inside knowing I can't see or touch my own dear wife until at least next spring? I want to live with her and await a darling little baby, not be stationed here as though nothing ever happened!"

"Don't you trust your own son's judgment?" Elma asked. "Has he ever been the type to marry someone on a whim or fall for someone just using him for a visa or money?"

"Even our names are perfectly matched," he choked out as he rubbed his hands over his eyes. "Our Biblical namesakes waited fourteen years to get married, and they never stopped loving each other. I love my Gepje even more now that she's so far away from me. I never thought I could ever love a woman that much. You told me I had to be a man and find a woman to take your place, and I did." He closed his eyes and remembered how good it had felt when Rachel touched him for the first time, how soft and loving her hands were, how special it was she was the only woman who'd ever done anything so personal with him.

Luisa put her arm around him. "I don't want to make you cry, Jaapje, but any mother would be concerned. For your sake, I hope I'm wrong and that your wife is the daughter-in-law of my dreams. I want someone who'll take care of you and love you."

"Rachel does love me. Oh, she's such a beautiful girl, with the most intense green eyes, pretty blonde curly hair, skin like alabaster, a soft, petite mouth like a pink rosebud, the softest, most loving hands, and—"

"Yeah, I think he's in love alright," Floor said. "We should all trust his judgment instead of acting like he's committed the worst sin in the world. I'd jump at the chance to marry a man I loved even if I hadn't known him very long. We have to make new families and replace all the murdered. We no longer have the luxury of courtships lasting more than six months. All I care about is finding someone who knows the kinds of sorrows I've experienced."

"Thank you, Floortje." Jakob stuffed his hands in his pockets and walked ahead of everyone. "I forgive you for insulting my wife, *Moeder*. I'm too happy you're alive to be angry at you. But can you please keep your opinions to yourself unless I ask for them? I can't last through this long separation if you constantly criticize us."

"I'll try," Luisa promised half-heartedly. "But remember, I have your welfare in mind. I'm not saying these things to be mean. Falling in love is the most natural thing in the world. I only hope this woman treats your beautiful heart like the treasure it is instead of giving it back to you with a stake in it."

No one said anything during the rest of the walk to Kees and Bram's apartment. Jakob knocked on their door, explained why he was there, and stepped back to give them privacy for their reunion. He felt like he were intruding when he overheard them crying. When they emerged after thirty minutes, he tried not to look at them, but he could see Kees and Bram looked very shaken-up. He couldn't blame them, after seeing what had become of Gusta.

Everyone remained silent during the walk to the graveyard. Jakob showed his mother the makeshift marker and stood back for a respectable period. He was glad Luisa wouldn't have to see Ruud's dead body like he had, though it had been fixed so well, it didn't look like he'd been shot. After what she'd been through, she didn't need to see any more dead bodies.

"Have you said Kaddish for your father yet?"

"Oh, no. I wanted to wait for the real grave to come in, and I don't think I remember the words. I don't even have a siddur."

"We don't have ten people either," Sander said. "We're one short."

"I don't think the Progressive Movement started counting women in a minyan since we've been away. We only have five men. It'll only take a few minutes. We can make it a special occasion and round up some other survivors. Look, I'm wearing *Vader*'s watch. The neighbors who buried him gave it to me."

"I think God will hear prayers even if only one person's praying," Elma said. "In the times of the Temple, sometimes full services were held with six or seven people. It's best to have at least ten, to have more of a community, but you can't always have that many if you're in a small community. We no longer have that luxury. I heard people in the camps saying Kaddish by themselves. They didn't care they weren't men or couldn't find ten."

"We're already here," Luisa said. "Someone can go looking for people. Not all the synagogues were destroyed, were they?"

"I guess not," Jakob muttered. "I've seen people going to the Portuguese Synagogue and the Gerard Dou Synagogue."

"I'll accost people for you," Bram volunteered. "I see people walking in the graveyard. I'm sure they'd be happy to fill in our gaps."

Jakob watched as Bram approached several strangers who all looked like the people he helped at the depot. He had no idea what to say to the others to break the ice. Even if Luisa hadn't criticized his judgment in marrying Rachel, he'd still feel alienated from her. His euphoria at still having a mother had quickly ended. The chasm he felt between himself and regular people now existed even wider between himself and his mother and old friends. They had seen, smelled, heard, tasted, felt, and experienced things he could only begin to imagine. That foul travelling coffin had only been the tip of the iceberg in the parade of macabre horrors they'd survived.

"I found seven," Bram announced. "They'll be honored to help you."

"Are you sure we should allow strangers to say prayers for my father?" Jakob looked meaningfully at Luisa. "After all, we haven't known them for years, and have no way of knowing what's really on their minds."

"They're helping you say Kaddish, not marrying you," Luisa whispered.

"I don't remember the words. I never had to say it for anyone before, though I've heard the words many times."

"Is it okay if we also say Kaddish for our friends and relatives who don't have graves?" Sander asked. "Afterwards, someone can say El Malei Rachamim for each individually."

"I don't have a prayershawl anymore. I rarely wore the one I had, since I'm not Orthodox."

"What are you afraid of?" one of the volunteers asked. "God will understand if you stumble over some of the words or need prompting. Here, have my siddur. I know the service by heart." He pushed it into Jakob's hands. "Can you read Hebrew?"

"What am I, an idiot? And I don't want to say any prayers for Luuk. I feel bad for how he ended his life, but I'm not going to pretend he was my friend just because he's dead."

"Only God can judge him now," Luisa said. "He had his own reasons and motivations that weren't for you to understand. I suppose at least death by electrocution is quicker and more merciful than death by gas chamber."

Jakob read the service at his own pace, mostly reading from the Dutch side of the page. He couldn't keep up with most of the other men, who tripped through it with a kind of high-speed mumbling and buzzing. It seemed impossible to read and understand the words if one were speed-reading them. He was still at the top or near the middle of most of the pages by the time he saw the non-Progressive people turning the page. It wasn't that he didn't know how to read Hebrew or understand the basic meaning of a fair amount of the words, but he'd never been taught to read them so lightning-quick.

For the first time in his life, he said the words of the Mourners' Kaddish. As the ancient Aramaic words tripped off his tongue, he pictured his father, and all the other people who'd never be coming back —his extended family, the Antemas, Elma's parents, Sander's parents, Debora, his classmates and teachers, everyone who'd been so alive and vibrant only a few years ago. They had no idea their lives were about to end, that they'd be forced to cram so many memories and experiences into only an inch of time and space. If they'd known what was coming, would they have escaped, hidden, or fought back as he did? Did they regret now, from the other world, not taking his warnings and urgings seriously?

7

Monday after he came back to headquarters from the depot, Jakob found a letter on his bed. His heart beat a little faster when he saw it was from Rachel, postmarked Atlantic City, New Jersey, USA. Ben curled up next to him as he carefully, gently, lovingly opened the envelope and guided the letter out. He also found a picture of Rachel on the beach with a slightly younger, dark-haired girl. The inscription on the back said she was the little sister of Rachel's former beau, Katherine Brandt.

15 June 1945

My dear husband Jaap,

I set sail on 30 May and arrived in America on 12 June. One of the other soldiers' wives was nice enough to help me get on a Greyhound bus going to Atlantic City. I wish Pietje's family had settled in a big city like New York, Boston, Newark, Chicago, or Pittsburgh, but it's not like Atlantic City is a backwater hamlet. They even have several synagogues for me. Progressive Judaism is called Reform here in America. They're not quite as religious as the European equivalent, but I suppose I'll get used to it.

You'll never guess who I found at the refugee center in Terneuzen before the ship left! My dear friend Juli van Acker! She looked so pitiful, I didn't recognize her at first, and was horrified when I heard this wretched woman plaintively calling my name. The poor dear was covered in bruises and scars from recent frostbite and burns, and also bears scars and welts from various beatings. I told you she's so shy and timid, she's practically scared of her own shadow. It should've been me and not Juli who was sent to the East. I could've handled it better. Now my dear Juli is even more scared of the world, and afraid Pietje's brother Fritz (Gary in America) won't love her anymore when she immigrates. She was manhandled and cavity-searched a hundred thousand times, but never actually raped. I tried to tell her Fritz will understand she wasn't willingly groped and assaulted by all those evil men. She escaped from a death march, thank God. I wish I could've taken her with me.

The Brandts have warmly taken me in and put me up in their guest room. I've been spending a lot of time catching up with Pietje's sister Lotje (Kätchen), who's in high school. Her American nickname is Sparky. It's so strange how they changed their names every time they moved. No one's ever changing my name, though they do pronounce it differently in America. Pietje (Barry) is with a fellow Dutch immigrant, Henriëtte (Jet) Vos. She came over in '42. Jet looks as plain as a pump handle, and doesn't have a sparkling personality to make up for it. Who knows, perhaps she's much different in private.

They couldn't believe I'm married to someone I haven't known for even a month, but they weren't in Europe during the war. They could never possibly hope to understand what drove us to bond so closely, intimately, and quickly. I wish I had a tangible piece of you with me, but at least I have the privilege of being your wife, and I'll always have my memories of that lovely night. Maybe it's a little different for a man, since he derives his main sexual pleasure from intercourse, but I don't feel like a virgin anymore. I let you have all of me except for that one formality, and I can't go back to my former state of not knowing what it's like to be sexually touched and pleasured by a man.

I miss you so much, and wish your term of service were already up and you had permission to immigrate. It'll feel like forever till I have my heart-stoppingly handsome husband back in my arms to love and protect. And remember, you promised our children would take my name.

I love you so much,

Gepje

Jakob scratched Ben behind the ears. "Do you hear that, Bentje? My bride still loves me, even if my mother thinks she used me for a visa and military wife benefits." He reached for his fountain pen and a piece of paper, regretting he didn't have a picture of his own to enclose.

2 July 1945,

My dear sweet treasure Gepje,

I'm so glad to hear you arrived safe and sound in America and are being looked after by good people. I miss you every single day, and wish our separation were already over. Nothing can fill the empty, aching void in my heart till we're together again. I long to be with you like a husband is with a wife. All that time I was so angry at the world and obsessed with finding my father's killers, I was denying myself the world's most precious thing. I had so much love sealed and suppressed in my heart that I was deep down longing to give to someone. I hope I gave you enough of my love to tide you through the rest of our separation. As soon as you're back in my arms, I'm going to give you even more love for the rest of my life. I can't wait till we have a physical symbol of our love, our very own darling little baby. I don't care what it is so long as it's ours.

You'll never believe my miraculous good fortune. Please don't hate me or feel jealous. My beautiful mother is still alive. It's a miracle from God she lived at her age. She posed as our friend Gusta's midwifery assistant, and my friend Elma posed as the assistant in training. My friend Sander is also alive. So are Gusta's husband and two grown children. Poor Gusta lost much of her mind, but hopefully she'll recover her senses after enough time. Her children and husband want to take her to a sanitarium. What else could a doctor, nurse, or midwife do in the Hell they were in? She saved so many lives by killing babies and performing abortions, even if she was trained to bring life into this world, not to take it away for no medically-indicated reason.

I wish I could tell you my wonderful mother is happy to learn I found a wife, but it's important to be honest. Please don't think I'm trying to manufacture drama or bitterness between you and my mother. I'm just honestly reporting the current facts. My mother is beyond stunned to learn we married after such a short courtship and that we're not living together as husband and wife. She can't understand what drove us together and made us fall so in love so quickly. I would've known if you were only pretending to love me to get a visa and military benefits. You're not like those girls who pretend one thing while their hearts feel another, like those Vamps in the old silent films. One of the things I love about you is how forthright and brutally honest you are, how you hold nothing back in speaking your mind. You're not a girl who plays games or leads guys on. And you were so sweet on our wedding night. I could feel the sincerity and the love in your hands and other parts of your body.

I'm very torn over where my mother will live after we immigrate. On the one hand, after what she's been through, I don't want to be separated from her ever again. It's my responsibility as her adult son to make sure she's being taken care of.

But on the other hand, it's not right for a newlywed couple to live with parents. I know that's normal in some cultures, but it wouldn't be right. My mother herself told me, in that letter she wrote before we were deported, that she wanted me to find a woman to take her place as the number one woman in my heart. She knows a healthy grown man's top loyalty is to his wife, not his mother. No woman should have to compete with her mother-in-law for her husband's love and attention, nor to be the only woman of the house. And it would be incredibly awkward to consummate our marriage with my mother in the house.

Hopefully I can finish the rest of my term of service in Amsterdam. My friends and mother are staying in a hotel, but they're going to look for housing soon. I hope to set my mother up in an apartment with my salary and check in with her in my free time. Sadly, I haven't found any news about my sister yet. At least I have one person. A lot of these people coming home have no one. Someday I hope we'll have many descendants.

Please stay just as sweet, loving, and loyal as you are. I'll be a very good boy and will return to you as relatively virginal as I was when we parted. You're the only woman I'll ever let do those things to me. After I've experienced some form of sexual intimacy, I'm longing to do that again, but it would be meaningless with a woman I didn't love. Even if I admire beautiful women, I won't do more than look at them. Only you get to have all of me.

I love you until all the oceans run dry,
Jaapetje

Chapter 22: Dancing Back into the Fire

On the week-anniversary of his reunion with Luisa, Jakob was handed a note by one of his commanding officers as he returned to headquarters. His stomach turned to ice as he read it.

Lt. DeJonghe,

We very much appreciate your services in both wartime and peacetime in the Princess Irene Brigade and the Royal Army of The Netherlands. Because of your distinguished record in combat at Hedel, we feel your services in Amsterdam can only do so much for your talents. We feel you'll be better-served spending the remainder of your term of service in the Dutch East Indies. Since your year of service will be up in February, your tour of duty will be abbreviated to six months. We trust you'll distinguish yourself in combat once again and make The Netherlands, the Army, and the Queen proud.

The note fluttered out of his fingers and onto the floor. So this really was his fate. The Indies. The Japanese were still there. Japan hadn't surrendered yet. Not only that, but he'd have to face off against the natives. At least things weren't as brutal as he'd heard they'd been earlier in the Japanese occupation.

"Well, I guess we're going to the tropics, Bentje." He knelt down and absentmindedly petted his dog, now two years old. "You'll be a good dog for me and my buddies when we go back into a warzone, won't you? And you'll get to see our buddies Leendert, Govert, and Jeronymus again. I don't think our friend Dries will be out of the hospital soon enough to join us."

Jakob went over to his bed and started packing up his things. Since he was going to the tropics, he left out his winter clothes. He'd give them to Luisa for safekeeping, and keep the rest of his things at Vrouw Visser's house. No single-minded soldier needed his entire library or a full wardrobe of clothes during a six-month deployment. All he needed were his caul, his current sketchbook and art supplies, enough clothes to get by, the little stuffed rabbit, and a couple of books. As always, he included Luisa's *Tao Te Ching*. He'd grown very attached to it in the last two and a half years.

"Say, will my wife's letters be forwarded to me?" he asked his commanding officer.

"Of course. We know where we're sending you. She'll also be sent a letter telling her you've been deployed. Perhaps you'll advance while you're there. She'll be really proud of you if you come back to her as a captain or major."

Jakob darkly wondered if he'd be coming back to her in a coffin. Sometimes he regretted not giving her a child before they parted, so there'd always be a part of him in the world and to give her a forever reminder of him. If he knew he had a child to live for, he could survive against all odds, just as Luisa had survived for him.

2

Jakob's plane landed in Jakarta on 11 July. He'd spent the entire flight worried about what would happen to him, and hadn't been able to enjoy his first aeroplane ride. This wasn't the first plane ride he'd dreamt about. He'd spent most of his flight looking out the window and drawing clouds, panoramic landscapes, and cities all lit up at night, all while dreading the moment the plane would land and he'd be taken to a battlezone. This wasn't a personal fight like the liberation of The Netherlands. It was just a job, an order he had no way of refusing unless he wanted to be stripped of his military honors and rank.

He took his bag from the overhead cargo and headed down the aisle with the other soldiers. His heart thudded in his ears every step of the way. He barely cared when Ben came out of the smaller plane transporting war dogs and heavier cargo.

"Are we coming to a battle in progress as replacements?" he finally asked as they walked towards the assigned encampment.

"No, at this point we're mostly fighting against the natives, though we're still dealing with those barbaric Japanese. We're here to liberate our own from the Japanese, not help the natives get independence. The natives have begun agitating for independence, but we're not going to let our colony get away."

Jakob knew the Japanese had committed horrible war crimes against the Dutch in the East Indies, but he wasn't so sure anymore if his country needed to keep any colonies. An occupation was an occupation, even if the occupiers were enlightened and not in the business of throwing people in internment camps or massacring them. He'd fought to liberate his homeland from an evil occupying force, and now he'd be seen as part of a different occupying force to the people he was supposedly coming to liberate. It didn't seem moral. He'd also grown interested in the native culture after reading some of Louis Couperus's novels set in the Dutch East Indies.

His train of thought was broken by the appearance of headquarters. Instead of being in the big city, it was in a jungle. He wasn't sure if that were a good or bad thing. At least he'd be able to draw the native flora and fauna, and maybe make some new animal friends.

"Well, look who the cat dragged in," Jeronymus smiled. "Come in here and make yourself comfortable. What have you been doing with yourself for the last two months?"

"I found my mother and some of my friends." He shook hands with Jeronymus and Govert. "They're in Amsterdam."

"Really?" Govert asked. "What a miracle!"

Jakob threw his bag on the floor by the bed he was pointed towards and had a seat. He was looking around at his new surroundings when he realized what was missing. "Isn't Leendert supposed to be here too? Was he transferred to another area or sent home?"

"Our friend is in the hospital," Jeronymus sighed. "We came under heavy fire from the Japanese, and he was hit in the leg and chest. He's out for the count like Dries, and probably won't be allowed to come back to us for awhile."

Jakob's heart sank to learn this. Leendert had always been such a calming, soothing influence, and now he was in pain in the hospital. He wondered which of them would be next.

"So, you handsome devil, did you finally get any women in the last two months?" Jeronymus asked as he lit a cigarette. "We got a lot of women while you were on that relief assignment. One night I had three in a row. Leendert was lucky enough to get a virgin one night. The last time he had a virgin was the first time he slept with a woman."

Jakob looked at the roof. "I'm sort of married now."

Jeronymus inhaled sharply and began coughing on the smoke. "What! You go from total virgin to husband in only two months! And without me to give you any expert advice!"

"I, um, technically still am a virgin. My wife's in America, and I didn't want to consummate the marriage for fear of creating an orphan. We didn't have a religious ceremony, just the civil one. Some people might consider a child illegitimate if there's no religious marriage."

"What?" Govert asked. "You marry a woman and then don't even screw her? If I married a woman I just met, I'd make sure to get in a lot of action before a long separation! There are always ways to prevent pregnancy, or to take care of it if the worst happens."

"We did other things on our wedding night." Jakob started biting the rough dead skin of his writing callus. "She says she doesn't feel like a virgin anymore, and I don't feel like a total virgin anymore either."

"What kinds of other things?" Jeronymus pressed. "Things that resulted in ecstasy?"

He nodded, starting to blush.

"For you or for her? Or for both of you?"

"Both of us," he mumbled. "Do you really need to know all the details of my wedding night?"

"Are you sure it was ecstasy for her? Sometimes it's hard to tell if you're a virgin. You don't know the signs in a woman. But congratulations, I guess. You're more of a man than you were the last time we saw you. Now you only have one more thing to do before you're a full member of the adult club."

"I took hints from you, so I knew I was doing it right. I sometimes overheard you encouraging your lovers and coaxing it out of them when they seemed to be holding back. You didn't need to sit me down for a personal advice session for me to figure it out. I got her to ecstasy at least five times."

"Does this woman have a name?" Govert asked. "Any pictures for us?"

"Do you think she'd mind if you experimented with other women?" Jeronymus asked. "Sensible women understand a man has to do what a man has to do, particularly when they're separated for long periods. Think of it as picking up lots of sexual experience she'll be the lucky ultimate recipient of. You'll be sleeping with other women so you can be an expert on it by the time you really sleep with her. Oral and manual pleasure might be the main course to most women, but not for the average man. Don't tell me you tried anything else."

"I think that's enough of this conversation, and no, I'm not going to cheat on my wife while she's thousands of kilometers away waiting for me."

"I suppose this means you stopped obsessing about Rachel."

Jakob pulled his copy of the wedding picture out of his bag and handed it to them. Their eyes widened as they recognized the informally-dressed bride as the girl in the pictures Jakob had found.

"No way!" Govert said. "You actually found your dream girl and married her? Some dreams really do come true."

"I had to have her for my own. She's living with a former beau's family, but he's got his own girl now. She sleeps in a guest room."

Jeronymus laughed. "You agreed to let her stay with a former boyfriend? What do you think will happen? If she's probably going to attach horns to you, you might as well start screwing the local women. You'll be even when you're back together. Let her have one last hurrah with an old flame, while you pick up experience from many sources."

"I'm not committing adultery, and I know she's not either. You can give me personal advice if you want, but I'm not going to use it on any woman but my Gepje."

"You're too old-fashioned for your own good. But if you insist, I'll be glad to show you all my dirty books and give you plenty of pointers. By the time I'm done with you and you're back with this dream girl, you'd better be able to send her to the farthest reaches of the universe with the most intense climax ever."

"In the meantime, you gentlemen are here to defend our colony," the commanding officer interrupted. "Let's have less talk about women and more talk about how to secure the area and repel the Japanese and natives. The Netherlands might not be as great a power as Britain, but this colony means a lot to us. We're here to take back control, not sleep our way through the islands."

3

Jakob spent the first few months of his new deployment mostly scouting the areas they encamped in, and sometimes served as a sniper. He spent most of his time taking walks and drawing the flora and fauna, since there were no real battles to speak of. Already he'd amassed an ample collection of drawings of lizards, elephants, orangutans, rhinoceros, birds, trees, and flowers. A few times he'd gotten close enough to draw leopards. He often used scouting as an excuse and sat in a particularly beautiful spot to write to Rachel. Now that the Japanese had surrendered and the war was really over, they only had to worry about the natives, and Jakob figured his superiors would be humane and sensible and let them have their independence.

"You're such a neat creature," he smiled at a young orangutan. "Here, I've got some figs for you. Would you like to sit on my lap?" He extended a fig to the mother. "Don't worry about me, Vrouw Orangutan. I love animals, and would never hurt your baby."

He fed several figs to each of them, and was delighted when the baby climbed onto his lap and started playing with his face. Best of all, the baby let Jakob hug and cuddle it, and the mother examined his hair for bugs, as though he were her own child. As he pulled more figs out of his bag, he started thinking about what he might like to do with himself once he was a civilian. Perhaps he'd be an art history professor, or a primary school art teacher, or maybe work on a nature preserve or be a veterinarian. He was so lost in his train of thought, he didn't hear a menacing growl until he looked up and saw a flash of orange and black heading right in his direction.

Completely forgetting everything he'd been told about not moving and staying calm when a tiger approached, he leapt to his feet, stuffed his fountain pen and notepad into his bag, and began running as fast as he could in a zigzag pattern. He limped heavier than usual, the way he always did when he had to run very fast, and took ragged, gulping breaths. The tropical heat combined with his terror produced an excess of sweat he was unable to stop to wipe away. All the while, the beating of his heart was probably loud enough to call the tiger's attention.

As he was running far away from his encampment, by now positive he'd gotten lost forever in the jungle, he saw another horrifying sight looming in front of him. A machine gun nest. Quickly glancing back to make sure he still had some distance on the tiger, he reached into the left-side pocket on his bag as he ran, pulled out a grenade, removed the pin, and aimed right for the nest.

By the time he saw the first Indonesian guerrillas coming out of the woodwork in the wake of the explosion, he was as hopped-up on adrenalin as he'd been while crossing the River Maas. He couldn't go back and risk the tiger, so the only way out was forward. No matter how he felt about his country's colonization of these islands, the people pointing guns at him were enemies. There was no time to tell them he was more or less on their side.

He dropped to the ground, pulled his rifle off his back and held it in his left arm, and took his pistol in his right hand. He barely looked as he fired on both sides and propelled himself along on his stomach. When he ran out of bullets in his right-hand pistol, he switched his rifle to his right arm and pulled out his left-hand pistol. These people had probably never encountered a soldier who knew how to shoot with both hands, and if they were the superstitious type, as he hoped, they might think they were being attacked by an evil spirit, not a mortal man.

As he was struggling to pull out another grenade while keeping himself shielded from gunfire, he saw that flash of orange and black again. His heart was in his throat as the tiger raced towards his position in the tall grasses. He was imagining his mother dying of grief and Rachel wearing widow's weeds at only nineteen when the orange and black flash rushed right past him. This time the tiger hadn't noticed him because he was lying still. As the guerrillas began screaming and running away, he took courage, leapt up, and threw the grenade at them.

He was pulling the bayonet off his rifle when he heard gunfire and thudding footsteps coming up close behind him. He was positive his goose was really cooked this time, with assailants on both sides. He dropped his rifle and put his hands up.

"You dummy, it's us!" Govert shouted. "Continue what you were doing! We're here to help you!"

Jakob grabbed his rifle and assumed his position in formation with his comrades. From what he had time to make out in the heat of battle, the entire company hadn't come to his rescue, but there were about fifteen or twenty other people there.

It felt cowardly to shoot someone in the back, but when it was either kill today or be killed another day, he had no choice. As he reloaded his rifle and continued firing, he reminded himself he was a soldier doing a job he'd knowingly, voluntarily signed up for. Soldiers who killed in the line of duty weren't murderers. Even the Ten Commandments only forbade criminal murder. Killing in self-defense or combat was perfectly permissible.

"They seem to be all gone," the commanding officer finally announced through a haze of gunsmoke and the acrid smell of gunpowder.

Jakob stood at attention, his heart thudding even more violently. He was petrified of the dressing-down he might be about to get for wandering off and exposing them to an unnecessary attack. He didn't move from his position, too afraid to wipe the ocean of sweat off his face or take his helmet off to cool down.

"I can explain what happened, Major Reinders. I was out scouting—"

"You don't have to explain anything besides the fact that you're a military genius and more heroic in battle than many men twice your age. I don't know anyone who would've run right into the line of fire instead of running back to report the situation and get reinforcements. I can't believe the number of bodies we saw on our way to finding you. How did you know there were guerrillas in this area?"

"You really think I'm a hero and military genius?"

"How else do you describe a nineteen-year-old who hasn't even been an official soldier for a year doing what you've done?"

"Thanks for your vote of confidence, but I just did what I had to do to save my hide. I didn't seek out a battle. I was scouting when a tiger started chasing me, and I stumbled upon a machine gun nest. After I took it out with a grenade, all these guys came pouring out. The tiger saved my hide by catching up to them and not me." He knew enough to leave out the part about playing with orangutans when the trouble started.

"We couldn't find you anywhere, and knew it wasn't like you to desert," Jeronymus said. "So we set out with a search party, thinking you might've been kidnapped or fallen under enemy fire. You're a born soldier."

"We're having a ceremony for you after you get back to our base," Major Reinders said.

"No, please, I don't deserve to be singled out for anything. If I hadn't panicked and run from the tiger instead of staying still, I wouldn't have gotten into that mess."

"It'll be a promotion ceremony. You've earned the rank of captain with your skill, experience, and bravery."

Jakob's eyes lit up. "Really? You're advancing me already? Oh, boy, I can't wait to tell my wife and my mother the good news!"

4

Jungle stalemate and periodic guerrilla clashes could only continue for so long. The Japanese attempted to retake control in October, and then the British came to help the Dutch with their reoccupation and defense efforts. Jakob's heart was heavy when they received orders to move to Surabaya at the beginning of November. This time he was being used as a reinforcement for the British, not being asked to hold down a bridgehead or help to liberate his homeland.

"Why again did we volunteer to come here?" Govert asked as they slowly began advancing through Surabaya at dawn on 10 November. "These people aren't the Japanese. We should just let them have their independence and they'll leave us alone. We're bringing these fights on ourselves."

"I agree, but as your commander, I have to order you to do what we're told," Jakob said. "The Navy and Air Force have us covered."

"Why are there Indians among the British troops we're helping? By all rights, they should be fighting for their own independence instead of helping their occupiers help another occupying force! After the occupation we lived through, I can't go back to how I used to see colonialism."

Jakob pushed down the door of the nearest house and motioned his comrades inside. He hoped his tall height would make them take him seriously. He probably wouldn't want a nineteen-year-old kid to order him around if he were in his thirties or forties, even if that nineteen-year-old kid had a higher rank.

He forced himself not to vomit when he saw some of his own men falling at the hands of the Indonesians in the houses they swept through. Every time he exited another room of another house still unscathed, he gave thanks. This was what he'd been trained to do since he was seventeen, be a cold-hearted, calculating assassin and fighter. Good soldiers never wasted time feeling sorry for the enemy or thinking things out before they fired.

Half of the city had been conquered within three days, but the other half proved to be a little harder to overtake. Once he'd gotten used to being back in battle, the adrenalin was a lifesaver. He once again found himself leading his own charges through houses and streets, shooting and throwing grenades right and left, dodging and ducking bullets as he advanced, mercilessly killing as many enemies as he could get in his sights. There was no time to think of anything else but fighting. Even the hand-to-hand fighting didn't scare him anymore.

"These people just won't give up," Jakob muttered as he loaded enemy ammunition into his bag.

Jeronymus relieved a fresh corpse of his rifle and pistol. "At least some of the residents like us."

"What! Are you telling us you're still sleeping your way around the islands even in the heat of battle?"

"Guilty as charged. It's a little harder to find Indonesian women to couple with, since they see us as the enemy, but you just have to use the right language. I've had at least twenty women in the months I've been here, and at least five women since this battle began. A man has to have something to take his mind off of being a moving target."

Govert looked at one of the Indian fighters who'd fallen in the hallway. "Maybe I'm stupid, but I was surprised to learn people of other races bleed the same color we do. That's what we get for living in a country with people of only one race."

"Enough chatter," Jakob said. "We have to get out of this house and clear the next one."

He was used to stepping over dead bodies, and no longer distinguished between Dutch, British, Indian, or Indonesian. He'd never get used to seeing his own men fall in battle, but seeing someone who was now a corpse was another matter. Just so long as the corpse wasn't too bloody or mangled, and so long as he didn't have to see dismembered body parts. He always ducked and threw his hands over his face when he encountered one of the many severed limbs, hands, feet, and heads strewn everywhere.

As they were walking in the street, he heard gunfire behind them. He pulled out his rifle and began firing back as Jeronymus threw grenades and the other members of their company went off in various directions to return fire. With adrenalin coursing through his entire being, this felt like the life. His only regret was that Dries and Leendert weren't able to share in this latest battle with them. After what he'd gone through with his friends, he felt a bond to them he didn't even share with Rachel or his mother. Only people who'd been through the heat of battle could understand, the same way he couldn't understand what his mother had gone through in the foul, evil kingdom of Auschwitz–Birkenau.

He heard a bullet whizzing off his helmet and shot in the direction of the gunfire. The sky was lit up with orange and yellow, and he struggled to see straight. He could barely hear anything through the roaring din of gunfire and bombs. Only after the ringing in his ears slowly ceased after a shout of all-clear did his eyes start to readjust to their surroundings.

The first thing he saw after the smoke cleared and the street was secured was Govert lying on his side, his bloody hands clutching his stomach as he moaned. Jakob dropped to the ground, gently moved his friend's hands, and ripped open his shirt and the top of his pants. A gaping, bloody wound was in his abdomen, and Jakob saw the hateful gunpowder and metal shards. He was about to reach for his tweezers to try to pull it out when he remembered they'd been warned never to try to remove a bullet themselves, for fear of worsening the bleeding.

"It didn't go that far, buddy," he whispered. "We'll bring the medic over for you as soon as we can, and you just keep putting pressure on it till you get to the hospital. Looks like you'll be going home early."

"I wonder which of us will be next," Jeronymus muttered.

"We're going home soon, remember? Our year of service is up in February, unless you plan to renew your service or sign a longer contract."

"Even February seems so far away. I guess there's only one thing to do to take my mind off of what happened to Govert."

Jakob threw his head back when he saw the look in Jeronymus's eyes. Even the wounding of one of their few friends left wasn't enough to dissuade this playboy from his favorite pastime. He wondered if Jeronymus would still have that on his mind if he were the one fighting for his life in the middle of a warzone.

5

The Battle of Surabaya ended victoriously on 20 November, and Jakob and Jeronymus returned to scouting and fighting off periodic guerrilla warfare, feeling a little safer and more secure. Since they were now part of the victorious occupying force in Surabaya, they were able to go through the city and help themselves to anything they wanted in stores, restaurants, and the open-air markets. While Jeronymus preferred to scout for any willing women he could find, Jakob preferred to buy arts and crafts to ship to Rachel. Chanukah started on the penultimate day of the month, and he wanted her to have something nice, even if it arrived a little belatedly. The news that he was now Major DeJonghe, only two months after being promoted to Captain, wouldn't be as special to her as a gift she could actually hold in her hands and put to good use.

"You speak Dutch?" he asked a woman at a stall in the market.

She nodded, eyeing his uniform and decorations warily.

"I take your side, Mevrouw. I'm very unhappy my friends are being killed by your men, but I think your people deserve independence from my country. I fought to liberate my own country from an occupying force, and now I see why you want your own freedom. I just came here to do a job. I don't agree with the specifics."

"Are you here long?"

"Just since July. My superiors promised me an abbreviated tour of duty, since my year of service is up in February. I'm not going to join up again for a longer term. I've had enough soldiering for a thousand lifetimes." He pulled some bills out of his pocket. "Do you accept guilders? I'm afraid I never had a chance to get native currency."

"As long as you pay what you owe. What are you in the market for?"

Jakob pulled out the latest picture Rachel had sent him. "This is my beautiful bride, who's waiting for me in America. We didn't get a real ceremony, and couldn't even properly consummate our marriage. We have a holiday coming up very soon, and I want to get her a really special present."

"Oh, yes, St. Nicholas Day. There used to be a man who dressed up as Sinterklaas who came through the city before the war. What would you like your bride to get from Sinterklaas this year?"

"Oh, no, Mevrouw, we don't celebrate Christmas. Our holiday is called Chanukah. It celebrates a military victory our ancestors in Israel had over the Greeks, who tried to make them abandon their heritage. When they rededicated the Temple, there was only enough oil to light the seven-branched candelabrum for one day, but a miracle occurred, and the oil lasted for eight days. Today we use a candelabrum with eight branches, and one in the center that's a little higher, to help with lighting the main branches. It's traditional to eat foods fried in oil, because of the miracle. It's not a traditional custom to give gifts, but who could object to getting presents?"

"Oh, you're Mosaic. They have church and cemetery in this city, but I don't think many of your people are still here to use them."

"I don't blame them for getting out. When I go home, my mother and I will ask for permission to go to America. We can't stay in a place where so many people helped our oppressors. We know who our friends are, but we can never be too sure who secretly helped our enemies."

The merchant set a large basket on top of her stall and began pulling out various embroidered and painted cloths. "Do any of these appeal to you?"

Jakob admired them. "Those are very pretty. My bride would probably love to put them in frames or use them as table runners."

She assembled the fabric art in three piles. "The shimmery gold and silver cloths are called songket. The cloths with bright colors and patterns are called ikat. The others are called batik."

He considered how much money he had and how many presents it would be considered appropriate to send. "Maybe I should buy several of them but not send them all at once. I can send her a package every month, and each month it'll have different presents. I'll get her more gifts when I'm back in Amsterdam, but it'll be nice to send her a lot of exotic things while I'm still stationed here." He started pulling out the cloths, tapestries, and shawls that appealed to him most. "She won't like anything that's too delicate and subtle, but she doesn't like things that are too loud and flashy either."

"Maybe you can buy her some jewelry too. I'll give you discount, for being nice customer and wanting my country to have independence."

His eyes fell upon a beaded necklace in various shades of blue and green, with a pretty dark green pendant in the middle. "That'll be perfect for her birthday in March. She'll be twenty."

"No jewelry for holiday?"

He looked around till he saw a green beaded bracelet. "Sure, I'll have that as well. I'll give her the fancier one for her birthday, and this for Chanukah."

After he paid, he stuffed the jewelry and textiles into his bag and imagined the look on Rachel's face when she opened the package and saw what her war hero husband had bought her. Then he remembered Luisa would expect a present too.

"Sorry, I forgot to get something for my mother. She went through so much, and I'm so lucky I still have a mother. My mother didn't have me till she was forty, and then she lost my little sister. I'd be a very bad son if I didn't get my lovely mother something special too."

"Of course." The merchant laid out a pair of beaded indigo earrings and a matching necklace. "You think this will make your mother happy?"

"Yes, very." He put his remaining money on the counter. "I hope you have a very happy New Year, and I hope your country achieves its independence without much more bloodshed."

6

The seventh night of Chanukah, 5 December, was St. Nicholas Day. Jakob felt a little better about receiving gifts at headquarters since the holidays coincided. He didn't think he'd be able to accept gifts given to him as actual Christmas presents. Without a chanukiyah, he'd had to make one out of hollowed-out jackfruits. His makeshift chanukiyah paled in comparison to the brightly decorated and lit tree the commanding officer had had shipped in from somewhere, but it was more special to him since it was made from scratch, and it was the first time he'd been able to publicly, properly celebrate a holiday since the occupation.

As Jakob and his comrades opened the modest presents, Jeronymus lay prostrate on his mattress, refusing to take part in the festivities. Ben tried to cheer him up by licking his face and rubbing his muzzle against his face, but Jeronymus covered his face and gently pushed him away.

"I think I had bad food," he moaned. "Why did I have to get sick on a holiday?"

"When did you start feeling sick?" Jakob asked. "Do you know what kind of food it was?"

"How should I remember? It's not like I got sick immediately after eating whatever it was. I never thought food poisoning could last this long."

"You mean you've been feeling ill before this and never told us?"

"What for? It's not like I was shot. I figured I could get through the pain and then be back to normal."

"What exactly are your symptoms, besides an upset stomach?" one of the commanding officers asked. "Knowing you, I bet it's something other than bad food. It's probably a bad woman, or bad women."

"Do I have to discuss such delicate matters in front of everyone?"

"You were the one who wanted to give Major DeJonghe explicit sexual advice when you found out he was married! Now let's hear just what's wrong with you. At least your womanizing never impacted your performance as a damn good soldier."

"That's impossible. I never sleep with dirty women. I've never screwed a hooker or camp prostitute, only clean local girls. I'd know if I were sleeping with a woman of ill repute. And for your information, I don't have a stomachache. It burns when I urinate, and I'm having other sorts of personal pain. I never knew bad food could have those kinds of effects."

"You have venereal disease, Lieutenant. I don't think anyone needs to examine you to know for sure, though you'll be going to the hospital for treatment as soon as possible. We can't have sick soldiers in our company. At the rate you go through women, you probably have several venereal diseases. You can't always tell who has them, and you don't always have symptoms right away. Why again haven't you used any of the numerous free prophylactics we have available?"

"Because I didn't want to. It's not my concern if a girl isn't careful enough. If I'm not marrying her, I shouldn't help her get an abortion or take responsibility if she doesn't have a diaphragm or pessary, or whatever else women use. And it's not as fun with a sheet of rubber in the way."

"Was all that fun worth it now?" Jakob asked.

"You bet. I'd do it all over again, and I will do it all over again till I'm ready to be married."

Jakob smiled when he unwrapped his present from Jeronymus, a Dutch translation of the fifteenth century Arabic sex manual *The Perfumed Garden*. "Looks like I'll be enjoying a lovely perfumed garden when I get home to my bride, while you'll be lucky if anything in your garden can still grow."

"Speaking of your perfumed garden, you've got a holiday package from her." The commanding officer tossed a package at him. "She has a leg up on your mother, since her package came first. Next time you write to your mother, you can tell her the wife she disapproves of so much sent her holiday package early enough to arrive on time."

Jakob began ripping open the box. "Having my mother still alive is present enough. I don't care if I get another gift from her ever again." He pulled out several chocolate bars, a box of candied fruit slices, a ceramic sandcastle painted orange and blue, ten tubes of oil paint, and a wooden palette. At the bottom of the box were several pictures and a letter.

3 November 1945

My dear sweet husband and beshert *Jaapje,*

I'm sending this out so early just to make sure it reaches you in time. What little I can find about the fighting in the Dutch East Indies in the American papers isn't good. Every single day I worry about you, having to risk your life against people you never did anything to. It's always a good day when I get another letter from you and don't get any official letters or telegrams from the Army. Pietje's sister Lotje is still worried about her sweetheart Lazarus, and she's jealous of me because I know you're alive somewhere. We haven't heard anything from Juli either. Fritz (Gary) is convinced something happened to her after I saw her, that she succumbed to a disease or were attacked.

Sometimes I start thinking about how I'm married to a near-stranger, how we've been married longer than we've known each other. Married for six months, and we only knew each other for perhaps one month all totaled, counting both our first brief meetings and those two weeks in May. I still can't really believe it, how I agreed to marry someone I barely knew and let you have all of me, even if we didn't properly go all the way. I often wonder if you still really feel the same way, in spite of how you profess your undying love in such sweet words in all your letters. Absence does make the heart grow fonder, but what if you feel differently when we're together again? Maybe you only love me in the abstract, but when you see me again, you'll wonder whatever possessed you to marry a stranger. You probably forget how to kiss by now, and I'll have to teach you all over again.

I'm working hard on learning your mother's recipes to perfection. Every time Vrouw Brandt lets me use the oven, I make something from your mother's recipes. So far, everyone likes my cooking. I wish I could send you some of my cooking and baking, but I'm sure it'd be stale or all broken apart by the time the package reached you.

Now that it's winter, Lotje isn't on my case so much anymore about shaving my legs and underarms like she and all her American friends do. I've told her you didn't mind, and that I keep my underarm hair very short and trimmed instead of as long as a man's, but she acts like it's a cardinal sin for a woman to have body hair. Poor girl has been away from Europe so long, she doesn't remember I'm merely doing what's normal in our homeland. I'm still in shock over the fact that Lotje and almost all her friends shave everything, if you know what I mean. Even if I'm going to be an American citizen one day, I never want to pretend I'm someone I'm not. I wouldn't be me without my body hair. God put it there for a reason, and it makes me feel so womanly.

Speaking of being womanly, I long to feel womanly with you, not just for myself. Even if I'm in a beach city, it still gets a little bit colder in the winter. I wish I had my husband to warm me up at night, go ice-skating and sledding with, and to go to the movies and out to eat with. I hope so much you really do want to continue as my husband once you're here. A girl my age should be going out with her fellow, not just her friends. There are some other young survivors who've moved here, most notably a family of twelve siblings from Warsaw and their Dutch adopted sister, and we like to go out and do things. I'm sure they'd love to meet you and thank you for your service.

I hope you have a wonderful Chanukah out in the jungle, and that you're back in Amsterdam soon. They'd better not make you wade through reams of red tape before you can join me, or I might have to go over there and throw a few punches!

I love you so much, even if we can't be together for a long time,

Gepje

He pulled the wrapper off the largest chocolate bar and began eating it as he wrote her a letter.

5 December 1945

My lovely bride Gepje,

Thank God, the big battle is over and we're not so much in harm's way as we were a few weeks ago. I'm writing this from the comfort of headquarters. Sometimes we still have to deal with guerrillas, but we haven't been called back to any frontlines yet. We can't predict the future, but I hope it continues like this for the rest of my term here. When I'm in the heat of battle, I feel so alive and immortal, but then in the aftermath, I realize what I've done and what I've lived through. You have to have a sense of fearlessness and audacity to get through a battle. You do things you'd never dream of doing, or see yourself doing, in normal time. I've done so many things here and back home that I'd think insane in anyone else. Sometimes I have a hard time believing I've done a lot of these things under fire.

My playboy buddy Jeronymus, to absolutely no one's surprise, has come down with a raging case of VD. You'll never have to worry I'll end up like that. I've been completely faithful to you our entire separation, and I know you have too. Even if you hadn't told me that detail about what you did to yourself when you were younger, I'd still have complete trust in you and not subject you to one of those hypocritical, disturbing "virginity tests." I don't want a strange man looking at and touching my wife. If there's no trust between a husband and wife, even when they're far away for a long time, there's no basis for them to continue in their marriage.

I think of you all the time, and hope my Chanukah package reached you in time for the holiday. After that arrives, expect a lot of other gifts I've bought for you. I bet you never thought you'd be the lucky recipient of jewelry and arts and crafts from the Dutch East Indies. When will I ever again get a chance to buy you such exotic presents? I hope you enjoy the drawings I've sent you too. Every time I see a mother orangutan with her baby, it makes me think of you, imagining you with a cute little baby. Don't worry, I think orangutans are really cute, neat creatures, even though you're not covered in orange hair.

Please don't talk about our marriage just being a pipe dream. You're my dream girl, the one I was destined to meet before I was born. Everything about our meeting and our reunion so much time later proves it. You don't meet someone, start thinking about her all the time, and then meet her again for no reason. I can't wait to make you my wife all over again in the coming year. Maybe it'll be strange to get used to living together and being a real husband and wife, but we'll have pure, sweet love to get us through the awkward early days. No one ever really loves someone, with real, mature love, in the beginning. You can have lust or a strange, uncanny feeling and connection, but that's not the same as love that's been tested through years. If you still love me after all this time, we're halfway there. You don't have any obligation to keep loving me and staying faithful, but you are. You'd better be careful when I see you again, because I'll have so much pent-up love and passion to give you. I know you'll unload your love and passion on me in equal measure.

I love you exactly as you are. Don't let any of these American girls, or girls who've become more American than Dutch, influence you. When I touched you, I knew I was touching a real woman. It would've felt extremely unnatural and even deviant if I'd touched you and not felt any hair on your legs or under your arms. I can't believe some American girls shave even more than that. Whoever started that trend needs his head examined!

I hate being so far away from you. At least back in The Netherlands, I'll be a little closer to you, kilometers-wise. None of the adventures I've had out here could possibly ever hope to compare to the life I'm going to enjoy with you. I'll take you on so many dates, cuddle with you at night when it's cold, cook with you, and treat you like a queen after what you've been through. I'm so excited thinking about how we might be expecting our dear little baby by the end of next year. When I was young and didn't know any better, I thought birth was women's stuff, but now I want to be there to see our future child being born. After I lost my father when I was only four-teen, and knowing he waited forty years to have me, I can't wait to be a father my-self and give our baby all the love my father can no longer give me.

I'll see you in my dreams, my beautiful bride. It'll be forever till I'm safely back in your sweet, loving arms and breathing in your sweet feminine scent. I still can't believe I was lucky enough to get my own blonde bombshell, and a girl with a beautiful heart, soul, and mind beneath the gorgeous exterior.

I love you more every single second we're apart,

Your loving husband Jaapje

Chapter 23: Amsterdam Reacquaintance

There was no victory parade for Jakob as he got off the plane with the other returning soldiers at the end of December. In spite of the letter he'd gotten praising his valor during the Battle of Surabaya, he wasn't being treated to a hero's welcome. The Dutch people were still recovering from the occupation. The struggle in the Dutch East Indies was serious business involving their sons, brothers, fathers, uncles, nephews, and cousins, but it was so far away and didn't seem so personal. All he cared about now was that he'd be able to finish the remaining two months of his service in a noncombatant capacity.

His first stop after arriving home was the apartment where Luisa lived with Floor and Elma, in the same building as Kees and Bram. Sander and Willem were down the hall. He knew from Luisa's letters that Gusta had been committed to a sanitarium shortly after he'd left for the Indies, and was secretly relieved he wouldn't have to see her again.

"You recognize me after almost six months?" he called as he opened the door and leaned in unannounced.

Luisa shrieked and dropped her knitting. Jakob smiled and held out his arms as she ran towards him.

"I love you, Mama, I love you so much. Now I can finally tell you in person again. I've brought back presents for you." He was happy to feel substantially more meat on her bones than there'd been six months ago. "As soon as the Army's done with me, I'll move in with you and help you cook. You'll gain even more weight with me as your chef. I was a very good cook in the partisans."

Luisa laughed slightly as he released her. "If you love me that much, you'll be happy with the normal weight I'm at now. I was too skinny last year at this time, but I don't want to get too fat in return."

"Now you can come to Willem's and my wedding in April!" Elma said excitedly. "We're getting married on the fifteenth of April, the year-anniversary of our liberation. Hopefully we'll figure out who'll live where after that. That day is Erev Pesach this year, and Ta'anit Bechorot, but the rabbi we found said it's fine to marry on that date, though it is cutting it close. We couldn't imagine any other date."

Jakob hugged her next. "I didn't forget you. I got a wedding present for you in the Indies. You're invited to my own wedding, of course, whenever that is. Are you planning to stay here or go to America?"

"Sander, Willem, and I are going to Palestine after the British go away. That's the only place we can really belong. As much as we love our country, there are too many reminders of everyone and everything we've lost. Like you've said, we can never be too sure who was in the NSB or doing other evil things to hurt us. Even silent collaborators are everywhere. People in America could never really understand. Does that interest you? I'm sure your Rachel will want to go wherever you go, even if she's gotten used to America."

He shook his head. "I'm committed to going to America. I love the idea of going to Palestine and bringing the State of Israel back after two thousand years, but I can't go anywhere without my mother. That's not a place for people her age. America's already built. They don't make new immigrants drain ditches, farm deserts, and take up arms against surrounding enemies. After I'm done with the Army, I hope to God I never have to fire a gun or throw a grenade at anyone ever again. Three of my buddies could've gotten killed in battle. Thank God, Govert and Leendert will probably be sent home soon, and the word from Hedel is that Dries recently was released and given an honorable discharge. My other closest friend is in the hospital with something else, but he'll probably be coming home soon too."

"Something else?" Luisa asked. "Was he attacked by a wild animal? I still can't believe you outran a tiger and got close enough to draw leopards. It must be your caulbearer's luck."

"You know Jeronymus loves the ladies. The word is that he has gonorrhea and chlamydia, and possibly one or two more venereal diseases."

Elma giggled. "Somehow I knew that would happen to him from the first time you told me about how many women he's bedded. You don't sleep around for so long with no consequences. He's an idiot for not taking precautions and thinking nothing would happen to him."

"Where are you going from here?" Luisa asked, looking uncomfortable at the topic of conversation. "You can't live with me till you're free."

"I was told I'd serve as a cook in a soup kitchen in Amsterdam. Finally, no getting shot at or constantly protecting my hide. I'd prefer to serve as a guard at a beach resort or work in a military bookstore, but it's good enough for a noncombatant position."

"Do you get to keep your uniform when they're done with you?"

"Of course. Both my dress uniform and my khakis, and my helmet, boots, cap, and a side arm. I guess I get to keep my bag and the supplies in it. I don't want to give a new recruit a used razor or a half-empty can of shaving cream."

Luisa ran her hands over his face. "You never had much of anything you needed to shave. Even after you started getting facial hair, it was so sparse and fine. You naturally have a soft, baby face. I don't think you'd look very good if you tried to grow a moustache or beard."

"I'd probably have to go at least six months without shaving if I wanted a real beard. My time in the partisans and Army is proof enough of my manliness."

"What about that beautiful dog of yours?" Elma asked. "Do you have to leave him to the Army once you're demobilized?"

Jakob smiled. "Bentje's all mine. He doesn't mind being left at headquarters or going on missions with other guys, but he's always thrilled to see me again. Both of us have had enough of warfare for a thousand lifetimes. Bentje doesn't like getting shot at or dodging grenades either. You don't mind, do you, *Moeder*? I always wanted a dog, and now you can't argue I'm not old or responsible enough for one. He'd be so sad and lonely without me, and he'll keep you company while I'm at work."

"I am kind of lonely while Floor and Elma are at work," Luisa admitted. "I won't mind your dog staying if he's well-behaved."

"Oh, he'll be the best-behaved dog ever! And before you know it, all three of us will be headed to America!"

2

28 February 1946 was one of the most bittersweet days of Jakob's life. He'd been looking forward to rejoining civilian life for such a long time, and now that it was finally here, he felt a gnawing longing to be back in the Army. He knew life as a soldier, both in battle and in a noncombatant capacity. It had been so long since he'd been a true civilian, and he'd been so young the last time he'd been a civilian. He didn't know how to do anything as an adult but be a soldier. Now he was expected to go out into the world and find a non-military job to support himself and Luisa until they got permission to immigrate. Rejoining the Army on a month-by-month basis was impossible. Either

he'd accept the honorable discharge or sign back up for a longer term, and only one of those things ensured he'd get back to Rachel sooner rather than later.

"Congratulations, Major DeJonghe. It's been an honor to serve with you. The entire nation is grateful to you for your service in the Dutch Resistance, the Princess Irene Brigade, and the Royal Army of The Netherlands, both at home and in the Dutch East Indies, in wartime and in peace. We'll miss your service and company very much, and wish you well in your future life as a civilian. Please accept this certificate of your honorable discharge, and these several letters of recommendation, to use in any way you want in your future endeavors. Had you chosen to remain in the Army, you could've easily become a general by the age of twenty-five. Our canine soldier Bernhard is also respectfully, honorably discharged of all former duties and obligations."

Jakob shook his commanding officers' hands. "Thank you very much. It's a shame current Dutch law doesn't recognize most dual citizenship, even if America does. I'm so proud of my service, I wish I could remain a Dutch citizen even after I'm in America."

"You'll retain your distinguished record of military service and all your citations and decorations. Any future employer will look very favorably upon that. Should you want to go to university, your record will look very promising. Anyone who has your kind of skill, bravery, and expertise on the battlefield is more than capable of succeeding academically."

He proudly walked over to Luisa and his friends after the ceremony, holding his honorable discharge and beaming a mile a minute. Savoring the chance to put his dress uniform to good use, he obligingly posed for pictures. One of his now-former comrades took several group shots, then took pictures of Jakob standing individually with Luisa, Vrouw Visser, Elma, Sander, Floor, Bram, and Kees.

"Do you think it'll be okay to wear my uniform at parades or events on the American Decoration Day? Even if I'm not a veteran of the American military, I was still in an Allied armed force."

"I'm sure you'll be welcome to don your uniform on special days. It's not like you'd be wearing a Wehrmacht or an Imperial Japanese Army uniform. You're also welcome to wear your uniform when you have your religious wedding with that beautiful wife of yours."

Jakob smiled and closed his eyes, picturing the look on Rachel's face when she saw him standing at the door in his dress uniform, with all his decorations and insignia. He didn't want to wear the traditional kitl on their real wedding day. Why cover up the uniform he was so proud of? He could always wear a kitl on Yom Kippur if he so wanted it, but he'd only get one chance to stand under the chupah and have a good time at a wedding reception. Maybe he'd wear it to each of the Sheva Brachot celebrations, to milk it for all it was worth.

3

Jakob's first act after receiving his honorable discharge wasn't to immediately find a job, but to go with Luisa to the American Embassy in Amsterdam to ask for permission to immigrate. He shuddered as they drew closer to the building at Museumplein 19, knowing this had been the German Embassy during the occupation and that adjacent buildings had been used for the Wehrmacht and police. There were still four bunkers in front of the building. Had it only been a year since they'd been under enemy occupation and their homeland had been a dangerous warzone?

While he and Luisa waited in the lobby, he saw a young woman covered in various types of scars, and with a haunting, heartbreaking look in her eyes. She carried herself as though she weren't quite sure if she belonged in this world or had already passed over to the next. He was even more horrified when she began walking over to him.

"I see you're a soldier," she said in a frightening tone of voice as she clutched his arm. "You have to help me. I've been begging at so many offices, and no one can help me! I know I shouldn't expect a free ride, but my sweetheart is waiting for me in America! He might think I'm dead, and I've forgotten his address!"

"I'm trying to immigrate myself. I'm the last person you want to ask." He edged away from her, trying to free his arm.

"But you have a kind face. They don't want to let anyone immigrate, and I don't want to spend years on a waiting list! You'd think I'd be given first priority because I look so awful, and I looked even worse when I first started begging! And I'll never go to a DP camp! Those places are former Nazi camps!"

He backed even farther up in his seat. "I'm sorry for you, but you have to obey the rules and do things the approved way. It's not as though our lives are at stake anymore."

"Major Jakob DeJonghe and Vrouw Luisa Hartog?" an official

called.

Jakob was relieved to be rid of this terrifying-looking woman. He pulled free of her and took Luisa's arm as they were ushered into the office.

The official beckoned them to sit down. Jakob helped Luisa into her chair and pushed it closer to the desk, then took a seat and helped himself to some of the chocolates on the official's desk. He passed a few to Luisa.

"I see you and your mother are looking to immigrate to the United States, and you're in a military uniform. Isn't wanting to immigrate a conflict of interest if you're serving in your country's armed forces?"

"I was just given an honorable discharge, Meneer. My year of service is up. My superiors knew I wanted to immigrate afterwards. See, they gave me these letters of glowing recommendation, and this is my honorable discharge." He set the papers on the desk, positive he'd be given priority.

The official took some time to read all the documents, then set them back on the desk. "It looks like you've had a very distinguished, memorable military career in a very short time. Can you explain why you're trying to immigrate after everything you've done in the service of your country?"

"I love The Netherlands, but after the war, my mother and I can't be too sure of who our friends really are. We know who helped us and who warmly welcomed us home, but we'll always wonder who hated us all along, who was in the NSB or stood by without protesting during the occupation."

"My son has a wife in America," Luisa said. "He's very eager to get back to her."

"How long has this wife been in America?"

"She arrived last June, Meneer," Jakob said. "We got married last May, and she went there on a ship for wives and other relatives of servicemen. This was a very opportune chance, and she took it. She's been living with old friends in Atlantic City." He put the marriage certificate on the desk, followed by his and Luisa's legal documents and passports. "My mother and I gave our most important possessions to friends before we went to Westerbork. That's how we still have these papers."

Jakob struggled to keep up with the questions being thrown at them after the basic introductions. Where they lived, their full names, dates of birth, how they planned to support themselves, how much money they had, the names of their parents, education, any friends or relatives in the United States, health, religion, how often Jakob and Rachel sent and received letters. It was very embarrassing to have to answer personal questions in front of his mother, and to listen to her answering the same questions. At least he wasn't like Jeronymus and could honestly say he'd never had VD, visited a prostitute, gotten or received money for sexual favors, or engaged in unnatural sex acts. He figured "unnatural" referred to Greek love, not the things he'd done with Rachel. The more left unsaid, the better. He might not be granted a visa if it came out he'd never consummated his marriage and that Rachel lived with a former boyfriend's family.

The official reviewed all his notes at the end of the long interview and read them again and again. Finally, he looked up at Jakob and Luisa.

"So far you've passed with flying colors. Now you need to make an appointment to see a doctor and report back here in about a week. We'll review the medical findings and see if everything checks out."

Jakob didn't want to see a doctor or subject Luisa to that, but kept quiet as he shook the official's hand. He'd figure out a way to get around that bit of business without completely ignoring the medical requirement.

"Do you remember the name of the doctor who was Gusta's primary backup if one of her births went wrong?" Luisa asked as they walked down the street.

"No, and even if I did, he's not a general doctor. I think they want us to see someone who services everyone, not just pregnant women. You don't really want to subject yourself to that, do you? After what you went through? I don't want a lecherous man looking at and touching my mother, and I'm not about to let someone conduct any invasive exams on me either. The Army never would've kept me in for my full term if I'd been unhealthy. Who the hell did that interviewer think he was, asking a woman if she's ever been a prostitute, and in front of her son no less?"

"They have to ask those questions to everyone. It's not personal, just like it's not supposed to be personal when a doctor looks at and touches someone."

"I never believed that. A hundred years ago, it was considered an inexcusable, unseemly violation of modesty to do what some doctors get away with these days under the claim of just doing a job. Gepje says one of her new American friends, one of the girls Lotje is friends with, is always talking about things like that."

"Whatever your thoughts on the matter, we have to go to some type of doctor. It's not like I'll be standing there exposed for hours like I was in the camps."

Jakob kicked pebbles along the ground with his left foot as they continued walking toward their apartment in Jordaan. All around him, he saw signs of the war and occupation, of an Amsterdam still struggling to heal raw, open wounds. Only six years ago, these streets had been alive, not full of bombed-out buildings, pieces of shrapnel, deserted stores, trenches, bunkers, roadblocks, and barbed wire. Now the streetcars didn't even run anymore. At least the streets had shown signs of a vibrant city during the February Strike, in spite of so much coming to a standstill.

His eyes lit up as they came up the stairwell of their building. "It might be a bit of work to go to him or get him to come here, but I'm sure the nice doctor who helped me after my accident would agree to help us and forge papers if need be. Dr. Gustaaf Xylander. I assume he's somewhere in the vicinity of Winschoten."

"That doctor you told me was pulling and pushing on your poor broken foot without any pain relief?"

"Yeah, that was really painful, but my buddy Leendert was right. It only lasted a short while, and as soon as he was done, I could start to get better. Now it feels like a million years ago, and I can't remember the pain."

Luisa unlocked the door to their new apartment, the fourth one on the floor where their other friends lived. Now Elma and Floor lived alone, and Sander had volunteered to move to one of the other floors after Elma and Willem's marriage next month, so the newlyweds could have their own space. Jakob thought these living arrangements were the stuff of the dinosaur era. Surely a realistic, reasonable modern person shouldn't find anything scandalous about unrelated men and women living together, or a cohabiting affianced couple. People these days knew such things existed, not like in the days when piano legs were covered.

"I'll help you make dinner, and then I can go to the nearest store or hotel to call Vrouw Visser to arrange for Dr. Xylander's services. Don't worry, *Moeder*. Leave things up to me, and everything will be fine."

4

A week later, Jakob and Luisa returned to the depressing-looking Embassy with their papers from Dr. Xylander. Since Dr. Xylander had been in the underground, he was no stranger to falsifying papers and lying on official documents. He'd conducted a basic examination for each of them, but hadn't asked any humiliating personal questions as the interviewer had, nor had he conducted any invasive, immodest tests or made them take any clothes off. Jakob was glad some modern doctors thought it was crazy to examine a naked person or subject him or her to invasive procedures when they were asymptomatic.

Jakob pulled out the latest picture of Rachel as they took their seats in the lobby. He gazed at her image and sighed, tracing his fingertip along her face and hair.

"Are you sure this woman is really waiting faithfully for you?" Luisa asked. "After such a quick courtship, don't you think it's a bit unrealistic to expect her to still feel the same way after so much time has passed?"

"Why would she still be writing me letters almost every day if she weren't still crazy about me? And I still love her to pieces. Sure I admire beautiful women, but I'm not tempted to do more than look. I'm no Jeronymus. When you meet her, you'll see what a smart, intelligent, sweet person—"

His train of thought was broken by a scream. Jakob jumped up and ran across the hall. He peered in and saw the woman he'd seen last week. She was on her knees, sobbing incoherently.

One of them had a lecherous look in his eyes, the same leer Jakob had seen on the tall, thin NSBer who'd frisked Luisa. "If you want to immigrate so badly, you can sleep with us."

Jakob was incensed to see one of them taking off his belt to whip her across the face. He'd been taught to never lay his hands on any woman. The disgusting words they were using turned his stomach. These words were downright misogynistic vulgarity. These were the kinds of words not even the most hardened soldiers in his company had used.

He was terrified of what might happen to him if he intervened. He'd left his pistol and knife at home, and now wore street clothes instead of his regulation khakis. These sadists wouldn't know or care he was a combat veteran of two wars or an honorably discharged major in the army. Sick to his stomach, he slunk back to Luisa and put his arm around her.

"Don't you think we should report those men?" Luisa asked. "Saying they're behaving unprofessionally doesn't even begin to describe what's going on in there. What, do they suspect she's a spy?"

"I wouldn't be too surprised to find out they're former NSBers. This is one of the reasons we're leaving. We know who our friends are, but we'll never be able to find out who was on the other side, either openly or silently."

She was pushed out of the office and landed on her knees, her blouse pushed far up enough to reveal a nasty scar on her back. Jakob ran to help her up when he saw the assailants hadn't followed her and had slammed the door.

"I was just thinking those men are probably former NSBers who never changed their spots. I wish I could help you, but I'm just an ordinary Dutchman. Even if I were still active duty, I'd have no sway."

She pulled her blouse down and dried her eyes. "No one's given me a visa, and I can't live in a refugee center forever. And I can't start a job, since that would waste valuable time I could spend begging at immigration offices. I'd accept a visa for anywhere in the world, so long as I'm ultimately able to go to America. My boyfriend might already think I'm dead." She started sobbing again.

"Do you have any idea what his last address was?"

"He's a student at Princeton, and his family lives in Atlantic City."

Jakob stared at her in amazement. "That's where my wife lives, and her former boyfriend's older brother is also at Princeton. I could ask her if he knows your fellow. Maybe there are more Jewish families in Atlantic City than I thought."

"Friedrich Brandt," she sniffled. "He goes by Gary now."

It suddenly dawned on him. "Are you Julia van Acker?"

She smiled weakly. "Please, call me Juli. So you're the one who crashed our Yom Kippur service by the river. Your puppy gave me such a fright. Boy, Gepje was right when she said her husband was so handsome."

He pulled out his notepad and fountain pen and wrote Rachel's address. "You have to get away from these people. I have no idea what they're doing in the Embassy, but I'm sure they'll be expelled and punished once they're caught by their superiors. Stop wasting your time with these *kankerhonden* and just write to your beau. He'll be horrified to learn what's happened to his woman."

"I told you, I have no address. I live in a stupid refugee center. I have to keep trying until I get a positive response, which I hope will be very soon. Maybe they'll let me immigrate after enough beatings. At this point, I'm so desperate I would sleep with them."

He couldn't believe how delusional and fatalistic she was, even when he was dangling a golden carrot in front of her. "If anyone had beaten my Gepje, used such repulsive words, or told her she could only immigrate in exchange for sexual favors, I'd be in prison for murder. Why don't you report them?"

"Why should I report people in a position to help me?"

"You can't let yourself get pushed around, Mejuffrouw. Stand up and be a Maccabee, not a Zealot. Now the world knows at least some of us believe in fighting back instead of meekly going like sheep to the slaughter. After what our community just survived, we should never let anyone abuse us ever again. We have to stop such behavior before it's too late."

"It's a small price to pay for a visa. It's not as though I've never been beaten before. You must've seen the scar on my back. I was beaten with a club during the death march I escaped, and many times before that. Before long I'll be with Gary, and he'll never beat me. He's the exact opposite of those animals."

He ripped out the page with the address and handed it to her. "You know what to do. This is your freedom. I knew a guy who was as fatalistic as you, but he wanted to end his life on his terms. He didn't want to put up with beatings and abuse in exchange for freedom. Please, Mejuffrouw, my wife was your best friend, and her friends are my friends. Stop playing the victim, and control your own destiny."

"Major Jakob DeJonghe and Vrouw Luisa Hartog?"

Jakob looked meaningfully at Juli as he and Luisa went into the office. He couldn't get rid of the images of those animals beating and verbally abusing Juli, the girl Rachel had said was practically scared of her own shadow. It made no sense to put up with such abusive, odious behavior, particularly when she'd been given a chance to escape. And what kind of woman would let her devoted long-distance sweetheart think she were dead or not even contact him? That was cruel and incomprehensible beyond words.

The official looked at their partially-fraudulent papers from Dr. Xylander, then reviewed the notes from the interview, Jakob's letters of recommendation, and his honorable discharge. "You're as healthy as a mule, Major DeJonghe, in spite of an old foot and ankle injury. A limp isn't a big deal next to some of the medical conditions these people think they can immigrate with. Your mother seems as healthy as a woman of her age can be."

"Yes, Meneer, we're very healthy stock. How else could my mother survive four camps at her age if she weren't healthy?"

"And you'll be working once you're in America?"

"Yes, Meneer. I'd like to go to university, but I'll take a job as well. I'll support my mother as well as my wife."

"You intend to live together?"

"No, but I'll set my mother up in her own house or apartment. I'm sure you can understand why I don't want to have my wife and mother under the same roof."

The official smiled. "You're a wise man, Major DeJonghe. No woman should have to compete with her mother-in-law to be the woman of the house. Have you gotten work since I last saw you?"

"He's getting a job as soon as we leave here," Luisa said firmly. "We have enough money from his Army savings to live on for awhile, but I want my boy to be productive. He can't sit around doing nothing just because we don't have much time left here."

"And you're a wise woman, Vrouw Hartog. I'm sure you can find decent work in the time you have left, Major DeJonghe. You probably won't find a ship leaving immediately. Might as well put yourself to good use in the meantime." He stamped "Approved" on their applications. "Your visas will be in the mail within a week."

Jakob stood up elatedly and shook his hand. "Thank you very much, Meneer. You have no idea how much this means to us. Oh, boy, I can't wait to tell my Gepje we'll be together again before the end of the year!"

Chapter 24: Last Months in Amsterdam

"This is where you'll be working most of the time, Major DeJonghe. It's a bit austere, but after what some of these children have been through, it's a paradise." The orphanage director led him down the hall. "Some of our children are more traumatized than others, and many of them can't remember their parents or a time before the war. Are you sure you can handle them?"

"Yes, Meneer. I think they'll like me, since I went through a lot of what they did. I'm sure my dog will help cheer them up. Animals have a sixth sense and comfort people who are hurting. He attached himself to me when he was a puppy because he saw my limp." Jakob looked down each hall, hoping against hope Emilia might show up or that someone might've seen her somewhere, anywhere.

"Are you planning to be a teacher or social worker after you're in America?"

"I'm not sure yet, but I think I'll go to school for art history, animal studies, or primary art education. My ship leaves at the end of July, so I've got some time to think. When I saw your ad in the paper, I knew I had to take the job. I really want to help these precious children who've lost so much. They need to see good people still exist."

"No disrespect intended, Major, but what you went through doesn't compare to what many of these children have gone through. They didn't have the option of jumping off a train and joining the partisans. We have a number of young survivors of Terezín and Bergen-Belsen. I don't believe we have any survivors of other camps, for reasons I'm sure you're aware of."

His heart twisted as he pictured little Emilia alone and scared in her final moments, far away from her parents and big brother, no one to love and protect her as she was shot, gassed, burnt alive, or electrocuted. He wondered if he'd still have a mother if Emilia hadn't disappeared. Luisa was the best mother he could've asked for, the kind who'd do anything to protect her children and sacrifice anything for them. She probably would've gone to the left with Emilia instead of pretending to be Gusta's assistant. He blinked quickly and pretended he had an eyelash in his eye.

"These children need someone with a lot of patience and understanding. I can't have anyone who loses his temper or punishes them.

They've suffered enough, and generally aren't misbehaving on purpose to annoy you."

"I'm totally against corporal punishment, and would only raise my voice to a child in extreme circumstances. I'll try my best to give them all the love they need."

A little girl holding a teddybear with a hole in it screamed and started running away when she saw him approaching.

"That's five-year-old Ursula, Urseltje. She's very scared of strangers, and doesn't like tall men. Her mother pushed her into a hole in the wall while the family was being rounded up. She was later found by a neighbor and hidden. That teddybear is the only thing she has of her former life."

"Are they all like that? So scared in a safe place?"

"Some of them wet the bed and have nightly nightmares. Are you absolutely sure you can handle this job for the next few months?"

Jakob went down the hall and sat down so he was Urseltje's height. "I want to be your friend, sweetheart. My name is Jaap, and I fought in the big war to chase the bad guys out of here. I lost my father and my little sister, and almost lost my mother. Does your bear have a name?"

"Teddy." She clutched her bear and eyed him warily.

"Would you like me to sew the hole in Teddy? Your old friend shouldn't have a hole in him. You'll be able to love him even more when he's whole again. You can hug him as tightly as you want, and none of his stuffing will fall out."

"Do you have children?"

"Oh, no, I can't have any children till I'm with my wife. But I do —did—have a little sister. Her name's Emilia." He pulled a picture out of his pocket. "She'd be nine years old this year. I haven't seen her in a very long time, and I miss her very much."

Another little girl came down the hall and tugged on his sleeve. "Are you going to be our new teacher? I had a nice teacher at Terezín, but she went away and didn't come back. Some of my friends went with her."

A little boy carrying a wooden spoon with a doll's body over the handle came up next. Jakob winced at the homemade toy. Surely they had better toys than that at this orphanage.

"Did your parents make that for you?"

"One of the big girls made it for me. I lost all my toys when I went into hiding. I could only take clothes and pictures."

"I used to have a beautiful doll," the other little girl said. "She had dark brown hair in braids, with dark blue ribbons, a green dress, green eyes, and blue shoes. And I had a stuffed doggy, a stuffed parrot, and a jigsaw puzzle my papa made for me."

"I used to have a clown doll," another little boy said. "Do toys still exist?"

"Of course they still exist." He patted the boy on the head. "Something tells me you'll all have a lot of toys very soon. Nothing can ever replace your old friends, but I'm sure you'll grow to love new friends." He stood up and walked back to the director. "I'll take this job, Meneer. I'll do everything I can to make sure these children get everything nice in life after what they've survived."

2

Jakob arrived at his first official day of work on his bicycle, feeling happy and confident he was finally starting to ride it naturally again. He no longer abruptly braked every twenty seconds for fear of falling off, or got scared when the bike began going a little fast or he came to a corner. It was a little difficult to initially push off and get his gimpy foot on the right pedal, but once he started, it was usually smooth sailing.

He went right to the kitchen after parking his bike in the hall. On his way back from the orientation yesterday, he picked up some ingredients at one of the few groceries that had reopened since the liberation.

"You don't need to cook, Major DeJonghe," the director said. "We have several cooks, and they observe kosher as best they can. Most of these children don't know or care about the details of kosher."

"It's not about that. I'm a pretty good cook, and I wanted to make the kids something special. When was the last time they had sweets?" He began unwrapping his parcels. "I'm sure they'll love me after I make them a cake."

"Can we help you?" one of the cooks asked.

"No, Mevrouw, I've got this covered. I've been cooking and baking since I was at least ten years old. My parents wouldn't hear of me not learning to cook. I'm not a spoilt mama's boy who can't do jack for himself."

When lunch was called, Jakob brought out the large cake he'd made. It felt so good to see the smiles on the children's faces. As he cut the cake and put a slice on each child's plate, he made eye contact with every one of them and gave each a compliment. He was grateful to see a number of them returning the smiles and saying a few words back.

"What kind of cake is this?" Urseltje asked.

"Cinnamon spice with raisins. I'll make you delicious soups, salads, cookies, pies, and all sorts of other things too. Just tell me what you want, and I'll see if I can't make it."

"Just don't cook us any tulip bulbs or sugar beets," an older boy said, wrinkling his nose. "I'd rather eat really strong maror than ever eat those things again."

"Don't worry, I'll never cook that nasty stuff. I hated tulip bulb purée and sugar beet pancakes too. We'll never go hungry again, now that the bad guys are gone."

"You ate tulip bulbs and sugar beets too?" a little girl asked.

"Yes, everyone starved together. But now that we're free again, no one will ever make us starve. You're all going to grow up in a safe world full of love. What we lived through will never happen ever again. Mark my word."

3

Gradually, the children came to like and trust Jakob. They especially loved when he brought Ben, who always sensed which children were the most wounded and spent extra time with them. Now he was glad Ben was a Kooikerhondje and not a Dutch Shepherd. These traumatized children might associate a Dutch Shepherd with a German Shepherd, and be set even further back.

Every week, he tried to cook or bake them something special, and was always rewarded with happy, grateful smiles. He liked to give them sweets too—chocolates, candies, peppermint sticks, raisins, sugar cubes. Whatever he could find and afford, he went out of his way to get for them. After he'd worked there for a month, he went to the nearest toy store he could find and spent almost his entire salary. He knew what Luisa's reaction would be, but he'd set aside enough for rent and groceries, and he'd already gotten Elma a wedding present in the Dutch East Indies. It was important to buy these precious children replacements for the belovèd toys, stuffed animals, and dolls they'd lost.

The children lined up in the living room when they saw him coming in with several large bags. Their eyes widened when he set them down and started pulling out cuddly new friends.

"Are those really for us?" a little girl asked.

"Of course they're for you, sweetheart. Most of you don't have any toys, and all children deserve toys. I had a teddybear when I was a little boy, and my mother put it in the suitcase of special belongings we gave to a nice Christian neighbor. I can't wait to give my child that teddybear someday. But in the meantime, I'm giving you toys."

He went through the orphanage, calling names and giving out toys. It meant the world to him when many of them exclaimed their new dolls and stuffed animals looked just like the ones they'd lost. Even the children who already had real toys got new friends. It wasn't fair to give only some of them toys.

"I don't want to get rid of my wooden spoon doll," the little boy he'd met on his first day announced. "He's special to me."

Jakob's heart ached at a child who cared more for a bad home-made toy than something from a real toy store, who didn't remember what it was like to have a real toy. "Sure you can keep the wooden thing, but now you have an even better friend. This one you can cuddle at night, and he fits in your arms instead of only your hand."

"So he's like a friend for my spoon doll?"

"And for you. It's so much fun to have a cuddly friend you can take everywhere with you. Some girls collect fancy dolls, but the ones they play with are the cuddly ones. Each has a special purpose."

Urseltje got her new friend last. Jakob knelt before her and presented her with a ragdoll dressed in a traditional Dutch costume. He'd bought two of them, one for Urseltje and another for a potential future daughter. The second doll had just been shipped off in his latest package to Rachel, along with Luisa's wedding dress. He hadn't told his mother he'd sent his wife her wedding dress, knowing what her reaction would probably be. It was better to do it without asking permission and deal with the fallout later. Luisa wouldn't have agreed to it when she didn't approve of the marriage.

"Teddy gets a friend?"

"Best of all, you get a new friend! Now you have one for each arm. There's never such a thing as too many toys for a child. Look how pretty she is. She's just waiting for you to love her and make her Real."

"Dolls can come to life?" a four-year-old girl asked. "Are they nice or mean when they come to life?"

He smiled. "Oh, no, sweetheart, dolls don't really come to life. It's an idea from a children's book. When a toy is loved enough, a special magic turns it Real, but not by becoming a live person or animal. Urseltje's Teddy is Real because he's so worn by love. You have to love a toy a lot to make it Real, and when a toy is that loved, you don't care how worn it is."

"Can you read that story to us?" a little boy asked, hugging his new boy doll. "I love when you read us stories. You always read the best stories."

"I don't think I've seen a Dutch translation of that book in any of the bookstores that reopened," he lied. He'd always found *The Velveteen Rabbit* a very sad story, and didn't want the children to suddenly respect him less if he cried in front of them. Not that he minded them seeing a man crying, but seeing anyone crying might set them back a great deal. They needed no disturbances.

"Does this mean you're not going to fix Teddy for me?" Urseltje asked. "Maybe he won't have that magic if he's fixed."

Jakob gently took Teddy out of her arms. "Of course I'll still fix him. I'll do it today if you'd like. A rocking horse in that story says that once you're Real, it lasts for always. The magic has already been worked, even if a hole is fixed or the child grows up. Love never dies."

"Can you use thread that matches his skin? I don't want it to look like he had surgery."

"Sure. You can watch me doing it, to make sure I'm being a good teddybear doctor and taking good care of your special pal."

After lunch that day, Jakob kept his promise and found a needle, thread, and scissors in one of the older children's rooms. He sat on a chair next to Urseltje's bed as she looked at a picture book.

"Are you sure you don't have any children?" Urseltje asked as he made a knot and pulled the thread through. "You act like a father to us."

"I'm glad you think so nicely of me, but my wife and I never did the thing that makes babies. It wouldn't be right to make a baby who wouldn't see its father for a long time, or to make a good woman be pregnant alone."

"We've all lost our parents, and it hasn't been the end of the world."

He continued stitching. "No child should ever get used to being an orphan or only having one parent. I never want my little boy or girl to know what it's like to not have both parents. Even if a baby can't remember, it can sense when something's wrong. A newborn needs two parents most of all. Besides, we didn't have a religious wedding. Some people think bad things about a baby born to people married only in a civil ceremony, and they think even nastier things about the mother."

"That's not nice. We need all the babies we can make after what the bad guys did to us. They tried to kill all of us, and we have lots of people to replace."

His heart ached for a child who knew about such things and spoke of them with such casualness. "We're already starting to replace the people we lost. A dear friend of mine is getting married in a few days, and she and her husband will be moving to Palestine with another friend of ours when it's safe. They're probably going to have a lot of babies as soon as they can."

4

Elma and Willem's wedding was held in the courtyard of their apartment on Monday, 15 April, with a young survivor rabbi from France. Everyone found it too depressing to go back into their old neighborhood to hold the ceremony in the Portuguese Synagogue. Almost all of the buildings had been looted and ransacked during the *Hongerwinter*, and the four Ashkenazic synagogues were no more. And it seemed insincere to use a Sephardic synagogue when they were Ashkenazic, and to have an Orthodox ceremony when they were Progressive. They'd briefly considered going to De Pijp to use the Gerard Dou Synagogue, which had survived because of its inconspicuous position between two rowhouses, but they felt it'd be best if they had the kind of ceremony they were used to, in a place where they weren't reminded so sharply of everyone and everything that was no more.

Elma wore a light gray dress, the first new article of clothing she'd had since Westerbork, and a veil Floor had crocheted for her. Willem had found a cheap suit at a consignment shop and bought two gold rings at the only jewelry store he could find in the area. Jakob, Sander, Bram, and Floor held the poles of the chupah, which Elma, Floor, and Luisa had embroidered with flowers, trees, leaves, and butterflies.

Jakob almost dropped his pole when he saw the second ring coming out during the ring portion of the ceremony. He watched and listened, astounded, as Elma proceeded to give Willem a ring and utter the traditional marriage formula, modified for sex. All the Progressive couples he'd ever known had both worn rings, but the husband had never gotten his ring under the chupah. He decided then and there he'd have a double ring ceremony too. Not that he'd mind having to give up the wedding ring he had now. That was just a cheap ring given to him in a quick, secular ceremony. A ring given to him in a proper religious ceremony would feel more sacred and meaningful.

After Willem smashed the glass, he pulled the veil from Elma's face and demurely kissed her. For a moment, Jakob flashed back to that last night in Westerbork, his last full day without a limp, when Elma had begged him for a kiss and he'd agreed. Part of him wished he hadn't done it, so his only experience of kissing a woman could be Rachel. Even if he hadn't loved Elma, that was something he could only do for the first time once. He was jealous of the other guys Rachel had kissed, and that another guy had touched her breasts before he had.

"Congratulations," he smiled when he came back to himself. "May you and Willem live in peace and happiness for a thousand years and have a hundred children."

"We're not Chinese or Hindus," Elma said. "But I appreciate your good wishes. I hope you and your wife live so long and have many children too."

Under halacha, one was supposed to stop eating chametz by a certain time on the day before Pesach, but since they were Progressive, and this was a wedding, the courtyard reception contained the last of their chametz. Bread, cake, pie, cookies, tarts, dumplings, all the good things they'd soon have to abstain from for eight days.

"Do you mind there's no music or dancing?" Jakob asked as they sat down to eat by the tulips. "After what you went through, you deserve a really fancy wedding."

"Marrying Willem was all I really wanted." Elma stuck her fork into a piece of chicken. "The only things that make a couple married are the exchange of rings and recitation of the marriage formula. Not a fancy party or expensive band. Don't you remember I was never the type of girl to want those things? A lot of people don't realize a wedding is about creating a marriage, not hosting a fancy party. Even if we had the money and there were as many things to choose from as there were before the war, I still wouldn't want to shell out thousands of guilders on making a silly party."

"That's my opinion also," Willem said. "And we'll need to save up all the money we can for immigration to Palestine and starting our lives there. I wish you and your mother would join us."

"Floortje and Brammetje aren't going either." Jakob smiled when a crumb fell off of Kees's plate and he didn't immediately dive to retrieve it. "When you have parents to look out for, you can't go to a place that needs pioneers."

"Not everyone there is young. A lot of people were born and raised there. Normal people understand the older generation isn't meant to farm and soldier."

"I'm not going to be a soldier or farmer," Elma said. "Before we were separated, Gusta taught me a lot. She might've lost her mind, but I didn't. Even if she never serves as a midwife again, I can use what she taught me. There'll be so many women having babies, to replace the murdered. It's my perfect calling."

"What are you going to do in America?" Willem asked. "Work in another orphanage or be a teacher?"

"Maybe I'll be a primary school art teacher or a zookeeper. My ship won't leave till the end of July, so there's still time to think. Americans have something called the G.I. Bill, which pays for veterans to go to school. I hope they let me have some of that money too, since I fought in the Allied forces, and I'll be becoming an American."

Elma set her plate on the ground after she finished eating. Willem followed her to the gifts table. It was hardly groaning under the weight, but the most important thing was that they'd been given gifts. Exactly a year ago, they'd hovered near Death. A wedding hadn't even been on their radar screen.

"Oh, how beautiful!" Elma held up Jakob's gift, an ikat tablecloth with an elephant motif. "Did you get this in the Indies?"

"I sure did. I wish I could get you a piece of Judaica, but I hope this is good enough."

"Of course it's good enough! I can't wait to put it on our table at the Seder tonight! I assume this can be washed?"

"Use cold water and salt if you absolutely have to wash it. Otherwise the dye will run. And dry it in the shade." He refilled his bowl with tomato soup and dumped in a generous handful of croutons. "I guess we're using an ordinary plate tonight. I hope someday Amsterdam has Judaica shops again."

"If it does, we won't be here to see them. This year, we really will mean it when we say 'Next year in Jerusalem.'"

5

That night's Seder was hosted by Bram and Kees. Jakob looked around at the other seven people at the table, and his heart ached for everyone who could no longer be there. He'd give anything to be back at the Antemas' if it could only mean everyone would still be alive and together. Even an insufferable little prat like Luuk.

Luisa lightly touched his arm. "Look at this, Jaap. It seems like you're once again the youngest. Would you like to ask the Four Questions?"

He thought for a minute. "Is it okay if I offer a modern version? I promise I won't make a scene like last time."

"What exactly are you planning?"

"Something good, *Moeder*. The Progressive Movement is supposed to be all about taking old stuff and making it seem new and relevant."

"Do you promise you're not about to embarrass me like you did last time?"

"On my word of honor." He stood up, this time only banging his chair against the wall. "Why is this night different from all other nights? On all other nights, we lived under an evil occupying force, but tonight we're free in our homeland once more, and our Queen is home. Why is this night different from all other nights? On all other nights, we were separated from our dear ones and not sure we'd be reunited, but tonight some of us are back together and closer than ever. Why is this night different from all other nights? On all other nights, we were deprived of our religious freedom and basic human rights, but tonight we're once more able to freely, publicly practice our religion and have the same rights as all other Dutch citizens. Why is this night different from all other nights? On all other nights, every second was precious, and Death or imprisonment lurked around every corner, but tonight we're in new homes close to our old neighborhood, without barbed wire and police checkpoints, and we have enough to eat and plenty of fuel to keep warm. May we never take these freedoms for granted ever again. Amen."

6

On his way home from work during the week of Pesach, Jakob

saw several signs advertising an art store's grand re-opening. He was eager to get to the fifth Sheva Brachot meal for Elma and Willem, tonight hosted by a young survivor couple on the second floor, but he just couldn't pass up the opportunity to check out an art store. Perhaps he could stock up on supplies before he went to America. Already he was running out of room in the sketchbook from Vrouw Visser, since he'd done so much drawing in the Dutch East Indies and drawn so many pictures of the orphans and postwar Amsterdam.

He dismounted his bicycle and locked it on the empty bike rack next to the store. None of the signs indicated an opening time, but it never hurt to be early. He peeked into the windows, trying to see if anyone were inside and what kinds of merchandise were on the shelves.

"May I help you? If you're here for the grand re-opening, you'll have to wait two more hours."

"I'm sorry, Mevrouw, I just wanted to see if you were open yet. I have to be somewhere soon, and I wanted to check it out early. Are you sure I can't reserve any merchandise and then come back?"

She gasped. "Jaap, is that you? I'm Vrouw Daube. My husband and I ran an art store before the war, but we lost our building in one of the bombing raids. Are you the young man I think you are?"

He broke into a smile. "Of course I remember you, Vrouw Daube. I made a lot of good use of that sketchpad and those art supplies you gave me the last time I saw you. I finally got a new sketchbook, but I'm running out of room in it. Oh, you wouldn't believe what's happened to me since I saw you. I fought in the war, met the Queen, killed Nazis and NSBers, fought in the Indies, got chased by a tiger, got married—"

"Slow down, dear boy. You'll have plenty of time to tell me these stories later. I'm just happy to see one of my best customers is still alive after what happened to your people. You got so tall and handsome. Where do you live now?"

"I'm in Jordaan with my mother and some friends. Thank God, my mother survived. We're going to America at the end of July. My wife has been there since June. I haven't seen my wife since the day after our wedding last May, and I'm dying to finally see her again and marry her all over again." He pulled one of Rachel's latest pictures out of his pocket. "Can you believe it, I got my very own Rachel, just like my namesake."

"She's very pretty. Are you sure you can't come to our grand re-opening? A lot of the merchandise came from our old store. We saved whatever we could and stocked it in our basement."

"My old school friend Anselma Specht and her new husband are having a Sheva Brachot meal, and I can't miss it. For the first seven days after a wedding, you're supposed to host the newlyweds for cele-bratory meals and repeat the seven blessings said at the marriage. Even if it's Pesach, we still have nice food. We don't hold by the archaic rul-ing against eating stuff like beans and dairy, so we're able to have a better banquet."

She pulled a key out of her pocket. "I've already broken the rules for you once; I don't suppose it makes much difference to do it again. We can go in the back, and I'll let you pick out what you want."

Jakob's eyes lit up at the sight of all the sketchbooks, paints, brush-es, easels, colored pencils, charcoal, wooden models, and all the other art supplies lining the shelves. He still had plenty of use left in his art supply kit and the Conté crayons, but it'd be nice to have some extras.

He paused in front of a shelf with felt-tipped colored pens. "I don't think I've ever drawn with these. Are they new?"

"My husband got them from an American soldier in the area. They're a relatively new invention, but I'm sure you can make nice pic-tures with them."

He picked up a package of the pens and moved to another aisle. "Can I have these crayons? It's probably at least a few years away, but it'll be nice to have beginning art supplies for my future child. My mother is convinced Gepje is attaching horns to me with her former beau, but she's still writing me letters almost every single day. She's the one who's often asking me if I'm still sure I want to be her husband after so much time apart. I'd know if my own wife didn't love me any-more."

"You're a brave man. I don't think I could've handled marrying my husband and then going away for a year. Have you really not changed your mind in all that time? It's not like you courted her for years, is it?"

"My mother's right in that she's little more than a stranger, but lots of people have gotten married when they barely knew each other. That used to be the norm. We'll have the rest of our lives to get to know each other, but we didn't have the option of a very long courtship. All we cared about was that we seemed like a perfect match, and we knew it was love that soon."

Vrouw Daube opened the cash register. "It's a mother's instinct to protect her child. I'm sure once the babies start arriving, your mother will change her mind and come to love your wife."

"I hope so." He plunked the crayons and pens onto the counter and went in search of a sketchbook.

"Remember what you promised me, Jaap. You have to show me your drawings in the last sketchbook I sold you. I expect to see marked improvement in your drawing ability, with so much free time and all those professional paints and pencils."

"Oh, yes, Mevrouw. I'm thinking about studying art history or teaching primary school kids art. I've drawn and painted tigers, leopards, elephants, rhinos, birds, orangutans, flowers, battles, Westerbork, my soldier buddies, you name it." He came to the register with his new sketchbook. This one had a purple border and a replica of Pieter Bruegel the Elder's *Tower of Babel*.

"You're welcome to come back when I'm closed for lunch or after hours. I can't wait to see all the artwork you've done in the last four years."

He took the paper bag with his purchases. "Thank you very much for being so nice to me and remembering me after so much time. I know you were one of the good people. A lot of these people I can't be too sure about."

When he got home, Jakob dragged his bicycle up to the apartment and set the bag on his bed, ignoring Luisa's usual complaints about how he insisted on keeping his bicycle safe indoors and how he was late. He threw his day clothes in a heap on the floor and pulled on fresh formal clothes for the Sheva Brachot, daydreaming about when he'd be the guest of honor at his own week of Sheva Brachot celebrations.

His eyes fell on the letter on his bed after he finished getting dressed. His heart skipped a beat when he saw it was from Rachel. He got a letter from her almost every day, but never ceased to have the same sense of excitement at seeing her name. Though he was wearing shoes, he lay down on the bed to read it. His door was closed and locked, so it weren't as though Luisa could barge in and chew him out about putting dirty shoes on the comforter she'd just aired.

1 April 1946

My darling Jaapetje,

I have very good news to share. I just passed my gymnasium equivalency test! Heer and Vrouw Brandt took me out to celebrate and said they'd help pay for my university education if I need help. I told them they didn't have to put themselves out like that, particularly since they're paying for Pietje's upcoming wedding and buying him and Jet a house, but they insisted. I haven't decided yet when I'll go to school, or where. There's a local college a lot of people go to, but it seems like a glorified junior college, not a real university. I like this place so far, but it's so old-fashioned and provincial to never want to leave your hometown, not even for university.

I see so many girls with their sweethearts, and feel so insanely jealous. Lotje even has one friend who's engaged, and she's the youngest girl in Lotje's circle of friends! All I have to cuddle at night is my old ragdoll. Seeing your beautiful pictures arranged on my nightstand isn't the same as seeing your beautiful face in person. Some ships travel very slowly. It might be September or October before I see you again.

You can tell me if you want your freedom. A year is a very long time for any-one, of any age, to wait for someone. Maybe you say you still love me, but when we're together in person, you might come to regret our impulsive decision to wed. I just wish I knew for sure you really do still love me, that I didn't have to guess and read between the lines. I love you so much I'd wait for you for ten years, but I wish I didn't have to be so alone and celibate in the prime of my youth. You probably resent having to be celibate too. A woman would have to be blind to not notice how hand-some you are. Being marked as your woman and belonging to only you doesn't mean much when you're so far away.

Forgive me, I'm rambling and not making much sense. I just feel like I'm going crazy after so long without my husband. Touching myself doesn't feel as good as it used to, remembering how much nicer it felt when you touched me. And I have no one to touch in return. It seems selfish now, and just makes me depressed. How much longer do I have to live this agonizingly celibate life and be the loyal wife thousands of kilometers away?

I feel as though I'm running out of things to say to you. Your life sounds more interesting than mine. You get to work at an orphanage and explore a big city, while I'm stuck learning English, making up for so many years of missed schooling, get-ting used to American life, and living in another family's house.

Have a nice day. I'm sure it'll be more interesting than mine. If you want to take some girls on dates, I won't blame you. Men have needs just as women do. Some won't consider us really married since there was no religious ceremony, and we never consummated it properly. You'd probably love to fulfill your physical needs with a willing warm body. Don't feel like you have to stay faithful to me if it's not what you really want deep down. It's not normal to be married far longer than you've known each other.

I love you so much, and wonder if the spark will spring back to life with a vengeance when I see you again, or if I'll wonder what the hell we were thinking. Perhaps I should've stayed in The Netherlands to be near you, and we could've immigrated together. I don't mean to upset you; I just want you to be realistic and not feel obligated to me if you feel you've grown apart from me in all this time.

I do still love you,

Gepje

His heart sank as he picked up his fountain pen and notepad and took a seat at his desk. It all seemed like a strange dream sometimes, but the feelings in his heart told him he was still in love so much time later. If only the fine line between love and lust weren't so hard to figure out. All he knew or cared about was that this woman had been on his mind since the first time they'd met, and it had to mean something that they'd crossed paths again so much time later.

20 April 1946

My beautiful bride Gepje,

I know this separation can't be easy on you in any way, but I'm suffering too. It makes me sad to read your thoughts on the matter. If I haven't fallen out of love with you or considered dating other girls yet, I don't think it's magically about to happen. You need to continue staying strong for both of us, and in a few more months, we'll be together again and have all the time in the world to make up for all the things we've missed. It's so, so special to me that you've been patiently waiting for me. I like knowing you're saving your sweet kisses and caresses for only me. It meant the world to me that you were waiting for me and sending me letters while I was in the Indies. What my buddy Leendert told me when I was having my foot set was so true. As painful as it is at the time, in the grand scheme of things, it really will be over before you know it, and before long, you won't be able to remember the pain.

My friends Elma and Willem are still having their Sheva Brachot. Soon enough we'll have our Sheva Brachot, and you'll be dressed in my mother's wedding gown. A modern woman like you would probably prefer to choose her own gown, and pick a more original color than cream, but I'd be really disappointed if you don't wear it. My mother saved it because she wanted my bride to wear it someday.

I'm counting the seconds till we can be together again. It feels like eternity till

I'm with my bride again, but every second we're apart brings us one second closer to our reunion. It'll make us love and appreciate each other even more, since we had to be alone and lonely for so long. The best happy endings have to be earned and aren't handed to us on a silver platter. Whenever we have hard times in the future, we'll only have to remind ourselves of our difficult first year of marriage and how we got through it. If we can make it through a year of separation, we can get through anything.

How can you even doubt I'm still crazy about you? Absence is making my heart grow fonder every single second. Why would I send you love letters every day and packages full of presents every month if I no longer cared for you? I'd never waste so much time and emotion on a woman who meant nothing to me. I'd be a man and write you a Dear Johanna letter, as I'm sure you'd be woman enough to write me a Dear Johan letter. Remember, the hardest time is just before the sunrise. Romance novels and movies would be really boring if the couple never had any problems and they had a happily ever after as soon as they met.

I assure you, by the end of the year, I'll be with you under the chupah and making you my wife all over again, properly this time. I can't wait for our wedding night. All that love and passion we've been storing up will finally have a place to go. I probably won't be an expert the first time around, but you have to do something many times to get good at it. I don't think we'll be getting any sleep on our wedding night!

I don't ever want to let you go after we're together again. I never expected to see you again, and when we met again, I knew I couldn't lose you again. All this time, you've been the only woman in my heart, soul, and mind. I'm saving up all my love for you and only you. It doesn't make our separation any easier when you voice such depressing thoughts and doubt our relationship.

After you get this letter, can you please, please, please try to send me happier letters? Someday our grandchildren may read our love letters, and I don't want them to think Opa *and* Oma *were ever anything less than 100% in love. I don't want them to get an unrealistic picture of relationships always being perfect and never needing work, but I don't want them to think we stopped loving each other during the most difficult phase of our relationship. This is the time when we're supposed to be most in love of all, since we're so far apart.*

I love you even when you break my heart by doubting me,
Your loving, loyal, faithful, hopelessly devoted husband Jaapje

Chapter 25: Change in Fortune

When Jakob came home from work shortly before his twentieth birthday, with Ben at his side, Luisa breathlessly greeted him and hugged him very tightly. When he looked over her shoulder, he saw she'd begun packing one of her new suitcases.

"God has been so good to us, Jaap. I just found out about a ship that's leaving in two weeks, and it's got room for us! Now we won't have to wait till the end of July, and we might even be in America in time for Shavuot!"

"What? When did you learn about this?"

"Just today! Bram came in during his lunch break and told me he found out this information from a colleague. He showed me the newspaper advertising the ship, and helped me call the company and purchase two tickets. It's a good thing we didn't yet pay for the tickets for the July ship."

Jakob slowly came into the apartment and looked at his surroundings. This had only been his home for a few months, but already he'd grown attached to it. As much as he longed to be with Rachel again, his heart somersaulted at the thought of leaving behind his new home and his only surviving friends. And the children would miss him so much.

"Well, what are you waiting for? We have two weeks to pack up. Everything we don't need can go in a suitcase or trunk. Things like clothes, dishes, and linens can wait till the last minute. But don't leave all your clothes unpacked. I do laundry once a week, and you don't need that many clothes to get through a week. I don't know why you think you have to throw your pants in the laundry immediately instead of wearing them several days in a row. They're not like socks or shirts."

"What about Bentje? Can he stay in our cabin, or do pets have to be in the hold?"

"We'll find out more details when the date gets closer. In the meantime, we need to start packing. Anything we don't need can be sold."

Jakob protectively put his hands on his bicycle's handlebars. "I can bring this, can't I? I'm not about to leave it behind when I'm lucky I still have it."

"You and that bicycle of yours. Yes, you can bring it, but things like furniture will probably have to stay. We don't have the money to ship them, and it takes longer for them to arrive if they're going on a cargo ship and not with you."

As he went into his room and pulled out his new suitcase, he flashed back to that day in August 1942. He shut his eyes and began gasping for breath as he saw the pictures, religious articles, linens, and smashed dishes and records lying all over the floor, while he was helpless to save his mother from the intruders who'd beaten and frisked her like a dangerous, degenerate criminal. Then the images were replaced by even more horrific ones, packing up that final night in Westerbork. How many other people had packed their final suitcases and parcels there, little knowing the next day's journey would take them to the end of the road? He'd seen the images in the newsreels, of the mountains of ownerless suitcases, and all the confiscated belongings. Some people probably hated him for his relatively good fortune. Most people hadn't been able to jump off the death trains, let alone become soldiers.

He put his shaking arms around Ben when he felt the moving furry object crawling onto his lap. "You're a good dog, Bentje. You always know when someone's in pain and how to comfort him."

"Jaap, do you have any idea where my wedding dress is?" Luisa called. "It's been hanging in my closet since we moved here, and I don't remember reports of a robber in the building."

He didn't answer and continued cuddling Ben and gasping for breath. Several minutes later, Luisa knocked on his door, and he still didn't answer. She finally tried the door and came in to find him slumped over on the floor as Ben protectively sat with him.

"Dear God, what happened to you? Shall I call a doctor?"

He propped himself up and shook his head. Luisa knelt beside him and rubbed his shoulders till his breathing returned to normal. He flashed her a grateful look as he started to regain his senses and the images faded back into the past.

"Thank you for surviving for me, Mama. I don't know what I'd do if I were alone in the world. God gave me such a special woman for a mother."

"Were you thinking about the last time you packed a suitcase?"

He nodded. "Do you think the bad memories will ever go away? I'd like to throw them all into a sealed iron box and throw it into the ocean when we're on the ship."

"The bad memories will live as long as your good memories. The person you were when you experienced all these things will live as long as you do, no matter how much you want to dump that hideous reminder of the past into the sea. I think you'll be reminded of these things less and less as you get older. In the grand scheme of things, those years will come to represent a very small percentage of your life."

"Do you have these memory flashes too? You went through worse things than I did." He tenderly caressed the number on her arm.

"Sometimes I have nightmares, and little things remind me of the past. You wouldn't be normal if you were never reminded of these awful things. At least we didn't lose our minds like Gusta."

He winced when he thought of how they'd probably have to say goodbye to her before they left. He wasn't looking forward to seeing her again. Perhaps she'd gone even madder in the sanitarium.

"Now that you're feeling better, can you tell me if you know what happened to my wedding dress? I'm positive we weren't robbed."

"Oh, that. I sent it to Rachel in one of my packages awhile ago. You told me you wanted my bride to wear it, and I wanted her to get it ahead of time in case it needed tailoring or something."

"What! You sent my dress to that strange woman! Now we might never see it again! She might wear it at her wedding to that former beau for all you know!"

"*Moeder*, please. Gepje's my wife, and you promised you'd stay quiet about your feelings on the matter. Don't rub salt into our wounds."

"This isn't just your business anymore! You gave her my wedding dress! Now it's my business!"

"But you said you wanted my bride to wear it, and we didn't have a religious wedding yet. Her former beau's marrying his girl soon. Maybe we can have a double wedding."

"Perhaps that's her way of saying he's marrying her. You could come to the house to find her in bed with that other fellow, or divorce papers waiting for you. I'm sure most judges would grant an annulment if the marriage is never consummated and the couple has been apart for an entire year. You don't really still consider yourself married, do you?"

"Of course I do! Gepje's the other half of my soul, the one I was destined to be with before we were born!"

"Look, Jaap, I never had any doubt you love the girl. You can't fake that kind of lovestruck look or so much devotion. But I can't know she loves you when I never met her and you married after a lightning-quick courtship. Maybe if you'd courted for years, I'd be more inclined to believe nice things."

"If this ship leaves in two weeks, I'll see her again next month. I'm positive I'll find her thrilled to see me again. You'll eat all your cruel words once you see how crazy she is about me."

"I hope so, Jaap. I hope so."

2

9 May, Thursday, was Jakob's twentieth birthday. His ship would leave in exactly a week, and most of the apartment had been packed up. As he rode his bicycle to work, he thought about how he'd been on top of the world on his last birthday. Nothing could ever beat being the star of a victory parade.

The older children greeted him at the door with a large birthday cake. "*Gefeliciteerd met je verjaardag!*"

He smiled at them and let them each hug him. It felt so good to know that in only two months, he'd earned so much love, respect, and trust from these children who'd never really be normal again. He was very sad to have to leave them in a week, after making so much progress.

"We all got you presents!" a little boy announced, jumping up and down. "And our cooks made you the cake you said you always had on your birthday!"

"Chocolate with strawberry filling?"

"That's the only cake you said you had," a little girl said. "I hope the cooks made it as nice as your mother."

"Now you get two birthday cakes!" Urseltje said. "One from us and one at home!"

"You don't have to do any work today," another little girl said. "But Heer Prinsen says he'll still pay you for today."

Jakob ruffled her hair. "I don't think of this as work. It's too much fun making children happy. Work was what I did for the Army."

Some of the older children led him to a plush chair decorated with colored streamers. One by one, the children came up to him and gave him their presents, wrapped in newspaper and colored tissue paper. He thanked each of them for the things they'd made in art class and on their own time, things like coasters, picture frames, tea cozies, decorative storage boxes, potholders, artwork, painted plant pots, scarves, and fancy soaps. In years past, he would've been insulted at getting so many cheap, homemade gifts, but after everything he'd lost, this was a small fortune.

"We'll get you more presents on your last day next week!" a little boy said. "We'll also give you something to give to your wife!"

"Can you adopt some of us and take us to America with you?" a three-year-old girl asked. "We'll miss you a lot."

"I'm afraid I can't do that, sweetheart. I'm sure you'll have a nice life here, and I'll write letters to you. Maybe someday I'll come back to visit. I do have some friends here I'd love to see again."

"Will your puppy come here on your last day too?" Urseltje asked. "I'll miss Bentje too."

"Of course." He'd given up on trying to explain Ben was probably almost three years old and no longer a puppy. To Urseltje, all dogs were automatically puppies.

"Can we take pictures with you on your last day, to keep for always?"

"Sure. Now that the bad guys are gone, you should preserve all the memories you can."

While he ate the cake and birthday lunch later in the day, he thought about how so many of the people he'd known would celebrate no more birthdays. Many of these children's friends and relatives would also celebrate no more birthdays. He could barely believe that not too long ago, birthdays marking fairly young ages had been their owners' last.

The best birthday present of all would've been a magical ship to transport him across the ocean to his bride, but Jakob made do with the letter that awaited him on his bed when he returned home. This time it was accompanied by a package. Rachel didn't know he'd be on his way sooner than expected. He was sick to his stomach over Luisa's reaction to this. Instead of agreeing it would be a great surprise for his loyal wife, she thought it was a good way to catch her unawares and bust her for potential cheating.

20 April 1946

My sweet Jaap,

Given the rate at which our letters seem to be arriving, I'm timing this to coincide with your birthday. I hope you enjoy the presents too. Your gifts to me are always so nice, and you probably won't think my gifts are much, but every husband deserves a birthday present from his wife. And you gave me such a beautiful birthday present. I wear that necklace almost every single day. Maybe someday, after the Dutch East Indies are no longer a colony and the war has stopped, we can visit there and I can see all the beautiful things you did.

I've been so depressed this month. Part of it is because I miss you so much and feel nagged by doubts about how much you could still love me, but it's also because Juli's birthday was this month. She turned 22 on 2 April. I can't believe someone so shy, quiet, and timid is an Aries. She must have a very strong opposing sign rising, to mask the usual characteristics of her sign. And I think of how you described her on your meetings at the Embassy, and wish I could do something, anything, to help her. Her ordeal must've really done something to her head, and now she thinks she deserves mistreatment. Her parents, particularly her father, were very emotionally abusive, but they never beat her. And she did get a fair amount of verbal harassment from boys, coupled with a worthless beau before she met Fritz (Gary). If only she were able to go to America with you! I know her birthday was a horrible day.

I hope to God I'm able to hold my sweet husband in my arms on your next birthday. I give you so much love in all my dreams, but you're never there when I wake. These pictures I send you all the time can't be enough to tide you over. Looking at me must make you mad with anticipation and desire to touch me. Don't worry about the cost of film; Lotje's friend Kit takes many of them free of charge. She's what the Americans call a shutterbug, and she's very wealthy. A lot of people in this town are rich, which makes me feel rather shabby. I know we'll never live in a mansion, have servants, or eat caviar for breakfast.

It sounds like you're a very good fit at the orphanage. Maybe you can study to be a teacher here. I'm still not sure what I'm going to do. I just want to go to university for the experience and to learn about many subjects. And I'm not sure if it would be a good idea to go to university right away. Perhaps I can do the American woman thing once in my life and help put you through school first, then take my turn. Assuming you still want to be married, I'd like to have a child as soon as possible. Bringing up a baby and going to university don't mix, and I don't want to hand my darling baby over to a nanny or nursery just so I can get an education. Our baby belongs with us at all times. I won't even put it in a crib or cradle, which the Brandts think is rather strange. After what I went through, I need to know my baby is safe at all times, and a family bed was the norm till relatively recently in human history.

Speaking of beds, I want you in mine as soon as possible. I wish I were able to go out as a woman alone and buy or rent a place, but women in this country need their husband or father to do just about anything. It's so obscene. It's the 20th centu-

ry. Women aren't supposed to be men's chattel anymore. If a woman is educated and earns her own money, she should be able to open bank accounts, sign for loans, buy houses and cars, check into a hotel alone, do anything. Many people might falsely assume we're not married because we have different surnames.

Sometimes the Brandts go to Judaica stores in Atlantic City and on Cape May, and I admire all the pretty things. I wish you didn't feel like it were your responsibility as the man to acquire all the ritual items we need. You certainly no longer have Judaica stores in Amsterdam. I wish you'd let me start getting all new items for our household. That way, we'll already have some by the time you arrive. We'll probably get some as wedding presents, but it's never a bad thing to have multiples. Most households can't function with only one of each item.

I'm continuing to learn your mother's recipes, and leaving onions out. I hope I make all your favorite foods to your liking. You'd better choose me over your mother. I'm glad our children will have one living grandparent, but I hate knowing she hates me and thinks I used you for a visa and military benefits. But I only care about pleasing you, not her.

In the meantime, enjoy your birthday presents. I'm sure you'll be making love to me in your dreams tonight. You'd better be telling me the truth that you still love me and only me, and that other women don't even tempt you.

I love you with every breath I have,

Gepje

He pulled open the box and found a tracing paper notepad, a box of twelve graphite pencils, five painting knives, a set of twenty-four watercolors, and a scrapbook. His scrapbook documenting the occupation and the war was now full, and sitting in one of his suitcases. He couldn't wait to start filling the new one with pictures, mementos, and clippings documenting his life in peacetime.

He was sitting down to write to Rachel when the door opened. He put down his fountain pen and went to hug Luisa. Their friends were behind her, carrying parcels from the bakery.

"*Gefeliciteerd met je verjaardag,* my sweet Jaap. I can't believe it's already been twenty years since I became a mother."

"And you don't look a day over forty-five. Are you sure you didn't have me till you were forty?"

"You know I don't look that young, but it's nice to know you think I don't look sixty. I'll take your cake and the dinner out of the refrigerator, and our friends can set the table and put out the other sweets. If you'd like, you can go into my room and get your presents in the closet.

This time you have permission to go into my room."

"You went into your mother's room without permission?" Elma asked.

"I had to get her wedding dress to ship to Gepje. Boy, I can't wait to see my beautiful bride wearing it. Maybe we can get married again next month, if the ship travels quick enough. She has a bunch of rich friends. Maybe they can help with money and make it possible to plan a wedding on such short notice."

"I wish I could go to your wedding. I hope you'll be happy with getting a present in the mail."

"You'll be there in thought." Jakob rushed off to Luisa's room and flung open the closet. He broke into a smile when he saw how many presents were waiting there. "Are all these for me?"

"Who else would they be for?" Luisa asked.

He came back with six parcels in his arms and put them on the davenport. Besides the gifts from Luisa, Elma and Willem, Sander, and the ter Avests, there were also packages from Vrouw Visser and his Army buddies. He knew what the realities of postwar travel were, and was grateful he'd been sent packages.

"It's been so long since I saw my friends. I guess they got my address from headquarters."

"Maybe someday you'll have a reunion," Sander suggested. "My father used to have reunions with his buddies from the Great War."

"Yeah, but I'll be in a different country soon. Teleportation is the stuff of science fiction. Maybe someday I'll have enough money to take a boat or a plane home." Jakob opened Luisa's gift first and pulled out a photo album. "Thank you, *Moeder*. May I use this for my photos of Gepje?"

"You needed somewhere to stick them. God knows, she sends you so many. But don't take this as my blessing on the paper marriage. I have yet to meet this woman and see if she deserves you."

"You'll love her as much as I do." He set the photo album on the coffeetable and moved on to the next package, from Sander.

"You don't need to open everything at once. Come to the table and enjoy your birthday feast."

He dutifully left the presents and took a seat. "Thank you so much for making a nice birthday for me, *Moeder*. God really knew what he was doing when he gave me you for my lovely mother."

3

Luisa had made a checklist of things to do before leaving Amsterdam, and Jakob's heart sank a little more each time he saw one more item checked off. Each check mark brought him one step closer to leaving behind his homeland, the place he'd fought so hard to help liberate, the only home he knew. Now he was sick with terror at one of the final to-do items.

"It's not Bedlam," Luisa tried to say as they were ushered into Gusta's sanitarium. "These people are treated very fairly, and some of them get better enough to go home. Maybe she'll feel better when you tell her she inspired Elma to become a midwife."

He stood back in fear at the sight of the people in beds and chairs. Some of the people walking the halls were babbling. At least no one was chained to the wall or lunging at him.

"Vrouw Kikkert, you have visitors," the warden said gently. "These are your old friends Jakob DeJonghe and Luisa Hartog. They've come to say goodbye to you, since they're going on a very big trip tomorrow."

Gusta sat bold upright in bed. "A very big trip? Who's making you leave? Don't you dare let them take me! I'm not going to kill even more babies!"

Luisa softly touched her arm. "Jaap and I are going to the United States. His so-called wife lives there. We'll write to you once we're there. You'll still have plenty of visitors after we're gone. You have a husband and two children, and a few friends."

"My friend Elma wants to be a midwife in Palestine because of you," Jakob said, avoiding looking her in the eyes. "She learnt a lot from you, and wants to use those skills for a good purpose."

"The only thing Anselma learnt from me was how to kill babies and perform abortions with her bare hands! No one will want to hire her when she only trained under a murderer! At least your mother was my assistant when I was actually delivering babies instead of smothering them, breaking their necks, injecting them—"

"Gusta, that's enough," Luisa interrupted. "Those days are in the past. God knows, you were innocent and forced into an impossible position. You saved so many lives. Would you rather have let those women die because they were pregnant or had infants? I'm sure many of them survived and will have many more babies."

"I should've refused! I should've died an innocent, holy martyr rather than survive with blood-soaked hands! Then I'd be remembered as a good person who chose death over violating all the principles of her profession!"

"God wanted you to survive for a reason. You should be bringing more life into the world, to make up for all the lives you were forced to end before they began. Even if you only deliver one baby for the rest of your career, that baby could be the start of a thousand more people. The Talmud says one life represents the entire world. That one baby you deliver could save the world."

"And it also says killing one person is tantamount to destroying the whole world! I destroyed hundreds of worlds!"

Jakob gingerly touched her hand. "I know you're not insane, Gusta. If you'd really gone mad, you wouldn't be able to remember things like that. I'm sure you can recover some of your mind and return to your old profession. Maybe you can help Floortje when she has children, and Bram's future wife."

"You weren't there! You have no idea what I was forced to do! I should've jumped off that train with you! How could I have believed we were going to a normal place!"

"No one really knew what was going to happen. Even I didn't suspect what those people were really capable of. But now it's over. We're safe, and our Queen is home. I'm sure you'll recover your mind with enough time."

"Do you have a rabbi or chaplain here?" Luisa asked. "It would do you a world of good to talk with someone who's nonjudgmental. He might get you to see you're innocent, and there's a life for you after what we survived."

"Maybe drawing or writing would help you. Drawing has helped me a lot. I have so many paints and colored pencils, I could let you have my extras."

Gusta gave him a disgusted look. "What exactly am I supposed to draw, the murder of babies? The gruesome procedures I did to induce preterm labor and perform abortions? A sky full of smoke, fire, and human ashes?"

"You can write or draw whatever's on your mind," Luisa said. "Even if it's not nice, it'll help you get it out of your system. If it sits inside bottled up, you'll only prolong your recovery."

"I don't deserve to recover. I'm a murderer who went against everything I was taught to do. If Anselma is smart, she'll find a real midwife or doctor to give her training instead of trying to copy a murderer."

Jakob checked his watch. "Would you like us to stay with you through dinner?" He wanted to get out of this place as soon as possible, but didn't want Luisa to think he were disrespecting Gusta or in a hurry to leave.

"What the hell kind of place do you think this is, a five-star luxury hotel or restaurant? The dining hall is barely better than the death rations in Poland!"

"I'm sure the food here can't be that bad," Luisa said. "These people can't be serving you watery soup with glass, string, worms, and God knows what else."

Jakob recoiled. "That's what they fed you, Mama? Why didn't you ever tell me? Now I'll have to work overtime to make you healthy, hearty meals! How dare anyone make you swallow broken glass, worms, and string!"

"We eat what we eat when it's all we're given. You ate tulip bulbs and sugar beets when you had nothing else."

"That was more nutritious and filling! No wonder you were so skinny when I saw you again!"

"Leave it in the past, Jaap. We're starting our journey tomorrow and putting an ocean between ourselves and those memories." Luisa squeezed Gusta's hand. "Kees, Floortje, and Brammetje all send their loving regards. Maybe someday we'll see you again, when you're ready to be a part of society. Your husband misses you so much. Think of him and your adult children, who need you."

"I don't deserve children of any age, or any husband. Leave me in my grief. You know as well as I do we'll never meet again, and you'll be glad you never have to deal with me ever again."

"Of course we'll see you again someday. You're only fifty, and perfectly healthy otherwise. Someday, when things are different, we'll come home to visit and find you in a much better state."

"I'll believe that when Hell freezes over."

Jakob was relieved when they left the sanitarium and were back on the street. As sorry as he felt for Gusta, he was glad he wouldn't have to deal with her again anytime soon. At least she'd only lost her mind, not her life.

He felt his foot hitting a rock on their way home in the twilight. When he squinted his eyes to see better, he saw it was heart-shaped. He smiled as he picked it up and put it in his pocket. As soon as they got home, he'd paint it red and put thin little white swirls on it, as a present for Rachel.

"Now you're a rock-collector?" Luisa asked. "Thank God you're just starting this hobby now, or your luggage would be weighed down by all those rocks. If you want to collect something, why not coins, stamps, or postcards?"

"It's a present for Gepje. I'll show you when I'm done making it look pretty. Maybe I will start collecting rocks after we're in our new city. There are so many pretty rocks and shells on the beach, and I can use them in artistic ways. Her friend Isaiah, one of the two people who wasn't caught in hiding, had a big marble collection. She used to tell me about what a marvellous collection he had, and how they'd play with the marbles in hiding."

"Oh, another male friend of hers. I never had that many male friends when I was a young girl. Men and women might be equal, but that doesn't mean young people are immune from natural urges. Do you think you'll return to find your paper wife still a virgin, even if she's still legally married to you?"

"Of course! When you meet her next month, you'll see what a nice girl she is. Like it or not, she's going to be the mother of your grandchildren."

Luisa looked back at the sanitarium. "I've heard most American women these days have babies in hospitals. Assuming this woman is still waiting for you and she's a normal Dutchwoman, it might be hard to find a real midwife. It's a shame Gusta is so out of it. Perhaps she would've liked to immigrate with us and help immigrant women who want to do things the old-fashioned way."

"Maybe she's needed more here. We can't give the Nazis a post-humous victory by all leaving. Some of us have to stay to keep our communities alive. Europe shouldn't lose its venerable Jewish presence by either death or immigration."

"I'm surprised anyone wants to stay in Europe after what happened. Perhaps the ter Avests will join us someday, or go with Sander, Elma, and Willem after the situation in Palestine calms down."

"Perhaps." He curled his fingers around the rock in his pocket. "But my heart is in America, and we're going to start all over again there. Just you, me, and Gepje. Someday we'll have a great big family again, and even stronger than it was before. No one will ever be able to cut down our family tree ever again, because it'll be composed of the strongest surviving branches."

4

Jakob went to the orphanage for the final time the next morning, riding his bicycle one last time through the streets of Amsterdam, as Ben ran beside him. He almost wished he didn't have to go, so he wouldn't have to see the faces of the children as he left.

"You brought Puppy!" Urseltje rushed forward and hugged Ben around the neck. "I'll miss you, Bentje. I wish you had a Vrouw Puppy who could give us baby puppies to love and play with."

"Maybe he'll find a wife in America, and we can send the puppies over on a ship," Jakob promised half-heartedly.

One of the oldest girls presented him with a wrapped package. "This is our gift to you from all of us. There are a few smaller things in there too. It's our way of showing appreciation for everything you've done for us over the last two months. We've been so happy to have a teacher and friend who went through some of what we did."

He sat down to open it and found a large scrapbook. One of the older boys pulled on his hands when he started flipping through it.

"Don't read it now. We wanted you to look at it on the ship and while you're in America. It's full of notes, drawings, and pictures for you to remember us by."

"You went to all that trouble for me?"

"We all wanted you to know how much we love and appreciate you," a little girl said. "You're a really nice grownup friend."

"We've got a special meal for you too!" a little boy shouted.

As sad as he was to be leaving, Jakob savored every moment of his last day at the orphanage. He was being treated like a king for probably the last time in a long time. Soon enough, he'd be just another new immigrant, and probably treated less than nicely by certain people.

Heer Prinsen took a group photo of Jakob and Ben with the children before he left a little earlier than usual. Jakob hugged each of the children and put the package into his bicycle basket before he left. All the children rushed to the windows and waved at him till he was out of sight. At least this time, it wasn't a permanent goodbye. He'd had too many permanent goodbyes during the war.

Once he got home, he packed up his remaining things and conducted two final walk-throughs with Luisa before locking up. Sander, Bram, and Willem helped them carry their luggage downstairs. Ben jumped into the backseat of Kees's car, the car Jakob had stuck his neck out to save four years ago, while the luggage was loaded. This time, they were taking a lot more than they'd taken either to Westerbork or when they were deported. Jakob lifted his bicycle into the car last of all. It was now a little too small for him, after how tall he'd gotten, but he couldn't dream of leaving it behind when he was so lucky he still had it.

Kees drove to the port, with Bram and Floor on the front bench and Jakob, Luisa, and Sander in the backseat. Elma and Willem followed them on their new bicycles. During the entire drive, as Jakob watched his native city going by him one final time, no one said anything.

Slowly, the sight of the large boat filled his eyes. The boat that would finally take him to Rachel and end over a year of loneliness, the boat that would put an entire ocean between his new and old lives, the boat that should've been there for so many millions of people before the Nazis devoured them all.

"There it is," Luisa breathed. "If only Emilia and your father could be here."

"Did you ever find out anything about Emilia, by the way?" Sander asked. "I don't mean to pry, but surely something is public record by now."

"Nothing." Luisa dabbed at her eyes. "The Peerenbooms seem to have dropped off the face of the Earth along with her. Now only God knows what happened to all of them. At least my Ruud is now respectably buried among our ancestors. Will you please visit his grave in our stead on Yizkor days, holidays, his birthday, and his Jahrzeit?"

"Of course," Elma promised. "We'll do it till we immigrate ourselves."

They started unloading the luggage and heading toward the gangway. Jakob moved as slowly as possible as he pulled his bicycle along, while Bram put a collar and leash on Ben for the first time in his life. He kept his ticket in his pocket, along with his passport and visa.

As he walked, he tried to remember the cabin number they'd been assigned.

"Jaap, don't leave yet! I've got something for you before you go!"

He turned around and saw Vrouw Daube running towards him with an oversized parcel in her arms. He stopped and let Willem take the bicycle the rest of the way.

Vrouw Daube thrust the package into his arms. "This is for you, one final present from my store. I couldn't let one of my best young amateur artists move an entire ocean away without a farewell token. You might not be able to use this on the ship, but once you're on dry land, you'll be able to put it to good use."

He felt the shape. "Is this an easel?"

She nodded. "Maybe you'll never be the next Vermeer or Rembrandt, but you've improved a lot over the years. I think you're ready for the next level, a larger canvas. There's a painting smock in there, and more paints, oil and watercolor. You've got more than enough art supplies to keep you stocked for a long time to come. Don't forget to send me some of your artwork every so often. I want to keep up with your progress."

"Yes, I'll keep in touch with everyone." He set the package down to hug her. "Thank you so much for being so generous with your merchandise."

"You're one of my most devoted amateur artists. If I had an international catalogue, I'd put you on my mailing list."

After all the luggage was in the cabin, Jakob and Luisa hugged their friends and lingered by the gangway till the last call for boarding. Having no choice but to obey, Jakob took Luisa by the hand and took Ben's leash in his other hand. He cast looks over his shoulder the entire walk up the gangway.

"Don't cry in front of all these people," Luisa whispered. "Wait till we're in our cabin. Remember, this is a happy-sad goodbye, not like the goodbyes we said to so many other people."

They stood by the guardrail and smiled down at their friends. As the anchor was pulled up and the ship began plunging through the waters of the North Sea, they waved until their friends and Amsterdam were a blur on the horizon. Before Jakob knew it, they were surrounded by water on all sides, no land in sight. He began breathing heavily as he flashed back to that foul railcar, bathed in sickening, unnatural darkness.

Luisa rubbed his back. "Remember where you are, Jaapje. We're on our way to the land of freedom and our new lives. Maybe it's only two of us, but we're still a family, safe, alive, together. That's the only thing that should matter."

"Three of us," he gasped. "We've got Bentje now."

Luisa laughed. "Yes, we've got a furry member of our shrunken family now. I can't believe you ended up with the dog of one of our tormentors."

"It served him damn right to lose his puppy. I saved Bentje from a horrible fate as an attack dog, and gave him a nicer name. Maybe there really will be a wife for him in America, and some puppies."

"Perhaps. You'll be having your own babies in America, whomever you have them with, and they'll never know anything about what we went through. Can you promise me that if this paper marriage of yours turns out to be over, you'll only marry another survivor?"

He tried to ignore her dismissal of his marriage. "I'd never marry a stranger. A husband and wife need something in common. I couldn't have such a big chasm between us. I need someone to talk to about that, who can understand what happened."

As they headed down to their cabin, he thought about the chasm that already existed between himself and ordinary people. There might be a chasm between himself and most other Dutch people, but they'd all lived through the war, the occupation, the *Hongerwinter*, and the difficult first postwar year. These people he was going to live with in America hadn't been through any of that. All they'd had was a homefront. Worrying about rationing, collecting scrap metal, and sending their sons, brothers, and husbands off to war couldn't come close to what he and Luisa had survived.

But for now, the only thing he needed to worry about was crossing the Atlantic. The most important battles had already been fought and won. Except one thing.

"*Moeder*, may I open the window?"

"What for? Do you want to drown us?"

"Our cabin isn't in steerage. No water will rush in. I have something I'd like to do."

She shrugged. "I suppose, if you don't leave it open too long. I don't like salty air."

Jakob reached into the side flap of his schoolbag, the one he'd had with him since their arrest in August '42, and pulled out one of two yellow stars he still had left. The other was glued to a page in his scrapbook.

"Lord our God, Ruler of the Universe, please save me from too many reminders of the past, see my mother and I safely across the ocean, let me find my beautiful wife still in love with me and ready to really start our marriage, bless us with a beautiful baby by next year at this time, and most of all, please, dear God, never let anything like the Nazi horror happen ever again, so long as the world is turning." He opened his palm, released the star, and watched the fiend fly away. "Amen."

The Story Behind the Story

Rachel and her friend Juli were first mentioned in one of my Atlantic City books in early 1995, when the year was 1942. Rachel made her début as a character later that year, shortly after the end of the war, when she came to America as Jakob's fiancée (not wife). By the end of 1995, when it was 1950, Jakob himself had made his first appearance, along with their firstborn child. Eventually, Luisa was written in as well, and Jakob's limp and the reason for it. In 1981, while in Israel for his firstborn child's wedding, Jakob finally discovered what happened to Emilia.

Starting in 2006, I began writing a lot of long short stories/pieces of backstory about my Shoah characters (both during and after the war), to be periodically inserted into my Atlantic City books set at the same time. Originally, they were intended as fairly short pieces serving as a sobering alternate trajectory to the fairly unburdened lives of these American teens who only think they have it difficult, until these characters ultimately linked up after the war. They soon grew so long and involved, they threatened to overwhelm the books they were intended for, and took the focus off the real main characters and their storylines. I realized I needed to spin all these interconnected characters off into their own series.

I started by expanding the story about Jakob (and, later, Rachel) into a full-length novel. Not only was it one of the fairly shorter ones, but it was more straightforward due to its lack of an ensemble cast. It was easy to flesh out all the long passages summarizing events, and to fill in the many blanks. Because of Jakob's age, it also seemed perfect to query as YA (albeit upper, mature YA). Hence, the fade to black in the wedding night scene, and my decision to make it into two books instead of one very long book like I usually do.

I initially intended it to be one book, but because I wanted to pursue traditional publication at the time, and was cognizant it had reached the upper acceptable wordcount limit for historical and upper YA, I felt it would be best if I created two volumes. The most perfect ending opened up, and I was able to turn the rest of the material in the originating story into a somewhat shorter volume about Jakob's first year in America, and his and Rachel's first real year as husband and wife. Each volume truly has its own focus, and the second one reads more like New Adult than Young Adult.

While I was writing the first volume, I hit upon the idea of Jakob and Rachel having met before their emotional encounter at the liberated Westerbork. The story took on a much more interesting direction thanks to Jakob running into her in 1943 and becoming obsessed by this mysterious dream girl. If they'd only met after the war, there wouldn't be much of a compelling story. Many survivors forged lightning-fast pair bonds with people they barely knew, but their earlier encounters and Jakob's unexplainable pull towards her added a more compelling level.

Jakob's limp and the story behind it were written into one of my Atlantic City books in 1998 (1981 for him), five years before my own serious accident that left me with a limp. My depictions of that intense pain; the feelings of helplessness and anguish during a long period of immobility; the tricks of getting up and down stairs and managing other tasks; the terror and uncertainty of bearing weight again and relearning to walk; and the humiliation of realizing a limp is permanent were all drawn from my own firsthand experiences. Just as Jakob gets a huge shot of pride when he's reminded his namesake had a limp, I too felt much better about my limp when I discovered Curly Howard had a real-life limp. He's my limping hero.

Had I chosen to write this story as one continuous book, or as adult literature that just happens to feature a young protagonist, I would've made many chapters much longer, or added more chapters. With the second volume in particular, I would've featured my Atlantic City characters much more prominently. But ultimately, this story assumed the form it was meant to.

I look forward to resuming the story of Jakob, Rachel, and their children in other volumes, concluding with their discovery of just what happened to Emilia.

Sources Consulted

Stone, David J.A., et al. *World War II Chronicle*. Lincolnwood, IL: Legacy Publishing, 2007.

Harran, Marilyn, Ph.D., et al. *The Holocaust Chronicle*. Lincolnwood, IL: Legacy Publishing, 2007. (http://www.holocaustchronicle.org/)

http://www.februaristaking.nl/: Dutch-language resource about the February 1941 Strike.

http://www.holocaust-lestweforget.com/: Extensive resources about the Shoah in The Netherlands, including a detailed timeline.

http://www.deathcamps.org/reinhard/dutchclashes.html: Information about the pivotal month of February 1941 in The Netherlands.

http://www.jhm.nl/culture-and-history/amsterdam: Information about Jewish landmarks in Amsterdam, such as synagogues, schools, cemeteries, and the Waterlooplein market.

http://www.jhm.nl/culture-and-history/amsterdam/dockworker: Information about the February 1941 Strike and the uprising by Koco's ice-cream parlor.

http://www.nieuwsuitamsterdam.nl/English/2009/01/koco.htm: Brief article about the uprising by Koco's.

http://www.behindthename.com/names/usage/dutch: Extensive list of Dutch names, both common and lesser-used, including nicknames and alternate spellings.

http://surnames.behindthename.com/names/usage/dutch/: Long list of Dutch surnames, both common and lesser-used.

http://www.hebcal.com/: Perpetual Jewish calendar, a handy tool for figuring out when the holidays in any given year fell.

http://www.louiscouperus.nl/: Dutch-language site about Louis Couperus, widely-regarded as the greatest novelist of the Dutch language and The Netherlands.

http://stadsarchief.amsterdam.nl/english/amsterdam_treasures/second_world_war/index.en.html: Historical artifacts and documents, in both Dutch and English.

http://operationmanna.secondworldwar.nl/: Extensive resources about the *Hongerwinter*, in both English and Dutch.

http://forums.wildbillguarnere.com/index.php?/topic/2491-royal-netherlands-brigade-princess-irene/: Information about the Princess Irene Brigade.

http://thecanadianencyclopedia.com/articles/liberation-of-holland:
Information about the Canadian liberation of The Netherlands.
http://www.godutch.com/newspaper/index.php?id=295:   Extensive
timeline of The Netherlands under occupation, and the years leading
up to it.
http://www.prinsesirenebrigade.nl/: Primarily Dutch-language resources and personal stories about the Princess Irene Brigade.
http://www.gunsandbugles.co.uk/princess-irene.htm: More information
about the Princess Irene Brigade.
http://amsterdam.usconsulate.gov/history.html: A history of the U.S.
Consulate in Amsterdam.
http://www.amsterdamsights.com/amsterdam/neighborhoods.html:
Information about Amsterdam's neighborhoods.
http://www.youtube.com/watch?v=ng_B48HjIzs: Vintage film footage
of the Princess Irene Brigade entering The Hague; no sound.

Glossary

Afikomen: A piece of matzah which is broken early in the Seder and hidden, traditionally meant for children to find and get money or presents for. It's the last thing eaten during the Seder night, after which nothing else is supposed to be eaten.

Amidah: The long silent prayer which is the cornerstone of every service, and is said standing. It contains eighteen benedictions. Traditionally, the prayer is repeated aloud after everyone has finished saying it silently, except during Ma'ariv (evening) services.

Aramaic: A Semitic language which was the lingua franca of the Middle East during Antiquity. Some prayers, most notably the Kaddish, are retained in Aramaic.

Beshert: A Yiddish word meaning "destiny," in reference to one's soulmate.

Blockältester (female form *Blockälteste*): Block elder; appointed head of a barracks.

Bokkelul (plural *Bokkelulen*): An insult which means "ram's dick."

Chametz: Leavened food which is forbidden during Pesach. Very traditional people of Eastern European descent (Ashkenazim) also include foods such as corn, legumes, peanuts, dairy, and anything fermented in this category, though the liberal denominations and people of non-Ashkenazic descent only abstain from the classic wheat, barley, spelt, rye, and oats.

Chanukiyah (plural chanukiyot): The nine-pronged candelabrum used during Chanukah. One of the candlestick holders is higher than the others, and meant for the shamash, the helper-candle which lights the others. Contrary to popular belief, a menorah refers to the seven-branched candelabrum used in the Temple.

De Pijp: A prestigious neighborhood in southern Amsterdam. Its name means "The Pipe."

El Malei Rachamim: A traditional memorial prayer.

Erev: Eve, in reference to the time shortly before a holiday or the Sabbath.

Gefeliciteerd met je verjaardag: Happy birthday (literally, "congratulations on your birthday").

Geliefde echgenoot, zoon, broeder, en vader: Belovèd husband, son, brother, and father.

Gerard Dou Synagogue: A synagogue built in De Pijp in 1892, which escaped Nazi destruction due to its unassuming position between two rowhouses.

Gymnasium: Roughly equivalent to junior high and high school in many nations of Continental Europe, traditionally for the most academically gifted students and roughly equivalent to a U.S. prep school.

Hagadah: The book containing the Seder service.

Halacha, halachic: Traditional Jewish Law (literally, "the way to walk").

Hallel: Psalms of praise traditionally recited on festivals.

Heer (Hr.): Sir/Mister.

Jackfruit: An oval-shaped yellow or pale green fruit which grows on trees in tropical climates, including Indonesia, Malaysia, India, Thailand, and some places in Africa.

Jahrzeit: Death anniversary (literally, "a year's time" or "time of year").

Jodenbuurt: Literally, "Jewish Quarter." Formerly the oldest and largest of Amsterdam's three Jewish neighborhoods, in the central part of the city. Today the neighborhood is a pale shell of what once was.

Jodenbreestraat: Literally, "Jewish Broad Street." The painter Rembrandt lived there, and the philosopher Baruch Spinoza was born there.

Jonas Daniël Meijerplein: A square in Jodenbuurt, once bordered by five synagogues, named for the first Jewish lawyer of The Netherlands.

Joodenrat: Literally, "Jewish Council." This body governed the local Jewish population, and were widely seen as traitors and collaborators.

Jordaan: A traditionally working-class neighborhood in central Amsterdam, known for its many courtyards. Rembrandt spent his final years in Jordaan. Today the neighborhood is much more upscale.

Juffrouw (Juf): Miss.

Kankerhond (plural *Kankerhonden*): An insult which means "cancer dog."

Ketubah: Marriage contract, signed right before a wedding and often with beautiful calligraphy.

Kitl: A white robe traditionally worn on Yom Kippur, Seder nights, one's wedding, and a few other holiday services. It's also worn as a burial shroud.

Kol Nidre: Literally, "All Vows," the prayer chanted thrice on the night of Yom Kippur, nullifying any vows, promises, or oaths one may have made during the year.

Kooikerhondje (Kooiker): A Dutch spaniel breed originally bred for duck-hunting. Its coloring is orange-red and white. The breed is largely unknown in North America.

Linkshandig: Left-handed.

Machzor: Prayerbook used only for the High Holy Days.

Maror: Bitter herbs eaten during the Seder, usually raw horseradish, Romaine lettuce, or green onions.

Mejuffrouw: My young lady; only used in direct address.

Meneer: My sir; only used in direct address.

Mevrouw: My lady; only used in direct address.

Mijn liefje: My love.

Minyan: A quorum of ten required for certain prayers, or to conduct a full prayer service.

Moeder: Mother.

Moshe Rabeynu: Moses Our Teacher, a common appellation for Moses.

Museumplein: A public square in southern Amsterdam.

NSB: *Nationaal-Socialistische Beweging*, the Dutch Nazi party.

Oma: Grandmother.

Opa: Grandfather.

Oude Pijp: The original section of De Pijp, whose name fittingly means "Old Pipe."

Pesach: Passover.

Portuguese Synagogue: A large Sephardic synagogue in Jodenbuurt, built during the seventeenth century. Miraculously, it survived the Nazi occupation unharmed and unplundered, and is still in use today.

Schach: Greenery and branches used to cover the roof of a sukkah, the temporary hut constructed for the autumnal holiday of Sukkot.

Shavuot: Literally, "Weeks," the late spring holiday celebrating the receiving of the Torah, on which it's traditional to eat dairy.

Sheva Brachot: Literally, "Seven Blessings." During the first week after a wedding, a celebratory meal is held at which the seven blessings said by the chupah, the wedding canopy, are recited again.

Sh'ma (or Shema): Perhaps the most important prayer in Judaism, traditionally recited as one's last words, "Hear, O Israel, the Lord our God, the Lord is One."

Siddur: Prayerbook.

Sinterklaas: Saint Nicholas, the Dutch version of Santa Claus.

Sturmbannführer: An SS officer whose rank was equivalent to Major.

Sufganiyot: Jelly doughnuts, traditionally eaten during Chanukah because they're fried in oil.

Ta'anit Bechorot: The Fast of the Firstborn, observed on the eve of Pesach. Traditionally, only firstborn males have observed this. It originated as a way to commemorate the Israelites being spared the final of the Ten Plagues, the death of firstborns.

Tallit: Prayershawl.

Tallit katan: A small prayershawl worn under one's shirt, with the fringes hanging out.

Tefilah: Prayer.

Teshuvah: Literally, "return," usually translated as "repentance."

Tzedakah: Charity.

U'Netaneh Tokef: One of the central, best-known prayers of the High Holy Days liturgy. It speaks about humanity being judged and all accounted for, with various fates during the coming year, and about the tenuous, fleeting nature of humans in comparison to the Divine. An apocryphal story persists that it was written in Medieval Germany by Rabbi Amnon of Mainz, who refused his friend the archbishop's request to convert to Christianity and subsequently had all his limbs cut off. The story continues that Rabbi Amnon was carried into the synagogue on Rosh Hashanah, as he was dying, and recited U'Netaneh Tokef with his final breath. Three days later, he was said to appear to Rabbi Kalonymus ben Meshullam in a dream, where he imparted the words of the haunting prayer. Contemporary scholarship reveals it probably was written several centuries earlier in Israel.

Vader: Father.

Van Woustraat: A street in De Pijp.

Vrouw (Vr.): Madame/Mrs.

Waterlooplein: A square in Jodenbuurt, used as a marketplace since the late nineteenth century. It's still a thriving market today, though lost its Jewish character in 1941.

Wilhelmus van Nassouwe: The Dutch national anthem, written from the first-person perspective of Willem van Oranje, the leader of the Dutch revolt against Spain which began in 1568.

Yizkor: Literally, "Remembrance," a memorial service held during Yom Kippur, Shavuot, Pesach, and Shemini Atzeret (the last day of Sukkot).

Zwanenburgwal: A street and canal in Jodenbuurt. The painter Rembrandt and the philosopher Baruch Spinoza lived there.

Notes

The traditional Dutch custom is for women to legally keep their birth surnames, though some women go by their husbands' names socially. A child may take either parent's name, though it must be the same for all children. The title Vrouw and the style Mevrouw are used regardless, just as it was customary and considered respectful in the English-speaking world until fairly recently to call an adult woman Mrs., even if she retained her birth surname after marriage.

While it wasn't a common occurrence to jump from a death train, there are numerous verified cases, and of the escapees living to tell the tales. Jumping is a natural part of Jaap's character, in keeping with his desire to fight back instead of passively accepting occupation and slavery. If he'd stayed on that train, the story would've been much different. It might've been uncommon for a Jewish boy from Amsterdam to escape from a death train, join the resistance, and eventually find his way into the Princess Irene Brigade and the Royal Army of The Netherlands, but it's certainly more compelling and dramatic than the familiar trajectory.

From 17 April 1945–1 January 1949, Westerbork was a prison for collaborators, many of whom hid there during the final months of the war. Despite that becoming its primary function, many freed Jewish prisoners nevertheless remained there in the early period after liberation. They needed time to physically and emotionally recover, and some had no place to go yet. The Dutch military also had to question everyone on account of the numerous collaborators lurking in their midst.

Ruud's well-preserved state after almost five years of burial is explained by the copper coffin. Because copper is such a strong metal, it significantly slows down the process of decomposition. Embalmed bodies also tend to be preserved much longer. President Lincoln was still recognizable when he was exhumed after thirty-six years.

Though The Netherlands uses the metric system, I felt it simpler to mostly use American measurements for height. Perhaps someday the U.S. will finally adopt the metric system like most of the rest of the world.

About the Author

Ursula Hartlein, who also writes as Carrie-Anne Brownian, was born on the fifth night of Chanukah in 1979. Though a proud native Pittsburgher, she's lived most of her life in Upstate New York and has also lived in Pittsfield and Amherst, Massachusetts.

She earned a bachelor's degree from UMass–Amherst in History and Russian and East European Studies. Her areas of historical expertise are Russian history, the World War II/Shoah era, and 20th century American history. Her ultimate goal is to one day have a Ph.D. in Russian history, with a focus on GULAG and the Great Terror.

She is the author of *And the Lark Arose from Sullen Earth*, the sequel to this book, set from 1946–47; *You Cannot Kill a Swan: The Love Story of Lyuba and Ivan*, a sweeping saga set from 1917–24; *The Twelfth Time: Lyuba and Ivan on the Rocks*, its sequel, set from 1924–30; *Journey Through a Dark Forest: Lyuba and Ivan in the Age of Anxiety*, a four-volume saga spanning 1933–48; and *And Aleksey Lived*, an alternative historical saga about the greatest Tsar who never ruled. Under her other pen name, she is the author of *Little Ragdoll: A Bildungsroman*, a contemporary historical family saga set from 1959–74; *How Kätchen Became Sparky*, set in 1938, the first book in a series set in an unusual Atlantic City neighborhood; and *Movements in the Symphony of 1939*, its sequel, set during 1939. She has also had work published in the anthologies *Campaigner Challenges 2011*; *Overcoming Adversity: An Anthology for Andrew*; *How I Found the Write Path*; *The Insecure Writer's Support Group Guide to Publishing and Beyond*; and *The Cat Who Chose Us and Other Cat Stories*; and *Masquerade: Oddly Suited*.